"YOU ARE MY WOMAN."

Cora didn't resist. Adrian's hair fell forward, touching her face. Cora's hands went to his waist. His tongue ran along the line of her lips, between. Her pulse throbbed without mercy, beyond her ability to contain it. He kissed the corner of her mouth, then her face. His breath came swift but deep, sure. His fingers wound in her hair and unraveled what was left of her braid. He caught its length in his hand and eased her head back.

He kissed her neck, just below her ear. Her weak spot. He must have remembered. But who was this man? Was he the same as she'd known so well so long ago? She felt the tip of his tongue, then his teeth grazing her flesh. Her nerves scrambled and jumped, crashing in panic. He was the same, and yet, so different. Stranger. Surer.

"You are my woman," Adrian said. "You will give me sons." He paused. "Daughters, too."

"You have lost your mind."

"In exchange, I will give you pleasure. I'll leave no ache unsatisfied."

That sounds fair. . . . Cora shook her head to clear her ravaged senses. "I don't think—"

"Yes, you do. You think too much. You talk too much...." Cora braced herself, but Adrian drew her closer into his arms. "It's time for you to feel."

FREE FALLING

STOBIE PIEL

LOVE SPELL BOOKS   ▣   NEW YORK CITY

LOVE SPELL®

August 1999

Published by

Dorchester Publishing Co., Inc.
276 Fifth Avenue
New York, NY 10001

ISBN 0-505-52329-9

The name "Love Spell" and its logo are trademarks of Dorchester Publishing Co., Inc.

Printed in the United States of America.

To Barbara Fairfield, my friend, cousin, and kindred spirit, with whom I've shared capers and heartaches and memories to last a lifetime.

To Carol Weymouth, who knows me better than I know myself, and is *still* my dear friend.

And to Charlotte Parry, who understands romance better than anyone I've ever met, and who reminded me that to touch someone's heart with a story is the most wonderful thing of all.

Our father, the Whirlwind,
Our father, the Whirlwind—
By its aid I am running swiftly,
By its aid I am running swiftly,
By which means I saw our father,
By which means I saw our father.
　　　　—Arapaho

There are great whirlwinds
Standing upside down above us.
They lie within my bowl.

A great bear heart,
A great eagle heart,
A great hawk heart,
A great twisting wind—
All these have gathered here
And lie within my bowl.
　　　　—Papago

FREE FALLING

Chapter One

June 27, 2000
Scottsdale, Arizona

"I'm going to jump now and spare the world my splattered remains." Cora Talmadge leaned out the wide door of the small airplane and held her breath. "Don't try to stop me."

A tap on her shoulder distracted her from the leap. "Maybe you should wait until the plane takes off, Cora." Jenny pointed to the runway five feet below. "You won't do much skydiving from this height."

Cora's eyes narrowed as she glanced over her shoulder. "That's the idea."

Jenny laughed and pulled Cora back into the plane. "Sit down, girl. We'll be taking off in a minute, as soon as your guide gets here."

"Wonderful."

"It's not that bad, Cora. The first time I did it, I was terrified, too. But I can't wait to get up there now."

Cora repressed a groan. Jenny had always been overly enthusiastic, a fearless computer scientist who wanted to experience everything firsthand. "Your first jump was two weeks ago."

Jenny nodded. "Just before you came out to visit me. Skydiving is great. It will change your life!"

"Or end it."

"That's a change." Jenny grinned and hugged Cora. "Come sit, and think of something else. Besides death."

Cora cast a forlorn glance out the portal. The early morning sun glinted off the sign over the school, and her heart chilled. THE NOMADIC ADVENTURER SCHOOL OF SKYDIVING. Nomadic adventurer. Years ago, that had been a term of affection and teasing, applied to herself.

It could only mean disaster.

Cora steeled her nerves. She'd get out of it somehow. If she backed out before they took off, Jenny would apply guilt persuasion. Cora hesitated, then sat beside Jenny on the long bench.

Two business executives sat at the far end of the plane, talking business. As if they weren't about to plummet to their deaths. At the skydiving school briefing, they said it was part of a program to "challenge and unite" company executives.

So here they were. Challenged and united. Even in flight suits, they looked . . . executive. Short, clipped hair, well-tended. One blond, one dark. Bookends.

Cora didn't want to be challenged. She wanted to relax, to take time off from her struggling art gallery. She'd moved from Maine to Manhattan. Until now, that was the greatest leap of her life. She accepted Jenny's invitation with the in-

14

tention of visiting galleries in Phoenix, and finding some way of luring Arizona artists to her small business.

Instead, death loomed. Not sudden death, but the kind that required a long, torturous fall first. Free falling, indeed! Cora fiddled at her collar, fingering her necklace as she closed her eyes.

Jenny seized the pendant and examined it. "It's a turquoise fetish bear, right? It's nice. You've worn this ever since I've known you. You never take it off."

Cora eased the pendant from Jenny's fingers. "I'm used to it."

"Who gave it to you?"

Cora attempted a careless shrug. "I don't remember. I've had it so long . . . " And how did Jenny know it was a gift, anyway? She could have bought it for herself. She didn't, but Jenny couldn't know that.

Life is supposed to flash before your eyes just before death. That must be what's going on here. But there was one period in her life she refused to recall, death or not. The pendant was enough. The term "nomadic adventurer" had been too cruel a reminder. . . .

A small man with an Australian accent sat beside Jenny. He looked young and unreliable in the extreme. Cora was relieved that he was Jenny's guide and not hers. Especially after he explained that skydiving gave him the high that he missed when he gave up cocaine.

Cora's relief turned to guilt and she seized Jenny's arm. "Are you sure you want to do this?"

Jenny's eyes widened, too innocently. "It's my birthday present to you, Cora. I couldn't back out now!" Jenny paused, and her eyes looked even more innocent. "And I paid in advance."

Cora nodded stoically. Yes. Paying in advance. Cora fingered her pendant again. She remembered when another used that same reasoning to convince her to go white-water rafting. That day had been her birthday, too.

Cora fidgeted as she formulated a plan for self-preservation. Once up in the air, she had every intention of averting her hideous demise. Jenny and the two executives would jump first, as the guides explained at the briefing. Simple.

Cora would explain to her guide, if he ever arrived, that she felt suddenly dizzy. If necessary, she would simulate an effective fainting spell, and travel safely back to earth still encased in the airplane.

There was no way she would jump from a plane at ten thousand feet. Even if Jenny had paid in advance for the glorious fall. Never.

Jenny's Australian guide closed the large portal through which they were to jump. Cora's spirits soared. "I take it my guide can't make it?" She couldn't conceal the hopefulness of her tone.

He didn't answer, but he grinned as he indicated the small pilot's entrance.

"Oh." Cora forced her attention from the closed portal to the interior of the plane. It looked gutted, suspiciously like a military transport craft. No comfortable, reclining seats, no magazine racks. Just a hard, low bench to sit on. Parachute packs lay strewn on the floor, in too much disarray to possibly be safe.

They'd watched the skydiving school's video, they knew what to expect. It was disgusting, horrifying, but all too clear. The plane flies to ten thousand feet, then drops its passengers.

All too clear.

"Where's my guide?"

The propellers moved slowly, gaining speed. Cora resisted a surge of hope. She raised her voice to be heard over the plane. "Wouldn't it be a shame if he couldn't make it?"

Jenny smiled. "He'll make it. Don't worry. You got the best guide of the bunch. He's the owner of the school."

"Great. So where is he?"

"He probably had some other business to take care of."

Cora slumped. Something about the way Jenny averted her innocent, brown eyes incited Cora's suspicions, but her nervousness refused rational thought.

"So . . . we go up, we get strapped on the front of some guy, and we drop from the plane? That's what I got from the video."

Jenny nodded as if this were a pleasant image. "In essence. Don't forget to put your head back on his shoulder and arch back when you're free falling."

A low groan of misery was all Cora could muster. "Just how tight are we supposed to be strapped?"

"If he has a dime in his pocket, you'll feel it."

The groan repeated, louder. "This is excruciating."

Jenny patted Cora's knee. "You'll be too terrified to be embarrassed."

"What a relief!"

The propellers roared, and Cora's hope reached a pinnacle. Her guide hadn't arrived. Cora started to extract herself from the flight suit. "Looks like we're taking off without him. . . . "

The Australian guide leaned forward and waved out the pilot's door. "He's coming."

Cora's heart crashed and she refastened her suit, then slumped miserably back onto the bench. Curses! She glanced at Jenny for reassurance, but Jenny was watching the doorway expectantly.

17

Cora sat at the far end of the bench. The two executives were close to the door. They moved down to give the new guide room. Cora waited despondently, fingering her pendant. She hated disappointing people. This guide was bound to be disappointed if she refused to jump. He'd think he'd failed, and she hated making people think that.

A tall, dark man appeared in the doorway, crouching as he entered the plane. He wore a flight suit like the other guides, and goggles around his neck. He didn't wear a cap like the one that squashed Cora's hair against her head. His black hair, tied back, fell over one shoulder. He wore one long, beaded earring.

He glanced up as he sat and Cora's heart froze in her throat. Shock radiated through her, obliterating fear. Adrian de Vargas smiled slightly and held up his hand in a still wave.

Cora couldn't move, she couldn't breathe. His beautiful, dark eyes showed no surprise, just veiled humor. Cora still gripped her little pendant. If he noticed. . . .

No, that was too hideous to comprehend. She shoved it beneath her T-shirt and fastened her flight suit to her chin.

The plane was moving. Faster and faster. Too fast to leap off, too fast for any kind of escape. Cora pressed her lips together and snapped her gaze to her clenched fists. She felt the blood drain from her face until her nerves tingled from want of oxygen. Her fingers tingled, too.

She'd never expected to see him again. She hadn't, until now, known where he lived or what he was doing. She had known, because she knew him, that it involved the outdoors. Rafting or skiing or sailing. She hadn't taken her imagination to this extreme, but skydiving fit, too.

She guessed why he hadn't shown himself at the briefing, and why he had waited until the last minute to get on the plane. He must have seen her name on some roster, and considered the situation amusing. Or maybe Jenny had told him her name when she arranged the birthday present from hell.

It was too late to avert disaster now. Cora glanced out the window into the blue sky. The plane angled so she couldn't see the earth below.

Maybe the disaster would be prolonged a little. Maybe it would take a merciful while to reach ten thousand feet.

"Approaching target zone. Strap on."

Apparently not. Cora winced as the pilot's voice rasped over the speaker. Cora heard only snippets of his words, but the guides rose and positioned themselves beside their charges. Adrian put on his flight cap, but he waited for the others before approaching Cora. She kept her gaze casually glued to the window.

Her heart raced so fast that she felt dizzy. Her fear was as great as it would be if she actually intended to jump. Which, until now, was as unlikely as flying to the moon. But backing out in front of Adrian de Vargas seemed equally impossible.

Jenny touched Cora's shoulder. "This is it!" She seated herself on the Australian's lap. Cora's stomach churned as he loosely fixed his harness to Jenny's. Yes, it looked excruciatingly close. And he hadn't tightened them together yet.

Adrian stood in front of her, casting a dark, impenetrable shadow over her body. Cora didn't dare look to see if the shadow was real. He didn't talk, probably because she wouldn't hear him, anyway. The roar was deafening. A merciful situation.

He sat beside her and slapped his thighs. She glanced at his legs. They looked strong, even in a flight suit. He had always been athletic. His body did whatever he wanted it to. Unlike her own, which resented any activity beyond walking.

He could ski, skate, do any sport he wished, even manage

a raft through rapids, in a storm. . . . Cora felt sick. Everyone else was in position. One executive sat on a large man's lap. The other had jumped once before, and sat beside his guide. The executives didn't talk anymore. Both looked pale.

Cora bit her lip so hard she tasted blood. She drew a tight breath, and tried to will her body into submission. Not a muscle obeyed. *Get it over with. Tell him you're sick.* She felt his hand on her arm. She felt him lean close to her.

"Are you sure you want to do this?"

Despite the roar of the plane, she caught his patronizing tone. It was too much. She met his eyes, her lip curved in an angle of superiority.

"Who wouldn't?" *What am I saying? Oh, no!*

He smiled, then tapped his thighs again. His lap. She was supposed to sit on his lap. She looked into his face. The last time she saw him, he had been beautiful, but he had been a boy. She hadn't thought of him that way, but she knew now it was true.

Adrian de Vargas wasn't a boy anymore. He still had Navajo cheekbones and Spanish eyes. He had the same perfect, straight nose and sweet, well-formed mouth that haunted her dreams and memory. He didn't know his exact ancestry because he had been abandoned at birth, but it showed in his face.

He was the most beautiful man Cora had ever seen. More beautiful now than when he formed the center of her world. And she had to sit on his lap and be strapped so close that she would feel a dime in his pocket.

Or die of embarrassment and humiliation by bursting into tears.

A moment ago, the worst thing she could imagine was plummeting headlong from a plane at ten thousand feet.

She'd had no idea how bad the worst could be. Now, she would be plummeting with a nightmare strapped to her back.

And she would be plummeting. Because she'd rather die than back out in front of Adrian de Vargas. Get it over with. Her legs agreed, at last. Cora stood up, but the plane jerked, and she thumped down into his lap. Fate was unkind, this day.

He didn't comment. He adjusted her position on his lap, centering her, then fixed straps binding them together. Cora's heart beat so fast that she wondered if she might faint after all.

He felt solid and strong. In other circumstances, she might feel lucky to be attached to Adrian rather than Jenny's skinny guide. Then again, maybe a lightweight man wouldn't fall quite so fast. . . .

Oh, God, I'm really going to fall! She hadn't considered that as a possibility until now. Until now, she had planned to get out of it somehow. She tried to remember the video. She hadn't paid much attention because she had been plotting an excuse not to jump.

They'd plummet, "free fall." Her guide—Adrian—would pull a cord and release the parachute, then they'd float to earth. If they were lucky, a bird might fly close by, and it would be "magical." She'd hold up her legs, and they'd slide to the ground on their bottoms.

Cora released a small groan of misery.

Then she'd say, *"Thank you very much. What a wonderful experience!"* Maybe she would shake his hand. She and Jenny would laugh about their fear, then go off for drinks and celebration.

That was the plan. Jenny promised exultation upon landing. *If I died right now, I could get out of this.* The strap

21

tightened without warning. Her back pressed against Adrian's chest. The noise of the plane altered in what Cora considered a threatening fashion.

The plane was level, and some fool opened the large, gaping portal. Jenny and her guide were already shuffling together toward the opening. The executive strapped to a guide was already crouched in the doorway.

Adrian was doing something, too. They both wore parachutes, hers in case of emergency, his to support them both. Her straps went around and between her legs, not unlike a diaper.

What a nightmare!

Adrian didn't get up. Jenny looked wide-eyed and terrified, despite having jumped before. *Oh, that's comforting.* Fear had its purpose. Terror outweighed the horror and shock of seeing Adrian again.

Gratitude for small favors will see my way into heaven. . . .

Wind stung Cora's face and swirled inside the gutted plane. She felt Adrian's hand on her shoulder. He touched her chin. He wanted something. She glanced back at him to find out what.

He mouthed words. "Lean your head back." Cora had no idea what he meant. He eased her head back onto his shoulder. "Got it?"

She heard that. He was reminding her of their jumping position. She nodded, then sat quickly forward, separating herself from him as much as possible. She felt sure she heard him laugh.

Adrian stood up, drawing Cora with him. He was taller than she was by a few inches, but they matched well enough to be paired. She remembered that a first-time jumper was paired with a guide of a similar size. Her height had always been a liability.

The first-time executive and his guide dropped from the plane, out of sight. Cora's mouth dropped, too. Her muscles tensed, she leaned involuntarily back against Adrian. If she had really intended to do this, she might have been better prepared.

Instead, she felt like a cow awaiting slaughter. A cow that had been, up until the last minute, carefully planning its escape.

The second executive hesitated at the door, giving Cora a brief hope he'd panic and the plane would have to land immediately. The guide spoke to him, and the executive crouched into position. He dropped, too. His guide waited, then followed.

Only Jenny and her Australian guide remained. Jenny looked white and panicked. Cora offered a reassuring expression, in direct opposition to what she felt. It was a reflexive gesture, used often on the subway. *It's my duty to make others feel better.*

She'd only failed once. The man strapped behind her had proven bitterly how limited her abilities were. Because of her inadequacy, she'd lost the only thing she'd ever really wanted.

Adrian pulled up his goggles, then fixed Cora's over her eyes. She didn't resist. Blurred vision might be a good thing.

The Australian guide leaned forward, bending Jenny forward. Cora felt sure she heard a sharp cry of shock from Jenny. He was looking to see the other jumpers. Then, without warning, the guide and Jenny dropped out of sight.

Adrian shuffled Cora forward. Her legs moved because his moved, but her knees didn't bend. She looked out at the blue sky and wondered desperately if she could control her terror. Vomiting would be beyond horror.

I will not! I won't vomit, I won't cry, I won't scream. I'll drop and say "thank you" and go home to Manhattan.

Adrian eased her down, then bent her forward, and Cora's resolve faltered. The world looked very small from ten thousand feet. Arizona looked golden in the sun. Beautiful and ghastly. She stiffened, but Adrian was looking over her shoulder.

A dark lump below had to be Jenny and her guide. Smaller lumps indicated the executives in their respective positions. They fell very fast.

"Ready? Cross your arms over your chest."

Physical courage wasn't her strongest quality. If her body obeyed the way Adrian's did, it might be different, but she could never be quite sure what it would do next. Trip, fall, bang into objects. Being shy and tentative wasn't helpful. Being awkward was often humiliating.

Cora remembered Jenny's promise. "Do this, and everything else will be easy." Maybe even seeing Adrian de Vargas again. And saying good-bye. Again.

Cora closed her eyes and crossed her arms over her chest. She tilted her head back onto his shoulder. She heard his voice close to her ear. "A leap of faith, angel." Adrian leaned forward. Her body sank forward and dropped into a gust of wind.

Cora felt air coming through her feet. What an odd sensation! She kept her lips pressed together to keep her cheeks from flapping in the wind. That image remained from Jenny's description. Nothing else formed in her thoughts.

Twenty seconds, and the free fall will be over. He'll pull the parachute, and it's pleasant. Like hell!

Cora kept her legs tucked back between Adrian's. His legs felt strong and hard wrapped around hers. He felt relaxed. Cora fought the impulse to flail her arms and the desire to right herself.

She had nothing but him. She was dropping out of the sky, and the only thing between her and death was Adrian. His body steadied hers. The wind screamed in her ears. Cora opened her eyes. She was supposed to keep her eyes open, but they hadn't cooperated with protocol.

Her body faced down, but she was looking ahead. She saw the ends of Adrian's black hair whipping in the wind. She couldn't see his face. Cora counted. Fifteen . . . ten. . . . He would give her the "thumbs up" sign to indicate the parachute's release. But they kept falling.

Twenty seconds had never felt so long. Amazing that they hadn't smacked into a desert cliff by now. He reached around her body and offered the "thumbs up" sign. Cora did her best to nod. She couldn't remember if she was supposed to nod or not, but she didn't want to delay the opening of the chute.

The parachute released and jerked them up, hard. Jenny had warned of "wedgies," but it didn't hurt as Cora had feared. Her feet went down, her body moved into a pleasant, vertical position. *Who would think I'd be grateful just to be vertical?*

The wind stilled, the screaming silenced. She heard soft noises, like those of a sail. She peeked up. A red and yellow parachute gleamed in the sun above their heads. She was floating. Her heart resumed a slower, steadier beat.

I'm alive. I didn't splatter onto the desert. Cora looked down. A mistake. Her vision circled and she snapped her eyes shut. The desert was still far away. Farther than she wanted it, anyway.

Silence. Adrian didn't speak. Cora's relief at surviving the free fall turned to nervousness. Silence. She opened her eyes and cleared her throat. His thighs pressed against hers, his chest against her back. Her feet settled on top of his, a comforting feeling. She didn't allow herself to think about the rest of his body.

She couldn't see him. She felt him, and that was already too much. From the corner of her eye, she saw that he held straps. He was navigating, keeping them steady. Maybe they'd just float down out of the sky without saying a word to each other.

Cora's teeth chattered from nervousness. She was more nervous about talking to him than about falling out of the sky.

There's a way to handle fear: Replace it with a worse one.

Even at nineteen, he'd made her nervous. She'd never understood why he had wanted to date *her*, of all people. She'd taken a martial arts class at college, thinking it would be easy, and was about to fail. He had tutored her, and she had passed.

She had fallen in love. Stupidly and completely. He had decided she needed more "physical confidence." So he'd set about teaching her every sport known to man. She'd given all her soul to avoid disappointing him. And she had failed, every time.

Cora looked down at the earth. They were falling over Scottsdale, not far from the airport where Adrian had his skydiving school. Scottsdale blended into the even denser spread of Phoenix, and stretched endlessly over the desert.

She saw the canyon, the golden brown hills, the straight, wide roads below, river beds.

Odd. She thought they'd fall faster as they got closer to the ground, but they almost seemed to have stopped. But that wasn't possible. Cora waited a moment for evidence they were still dropping. Instead, she felt more and more certain they weren't going anywhere.

No, we're not moving. How can that be? Cora resisted the impulse to question Adrian. *He must know what he's doing. He owns the school, after all. If we've slowed, it must be normal.* Cora looked down again. The executives and Jenny seemed lower now. They were still moving. Jenny looked up and waved. Cora waved, too.

Cora saw the executives off to the right. That sort of man generally found her attractive. The younger one had asked her to meet him for drinks afterwards. Unfortunately, Cora's heart had no room for any man.

Except one.

Jenny shouted something, but Cora couldn't hear from that distance. She moved her legs to see if it made a difference. They just hovered. The urge to question Adrian grew stronger. If he didn't speak soon. . . .

"Happy birthday, angel."

Her heart skipped, her throat constricted. Hot tears burned her eyes. She wasn't sure why. His low voice came as if out of a dream.

"Thank you." Her voice was so small, she doubted he could hear her. He didn't say anything more. She tried to think of something light and casual to say. Anything would be better than tears.

"Long time, no see" sounded wrong. "Hey, how've you been, pal?" wasn't any better. And though Cora had, during college years, attempted to speak in some form of vernacular, it had never sounded quite right coming from her lips. "Cool" sounded forced and awkward.

Adrian could say anything he wanted and sound natural.

Probably because, unlike herself, he was born "cool." Cora sighed. *I'm hanging in the sky with the man least compatible with myself who ever lived.*

"Why did you leave?"

His question took her off-guard. Her throat tightened even more. He couldn't expect her to answer.

The cursed tears burned hotter. "We're not moving."

"We're still. Why did you leave?"

Cora glanced back, she saw his jaw. His hair. But not his face. "What do you mean, 'still?' "

"I've stopped us."

Cora felt like a deer caught by a hunter. The panic surfacing seemed extreme. "You can't stop us! That's impossible. No one, even you, can defy gravity."

"I'm doing it."

She couldn't see his face, but she knew he was smiling in that self-satisfied expression she'd once adored. Cora swallowed hard. "Move us."

"Why did you leave?"

Her whole body tensed. "It doesn't matter."

"If it didn't matter, I wouldn't ask."

Cora angled her head from any possible view. Tears fell beneath her goggles. *What do I say?*

"If you'd like, I can spin us, too."

It sounded like a threat. "I do not wish to spin."

He chuckled. "You were saying. . . . " He paused, and the parachute began to move slowly in a circle. Cora ground her teeth together. "We could hang here for quite a while, Cora Talmadge. You'd be amazed at the tricks I can do with a chute."

If she jammed her elbow back into his stomach, it might have an unfortunate effect on the parachute. Cora sighed in resignation. "You were going to Thailand. . . . "

"Nepal."

"Whatever."

They stopped moving, hanging still again. "You were coming with me, Cora."

"I wasn't."

"I guessed that much when you failed to show up at the airport."

Cora stiffened at his tone, but she had no response.

"I take it you flew home from Kathmandu instead."

Her teeth sank into the soft pulp of her lip. "Yes."

"Why?"

Cora's throat hurt. "I explained that in my letter."

"You said it was time for us to go our separate ways. That's not an explanation."

"I couldn't think of anything else to say."

"I guessed that when you didn't answer my subsequent letters."

She couldn't speak. She had answered, but too late. He had written sweetly of missing her, and she had caved. She had called him. The worst mistake of her life, because she hadn't been in time. His number had been disconnected, and all she'd had were memories and regrets.

"And when you moved, and I couldn't find you," Adrian continued.

Cora's mind went numb. She'd left the University of Colorado and taken classes in New York. She had wanted to forget. She never had forgotten.

"I'm surprised you didn't change your name. Enter a witness protection plan. . . . "

Cora had no response. Adrian sounded bitter, but it had happened long ago. Nine years. They hadn't dated long. From January to May. They'd met in their second year at the University of Colorado. He'd convinced her to travel to Asia with him that spring, and she had gone, knowing it would be a disaster.

She had left him in India, and they never saw each other again. Until now.

Excruciating. Cora preferred the fear over this. *I loved you so.* "Must we discuss this now?"

"Yes, we must." His tone mimicked hers. He made her sound Eastern.

"This isn't a good time, Adrian."

He hesitated. "Then later. Have dinner with me."

"I can't."

"Cora—"

"I have plans already."

"Then tomorrow."

"I'm going back to New York tomorrow."

Tears stung her cheek beneath the goggles. She expected more, but Adrian fell silent. The old ache resurfaced with such power that Cora knew it had never really left at all. She couldn't explain.

She'd set him free, because she hadn't been strong or confident enough to keep him. She wasn't any stronger now than she'd been nine years ago. But she accepted herself now, and didn't dream of being someone greater than she was.

Cora looked down. The others were far away, drifting closer to the ground. Phoenix stretched endlessly beyond. They were landing near the airport, outside Scottsdale. The mountains loomed behind. *It's so beautiful. . . .*

From a flat, jutting cliff to her left, Cora noticed a dusty spiral of wind and debris. How odd! It swirled on the ground, rising upward in a funnel. "What's that?"

"What?"

Cora pointed. "That . . . wind thing."

"I don't know."

30

Cora rolled her eyes. "What do you mean, you don't know? You've done this before. What is it?"

"I don't know."

He sounded serious. Cora cranked her head around to see him. He was looking at the spiral, shading his eyes from the sun. He shook his head. "I've never seen anything like it."

"That's very comforting." Cora looked back at the strange tunnel. "You know, it's getting higher. It almost looks as if it's reaching toward us."

Adrian didn't answer. He pulled on the straps and the parachute moved. It drifted away from the approaching whirlwind, and lowered. Cora relaxed. She heard a rushing noise from below. The blue sky turned hazy.

The wind tunnel narrowed and coiled, creating a sucking sound. The parachute wobbled, then moved in the opposite direction. Toward the whirlwind.

"Adrian . . . I'd think we'd want to move away from that . . . whatever it is."

"I'm trying."

Cora bit her lip. He meant it. His voice sounded strained. She glanced at his arms. His muscles looked strained, too. He was fighting the wind.

Something seemed wrong about this. Adrian shouldn't fight the wind, he should be part of the wind. She wasn't sure where this came from, but it felt like memory.

He swore, in a language she didn't understand. She guessed it was Navajo.

The parachute jerked toward the tunnel. The haze increased until small dirt particles stung Cora's cheeks. "It's like a little tornado."

"It's no tornado—" Adrian's words were cut off as the parachute yanked them upward, then spun them around.

His words were drowned in a sudden rush of wind. It **didn't**

31

scream as it had when they dropped from the plane. It moaned and howled. Cora grasped her straps, she closed her eyes. They spun faster and faster, caught with the wind.

She was really going to die. In a freak whirlwind, with Adrian. Adrian can't die. She felt him behind her, fighting to regain control of the parachute. But Cora didn't panic. Dimly, she wondered why not.

She waited, but panic didn't surface. She opened her eyes, trying to gauge their position. All she saw was the spinning debris of the whirlwind. And still, no panic. The wind seemed to lift them, to carry them.

Without warning, it shot them free. The parachute filled with air, just in time for Cora to see the ground. "Flare!"

She didn't know what he meant. "Pull the straps, Cora, now!"

Cora pulled her straps down, in toward her chest as she remembered from the video. Adrian pulled his, too, and the parachute collapsed. "Legs up!"

She pulled her legs up. They skidded down, then bumped on the tall, dry grass. Grass. Something about this seemed strange to Cora, but she wasn't sure why.

The parachute collapsed behind them. Cora tried to stand up. The bind to Adrian held her back and she flopped backwards on top of him. The earth was comfortingly solid.

Cora drew a tight breath and relaxed. "Well, that was eventful."

She felt calm, not wildly exulted as Jenny had promised. She felt relieved, true, but not wild. She waited for Adrian to unhook them. For a brief, painful instant, she wished to remain right where she was.

Adrian didn't move. Cora waited. Even through her flat pack, she felt his heart pounding against her back. She tried to look back at him. "Are you all right?"

He nodded, but he didn't answer. He unhooked her. His hands were shaking. Cora slid off him, righted herself, and sat on her knees, looking down at him. Adrian still lay on his back, staring at the sky.

"Are you hurt, Adrian? You look pale. I didn't . . . " She paused to wince at the possibility. "Squash you, did I?"

Only his eyes moved as he looked at her. "Do you know how close we came?"

"Yes. Six inches."

His brow furrowed in confusion. "Six inches?"

Cora nodded. "From that prickly thing." She pointed at a low, spiny cactus with a paddle-shaped fruit and long thorns.

Adrian followed her gaze. "Prickly pear."

"Is that what you call it? Pear? Are they edible?"

Adrian looked at her as if she had lost her mind. "Some varieties are edible, yes. You have to burn the spines off . . . " He stopped and shook his head as he sat up. "Cora, you and I just—"

Cora didn't want to talk about their lost relationship. It hurt too much. "Six inches off, and we'd have sat right on it. Well, you would have. I'd be on you."

Cora stood up and dusted herself off. She looked around. "I thought we were landing on some strip. Where is this place?"

"I don't know." Adrian rose to his feet and pulled off his goggles. He took off his flight suit while Cora watched. She held her breath. He wore a plain, white shirt and jeans that weren't too tight, yet somehow managed to show his strong, well-formed body to its usual perfection.

He wore light hiking boots, unlaced at the top. Adrian dropped his diving gear and studied the landscape. His brow furrowed as he looked around.

"Where are we?"

"I have no idea."

"What do you mean, 'no idea?' You've lived in Arizona all your life, haven't you?"

He nodded.

"So, where are we?" Her voice had grown higher. Not for fear of being lost, but of being alone with Adrian.

Adrian was staring at the ground. "What the hell . . . ?"

Cora looked down at the tall, dry grass, too. "What's the matter?"

"Grass."

"That's lucky, isn't it? Made the landing softer."

It was hotter than she remembered when they took off. Cora started to extract herself from the flight suit.

"You don't understand, Cora. It's not 'lucky.' It's impossible."

Adrian's attention shifted from the grass to Cora as she fumbled with her flight suit. She tugged her cap half off, and it became entangled with her goggles. She noticed her error before Adrian had to point it out.

The goggles came off, then the cap. A long braid of golden pale hair fell over her shoulder. Part had come loose and spilled around her face in soft waves.

She didn't look flushed. She didn't look frightened. They'd escaped death by the narrowest margin, and she showed no sign of fear. Cora, who refused to swim in water over her neck, had a peculiar reaction to skydiving gone awry.

"Impossible? Grass isn't impossible, Adrian. It grows everywhere." She had that same smug tone in her voice that he remembered. For a reason he had never understood, it had the peculiar effect of arousing him.

"We don't have grass in Arizona, Cora. Not like this. Not here. There was grass a century or so ago, but not now. It was grazed off."

"Then we're on a golf course." Cora kicked at the tall grass. "Most of it's over my ankles. I'd say you've got plenty of grass."

"Impossible."

Cora's eyes narrowed. "Did you hit your head when we landed?"

"No."

"You've got grass."

"I see that. It shouldn't be here."

"Well, neither should we." Cora looked left, then right, her hands planted on her hips. "Where's Phoenix? It should be around here somewhere. I remember seeing it before we got sucked into that wind tunnel."

She spoke casually. As if she expected Phoenix to rise up before her, a sprawling metropolis that had better explain itself now. Or else.

Adrian's heart constricted. There wasn't another woman like her in the world. He steeled himself against his reaction to Cora Talmadge. He'd attempted to bridge the endless gap between them, he'd admitted his desire to know what ended their youthful romance. She had avoided the issue. And him.

Fine. He'd let her go, he'd let her return to New York, never knowing. Seeing her again had been a mistake. The wound was reopened. Maybe it had never really healed at all. Since he'd known he would see her again, he'd thought of nothing else.

He'd half-hoped Cora Talmadge had changed. Maybe she'd become polished after her years in Manhattan, maybe she'd turned cold. But no. She was just the same as he remembered her. Everything faintly askew, singular and oddly alone. The effect was even stronger now than it had been at nineteen.

She was twenty-eight years old, and she still looked out at the world through those surprised gray eyes.

Her face was beautiful, maybe more so than he remembered. Her nose was still delicate and straight, her eyes tilted at the corners, soft and somehow vulnerable. Her chin was small and square, and he remembered how it quivered when she repressed fear or tried not to cry.

But it was her quick, fluid expressions that held his memory. Her face showed every emotion, but he never knew what she was thinking. She had been at nineteen, and was now, a poignant mystery.

At least she hadn't forgotten him. He'd been afraid that she would smile politely and offer small talk when they met again. But from the moment he saw her huddled in the plane, he knew she'd rather leap from the plane without the parachute than talk to him again.

Her abject horror reminded him of every reason she had lingered in his heart when every other woman was forgotten. But she didn't want him. She clearly had no interest in reforming a friendship between them.

Cora fiddled with her pack, waiting impatiently to get as far away from him as possible. She turned in a circle, one way, then back again.

"Where is everybody? Jenny and those businessmen and your guides? I don't see them." She looked up into the sky. "They had to land before we did, right?"

"They should have." Adrian gazed across the horizon. Nothing. The sky was empty. Yet the land formations indicated he stood just north of Scottsdale. Adrian shook his head. Nothing. Not a house, not a street. But grass, all over. The plants looked odd. Different.

"I didn't realize we were blown this far off."

Cora still sounded calm. She eased her parachute from her back and unbuttoned her flight suit. She squirmed free of it. She wore pressed chinos and a white T-shirt. He suspected they were the same pair of chinos she'd worn when they met, and every day after. She wore plaid sneakers, with paint splatters on the toes.

"Those are new."

She looked down at her feet. "I've had them for seven years."

"New to me."

Her chin lifted. "I have new flannel pajamas."

Adrian sighed and shook his head. "I was afraid of that."

"Aren't we supposed to fold up the parachute? That was in the video."

"Right." Adrian folded the parachute, while Cora attempted to assist, and instead, tangled the cords. He caught her hand. It felt small and warm in his. "Let me."

She stepped back, saying nothing. But she looked a little hurt. He put the pack on his back. She didn't meet his eyes, but sorrow touched the curve of her lips. Adrian remembered that look from their brief days in India. She'd looked defeated and sad, trudging along beside him.

And he had lost her. He had never known why.

"Well? Which way do we go?"

Adrian shrugged. "I'd say we're somewhere northeast of Scottsdale. We go west."

Cora looked up at the sun, held out her arms, then turned to the north and marched off. Adrian smiled. The nomadic adventurer strikes again. He caught up with her. "West,

37

angel. That way." He pointed and she nodded, though her expression appeared a little pained.

"In New York, there are signs."

"There's not much evidence of it here, but we have signs in Arizona, too."

"I'd like to see one."

"I would, too."

Chapter Two

"We're walking in circles, Adrian." Cora stopped, her hands on her hips, her hair falling around her face in careless disarray. Her cheeks looked pink from walking. "It's getting hot. Fortunately, I applied a high-SPF sunscreen this morning." She studied him intently. "I suppose you're used to the heat, so it doesn't bother you to be walking in circles all day."

She sounded suspicious, as if he'd lost them on purpose. Adrian turned and gestured back to the mountains. "If you find yourself facing Camelback, you can say we've turned around, Cora."

She considered this a moment, then nodded. "I suppose that's true." She paused. "So where is everyone? Shouldn't we be seeing houses by now?"

"We should be seeing Phoenix itself by now." Adrian turned in a full circle. Nothing, not for miles, not anywhere. "Those are the southern end of the McDowell Mountains.

Just north is Pinnacle Peak. This should be dead center Scottsdale."

"Very funny. Take me home, Adrian."

"We're lost."

She tilted her head back and drew a long breath of exasperation. Cora had a pretty neck, long and slender. Adrian looked away.

"Lost? You expect me to believe you've lost us?"

"I haven't 'lost us.' We landed somewhere . . . unexpected."

"You were born here, Adrian. How 'unexpected' can it be?"

"Actually, I was abandoned here. I have no idea where I was born."

"Don't quibble, Adrian. You know your way around, and I suppose you think this is very amusing." Her chin lifted and her eyes narrowed. "But I have plans for this evening."

"Do you?" He couldn't hide his irritation. "What plans?"

She hesitated. "I have a dinner engagement."

"Good for you." Adrian tried to stop himself, and failed. "With who?"

"With . . . with one of those businessmen. The blond one."

"Davis."

"Yes. Mr. Davis."

"Davis is his first name."

Cora's eyes cooled to blue, snapping with anger. "I didn't ask his name."

"Just agreed to spend an evening of bliss in his company. Well, angel, as soon as I can get you back to the airport, you can go about your business."

She glared. Adrian glared back. So that was the kind of man that attracted Cora Talmadge. Davis Sprague, a high-tech accountant.

"Thank you. I intend to do just that."

40

Her eyes narrowed to blue-gray slits. Her lip curled. Cora Talmadge had the most expressive mouth he'd ever seen. Not full or thin, but soft. He remembered kissing that mouth, and how she responded with such sweet vigor.

Adrian took a step closer to her. She stiffened, but she didn't back away. "I wouldn't want to keep you from such an important engagement."

"You have already."

Adrian touched her cheek. Her eyelashes fluttered, her facial features tensed. "I wondered if I'd still find you attractive."

He saw her swallow nervously, but she didn't respond.

"I thought you couldn't compare to my memory. But I was wrong, Cora. You're even sweeter than you were. I'm not sure why."

She pressed her lips together, but her chin quivered. That expression, he knew too well.

Adrian's gaze lingered on her mouth. He pressed the pad of his thumb against her bottom lip. He moved closer, and knew she held her breath. He caressed her lip, slow and light, until she gasped, almost imperceptibly.

"I wondered if I'd still trade the world to kiss you."

Her eyes widened, but she didn't speak. Her chest rose and fell over quick breaths. Adrian ran his thumb from her lip across her cheek, just above her ear. He slid his hand into her hair, untangling her loose braid until her hair fell over her shoulders. One long strand curled around his finger.

He wanted to kiss her. He longed to remind her of the passion that once burned between them. From the moment he met her, to the last night in her arms, it had never abated. But she had left, and he didn't know why. Until he understood that, he couldn't reclaim her heart, or settle his own.

Adrian leaned toward her, imagining his mouth on hers.

He felt her swift breaths as their faces drew closer. He imagined her soft taste, her warmth. Her eyes drifted shut. She was surrendering.

He didn't want her surrender.

Adrian drew back. She opened her eyes and her cheeks flushed pink. "Don't do that." Her voice shook.

"I didn't."

"Almost."

Adrian smiled. " 'Almost' isn't a kiss." But it felt like one. His body reacted as if she'd stripped and begged him to make love to her. He should have kissed her and gotten it over with.

Cora trudged on ahead. Adrian sighed and followed. She walked fast. Maybe living in Manhattan had strengthened her more than he realized.

"Did you ever find your biological parents?" Cora had a way of bringing subjects out of thin air. That characteristic hadn't changed, either. Adrian suspected she was trying to keep their conversation safe.

"No. After a few more failed attempts, I stopped trying. I'm probably better off not knowing."

She watched him intently. "Why?"

"The one thing I learned about my 'discovery' was that I was bruised and malnourished."

Her face paled, her eyes widened. "Oh, how awful!"

"I don't remember it, Cora. I was four months old."

Cora winced. He saw tears in her eyes. "So you still don't know your ancestry?"

"I was wrapped in an old, dirty Navajo blanket, tied to a cradleboard. I assume I am Navajo."

Cora studied his face, sighed faintly, then looked embarrassed. Adrian wondered what she saw that inspired pink cheeks. She turned her attention casually to a Palo Verde bush and plucked one of its golden blossoms. "Where were you found?"

"On a rock, in the hills around Carefree."

Cora's gaze snapped from the plant to him. "On a rock? Who would leave a baby on a rock?"

"That's why I stopped looking. I didn't want to find out."

The sky turned red as the sun rose higher across the desert. For a moment, Adrian wondered if somehow they had been walking in circles, after all.

"What about the people who adopted you, your parents? They must love you." Cora sounded hopeful.

"They adopted nine children. They're loving people."

Cora fingered the Palo Verde blossom. "It must be nice to have brothers and sisters."

Adrian remembered that she had none. Her parents divorced when she was ten, leaving her jostled between Maine and Nova Scotia. "Yes. They're good people. They adopted children no one else wanted, and they taught us our various cultures. So I speak Navajo, which presumably is my heritage."

"If they valued your culture, why did they name you 'Adrian?' Why not Bright Arrow, or something like that?"

Adrian laughed. "I was named for my grandfather."

"You grew up surrounded with people, and I got tossed from small town to smaller town. I wonder if that's why . . . " Cora stopped abruptly and looked away.

"How are your parents?"

Cora hesitated. Adrian hadn't met Cora's father, but he remembered her mother—a cold, silent woman who radiated disapproval. He had tried to convince Cora that her mother's opinion wasn't deserved. She had never quite believed him.

Cora dropped the yellow blossom and sighed. "My mother is still in Nova Scotia, but she moved farther into the

43

woods when the population went over a thousand. My father's still in Maine. Sometimes, I exhibit his sculpture in my gallery. They visit me in Manhattan. I visit them in the summer, sometimes."

Cora fell silent, watching his face. He wondered what she was thinking now.

"Jenny says your gallery is struggling."

A faint frown tugged at her lips. "It's small. Big artists want big galleries. I started it so I could exhibit my own sculptures." She paused and sighed. "I sold a few."

"I still have the one you gave me."

A sorrowful smile touched her lips. "Did you ever figure out what it was?"

Adrian smiled. "It's the wind, angel. Wind meeting wind. It's you and me."

Her eyes widened in surprise, her mouth dropped. Her cheeks flushed to bright pink, and she turned away. He'd guessed right, this time. Too late, maybe. But he'd guessed right. Staring at the peculiar object for hours on end finally had paid off.

"Shouldn't there be a road around here somewhere? I'm getting tired of carrying this pack. And I'm thirsty." Cora climbed up on a boulder, then climbed onto another. She shaded her eyes against the sun.

"Is that water clean enough to drink?"

Adrian eyed her doubtfully. "What water?"

She issued an impatient sigh. "The water in that river."

"What river?"

Cora pointed. "That one."

Adrian stared at her, then climbed onto the rock beside her. There, cutting through the empty desert that should be Scottsdale, a wide river flowed. Wide and sparkling, where the nearly dry Salt should run.

"Well? Can we drink from it?"

"No."

"Why not?"

"Because it's not there."

Cora drew a long, patient breath, then turned to face Adrian. He looked sane. He didn't appear injured. But the man was clearly confused. "Being a hero has finally taken its toll on you."

He eyed her doubtfully, the confusion furrowing his smooth forehead. "What are you talking about?"

Cora gestured at the river. "You just told me that river isn't there. It's there, Adrian. It's wide and swift, and I'm surprised you haven't been rafting on it."

Adrian looked back at the river. "That's the Salt, Cora. It's a well-tended aqueduct, not a damned river."

She angled her brow, waiting for him to accept the obvious. She cupped her hand to her ear, listening dramatically. "I must be mistaking the rushing sounds."

"Something is wrong. It looks like Scottsdale's landscape. The Salt River Reservation should be south of here, but . . . "

Cora sighed and shook her head. "A man can only maintain heroic standards for so long, Adrian, before he cracks."

"You've never been to Arizona, have you, Cora?" Adrian didn't let her answer. "What do you mean, 'heroic standards?' "

"You get me in trouble, then you save me." She braced her hands on her hips and tapped her foot. "You put me on a raft, in the rapids, in a storm—"

"I didn't know a storm was coming."

"It came. And you saved me." Cora paused as a sinking feeling washed over her. "Because I mishandled the paddles and overturned us."

A faint smile touched his lips. "That day was your birthday, too."

Cora shoved away the tenderness of her memory, and recalled the reality of their disasters. "You took me skiing, do you remember that?"

He looked uncomfortable. "You said you could ski."

"On beginner slopes, Adrian. I believe they're known as 'bunny hills.' You had us dropped onto new snow, over what I'd call cliffs." She paused for effect. "I ended up in a tree."

His smile deepened, though he obviously tried to contain his amusement. "You looked like a Christmas tree ornament."

"You saved me."

"I felt I had to."

"Exactly. And you saved me today. True, I wouldn't have jumped out of a plane if not for you, but—"

His brow rose, and Cora cringed. "You had no idea I'd be there."

"Let's be honest, shall we?" Cora braced herself and straightened, her chin high. She was thirsty and tired, and that had the unfortunate effect of reducing inhibitions. "I had no intention of jumping out of that ridiculous plane until I saw you. Generally, I avoid getting into them at all. Jenny had already paid—"

He grinned, wide and without remorse. "I know."

Her lips tightened. "You know?"

"Of course. Whose idea do you think this was? Jenny wanted to give you a special present for your birthday. She didn't think you'd go for skydiving, and I knew you wouldn't. I also knew, from past experience, that you have a weakness for the words 'paid in advance.' It's guilt, Cora. You don't want to disappoint. A residual of childhood, perhaps."

Cora stared in amazement. Her heart took strange bouncing leaps. "I see."

"I doubt that—"

"Did it ever occur to you that I wanted to be a hero, too?"

His self-satisfied expression faded, leaving him confused again. "What?"

"You were always saving me, Adrian. From trees, from rivers. Now, from the sky. I never saved you. Not once."

Adrian touched her face, gently. "That's part of your charm, angel. You made me feel heroic." His hand dropped to his side as he studied her face. "I take it I made you feel . . . less."

"You were the saver. I was the save-ee."

"Is that why you left?"

Cora hesitated. "In a way." She swallowed hard to contain her burgeoning emotion. She looked back at the river, squinting as the bright sun glinted on its surface. "If you know the name of the river, you know where it goes. We can follow it, and find . . . Where does this river go, by the way?"

"It goes through Tempe, on the south side of Phoenix. Cora, you don't understand. This river shouldn't be this wide, this full. Something's wrong."

"So maybe a dam burst. Let's go. It has to lead somewhere."

Adrian sighed. "Why do I think it won't be what I expect?"

They walked without speaking. The river ran on and on, birds dove and fed as if used to the water. Adrian stopped and surveyed the unchanging landscape. He gestured toward a sharp hill. "I've got to get a look around. You wait here. I'll climb up and see if I can locate our position."

"Good idea."

Adrian dropped his gear, so Cora dropped hers, then eyed the hill with misgivings. "It looks sheer."

"It is sheer. You wait here."

47

Cora nodded, then sank down and sat cross-legged beside the river. "I never was very good at rock-climbing."

"You only sprained an ankle, Cora."

She nodded again, but didn't comment.

"I'll be back."

Cora watched Adrian as he ran across the grassy desert toward the hill. How could he run? Her legs ached, her body ached. And he ran like a sprinter. She watched him scale the rocks, then disappear from her view.

Cora lay back and stared at the sky. She saw no airplanes, no streaks of white that indicated their passage. It was so quiet. It felt like a dream, strange and unreal. If her legs didn't ache so much, she might believe she imagined it all.

There was a time she would have given anything to be the right woman for Adrian de Vargas. If she thought it was possible, she might still allow herself to dream. She knew better now. She'd never change, and neither would he.

Cora closed her eyes. She felt the sun on her face. He'd almost kissed her. She was sorry he'd stopped.

"Cora, wake up."

Cora opened one eye. Adrian stood over her, the sun behind him. She smiled.

"Now, Cora."

He sounded agitated. Cora's smile faded, but she didn't get up. "What's the matter? Did you find Phoenix?"

"No."

"Scottsdale?"

"No."

Cora sighed. "Well? What did you see?"

"Indians, Cora. I saw Indians."

48

"Native Americans, Adrian." Cora sat up and yawned. "Did you ask them where we are?"

"I didn't speak with them."

"Why not?"

"They were riding too fast." His voice sounded very odd.

"What do you mean, 'riding?' "

"As one does on horseback. When hunting. . . . " He paused and his brow furrowed as if in pain. "Elk."

"Elk?"

He nodded. "Three men on horseback, hunting elk. With bows and arrows, Cora. They got one, too. Then headed off into the hills."

Cora's lips formed a tight frown of indignation. She scrambled to her feet and placed her fists firmly on her hips. "Do you mean they actually killed an elk? Is it hunting season?"

Adrian placed his hand on his forehead. "Elk don't normally roam the suburbs, Cora. A few have been introduced back into Arizona, but not here."

"We should report them!"

"When we find a warden, we'll do that, shall we?" His tone indicated he considered her comments peculiar. Cora stiffened.

"Did you see anything else?"

"There's a decrepit ranch just west of here."

"Oh! Good. They'll have a phone. We can call. Someone will pick us up."

"Don't hold your breath. They don't have roads, I didn't see any power lines anywhere. So a phone . . . "

"Of course they'll have a phone. Probably a cellular phone. Everyone has a phone."

* * *

49

"Well? Knock on the door."

Cora waited impatiently while Adrian assessed the small farm. It was a shambles, no question, but someone obviously lived here. Chickens scurried across the yard. Horses grazed in a rough pen. Only one looked suitable for riding. They all looked like they needed to be wormed.

"I may have to speak to them about seeing a veterinarian. Animals should be kept in better condition."

Adrian eyed her doubtfully. "Let's just ask for a phone, and get out of here."

Cora's brow furrowed when one of the horses broke into a hacking cough. "This is unacceptable."

Adrian seized her arm. "Right the world later, woman."

"I suppose it wouldn't be wise to insult the owner of this establishment before he helps us." Cora looked impatiently at the front door of the cabin. "What are you waiting for?"

"There's something wrong, Cora. Look, no trucks, nothing."

"Maybe someone took it to town." Cora decided not to wait for Adrian to act. She'd done that enough when they were young.

Time to take charge. She stepped up to the door, cleared her throat as if for a speech, then knocked twice on the door. She cast a triumphant glance Adrian's way, to be sure that he noted her confident attitude. He nodded, offering silent support.

The door opened a crack. The end of an old rifle poked through, half-way down the door. Adrian grabbed Cora's arm and yanked her back.

"We don't mean to bother you! But—"

"Cora, I think we should be going now."

The door opened wider and a small, red-haired boy appeared. "You git, or I'll call my pa."

Cora breathed a sigh of relief and smiled at the boy. "Hi, there! I'm Cora Talmadge, and this is—"

The boy eyed Adrian with a sneer that didn't conceal his fear. "He's red."

Cora glanced back at Adrian. "He's been running." He didn't look flushed to her. She turned back to the boy. "Are your parents home?"

"Ma's dead."

"Oh! I'm sorry!"

The boy shrugged as if it didn't matter. "Pa ain't here."

"You shouldn't tell that to strangers."

"Why not? He ain't."

"Yes, I know, but it's dangerous. Not now, because we won't hurt you, but—"

"Why you wearing boy's clothes?"

Cora's brow furrowed. "I'm not. What is your name?"

"Archibald Cramer."

"Well, then Archibald. Do you have a phone we could use?"

He looked blank at her request. "No."

Cora sighed. The child was right not to allow strangers into his home when his father was gone, true. But she was desperate. "It's not a long distance call, I promise. Maybe your dad keeps a cellular phone somewhere. In his truck, maybe? Do you expect him back soon?"

Archibald didn't seem to understand her question. He kept his rifle pointed at Adrian.

"You know, you really shouldn't point that at people. I know it's just a toy—"

"It ain't no toy."

Cora seized the rifle without preamble and set it against the cabin wall. "Then don't point it!"

Archibald's pink face went white, his eyes rounded like saucers. "Is he going to scalp me?"

51

Stobie Piel

"Scalp you?" Cora stared hard at the boy. Perhaps he had a learning disability that wasn't immediately apparent, but affected his judgment. "We're not going to hurt you, Archibald. We're just lost, you see. We were skydiving. You know, jumping out of an airplane. You may have seen that in movies or on TV—"

The boy eased back into his door, then slammed it shut. Cora rolled her eyes. "That child shouldn't be left alone out here. He needs supervision."

Adrian nodded. "You can say that again. Weird kid."

"Now what?"

"I have no idea."

"You keep saying that. It's getting dark." Cora knocked on the door again. "Archibald! Maybe you could just tell us how far it is to Scottsdale."

"You want answers, girl, you get 'em from me." A harsh, deep voice spoke from behind, and Cora jumped. A large, burly man with a red beard stood behind them. He aimed his strange, heavy rifle with more accuracy than his son.

"Git off my land, red man."

Cora rolled her eyes. "There's no need to be rude! I am Cora Talmadge, and this is Adrian de Vargas. He owns the Nomadic Adventurer School of Skydiving just outside of Scottsdale—" Cora stopped and turned to Adrian, her eyes wide. "You named it for me, didn't you?"

Adrian smiled. "What do you think?"

Cora gazed into Adrian's warm, brown eyes, forgetting the man with a rifle. A tiny smile grew on her lips.

"Cora, maybe we should discuss this at another time."

"Oh, yes." Cora gathered her senses and turned back to the rancher. "We're lost. A whirlwind blew us off course. If you have a phone we could use . . . "

The rancher looked her up and down in a way that made Cora feel like a horse at auction. Her words trailed and she eased down the steps to stand closer to Adrian.

"What'ch you want for her, boy?"

Cora's brow furrowed, she looked up at Adrian. He wore a bewildered expression similar to her own.

"No, you don't understand." Adrian paused. "We need a phone. Or just point us to the nearest road."

"You're on it, boy."

Adrian and Cora looked down at the hard-packed dirt, then at each other. Cora drew a tight breath. She knew where Archibald had inherited his disability from, anyway. "Well, thank you."

The rancher lowered his rifle and took a step toward them. "Give you that there horse for her."

A confused smile curved Adrian's lips. He glanced at Cora. "For . . . her?"

"That's what I said."

Cora gasped as she began to sense his offer. "What?"

The rancher ignored her. "It's a damned fine horse. A hell of a lot better than the nags your people round up." He gestured at the scrawniest of his animals.

Cora clenched her fist. "Perhaps we don't understand you, sir. You're not possibly offering a horse in exchange—"

"For the woman. Put you onto Tradman's trail, too. How's that for an exchange?"

Adrian eased his pack to the ground. Cora wondered if he was clearing his arms for self-defense purposes. "Tradman?"

The rancher's eyes darkened. "The scalper. Figured your kind would like to get your hands on him. Can't say I'd mind getting rid of him, either."

Adrian and Cora exchanged a doubtful glance. Cora

53

forced a smile. "We're not looking for tickets, thank you. Just a phone."

The rancher ignored Cora. "I could be persuaded to offer up an extra chicken for her."

Adrian offered a polite smile. "She's not for sale."

Cora breathed a sigh of relief and elevated her chin. "I'm not."

"Where'd you get her?"

Cora attempted to compose herself. She resented the way the rancher directed his comments to Adrian, as if she couldn't speak for herself. "We met at college, in Boulder, Colorado. They have a good football team, you know."

The rancher laughed, then spat at Cora's announcement. "College? You expect me to believe you've had schoolin'? A girl and a red man?"

Cora braced indignantly. "Now, look—"

"If you ain't selling her, git off my land, boy. But you won't get far stealing white women. Even if you dress her up like that, she's good-looking. Someone's going to come after you, when word gets out."

Cora eased closer to Adrian. "This is too weird. Maybe we should just go. I didn't know people like this existed."

Adrian just stared at the rancher, his face blank. But Cora saw a strange expression in his eyes, one she'd never seen before. "I've been told—"

"Let's go." Cora touched his arm and the rancher's eyes darkened.

"If you want to get a good trade for her, Indian, I wouldn't let it out that you've been between her legs."

Cora's face went white, then flamed to red. "I don't think that's any of your business." Her words choked out, but Adrian shook his head.

"Thank you for your time."

Cora whirled to face him. "You're thanking him? Have you lost your mind?"

Adrian cast a warning glance her way. "No. Have you?"

"Oh, right—" Her propensity for righting wrongs might see them killed. The rancher did hold a rifle. It looked odd, but Cora didn't know much about guns. Maybe Adrian did.

"I see you're a gun collector. That's an interesting gun. Is it an antique?"

"Hell, no! Best in the world, got it from a rebel soldier who passed through here. Left me a carbine, too, but I ain't got no shells."

"A rebel? From what country?"

"Texas."

Cora's eyes narrowed to slits. "Texas? Was he stationed in Bosnia?"

The rancher looked disgusted. "Young folks don't know nothing 'bout what's going on back in the United States. He was fighting in Virginia, of course. Got shot up by the Yanks, and had to come on back home."

"I see." The man was obviously crazy. Now what? Cora decided to give it one more try. "If you could just tell us which way to Phoenix."

"What's Phoenix?"

Cora's jaw tightened fiercely. So, he'd decided to play games. "The city."

"Never heard of it." He sounded serious. Cora glanced at Adrian, who shrugged. Cora began to wonder if somehow they'd been blown to another country.

"Scottsdale?"

The rancher shook his head.

"Tucson?"

"Girl, you're hell and gone from Tucson. That where you

55

come from?" He recognized Tucson, so they couldn't be in another country. How odd!

"I was born in Nova Scotia, when my parents were painting up there. It's beautiful in the summers—"

The rancher was staring. "Ain't that in Canada?"

"Yes. I'm not Canadian, though. I have American citizenship. My father lives in Maine, near Camden?" She waited to see if he recognized the coastal town. Apparently not. "It's a bit of a pain in summers there, but it's so pretty. Traffic is horrible on Route 1." Cora stopped and sighed. "I live in Manhattan now."

The rancher's eyes narrowed to doubtful slits. "How'd you get out here?"

Cora hesitated. "I flew out."

The rancher's brow angled as he turned his attention back to Adrian. "I'm attemptin' to get on with you people, but you don't make it easy on me. Ain't it just like an Indian to try to pawn off a crazy woman?" The rancher issued a clucking noise and shook his head in disapproval. "I ain't payin' squat for her. Not one chicken. Git her off my land."

Adrian seized Cora's arm. "If you don't mind, let me do the talking from now on."

Cora's mouth formed a tight circle of displeasure. Then she smiled. "All right, go ahead. Let's just see how far you get . . . hero."

Adrian looked poised as he turned to the rancher. "Is there another house nearby?"

"Got a raid planned? I ain't telling you nothin', red man. I made that mistake, trusting you people. Lost every chicken I had last year."

Cora chuckled, but made no comment.

"I'm sorry." Adrian cleared his throat. "I don't want any chickens . . . I could pay you." He withdrew a flat wallet and produced twenty dollars.

Cora fumed at the injustice. "I don't think we should have to pay just to find out where we are!"

"Cora—"

The rancher took the bill, then laughed. "What the hell is this?"

"Twenty dollars for your troubles."

The rancher examined the bill, then shook his head. "You people ain't no good at forgery. Can't even get the year straight. This says 1993."

Cora wondered what difference the age of the bill would make. "So, it's a few years old."

"A few years off, I'd say, girl. Say about a hundred and twenty-four."

"A hundred and twenty-four what?"

"Years, girl."

Cora drew a long, patient breath, then nodded. "Okay." She turned to Adrian. "I think you're right. We should go now."

"Good idea."

Another thought struck Cora, and she faced the rancher. We're not in a park, are we?" She paused, then laughed as the situation cleared itself. "It's a theme park! Very funny. Well, you certainly had me fooled. You carried it off very well."

Both Adrian and the rancher eyed her with misgivings. "Git, both of you."

"Cora, shall we go?"

Cora's expression changed. White fury boiled in her veins as she whirled to Adrian. "You're in on it! Oh! I should have

57

known. Well, Adrian de Vargas, knock it off, and knock it off now!"

"What are you talking about?"

"All this! This wacko man and his kid. This." She waved her arms and spun in a circle. "You landed us in some park, and I suppose you've had a good laugh—"

A horseman approached, distracting Cora. He looked like a cowboy, or a desperado. He wore a long mustache. He wore a Civil War uniform, which looked to be part Union and part Confederate. Probably the best costume he could come up with. He had to be an actor. A character actor used to playing villains.

He noticed Adrian and drew his horse up short. He moved slowly, drawing out another aged rifle. He aimed at Adrian. Cora rolled her eyes, then marched across the yard. Cora approached the rider, stood at the horse's shoulder and held out her hand.

"Give it here."

He glanced down at her through one eye. "Who're you?"

"Cora Talmadge. Hand it over."

"What?"

Her patience crumbled. "The gun."

The man looked shocked and confused. Cora stood on tiptoes, seized his rifle and yanked it from his hands. "I've had just about enough of this foolishness. Where's Phoenix? Where's a phone, and how do we get out of here?"

"Cramer! Who's the woman?"

The rancher shrugged. "Don't got no idea. This red man tried to trade her for a couple of my horses."

"He did not!"

The newcomer ignored Cora. "He armed?"

58

Adrian walked smoothly to Cora's side. "What do you think?"

Cora eyed him doubtfully. "Are you?"

His dark look silenced her. She crooked her brow in a dangerous fashion. "I'm armed, too."

No one seemed to care if Cora was armed or not. Her shoulders slumped. If Adrian staged this as a joke, it was a good one. Well thought out.

"What've you got, Cramer? I want more than this two-bit half-breed. We've gotten rid of the northern tribes. Time to take care of these." He waved in the direction of the eastern hills.

Cora began not to care if they were joking. No one called Adrian a "two-bit half-breed." Not in her presence, anyway. "If you can't say something nice, don't say anything at all."

Cramer didn't seem as unpleasant as the man on horseback. Cora decided to revert her questions to him. "Who's gone?"

Cramer shook his head as if she should know the answer. "The army took care of the Navajo, girl."

"Really? How nice. I didn't know they were moving. Where were are they going?"

"Fort Summer. Army folks figuring to keep them out of trouble."

The desperado chuckled. "I wouldn't say that, Cramer. Not so many reached the Fort as headed off."

Cora turned to Adrian. "What's he talking about? Where did the Navajo go? And where is Fort Sumner?"

Adrian kept his eyes on the rider. "Fort Sumner is in New Mexico. I believe he's referring to a time in history known as the Long Walk. It is an ugly period, when more than half of the Dineh population were taken captive and forced to walk

59

three hundred and fifty miles to what amounted to a concentration camp." Adrian's voice changed as he related the story. It grew hard and cold. "Where they were deliberately starved by their captors, and died of disease."

"Oh. I see. It's a reenactment sort of thing. What happened?"

"The Dineh were returned to their rightful land four years later—"

The desperado spat, just missing Adrian's feet. Cora suspected he didn't mean to miss. "They ain't coming back, red man. If I had my say, you and all your kind would be marching to hell. You tell your people up in the hills, eh?"

Adrian ignored him. "The Navajo Nation began as a few million acres around Canyon de Chelly."

Cora recognized the name. "That's one of the sites I wanted to see! Jenny was taking me to an exhibit of Canyon art tonight."

Adrian's brow angled. "I thought you had a date."

Cora blushed. "Well, I hadn't exactly agreed."

A slight smile curved Adrian's lips. "I must have misunderstood."

She didn't respond. "So, I'm right. He's pretending to be from the past." She glared up at the rider. "Well, we don't have time for this. It's getting late. I have an early flight to New York tomorrow."

The rider's eyes narrowed to slits. "What's she talking about, Cramer?"

Cramer sighed. "Girl thinks she can fly. The red fellow tried to sell me a lunatic."

"He never did! You tried to buy me. Adrian wouldn't sell me. Would you, Adrian?"

Adrian hesitated while Cora's mouth dropped. He grinned. "No."

She turned back to Cramer. "Can we just get back to normal here?"

The rider nodded at Adrian. "Has he got any connection to the Tonto, Cramer?"

"Damned if I know."

The rider grinned. "Got a few of your kind already, boy. Maybe you'd like to hand over the girl, or join your brothers."

Cora's brow knit. It sounded like a threat. "He just said I'm crazy."

Cramer nodded. "I did. I don't want this one, Tradman. I'll get me a wife somewhere else. Down in Tucson, maybe."

"A wife!" Cora shook her head vigorously. "No, no, and no. I don't think so. Now, this may be an authentic display of the male attitude in—what year did you say this is supposed to be?"

Cramer rolled his eyes. "1869."

"Of 1869. But I'm just not in the mood here." She paused. "Tradman? You must be the ticket scalper. Is there a concert coming up? Probably a sports thing. Well, I'm leaving tomorrow, so I'm not interested."

"See, Tradman? Talks gibberish."

"Woman don't need to be sane to be useful."

Cora's skin crawled as Tradman assessed her body. He meant sexually. Cramer came unexpectedly to her aide.

"This girl ain't worth getting into a brawl with no Indian."

Tradman drew a shiny revolver from his vest, and Cora groaned. "I wasn't thinking of brawling, Cramer. I was thinking more of adding to my collection."

He aimed the gun with expert ease at Adrian's head, while drawing a sack from his saddle. He unfastened a button, and it unfolded revealing snippets of long black hair, and a few thin braids.

Cora stared, then glanced doubtfully at Tradman. "That's

disgusting. I think you'll need to come up with a more polit-
ically correct display if you want to attract tourists."

"Mexicans pay in gold, girl. You'll be thanking me for
getting you away from the likes of this red devil."

Cramer stepped between Cora and the rider. "Not here,
Tradman. I don't want no trouble with Indians. They stay
clear of me, 'cept for taking a few chickens now and then. I
stay clear of them. You go shooting, and I'll have them all
over me."

"Shooting! Adrian!"

Tradman ignored Cora's outburst. "He's a loner. They
won't miss him. And I'll take the woman."

"He ain't no loner, Tradman. Look at him. He's clean. He
ain't skinny, he speaks English."

"He won't be speaking anything soon."

Cora didn't know what to do. It was probably a joke. But
something told her it wasn't Adrian's joke. He might not
have been raised a Navajo, but he would never allow others
to utter such evil slurs against his people.

It was possible they'd stumbled into some especially
peculiar faction of white supremacists. She knew Adrian
wasn't armed, and Tradman was. Plus, he had a horse.
Which was more than they had.

Cora eyed the horse's bridle. She didn't like the looks of
its bit. It was unnecessarily harsh. She noticed scarring
around the horse's mouth. *Well, we'll just fix that, shall we?*
She glanced up at Tradman, whose pale blue eyes remained
fixed on Adrian as he aimed his gun.

She glanced back at the horse, a nervous, beautiful bay
animal with a white star.

"Look, we don't want any trouble with you. We're lost,
that's all." Adrian was trying to reason with them. But men

62

like Tradman weren't capable of reason. Cora had seen that sort on New York's subways.

She patted the horse's neck, then his ears. Then she slipped the bridle over his head. Tradman wasn't holding the reins. They were wrapped around the pommel of his saddle.

He jerked around, too late. "What the hell?"

Cora hopped back and slapped the horse's rump. The horse startled, then bounded away. "See if you can act your way out of this!"

She chuckled, then dusted her hands on her chinos. "I hope he gets bucked off." She examined her palms and shook her head in dismay. "He never brushes that poor horse. If people can't take care of their animals, they should-n't be allowed to have them."

Adrian's mouth was open, he looked shocked beyond words. Cora wondered why. She faced Cramer again, utilizing the manner of a school teacher. "Which reminds me, Mr. Cramer. When was the last time you had a vet out here?"

"A what?" Cramer's voice sounded small.

"A veterinarian." He still looked blank. "Animal doctor."

"Crazy. Red man, I don't know where you found her, but if I was you, I'd put her right on back."

"The thought crossed my mind."

Cora glanced at Adrian reproachfully, then turned back to the matter at hand. "Your animals need worming. A few shots. It's expensive, but necessary for their care. I worked in a clinic when I was in high school—"

"Aw, hell!" Cramer's interruption brought a frown of displeasure to Cora's lips.

"What?"

Cramer fumbled with his rifle, but he looked white and terrified. Cora heard the noise of what sounded like riders, many riders. She turned. Across the desert raced a group of Indians.

Cora sighed. "When I said this day was eventful, I had no idea."

Cramer's hand shook. "Lord be with me and my boy." He sounded authentically terrified. Cora knew that only reflected his abilities as an actor, but like any good actor, his emotion was infectious. She endured a tremor of fear, too.

To hell with fear. I've just dropped out of a plane. How much worse can marauding Indians be?

Adrian stood in front of her, straight and fearless. He watched the approaching horsemen with a strange expression on his handsome face. It looked like admiration.

Cramer tapped Adrian's shoulder. "Listen—What'd you call yourself?"

"Adrian."

"Adrian, I'm figuring you're a scout, wherever you're from. But I didn't set Tradman on you. You got my word. Hell, you got no reason to believe me—"

Cora wondered how the rancher could possibly accuse her of gibberish after this weak display. "What do you want?"

"Tell 'em I don't mean no harm to your kind." Cora saw tears in the rancher's eyes. Real tears. "Maybe you can convince 'em to spare my boy. Tell 'em Archie's a good worker. Lord, please."

Adrian nodded, but he didn't look back. He kept his dark eyes fixed on the riders. They stopped and formed a semicircle around the entrance to the ranch. Their clothing wasn't much different from the rancher's. They wore bright scarves around their foreheads and their hair was long and black.

Cora wondered where their feathers were. A few carried rifles, but most had bows. Some wore beaded collars. They seemed surprised, probably by her unexpected presence in the theme park.

She held up her hand and waved. "Sorry we interrupted you. We're lost, you see." Cora paused. "I don't suppose any of you have a cellular phone?"

Chapter Three

Adrian stood still as stone. The men on horseback assessed him silently, then turned their attention to Cora. They seemed surprised. Baffled. That much, Adrian understood.

"It's been a bit of a long day, you see, and we're tired." Cora didn't sound upset. She wasn't frightened. Adrian glanced her way. She didn't look tired. She looked pert and beautiful, despite her hair being unraveled from its braid.

Every time he looked at her, his heart twisted. Every time. When she spoke, his muscles tightened as if anticipating a blow from a small fist.

Cora seemed confused by the Indians' lack of response. She glanced Adrian's way and shrugged. She faced the warriors again, casually. "I thought perhaps you could help us. This gentleman," She gestured at Cramer. Her eyebrow raised in a conspiratorial manner and her voice lowered.

"He isn't . . . equipped, shall we say, to point us in the right direction."

The Indians looked at Cora. They looked at each other. One young man spoke quietly to an elder, then eased his horse forward. He faced Adrian, ignoring the rancher. He seemed leery of Cora, and positioned his horse on Adrian's left, separating himself from Cora.

The young man cast a suspicious glance Cora's way, then turned back to Adrian. "We do not know you." He spoke in a language close to Navajo. Adrian wondered if he meant to keep their conversation from the rancher.

"I am Adrian de Vargas." He paused. This wasn't the Arizona he knew. "I am looking for the city. Phoenix."

He expected the doubtful gaze. "A white man's city?"

Adrian hesitated, uncertain how to respond. "A city of many people. All colors."

The young man didn't reply for a long while. "I am Haastin, of the Tonto Apache. Your name is not of The People."

"It was given to me by my adopted parents." Adrian wasn't sure how to answer. The young man studied him thoughtfully.

"We do not know you, but your face is known to us. Do you know the father, whirlwind?"

Just when he thought he was getting somewhere. Everyone in this place was crazy. "It was a whirlwind that brought me here." He sighed, expecting a reaction similar to Cramer's.

Haastin's eyes widened into both shock and joy. "The father awaits you." A new and deeper respect sounded in his voice. "Come with us."

Adrian hesitated. "I am lost."

The young man smiled. "Not lost, but found." He eyed

Cora again. "It is a great power that transports not only himself, but his woman. Did you capture her?"

My woman. A tremor invaded Adrian's spine, and ran through him like the wind. He liked the idea of capturing Cora. "You could call it that, perhaps. Where would you take us?"

"I will leave it to whirlwind to tell you."

Haastin's language was strange, altered from the Navajo Adrian knew. Maybe the word he had interpreted as "whirlwind" meant something else. It was spoken with reverence and pride, like the name of a god.

Haastin turned his attention to Cramer, who remained white and shaking. "What of that one? Did he do you harm?"

"He did no harm, other than confusing us. No more than you have done yourself."

Haastin seemed to understand. He even seemed amused by the situation. "We fear others follow him to this sacred land. We try to drive him away, but he is stubborn. He doesn't fight, so we do not fight."

"He stood against a man called Tradman."

Cramer heard the desperado's name and sucked in air as if it might be his last. Haastin edged the horse Cramer's way. A twinkle in his dark eyes told Adrian humor motivated his veiled threat. "We honor your courage Man Who Is Alone." Haastin spoke in halting English, his face expressionless.

Adrian caught the twitch of a smile on Haastin's mouth before his expression reverted to stone.

Haastin slipped back to Navajo. "He needs reminding of his place, I think."

Adrian smiled. "He is not entirely alone. He has a son."

"But no wife. She is in the ground by his hut, beneath a small stone." Haastin paused. "He sets flowers by the rock."

Cora tapped Adrian's shoulder. "What's he saying?"

"Haastin has offered to take us with him."

Cora's brow furrowed. "Where? To Phoenix?"

Adrian hesitated. He wanted to go with the Apache, to investigate, but Cora might object if he gave her the opportunity. "I believe they can help us."

Cora considered this. She obviously trusted his judgment, and Adrian endured a pang of guilt. He felt fairly certain Haastin's men wouldn't bring them to Phoenix. "Do they know I have a flight early tomorrow morning?"

Haastin listened to Cora's comments with a dubious expression. "Your woman talks much."

"My woman . . . " Adrian's voice trailed. He wanted it to be true. Some part of him had never let her go. His gaze shifted to Cora. Her cheeks were pink from the heat. She puffed a quick breath, and a portion of her long, curly hair elevated. If they had truly gone back in time, by a method a white man couldn't comprehend, yet seemed to offer no confusion to the Apache warriors, then maybe he didn't have to let go of Cora at all.

"My woman talks much, but she will go where I tell her to go." Adrian's voice wavered slightly at the last statement. He thanked the higher powers that Cora didn't understand Native languages.

Haastin nodded, then turned to the elder man. The elder man watched Adrian intently, but he didn't speak. He nodded once. Haastin waved to another warrior. "Ride two, and give this man your horse."

The warrior didn't hesitate. He jumped down and led his horse to Adrian. The horse was lean, black and white. It snorted and tossed its head as if eager to be off, at a high speed. Cora didn't like fast rafts, fast skis, or fast cars. Fast horses though . . .

"I'm afraid we'll have to ride—"

Her brow angled. "Riding is one thing I can do. I had a pony, you know."

"No. I didn't know."

She looked proud. "I won three medals for stadium jumping." She sighed. "I was in Pony Club." A far-away expression crossed her face. "I could vault on and off at the canter and ride backwards." She cast a proud glance at Cramer. Cramer appeared mystified, not without reason, but Cora didn't notice. "I was the best in my division. It's the only sport I was ever good at."

Adrian wanted to take her off, alone, and talk. He wanted to hear about this new, unexplored facet of her past. But he couldn't at this moment without alienating Cramer; the man already eyed him like an enemy. He didn't want the man to get violent. Adrian saw the rancher's fear, and realized he had never caused anyone fear before. He liked it. Despite everything he thought he knew about himself, he liked it. "Treat them with respect, and they will respond in kind," he mused aloud.

Cora tapped her lip thoughtfully. "Now, as I remember it, that wasn't always the case—"

Adrian seized her arm. "Not now, Cora."

She nodded. "Right." She offered Cramer a polite smile. "I'm sorry to have troubled you, Mr. Cramer. I hope you remember to call out a vet. And your son needs special ed, I'm afraid. It's worth the effort, I promise you."

She hadn't accepted the possibility of time travel. That much was certain. Adrian looked around, knowing he stood on ground that should be Scottsdale, and time travel no longer seemed impossible.

Cramer eased back toward his decrepit home. He stopped and turned back. "Boy—Adrian—you put off Tradman something awful. He don't forget, and he's got ties over at Camp McDowell. Just thought I'd warn you."

"I'm not afraid of Tradman."

Cora's brow furrowed tight. "I'm not, either. We'll report his bizarre actions to the authorities as soon as we reach Phoenix. I'll mention that he's been pestering you, too."

Cramer and Adrian exchanged a glance and sighed in unison. "Red man, you've got more trouble with this one"—he looked pointedly at Cora—"than Tradman could ever give you. Good luck to you."

Adrian turned his gaze to Cora. Her face knit in a tight frown, offended. "I'll need it."

He took the horse's reins, and Cora's frown tightened. "I suppose you want me to ride behind you?" He sensed a feminist argument approaching.

"I think we'd fit on the saddle better that way." Good. He sounded fair, reasonable. Cora looked suspicious, but she didn't argue.

"Okay."

Adrian tied their parachute packs to the saddle, then mounted. Cora climbed up after him. He offered his hand, but she didn't need it. She settled herself behind him, but she didn't hold his waist as he hoped. Her long legs dangled against his. Her chinos slid up revealing her ankles and calves over fluffy white socks.

Only Cora could make white socks sexy.

Cora noticed her exposed leg and bent down to adjust her

pants. "I hope I don't burn." She fidgeted behind him, fumbled in her pockets, and withdrew a tube of sunscreen.

Cora remained practical. Maybe her senses were rattled from the dive. Adrian considered this. He'd provoked fear, and liked it. He'd contemplated taking Cora captive. Maybe it wasn't Cora's senses that were rattled, but his own.

Haastin lead the Apache forward, and Adrian followed. They rode toward the McDowell Mountains northeast of where Phoenix should be. He hoped Cora wouldn't notice the direction.

"Toothpaste!" Cora's sudden comment startled both Adrian and their horse. It jumped forward, but Adrian reined it back to a walk. Cora didn't lose her balance, nor did she seem unnerved. "Sorry. But Adrian, what do we do about toothbrushes? Ask Haastin if there's a drugstore near where he's taking us."

"I don't think we can count on drugstores, Cora. But there are native plants you can use for that purpose."

"What about sunscreen?"

"We'll think of something."

"I hope so. I burn easily, you know. And I must brush my teeth twice a day."

Adrian nodded. It was possible that Cora was odder than he remembered. He didn't care. He wanted her, and he would have her.

Adrian's will turned to steel. Cora sat behind him. They rode among Apache warriors. She was his. As they rode forward, Adrian realized he didn't care where they were going. She was his.

They'd ridden for an hour, but Haastin had told him very little of their destination. They spoke of the whirlwind as if it were a living entity, a person, but no one would explain when he asked what it meant.

Haastin led his group higher into the hills, riding northward along a narrow but well-trodden path until the sun cast red shadows over the Sonoran desert. Cora didn't complain. She just listened to their voices, occasionally patted the horse's side, and asked about various plant life. She spotted a hare, and directed everyone's attention to it as if a wildebeest had passed by.

Adrian saw no javelinas, and his suspicions about their location grew. The javelinas were late-comers to Arizona, having moved north from Mexico in the early part of the twentieth century. He saw no dwellings, no roads, and no power lines.

"I feel fairly certain we're not heading for Phoenix. I haven't seen a single golf course."

Her calm assessment startled Adrian again, and she leaned forward and to the side to assess his facial expression. Adrian forced his features into stoic submission. "You are jumpy, Adrian. I've never seen you jumpy before. And you look tense. Are you hiding something?"

Yes. I'm plotting to take you captive, and make you mine whether you want to be or not. Adrian tried to clear his senses, to remember the rational mind he once possessed. "No. It's just that you keep popping out with things, out of the blue, when my mind is somewhere else."

"Where?"

"I was considering our predicament."

"Being lost?"

"Possibly. Or maybe something else."

Cora rolled her eyes. "You can't believe we've gone back in time."

73

"The evidence suggests we've done just that."

She snorted, then huffed. "Ridiculous."

"Maybe." He wanted to believe. If true, moving back in time might give him the one thing his life had been missing. Cora.

Adrian de Vargas had the most beautiful back in the world. Cora silently compared his shoulders to those of the other men. Haastin was tall and lean, but not as strong as Adrian. Adrian also had the most beautiful hair in the world, even in a ponytail. Black and thick and shiny. The other men had pretty hair, too, but it didn't look as well-tended, as clean.

Cora tried not to notice, to dwell on his physical perfection. It wasn't easy. She remembered what he looked like naked. She remembered him lying above her, his hair falling forward around his face. Adrian had admirable bone structure. Beautiful, brown eyes, tender lips. . . .

Cora sighed. Adrian tensed and glanced back. "Are you tired?"

"No. Yes!" She cleared her throat. "It's getting dark. How much longer are we going to ride? My bottom isn't conditioned for riding."

Adrian spoke to Haastin in what Cora assumed was Navajo. She liked the sound of their voices. The language was beautiful, somehow transcendental. No wonder they were such fine artists. Haastin chuckled at whatever Adrian had said. A grain of suspicion formed in Cora's mind.

They weren't heading for Phoenix, that much was certain. They'd gone out of their way to avoid any kind of civilization. Yet Adrian didn't seem concerned. He'd been acting peculiar, no question. Unlike the man she remembered from college.

Adrian had been perfect. Never nervous, never con-

74

fused—except occasionally in her presence, and that was her fault for being odd. His life had been perfect, too. He could do everything, get along with anyone.

Until today, of course. He didn't do very well with Tradman or Mr. Cramer. Before today, though, his life was sweet. He'd been raised in a well-to-do suburban home, by loving parents who attended all his sports events, who praised him and encouraged him. He'd become a successful businessman, owning his own company. Cora, on the other hand, verged on another depressing failure.

"I suppose your business is doing well financially."

Adrian startled again. Cora felt sure she'd never seen him startle before. Not once. "I am sitting behind you. You might expect me to make occasional conversation."

He drew a quick breath. "Out of the blue."

"Next time, I'll tap you first." She paused. "Well?"

"Well what?"

"Your business. How's it doing?"

He shrugged, as if he barely remembered he had a career. "It's fine." He paused, probably knowing she expected a more indepth reply. "I operate the skydiving school in spring and fall. I've got a few ties with ballooning. We do rafting and climbing, hiking—"

"No skiing?"

"Skiing in the mountains, snow boarding. We own a few cabins in McDowell Mountain Park." He paused. "A few over near Four Peaks."

"We?"

"My company."

"I see. It's successful."

"Yes."

"Where do you live? In one of those cabins?"

"I have a house in Paradise Valley."

Cora groaned. "Paradise Valley? On Pleasant Street, I suppose."

Adrian hesitated. "Actually, it's a Spanish phrase meaning, approximately, 'street without worry.' "

Cora groaned again. "I live in a small apartment in the Bronx. My neighbors are members of a gang, 'The Demons.' They're actually quite nice young people, in a way. They helped me get rid of the mice infestation—they have all kinds of weapons, you know—but I'm still fighting the cockroaches."

"Then you're in no hurry to go back." Adrian spoke with veiled satisfaction. Almost an elusive threat.

Cora's chin firmed. "I have a life." She paused. "Not much of one, true. But it's mine."

"No adventure, Cora?" His voice lowered, he glanced back at her again, and her heart took a small bounce.

"I don't do 'adventure' very well, Adrian."

"It might be more rewarding when it's unexpected."

Cora reached up, seized his ponytail, and pulled his head straight back. "You did this on purpose, didn't you? I want answers." The quality of her voice was admirable, low and threatening. Cora felt satisfied. "I want them now."

Adrian repressed a laugh, which was unacceptable. Cora tugged his long hair lower.

"I can't see where we're going, woman."

"The horse knows." Her voice remained dangerous. "Start talking. You planned this." Cora noticed the warriors' shocked looks. She glared at Haastin, who saw Adrian laugh. He shrugged and rode forward.

"I didn't plan this, exactly."

"You planned something."

"We'll talk later. Please?"

Cora sensed he disliked begging. His version of "please"

sounded like begging. She released his hair, slowly. "Very well. But I expect a full disclosure as soon as we stop." She waved her hand at Haastin and his friends. "I want them explained, too."

Adrian rubbed his neck muscles. Cora resisted the impulse to assist. "If I could explain what's happened today, I would. I have no clue."

Cora's fingers twitched as she again contemplated making use of his hair. "That seems unlikely. You've practically admitted you were scheming."

"I arranged to see you again. Not take you back in time."

Haastin stopped his men abruptly, preventing Cora's argument. He spoke to Adrian, who nodded. Cora tapped Adrian's shoulder. "Well?"

"We're stopping for a while. Haastin says they don't ride into their village during the light hours."

"Why not?"

"The village is hidden, moved often. Their strength is in stealth."

"So you don't know where we are, or where we're going?"

Adrian shrugged. "It appears they're taking us to the area I know as the McDowell Mountains, which is northeast of where I live. I know the area well, so don't worry."

"Why should I worry?" Adrian ignored her sarcasm, and swung his leg forward over the saddle. "That's not the proper method of dismounting, Adrian."

Cora squirmed forward in the saddle, and dismounted correctly, her right leg carefully over the back. She hopped down, proud, but Adrian was speaking with Haastin and didn't notice.

I finally do something well, and he couldn't care less. Cora sighed to herself, and took off the horse's saddle. "He's thin, but well cared for. Good." The older man smiled as if he knew she had complimented him, then hitched the horse with the others.

Haastin's men prepared a simple meal. Adrian assisted, but they shook their heads when Cora tried to help. She wondered if Adrian had told them about her inabilities camping, but she didn't dare ask. They produced dried meat and some sort of root vegetable, which they shared with Adrian.

Cora sat on a flat, sand-colored rock, waiting for her portion. Adrian sat beside her, and passed her the food. "It's elk." He sounded hesitant, but at this point, Cora didn't care what it was. Her stomach churned at the sight.

"It's quite tasty." She swallowed, and took a drink of water. She didn't dare examine it to see if it was clear.

Daylight ebbed away, fading to night. Haastin lay on his back, eyes closed. The older man stood as if on watch. Cora peeked at Adrian. He was watching her, too.

"So, are we sleeping here tonight?"

"So it seems."

"Oh." Cora felt nervous. She wasn't sure why. "Do they have blankets?"

Adrian smiled. "I don't think they'll provide us with sleeping bags, if that's what you mean." His dark gaze moved from her face to her body, then back. His smile widened. "A shame we don't have at least one." His voice lowered meaningfully. Cora knew why, and her face flamed.

A sleeping bag. She swallowed too fast, coughed, and took a quick gulp of water. Her face still felt unnaturally hot. He was referring to their first night together, when he took her up into the Boulder foothills, set up a tent beneath the Flatirons, and made love to her until dawn.

The best night of my life. Cora tried to concentrate on her sparse meal and failed. She'd thought then, innocently, that anything was possible; that if she tried hard enough, she would deserve his approval, that she would make him proud. She thought because love-making was bliss, because their passion seemed endless, that her confidence would carry through all parts of her life. It wouldn't, but she didn't know that then.

Cora stuffed in another large bite of dried meat, fighting to control her wayward thoughts. "So, are you going to tell me what's really going on?" Her voice came thick around a full mouth, but she had to redirect their conversation.

"Cora, I told you. I don't know."

She angled her brow doubtfully. "Adrian, I'm tired. I have a flight to New York tomorrow morning at eight o'clock, which I may possibly miss."

"I'm afraid so."

She looked into his eyes. "Please." *Curses! Now I'm begging.*

Adrian touched her cheek. "Cora, I'm not lying to you. I don't know what's happened to us."

Cora started to speak, but Adrian took her hand. "Come with me."

He stood up, and pulled her with him. "Where are we going?"

Adrian didn't answer. He led her from the campsite, through short, jagged bushes, over rocks. The night was clear, the moon a half crescent. Cora saw the ground just well enough not to stumble, but Adrian seemed to know where he was going.

He brought her to an open space, to the edge of a plateau. Beyond them stretched a vast, dark plain. "What's this?"

"This, Cora, is the desert just north of Phoenix." Adrian waved his arm back and forth. "Do you understand?"

"You know where we are?"

"Yes. I've hiked this path many times. I know this campsite. I've stood here, in this same spot, and watched the sun set. Up to the right is Pinnacle Peak. Just south is Paradise Valley. I live there, Cora. Do you know what happens at night?"

Cora swallowed, looking up at him as the night wind moved his hair softly from his face. *My love.* "What happens?"

"The desert looks like it's on fire, Cora. Every light blazes. It flames across the desert like magic."

"Are we talking about city lights here, Adrian?"

He smiled and leaned closer to her. "Yes. Fire."

Cora tore her gaze from his face and eyed the black desert. "So what's happened? A power outage?"

Adrian took her shoulders and turned her to face him. "There is no Phoenix, no Scottsdale, no Paradise Valley. No man-made lights. The city is gone, Cora. It's not here. There is only one reason."

"Not time travel! No, no, and no."

"Look." He eased her around. "You flew over this area, you've driven through it. It's huge, and growing. Where is it now?"

Cora stared, considering. "You can do a lot, I know. But I don't think even you could get everyone in Arizona to turn off their lights just to play a joke on me."

Adrian turned her back to face him. Cora felt like a doll in his hands. "I wouldn't play a joke on you at all. I wouldn't hurt you, nor make you feel bad, or . . . " His voice trailed as if he thought of something else he wouldn't do, and had reconsidered. A tremor of nervous agitation spilled through Cora's veins.

Adrian shook his head as if to banish a wayward thought. "You left me, and I respected your freedom. Do you know how much I wanted to hunt you down, to find you, and bring you back to me? To give you no choice, to keep you in my bed where I know you were happy?"

Cora's small, muted squeak stopped his words. Painful emotion flooded through her, leaving her weak. "I thought you'd be relieved to be rid of me."

He let her go so fast that she stumbled backward. Even in darkness, she saw his eyes blaze. "Relieved? Why? To be ditched in the middle of India?"

Cora winced. "It wouldn't have worked, Adrian. I wouldn't have gone farther than a mile up Mount Everest before something happened. I would have fallen, you'd have to carry me back down—"

His hands went to his hips, his lips tightened into anger. "So what? I didn't mind carrying you."

"You wouldn't have gotten to the top as you'd dreamed." Her voice was very small and wistful. Cora fought tears, and she won, for the moment.

"The top? What makes you think I wanted to get to the top without you?"

"You talked about it constantly. Your friends were going up, and they weren't afraid. You were so excited—"

He huffed. "Do you know why?"

Cora hesitated. "Well, no. I never quite understood that part."

"Then I'll tell you why." He sounded angry, hurt. Cora chewed her lip. "I was a fool, angel. I was nineteen, and climbing to the top of the world with you was the most romantic thing I could imagine."

Cora's face tightened into a protective ball. His hurt grew, and sank deep inside her. Dimly, she realized only a nineteen-year-old boy would consider sub-zero temperatures and near death conditions romantic, but her heart expanded on Adrian's behalf.

His jaw was set firm and angry. His eyes glittered. "If you didn't want to go, why didn't you tell me? Did you think I'd go without you?"

"No. I thought you would stay." Cora wanted to touch him. Instead, her fingers curled into a tight ball of restraint. "Don't you see? I didn't want that. I didn't want you to have to give up your dreams for me."

"My dreams." Adrian looked at the ground and shook his head. "Cora, it wasn't the mountain I wanted. It was you." He met her eyes, and she saw him as he had been at nineteen. Young and passionate and strong. "I was going to ask you to marry me."

Cora's mouth drifted open, her eyes widened. Her breath came slow and shocked. She started to shake her head. It was too much to imagine. Adrian took her shoulders again, more gently this time.

"I was nineteen, Cora. I wasn't thinking. I was in love, and it seemed right. I know we were too young. You would probably have laughed. . . . "

"I wouldn't have." She didn't want to cry, but tears stung her eyes. "I would have married you in a second, and been an albatross ever after."

He smiled, but he didn't look happy. He reached beneath his white shirt and withdrew a black necklace. On the end hung a narrow, silver ring. "Like this?"

Cora looked at the ring, then at Adrian. "What is it?"

"Your engagement ring. I bought it in Kathmandu."

Misery welled from her chest and erupted in a tortured moan.

"No." *I hurt you. Adrian.*

She knew now what had eluded her nine years before. She had believed she was acting on his behalf. But she had been acting for herself, instead. She couldn't endure failing him again, so she left. Not for him, but for herself. Adrian could endure disappointment. She couldn't.

She squeezed her eyes shut to stop the tears, but they emerged from beneath her lashes and fell to her cheeks. "I'm sorry."

Adrian cupped her chin in his hand and lifted her face. "It's not your fault, Cora. I wanted you. There's no reason you should have wanted me, too."

His hand slid from her face and he gazed back out over what should be Phoenix. "I took this"— He lifted the ring, then let it fall back to his chest—"I took it with me when I climbed the mountain. I made it to the top, and I stood there alone."

Cora's heart throbbed in pain, in remorse. *I'm not good enough, I'm not worth your pain.* She couldn't speak. She barely breathed.

"I meant to throw it as far as I could, to set you free. To set myself free. I couldn't do it." Adrian looked back to her. "I couldn't let go of you. So I flew home, and I wrote letters, and I waited like a fool for your answer."

Cora's knees went weak and she sank to the ground. She buried her face in her hands and cried. Adrian seemed surprised by her reaction. He knelt beside her and touched her shoulder gingerly. "I'm sorry, Cora. I shouldn't put this on you. You don't owe me anything."

She peered up at him, her vision misty from crying. "I caved." Her voice came as a broken sob. His brow furrowed. "Caved?"

She nodded. "I caved. I called you. I thought I'd been wrong, and maybe I could make you happy, after all. I missed you, too, and I thought I couldn't live without you."

"You called me?"

Cora stared at a flat, spiny cactus and prodded it with her

plaid sneaker. "You sent your letters to Halifax, but my mother was gone. I didn't get them in New York until three months later." She sniffed and dried her eyes. "I called, but you weren't home."

"You could have called again."

Cora met his eyes, silent for a moment as she steeled herself to the memory. "Once was enough. You had a new roommate—I didn't know him. He said you had gone camping in Santa Fe with your girlfriend."

Adrian groaned and swore. He raked his hands through his hair, caught his fingers in the black band that held it back, yanked it out and tossed it aside. His hair hung loose over his shoulders, and Cora fought to keep from touching him.

"I thought if you'd met someone else, then you probably didn't miss me anymore."

Adrian crossed his arms over his knees and stared out across the desert. "Ever heard of a rebound relationship, Cora?" He didn't let her answer. "There were several. I found it simpler to date women more intent on action than on introspection."

"Women the opposite of me." Cora crossed her arms over her knees, too. "I thought you would prefer someone like that."

Adrian issued a derisive snort. "They were safe. Nothing lost, nothing gained. Nothing."

Cora didn't know what to say. "Weren't they more fun than I was?"

He eyed her irritably. "No, they weren't more fun. They were boring. I didn't care if I woke up next to any one of them, if I ever saw them again."

Cora considered Adrian's love life after she left. It wasn't what she'd expected. Since that disastrous phone call, it hadn't occurred to her that his pain lasted, that he even remembered her. He was too sane and too perfect to miss her for long.

But she was wrong. "Didn't you date anyone sensible?"

"After college, when I came back here, I focused more on creating a business, but my taste in girlfriends didn't change much. I bought some cabins in the mountains, as I told you. The woman who ran them was Apache. She loathed me. I loathed her. But she made me see that I was hiding."

Cora studied his face. "You didn't loathe her."

"After a while, I grew to care for her. In a way, I loved her. We were together for three years."

Cora's heart beat slow. Three years seemed far more significant than one spring. "Why didn't you marry her?"

"She wanted to marry, to start a family. I wanted to want that, too, but I didn't. She understood, and we ended our relationship. She married a man from Albuquerque about a year later. They have a daughter."

"Do you miss her?"

Adrian looked at Cora, then shook his head. "No. I cared, but it wasn't love. We stayed friends, but there was no ache when she was gone." He turned away and sighed. "After that, dating seemed pointless. I developed my company, and I bought a bigger house. I sent my parents on vacations, but I didn't travel."

"I didn't travel much, either. Once to Paris on a gallery tour."

Adrian picked up a stick and made circles in the dry earth. "Alone?" He winced as if he wished he hadn't asked.

Cora smiled, then resumed a more serious expression. Adrian cared. She mattered to him, even now. "No, not alone. I went with a group of women, and two gay men. We had a good time. I enlisted a Parisian artist to my gallery, but he drank too much, and never submitted anything further."

"Good." Adrian caught himself and tossed the stick aside. "Jenny said you weren't dating anyone."

"You asked her?"

Adrian shrugged. "I was mildly curious."

"Oh." Cora paused. Adrian was more than mildly curious. It didn't seem possible, or right, but Cora began to feel powerful. Dangerously confident. It couldn't last, but she couldn't subdue her elevated self-esteem. "I dated a bit, when one of my friends would set me up or I couldn't get out of it without hurting some man's feelings. But you're the only one I slept with."

Adrian turned slowly. Cora clapped her hand to her forehead and issued a long, tortured moan. *Never let yourself feel confident, Cora. It is now, and always has been, disaster.*

"The only one?"

Cora tried to think of a way to extract herself from her admission, failed, then nodded. She didn't dare look at him, but she knew he was smiling.

"I was the first." Adrian sounded happy. Proud. "Which means there has been no other." Even without seeing him, Cora knew pleasure radiated from his body. "Well, well."

She looked up at him, and she remembered what it was like to hold him, to kiss him, to quake in delirious pleasure beneath him. Her mood altered unexpectedly, but she didn't resist the change. Her eyelids lowered, and she leaned to kiss his cheek. He held himself still, surprised, and she touched his chin, directing his face to hers.

Very softly, Cora touched her lips to his. Her mouth parted against his, and she felt his shocked breath. Cora drew back and gazed into his eyes. She reached beneath her tee shirt and drew out her own necklace, the bear fetish he had given her nine years before, on her nineteenth birthday.

Adrian's expression changed when he saw what she held. "Cora."

Free Falling

Cora smiled. "You see, I've been carrying an albatross of my own."

They sat together, staring silently across the dark desert. "Do you really believe we've gone back in time?"

Adrian barely heard Cora's question. She'd kissed him. For all the moments he'd thought of kissing her, she kissed him first. "What?"

Her brow furrowed slightly, as if she found his reaction odd. "Time, Adrian."

"Oh, that." He forced his gaze from her lips. "I can't think of any other explanation."

"Unless Elvis stole Phoenix and gave it to alien invaders."

His mouth opened. Cora was smiling. She had no fear, even at the thought they were lost—not on land, but in time. "Did the Indians say anything about it?"

"They speak of the white man like strangers, they say he fought a war in the east, and will one day destroy himself. I think they mean the Civil War."

"Mr. Cramer mentioned the Civil War, too. I guess we know our time period, then." Cora paused. "Yuck. Corsets. I'm glad we didn't land in Virginia."

Cora's references weren't predictable. Corsets. "Haastin and his men seem reasonable."

"Apaches. Adrian, weren't the Apaches in some sort of trouble round about now? I saw a movie about Geronimo—"

"Different tribe." *I hope.* He knew more about the Navajo, but there was no need to worry Cora with past violence.

He looked into her eyes and saw a woman where there once was a child. Cora had changed. He wondered if even she knew how much. She had kissed him. He wondered if she'd do it again, if she meant it to stir his senses. Or was it an act of pity?

He shouldn't have incited her sympathy with his youthful heartache. It wasn't beyond Cora to surrender herself out of guilt. "The past is gone, Cora." Adrian patted her knee. "Maybe we can put it to rest and be friends."

Her face changed. The confidence in her silver eyes wavered. The sorrowful, faraway look returned, but she smiled and nodded. "I would like that."

Adrian stood up and held out his hand. She took it, and stood up, too. They looked at each other for a moment. He longed to kiss her, but not on the weight of her sympathy. He couldn't take her captive, or force her to stay by his side, despite the compulsion to do so.

Somewhere, deep in the back of his mind, a divergent thought seized Adrian's imagination. *Why not? She is here, mine . . .*

"Let's get some rest, shall we? Tomorrow can't be any stranger than today."

Cora glanced back at the empty Sonoran desert. "Adrian, I wouldn't count on it."

I kissed him. Cora woke with a start. Bright sun gleamed in her eyes. Adrian lay beside her, still asleep. She heard soft voices, and she sat up. The older man tended the horses. Another prepared food. Haastin returned to the campsite as if he'd been scouting the area.

He looked toward Cora and Adrian and his brow angled. Probably because Adrian still slept. Cora peered at him as he lay quiet beside her. Adrian had always been a late-riser. At first, she had considered the trait out of character, but he took life at his own terms. Early morning wasn't one of them.

Cora started to get up, then lingered as she watched Adrian sleep. His brow furrowed slightly as if he dreamt.

His lip curled at one corner. He looked devious. Cora had never seen him even remotely devious before, but he was scheming in his dream.

Adrian chuckled softly in his sleep. He sounded devious, too. His lip curled into a deeper smile. A peculiar warmth swarmed Cora's body. He said he hadn't lost them on purpose, nor arranged their bizarre circumstances, and Cora believed him.

But he was hiding something. It wasn't the circumstances, but his own intentions he concealed. Cora had no idea what they were. Then again, her own behavior had taken a strange turn, too. *What was I thinking? To just lean over, grab his face, and kiss him?*

He suggested they be "friends." Cora wanted that, because she had believed for so long they could be nothing more. Because Adrian was too perfect and well-adjusted. Until now. Cora watched Adrian sleep, and she envisioned an egg. A perfect, well-adjusted egg, its shell untarnished.

At the top, however, the tiniest of lines had appeared. A minuscule fracture.

Adrian was cracking. So he needed her help and protection. Even if he didn't know it himself.

"Talks Much" Haastin spoke in halting English, phrasing the words like a name. Cora eyed him doubtfully, then offered a polite smile.

"Hi. I'm Cora."

He nodded. "Talks Much, yes." He pointed toward the horses. "Leave soon. Whirlwind waits for him." He gestured at Adrian.

Cora stood up. "Okay." She cleared her throat, trying to decide how to handle the situation. "Um, I have a flight this morning." She checked her watch. "In about an hour. I suppose there's no chance of my making it on time?"

As she guessed, Haastin looked confused. "Leave soon."

"Right." Cora peered down at Adrian. There was no way she'd make her flight. Despite herself, she was glad.

"Very well. I'll wake him. Is there a place I can wash?"

Haastin's confusion grew. He shook his head.

"Water? Maybe a spring?"

He understood this. "Water. That way."

Haastin led her along the path, then pointed to a smaller path between juniper bushes. Cora followed the path and found a private spot behind a boulder, then went farther until she found a tiny stream. "Good enough."

Cora tested the water. It wasn't terribly cold, and it looked clean. She washed, used a leaf to scrub her teeth thoroughly, dampened her hair, then went back to the campsite. Adrian was still sleeping. Haastin and his men spoke in whispers as if afraid to wake him.

"He's a late-riser."

Haastin looked uneasy. "Leave soon."

Cora puffed an impatient breath. "You could have woken him yourselves, you know."

Haastin shook his head. He looked at Adrian with obvious respect, maybe even reverence. Cora wondered why. True, she once looked at him the same way, but for different reasons. She went to his side and gazed at his sleeping face.

She saw the same well-formed cheekbones, the flat cheeks, the strong, angular jaw, the proud forehead. She saw the same tender lips, and the long, black eyelashes. Cora blinked, and she saw an egg. An egg with the slightest of hairline fractures.

"Adrian." His mouth opened, smacked, and closed. "Adrian. Wake up! It's time to go."

Waking Adrian de Vargas had always been a trial. Cora bent down and prodded his shoulder. His lips smacked again, he issued a muted groan, breathed deeply, and reverted to sleep. Cora filled her lungs with air and prepared to shout. "Adrian!"

He shot up like an arrow, brown eyes wide, mouth open. Cora smiled. "Good morning."

He looked around, then up at her. For an instant, she saw his confusion. "Cora. . . . You're really here. We're . . . " He looked around again, and saw Haastin. "It wasn't a dream. We're—"

Cora sat down beside him, cross-legged. "We're still in the past. Hard to believe, but I checked when I went for my walk. The desert is still empty. By the way, there's a nice spring if you want to freshen up. Good, fat boulders for privacy."

Adrian just stared. He pushed his long hair from his forehead, and stared again. "Are you all right, Cora?"

Her brow rose. "I was just wondering the same thing about you. You seem askew."

"*I* seem askew?" He shook his head, then sighed. "I always liked that about you, Cora. There was always something a little out of place in you. Askew. If not for that, you'd be just beautiful."

Cora adjusted her position. "Thank you. Haastin seems eager to get moving. For some reason, he's nervous about waking you. True, it's your grumpiest time of day. I see that hasn't changed."

Adrian smiled. "I'm not grumpy, and no, it hasn't changed."

"I thought not."

Adrian's smile faded as he looked into her eyes. "I'm beginning to wonder if anything has changed at all."

Chapter Four

They rode through the morning, higher and higher into the hills. Having missed her flight, Cora relaxed into the events at hand. Adrian remained quiet. Cora checked his expression several times, but she didn't detect the devious look she'd seen while he slept.

Instead, he seemed to be debating something. Almost as if he was at war with himself. Cora tapped his shoulder, and he startled. "I told you I'd tap you before speaking. Maybe you'd like me to hum or clear my throat before tapping."

He drew a strained breath. "It's just—"

"I know. Your mind was somewhere else."

"Exactly."

"I'm almost afraid to ask where."

A shrewd guess. Adrian jerked around in the saddle, his eyes narrow with suspicion. "What are you talking about?"

"Guilty conscience, Adrian? Perhaps you'd care to relieve the burden by confessing."

His jaw hardened, his brown eyes darkened. He faced ahead again, but his back looked tense. Yes, she was right. Adrian had shown more peculiar sides to his personality in one day than all the time she'd known him before. "I see. You're not ready to squeal. Well, we have time." Cora sat back in the saddle and crossed her arms over her chest. It was an awkward position, but she liked the image.

Adrian looked over his shoulder. "You're looking smug, Cora." His gaze whisked to her lips. "You have the strangest effect on me."

"What effect?"

Adrian glanced forward toward Haastin and the others, then back to Cora. "You're arousing me."

"Oh!" Her voice came as a squeak. His peculiarity was having a similar effect on her, but she decided not to mention that just yet. She eyed their saddle meaningfully. "How uncomfortable for you."

His eyes darkened still more. He wasn't used to her teasing him. He must remember a shy, nineteen-year-old girl. She had been swept away by passion, but she didn't plan it, or instigate it. Suddenly, Cora imagined what it would be like to instigate everything.

I could kiss him here, riding. She bit her lip, then dampened it with a quick dart of her tongue. Adrian swallowed hard, and his breath came quicker.

Haastin stopped his horse, and spoke to Adrian. Adrian rolled his eyes. Cora waited while they conversed in their low, rhythmic language.

At nineteen, she'd been attracted to Adrian, she'd admired him, worshipped him. When he touched her, she'd felt honored. But it was like kneeling before a king, someone so vastly superior that she could do no more than answer his desire.

This was different. She didn't feel weak or small or insignificant. She matched him, and urged him, and felt free to say so. Curse Haastin for interrupting! Something had changed. Cora suspected it was Adrian. Maybe he bumped his head in the fall, maybe the transition in time had rattled him unexpectedly.

It hadn't rattled her. Cora pondered this while Haastin conferred with Adrian. Why wasn't she shocked, or frightened? She accepted they might indeed have gone back in time. But she wasn't nervous or panicked. She felt just the same. Maybe stronger, because now she knew she could handle falling from the sky, losing herself in time, and most of all, seeing Adrian again.

The horses moved forward. Cora cleared her throat and hummed. At times, life was enjoyable. Adrian glanced back, his lips curved in a smile. "Yes?"

"What did they say?"

"We're approaching their campsite."

"Good. So what?"

Adrian hesitated. "I'm not sure. Haastin wanted to know if he should send someone ahead."

"Why?"

"Good question. He spoke as if I expected it, so they could prepare."

"Prepare for what?"

"I have no idea."

"You keep saying that."

Haastin turned his horse from the path, and cut left. They emerged at a sheer drop, and the horses filed one by one down its jagged edge. Short, bare trees and full junipers obscured the view below, but Cora endured a wave of premonition.

"Where are we going?"

Adrian guided the horse around a jagged boulder, then over a flat rock. "Haastin's village lies hidden below."

The horse slipped, and Cora seized Adrian's waist to steady herself. "My lady yields." Adrian spoke in a low whisper, as if to himself, but Cora heard. She couldn't think of anything to say in response. She slid her arms a little tighter around his waist and smiled to herself.

"I wouldn't call it yielding, exactly."

The horse slid again, then took a sharp corner to the right. Back and forth, they zigzagged down the cliff side. Haastin rode casually, as if he'd made this journey a thousand times. Cora turned her attention to their horse, who seemed likewise familiar with the path.

"This is fun."

Adrian glanced back at her. "Is it?"

Cora looked around. "Scenic." A fat, long-eared rabbit hopped out ahead of them, then disappeared behind a juniper bush. "There's another one!"

Adrian shook his head. "Jack rabbits are something we have in our time, Cora."

"Yes, I know. What about those little pigs?"

"They didn't come north until the early twentieth century."

"Too bad." Cora kept her vision alert for more wildlife. "What about roadrunners and coyotes?"

"We should see a few."

Cora scanned the horizon as they emerged near the base of the cliff. "Well, there's something you don't see every day."

Adrian looked in the direction Cora pointed out. A small

village lay sprawled in the valley bed. Its grass huts looked temporary, as if constructed to be easily moved. Children ran in groups, playing and shouting. Women mulled together, working on baskets and preparing food. Cora saw an animal skin stretched out on posts, with other skins beside it.

Horses grazed in a small pen, and chickens pecked around their feet. "I wonder if any of those belongs to Mr. Cramer?"

Adrian didn't answer. He stared at the village with a look of pure, childlike wonder. His brown eyes glowed, his lips parted. Cora waited for him to comment, but he seemed beyond words. "It's better than a reenactment, isn't it? I wonder what they have for bathrooms?"

Since Adrian didn't move, Cora swung herself off the horse and hopped down. She adjusted her chinos and smiled at the village children. They stopped short and stared at her. "Do Native Americans use toothbrushes?"

Adrian didn't answer. His expression hadn't altered. He looked vibrant and alive, passion filled his dark eyes. Cora realized she had never seen him this passionate before. She'd seen him excited and happy, she'd seen his eyes black with desire, but never like this. Never about life.

Life had been easy for Adrian de Vargas. Maybe too easy. Cora looked between him and the approaching villagers. She hadn't understood nine years ago, but she knew now. Her life had been the opposite. She knew failure, she knew loss. Nothing came easily, not her childhood, not her career. Not her first love.

Going back into the past was a breeze comparatively. But for Adrian . . . it might be a different matter. Haastin dismounted and spoke to an old woman. Cora liked the women's clothing. She expected short leather dresses with an attractive fringe, but the women wore long skirts and blouses as a pioneer might wear. They wore turquoise jewelry, and their hair was bound in a figure-eight twist.

Cora fiddled with her hair, wondering if she could do the same. The men of the village weren't dressed much differently from men of the future. Their pants resembled jeans, and they wore high, soft boots like worn cowboy boots. They wore big shirts in different colors, with beaded necklaces.

Before Adrian could dismount, Haastin took his horse's reins, and led him forward. The villagers saw Adrian's face as he passed by. Some gasped, some whispered. All watched him in awe.

Cora hesitated, then trudged along behind his horse, forgotten and ignored by the Apache. They led him to a round hut, the largest in the village. Above the narrow, cloth doorway, Cora saw an image engraved on soft wood. A whirlwind.

Her suspicions mounted. "Adrian, do you see that?"

Adrian nodded, but Haastin cast a warning glance her way. "Talks Much, stop." He looked to Adrian more respectfully and said something in his language. Then he went into the hut alone.

"What did he say?" Cora frowned. "And why does he keep saying 'Talks Much'?"

Adrian tore his gaze from the doorway, a veiled smile on his face. "Oh, I don't know. . . . "

"You know. What does he mean by it?"

"It's just a name. . . . " Adrian paused, grinning. "What they call you."

"They call me Talks Much? How rude!" Cora huffed. "It couldn't be something flattering, could it? Ha!" She fell silent a moment, fidgeting. "I don't talk that much."

Adrian gazed artfully toward the sky. "Haastin told us to wait here."

"I could think of a few names for him, too."

Haastin emerged from the hut and gestured to Adrian. Adrian swung his leg forward over the horse's neck and jumped down. Incorrect dismount again. Cora sighed.

Haastin stood by the grass hut and waited. Adrian walked to the door, but Haastin motioned to Cora. She placed her finger on her chest. "Me?"

Haastin nodded. "Talks Much, go first."

Cora shifted her weight from one foot to the other. "I don't know. . . . Is Adrian coming, too?"

"He follows."

"Oh. Very well." Cora entered the hut. It was small and dark, and had no furniture. A middle-aged man sat alone at the far end, his head bowed as if in prayer, cross-legged and silent. He wore a wide-brimmed hat with a red cloth bound around it. Long, black hair fell straight along his chest.

Cora looked around. Skins and woven blankets that looked Navajo hung on the wall. Spears and guns were stacked in one corner, a selection of knives in the other.

"Not entirely reassuring." Cora waited for Adrian to enter behind her. He bowed his head coming through the narrow doorway, then looked up. The sitting man looked up at the same time, and Cora's breath caught in her throat.

Wide, brown eyes. Bone structure that could make an artist weak with admiration. The man looked like an older copy of Adrian. Cora heard Adrian take a sharp breath. Apparently, he noticed the resemblance, too.

"Oh, my!" Cora took a step closer to the man. "Isn't this amazing? How do you do?" She caught herself. "What am I saying? No one around here speaks English."

"Talks Much, be silent."

Cora braced into fierce indignation. "Now, look."

He held up his hand. "I am Tiotonawen, Father of the

Whirlwind. I am leader of these people. We are of the Tonto Apache." He paused, looking proud, and even more like Adrian. At least, the Adrian Cora had seen in the last two days. "We are much feared by the White Eyes, and by weak tribes."

"Really? How nice. Well, we're lost, you see." Cora held up her hand, too. "Don't laugh, but I think we've been sent back in time. I know it sounds crazy. . . ."

"It is truth."

Cora stopped. "Is it? I mean, you know about it?"

A mystical and somewhat devious smile spread across the old man's face. "I know." His dark eyes whisked to Adrian, then returned to Cora. "Talks Much says much, but nothing. I will ask. You will answer. Keep answers short."

Cora puffed an annoyed breath. "Adrian speaks your language, you know."

"Talks Much will speak."

"My name is Cora." She set her jaw obstinately, but the old man wasn't impressed. "I can't pronounce your name, so I shall call you Whirlwind."

She felt smug, but the old man just nodded. "You are from away."

"I am from another time entirely. I'm also from New York. Well, I was born in Nova Scotia, but I grew up mostly . . ."

Tiotonawen held up his hand again and looked pained. "From away."

Cora frowned. "Yes."

He nodded toward Adrian. "You are this man's woman."

Cora chewed the inside of her lip. "Well . . . We dated briefly in college."

"College?"

"School. A university, for adults, for learning."

Tiotonawen looked at Adrian. "He went to school?"

"Yes." Cora guessed this wasn't usual for Native Americans of this time period. Or for women. "We both did."

"He learned many things?"

Cora sighed. "Of course. He was brilliant. He got A's in everything, special honors. He was a business major, so he could run his own outdoorsy company. Which he does now, so it must have worked."

Tiotonawen looked confused. Cora realized she'd seen that expression on many men's faces. *Men are odd, from any time period.* He probably didn't understand the complexities of the future. "That means Adrian owns his own business. Naturally, he's successful at that, too. That's not so easy, you know. I own my own business—an art gallery—and. . . ."

"Talks Much—"

Cora sighed. "I know, you don't want to hear about me. Well, what else do you want to know?"

"You are his woman. Where are his sons?"

"What sons?"

Tiotonawen's brow lifted as if she'd insulted him. "You have given him no sons?"

Cora glanced at Adrian. "He never asked for any." She chuckled at her own joke, but Tiotonawen wasn't amused. "Sorry. I only said we dated. We aren't married. I haven't seen him in seven years."

"He went on hunt and stayed on hunt?"

"No." Cora wondered what hunting had to do with anything. "We broke up."

Tiotonawen obviously didn't understand. "Did you put his clothes outside door?"

"What? Why would I do that?"

"You did not?"

"No, I did not. Why do you ask?"

"You lay together?"

"Oh, like that's any of your business!" Cora placed her hands on her hips, but Tiotonawen just smiled.

"You did. Did you share hut?"

"We shared an apartment for a while. We had to, you see, so we could spend time together. My roommate hated men. She hated women, too. I roomed with her because I didn't want to disappoint her by saying no, but she wouldn't let Adrian visit after ten o'clock. And his roommate was worse than a frat boy—"

Tiotonawen held up both hands. "He left you for silence."

"He did not! I left him."

"Why?"

Cora averted her eyes to her feet. "Because I didn't want to disappoint him anymore, and I was afraid to climb Mount Everest."

Cora felt Adrian's gaze intent upon her, but she didn't dare look at him. Curse this odd, look-alike man for asking!

Tiotonawen considered Cora's words, then nodded. "He did not go on hunt and stay away. You did not leave clothes outside door."

Cora turned to Adrian, who stood motionless, a strange expression on his face. She shrugged. "This time period is so odd." She eyed Tiotonawen. "Adrian wouldn't hunt. I know you people have to kill animals for food, but we have grocery stores. McDonald's. True, Adrian wouldn't be caught dead in a fast-food restaurant, but I have to admit to a certain fondness—"

Cora caught herself before he could stop her. "Sorry."

"You are his woman."

"That's a fairly primitive term, 'his woman.' Even if I

101

married him, I wouldn't call myself his woman, precisely." Cora straightened, determined to drag Tiotonawen, and any other man with his attitude, into the twentieth century. "Marriage is a union of two equally powerful adults, with common goals—"

"Talks Much speaks words of air, with no meaning. Talks Much thinks but does not see. You are his woman."

Cora suspected he had a point relevant to conceptual thinking. Her lips twisted into a frown. "Whatever."

Tiotonawen fixed his dark gaze on Adrian. After a long silence, he turned back to Cora. "Does he walk free?"

A touching question. Perhaps he feared his people would live in some form of future slavery. "He does. All men are free, black and white, rich or poor. Male or female."

"There are no female men, Talks Much." Humor infected Tiotonawen's voice and Cora glared.

"Very funny. Is there anything else you want to know?"

"Does he walk unseen?"

Cora's brow angled. "Unseen? Do you mean invisible?"

"Unseen."

Cora glanced at Adrian, whose brow furrowed as if he understood the meaning of Tiotonawen's bizarre question, yet was surprised by it. "Can you?" She shook her head. "Adrian can do a lot, but I don't think he can make himself invisible."

"You have not seen him do this?"

"Well, if he could, I wouldn't see him, would I?" Cora cackled at this, but Tiotonawen remained stone-faced. She detected a small smile on Adrian's lips, but he didn't speak. "Now, I've got a few questions, if you don't mind. Where are we, how did we get here, and why are you asking me all this stuff?"

"You are in a Tonto village of the Apache people. You

came by the sacred whirlwind. The whirlwind has returned my son to me."

Cora's eyes widened. "Your son?"

Tiotonawen returned his gaze to Adrian. Tears glittered in his beautiful eyes. "My son."

"No, no, no, no. You don't understand. We came from the future. Way in the future." Tiotonawen wasn't listening. Cora had to make him see reason. She sensed danger, not to herself, but to Adrian. "At least a hundred and . . ." She tried to remember the date Cramer had mentioned. Civil War. 1860s. "About a hundred and thirty-odd years. So Adrian can't be your son. Sorry."

"He is my son."

Cora rolled her eyes, annoyed. "He was born twenty-eight years ago."

"That is true."

"You're missing the point. Twenty-eight years ago, one hundred thirty-one years from now. He was abandoned, then adopted."

Tiotonawen's eyes flashed to Cora. "Not abandoned. I gave my son to the whirlwind."

"He was a four-month-old baby!" Cora wondered why Adrian didn't speak, to explain to the old man the error of his assumption. Maybe he was too stunned and rattled. So it was up to her to defend him.

"I gave my son to the whirlwind."

"That's crazy. What did you do? Wrap him in a blanket, strap him to a cradleboard, and toss him into a whirlwind?"

"Yes."

Cora clapped her hand to her forehead, then made a tight fist which she aimed at Tiotonawen. "You did not! He was a little baby. That would have killed him!"

"My son has the power."

"What power?"

"The power of the few Apache who walk in the shadow of the gods."

"And you could tell this about a four-month-old baby?"

"My son did not cry. He had no food. His mother lay dead. Our people died of sickness. He was sick. He did not cry."

Cora's eyes flooded with tears. "So you threw him away?"

"I had no food to give him. The white soldiers came and burned our food caves, but they gave us their food. They poisoned that food with sickness. Many died. My wife, many babies."

"Oh." Cora felt sick. She'd heard this kind of story before, but it was far away, in the past. *The past.* She squeezed her eyes shut to blot the image, but if that baby was Adrian. . . .

"I gave my son to the whirlwind, before all could die. The future may come, and none of my people will be in it. Only my son."

Cora wiped tears from her cheeks. "I understand."

"Good. Talks Much, leave us. I will hear my son alone."

Cora left the hut with every intention of eavesdropping outside. Haastin seemed to suspect her scheme and directed her toward a group of women. Cora glared, but Haastin remained unyielding. He spoke to a young woman who held a nursing baby.

Cora assessed the girl. She had wavy, black hair and shining brown eyes. She wasn't thin, but womanly. Her face was friendly and alert. She was beautiful. Cora wondered if Adrian's only long-time girlfriend had resembled this woman.

"I am called Laurencita. Please sit."

Cora breathed a sigh of relief. "You speak English."

Laurencita smiled. "I speak our tongue first, but I lived many years with the Yankee soldiers."

Cora swallowed. "As a captive?"

"Not exactly. My mother was wife to an officer, after my father was killed by his men."

"I don't like the sound of that!" *The injustice!* Cora clenched her fists into tight balls, but Laurencita laughed.

"My father killed many soldiers. It is a fair exchange."

Cora bit her lip hard. The past was brutal. "How did you get away?"

Laurencita patted Cora's arm as if Cora was the one who needed comforting. "Haastin raided their supply route, and took me captive." She sounded proud, so being a captive must be more pleasant than it sounded. Haastin passed by with another warrior, and exchanged a fond glance with the girl.

"Are you married?"

"We are. We have two sons, and a daughter, Haozinne." She pointed to a group of small boys, and a single girl. The little girl tried to play with the boys, but they seemed reluctant. Cora frowned.

"Why don't they let her play?"

"Haozinne is a girl. She should learn women's jobs, not to fight."

Cora clucked her tongue. "It doesn't sound entirely fair." She eyed the baby. "He's a beautiful child." Maybe Adrian looked like this, twenty-eight years ago. Here, in this time.

It seemed impossible. Adrian belonged to another time, another world. Not hers. But if that were true, then why did he fit into the future so well, while she remained a virtual outcast?

"You are Tiotonawen's son's woman?"

"You know Adrian is that old man's son, too?"

"Haastin told me so. He is known to us. The one of power, taken by the whirlwind. It is said that when he returns, our future is sure."

Cora tapped her lip thoughtfully. "I wonder why none of this was recorded in the history books?"

Laurencita's baby stopped nursing. His small head tilted back in sleep, his mouth open. She adjusted his position and softened his black hair. "Would our sacred truths be found in the white eyes's books, Talks Much?"

Cora drew a calming breath, slowly. "My name is Cora. Cora Talmadge. Not Talks Much."

Laurencita chuckled. "Don't let it bother you. My husband has names for many people. To him, I am Little Round Belly."

"Dear God! What do you call him?"

Laurencita sighed. "Haastin."

"In the future, men treat women as equals." Cora paused. "At least, that's the idea. Some are rather stubborn about accepting it."

Laurencita seemed neither shocked nor particularly elated by Cora's disclosure. "What of my people?" She spoke hesitantly, as if she feared the answer.

"Well, I'm not an expert on Native American culture, but Adrian certainly does well in the world. People seem really interested in the spiritual angle. Native American art sells like crazy." Cora crossed her legs at the ankles and stuffed her hands comfortably in her pockets. "I was hoping to enlist some Native artists for my gallery in New York. Some painters, sculptors—that sort of thing. The galleries in Scottsdale are fabulous. I could spend weeks visiting them."

106

Laurencita looked predictably lost, and Cora sighed. She'd found a new friend, and gotten carried away. "Of course, that was then, this is now. But if there's a way to travel through time, it shouldn't be too hard to get back."

"I don't know, Cora. Tiotonawen knows."

"I'm sure he'll tell Adrian, after they've had a chance to catch up. I'm in no hurry, though. This is all quite interesting." Cora eyed Laurencita's pile of reeds. "What are you making there?"

"A basket. Do you like it?"

Cora examined the basket. "It's beautiful. I could sell those. . . . " She stopped herself and shook her head. "Maybe you could bury a few, and when I get back, I could unearth them. . . . I'd have to find some method of paying for them in advance, of course."

Unlike the men, Laurencita seemed to understand Cora's reasoning. *Women are so practical, so logical. Men could learn from us.* "Tio—Adrian's father—said something I don't understand. He kept asking me if I left Adrian's clothes outside a door, and if Adrian had gone off hunting and never come back."

Laurencita set aside her basket, truly surprised this time. "Why would you want to do that?"

"Good question. But he was insistent."

"These things are done when a wife wishes to divorce her husband."

"But Adrian and I aren't married. We had a relationship, but it didn't work."

"Did you lay together and share a hut?"

"Yes. . . . "

"To my people, you are married." Laurencita eyed Cora intently. "Why do you not want that man? He is . . . " She

107

peeked up to see if Haastin was listening. Cora looked around, too. All clear. "He is strong of build and clean. His face shows no age, yet he must be near thirty years."

"He's cute, I know. But thirty isn't very old." Cora realized many of the people she'd seen looked worn, even the younger ones. "Sunscreen! That's it. Too much sun ages you. Adrian is careful, because I lectured him a great deal on the subject." Cora beamed. "I suspect he took my advice, and applies an SPF of at least fifteen. . . .

"The future is much changed from the now."

Cora nodded. "I suppose so." She looked around. Many people were smoking, in pipes and in rolled leaves. "That's a problem, too. Smoking. It's bad for your health, you know."

"Tobacco is sacred." Laurencita paused. "I am made sick by it, so cannot take part. By the age of twelve, all boys learn."

"Do they?" Cora's brow angled. "Well, this should prove interesting."

Adrian emerged from the grass hut with his father. He had changed. Cora felt it without talking to him. He stood taller, straighter. Less relaxed and casual than the man she knew. He looked like a king. An Apache king.

Cora felt light inside, shaky. Adrian had power. She had always known, but now he knew. The villagers rose and gathered around him. Cora got up and followed Laurencita. Tiotonawen spoke in his language, pride ringing in his voice. The people moved closer. Many reached out to touch Adrian.

Tears flooded Cora's eyes. He was home. He had found his father, and he was home. Adrian's gaze shifted to her. If she'd sensed his change from afar, it pierced her heart now. She didn't know him. She was seeing him for the first time, and his power seemed endless.

He moved through the crowd, never taking his eyes from hers. "Adrian . . . " Cora backed away involuntarily, but he caught her arm.

"Come."

She hesitated, but he edged her forward. "Where are we going?" Her voice sounded high, almost a squeak. "Um, Adrian."

He stopped and faced her. "My father has restored my true name. Tiyannandiwahdi."

Cora tried to count the syllables, and failed. "Oh, really? And am I supposed to call you this?"

"It is my name now. It means Son of the Whirlwind."

"Appropriate, but still unpronounceable. Unless I call you 'Tee' for short."

Faint agitation stirred in his brown eyes, then disappeared. "You may call me whatever you wish."

Cora scrutinized his appearance, trying to see what had actually changed. "Have you grown taller, or is it just me?"

His dark brow angled. "Come."

"Where are we going? Home?"

He smiled, a dangerous smile. "We are home, Cora."

This was it. This was what she feared. "The egg is really cracking, isn't it, Adrian? I mean, 'Tee.' "

He looked confused—the first expression she recognized since he had left his father's hut. "Egg?"

"You're cracking like an egg, pal. Okay, maybe that guy is your father. It's possible. I wouldn't have said so yesterday, but a lot has happened. But this isn't home. If you were born in, I don't know, Afghanistan, would you think you had to be in Afghanistan to be home?"

His brow furrowed. "I belong here, Cora."

"Do you? Well, I don't."

His dark eyes glinted. This expression, she had never seen

nor imagined in her wildest dreams. This wasn't her gentle and tender Adrian. This wasn't the nineteen-year-old boy she once loved. This man was a warrior.

Cora gulped. Adrian's sensual mouth curved in a smile, but suddenly, even sensuality seemed dangerous. "Come."

He took her arm in a firm grip and led her through his people. They stood back respectfully. Cora cast a desperate glance toward Laurencita, but her new friend just smiled. Just like Jenny when she informed Cora about her skydiving "gift."

"Oh, no!"

Adrian went to the hut nearest his father's, held back the cloth, and eased Cora in. Her heart raced, her breaths came swift and shallow. Fear, mostly. And excitement, though she wasn't sure why she should be excited.

"Well, well. Isn't this nice?" She eased to the far side of the hut. Adrian entered, again bowing low through the doorway. He set his pack in the corner, then stood blocking the light, huge and dark, his shoulders impossibly broad, his legs powerful. "Oh, dear."

His eyes burned. "My father has given me this dwelling. *Home.*"

"How quaint!" Cora backed farther, bumped into a pottery urn, and it tumbled to the dirt floor. Adrian smiled, but not out of humor. Out of something Cora didn't understand.

"So. . . . Did your father tell you how we get back?"

"Back where?"

"To the future!" Cora drew several short breaths that sounded like gasps. "If we came back, we can go forward. It only makes sense. I assumed you asked him."

"No."

"I can understand wanting to get acquainted and all. I'm not in a huge hurry. It's very interesting here. But, you know, I'd just sleep easier knowing it's, um, temporary."

"You won't have trouble sleeping."

"Won't I?" Amazing, the heights her voice could reach. "Why is that?"

He moved across the floor with such perfect grace, such innate power, that Cora stood spellbound. When he drew close, she snapped free of her trance and hopped backwards.

His dangerous smile widened. "You won't have trouble sleeping, Cora, because I will make love to you until you find sweet exhaustion."

"Oh, my God. . . . " She actually swayed as she stood.

He took another step closer. "I think you ache for me. I ache for you, too."

Cora felt drunk. Feverish. Her skin felt hot. "I thought we were going to be friends. . . . " Her voice cracked and she gulped.

Adrian laughed, low and husky. He caught her face in his hands and leaned toward her. "Do you know why you're here?"

"A long and unpredictable series of events, which I'm sure in some fashion can be explained scientifically. If I posed the issue to Carl Sagan, I think he'd probably say—"

His lips brushed hers, and her words vanished. "You're here because I brought you."

"You didn't know! You were just as surprised as I was!" Her voice came as a small, rushed whisper, desperate to maintain reason when reason fled like the wind.

His long, brown fingers caressed her face, over her lips, into her hair. "I brought you here, because it was my wish. What my mind didn't know, my soul arranged."

Stobie Piel

Cora's eyes narrowed to slits. "Does this have something to do with the power thing?"

"It does."

"Ah." She felt his warm, sweet breath on her face. Dimly, she knew Adrian must have cleansed his teeth, too. Man of the past or not.

"I brought you here, Cora. Because you're my woman." Adrian said 'my woman' triumphantly, eyes ablaze. Cora knew she should be offended, raise some kind of objection. She fought to think of one.

"Don't I get some say in the matter? Laurencita told me a woman can divorce her husband just by tossing his clothes outdoors. So I'm assuming . . . "

"For an Apache wife, that is true. For a captive—"

"Captive! What do you mean, 'captive'? "

"Isn't it obvious, Cora? There are different rules for when a man takes a woman of his own tribe, and when he takes a woman from his enemy."

Cora shook herself. His hands slipped to her shoulders, and she felt the vibrant tension in his touch. "*Enemy*? In what way am I your enemy?"

"Your world is white."

"My world is multi-colored!"

He looked unyielding. His gaze fixed on her mouth as if he'd abandoned thoughts of speech.

"Are we talking about ancestors here, Adrian?"

He nodded, still watching her mouth.

"Is that so? Well, at this time in history, most of my ancestors were in Scotland. I don't recall the Apache declaring war on Scotland."

"All Western European people."

Cora ran desperately over her family tree. "I've got you there, too! One of my ancestors was French Canadian, from

Nova Scotia. He was part Micmac. What do you have to say about that?"

His mouth met hers before she completed the sentence. His whole body seemed to envelop her, and she was losing herself inside him. Power. His strong arms wrapped around her, his lips moved against hers.

Cora didn't resist. His hair fell forward, touching her face. Cora's hands went to his waist. His tongue ran along the line of her lips, between. Her pulse throbbed without mercy, beyond her ability to contain. He kissed the corner of her mouth, then her face. His breath came swift but deep, sure. His fingers wound in her hair and unraveled what was left of her braid. He caught its length in his hand and eased her head back.

He kissed her neck, just below her ear. Her weak spot. He must have remembered. . . . She felt the tip of his tongue, then his teeth grazing her flesh. Her nerves scrambled and jumped, crashing in panic.

"Adrian, about being friends. . . ."

His mouth trailed a line from her ear to her shoulder, obscuring Cora's line of thought.

"You want this, Cora."

The power of suggestion. Maybe his father was right. Cora fought the notion. She tried to shake her head, but he caught her face in his hands and leaned close to her.

"Desire is stronger than fear. You want me."

"But what if—"

He touched her mouth, silencing her. "Do you want to be safe, or do you want pleasure? Do you want to hide?" His lips curled upwards, teasing and knowing. "Or do you want to writhe in bliss beneath me?"

Cora winced at his blunt assessment, her cheeks burned. "Dear God!"

113

"As I remember, that happened easily for you."

Cora opened her eyes, aghast. He had to remember every detail, and remind her.

"You've been alone for a very long time. Do you remember what it's like?"

Yes. "We don't have protection!" Her voice burst forth in a squeal of desperation.

"You owe me sons."

"Sons?" Cora's mouth dropped, then closed as she imagined a small, black-haired baby with big, brown eyes. A baby looking at her, his tiny fingers curled around hers. A smile began on her lips. "Wait a minute! What do you mean, 'owe you'? "

"You are my woman. You will give me sons." Adrian paused. "Daughters, too."

"You have lost your mind."

"In exchange, I will give you pleasure. I'll leave no ache unsatisfied."

That sounds fair. Cora shook her head to clear her ravaged senses. "I don't think—"

"Yes, you do. You think too much. You talk too much." Cora braced herself, but Adrian drew her closer into his arms. "It's time for you to *feel*."

"Oh, dear!"

He seized a worn blanket from the wall and dropped it to the floor. Before Cora could guess his intentions, he sank to the floor, bringing her with him.

"I was awfully afraid of this."

Adrian positioned himself above her, looking down. His hair fell forward. He looked exotic, a vision of masculinity. He looked like a man from another time. A time of warriors and life lived to its fullest. Never hedging in fear, but living.

"Is it truly fear you feel, angel?"

Cora nodded, but she couldn't answer. Adrian brushed his lips against her cheek.

"I don't think so. I think you're afraid I'm right, and that I'll give you such pleasure you'll never want to leave this place."

He moved his hips against hers, slowly and sensually. A raging, molten heat swarmed inside Cora's body, centering in her loins. She didn't care that she wasn't right for him, that she would eventually disappoint him, and prove herself inadequate. Her thoughts fled, and her desire seized control.

He kissed her mouth, and she answered. She touched her tongue to his, then sucked, inviting him inside her. His kiss deepened, his breath quickened. She affected him, too. That was all she wanted to know. She felt his rigid male length pressed against her, and she squirmed to center him against her own core. He moved with deliberate persuasion, until her hips rocked beneath his.

This, they had never done before. They were both clothed, yet she hovered on the verge of orgasm. She felt his concealed erection as it pulsed, even beneath his jeans. Maybe he felt her, too. He lifted himself above her, still kissing her lips, and fumbled with the clasp of her chinos. It was a button, which he was trying to unsnap.

"Button, Adrian. Button."

He murmured understanding, and the button came undone. "Oh, Cora, it doesn't take much, does it?" She wasn't sure what he meant by that, but when he kissed her neck, she didn't care. "Maybe I didn't do this enough before."

How could it be enough? Nothing would ever be enough. She would always want more.

"Don't worry, angel. I'll satisfy you until no other thought can find its way into your muddled brain. You'll never leave me again."

Cora's eyes drifted shut. *Never again*. Her eyes popped open. "What do you mean, 'muddled brain'?" She attempted to remove herself from beneath him, but Adrian didn't release her. "There's no need to be insulting!"

Adrian gazed down into her eyes. His dark face was flushed from passion, yet he studied her calmly. She felt his heartbeat, swift and powerful. A heartbeat fueled by desire.

"I want you, Cora."

I want you, too. She couldn't say the words aloud. Cora felt suddenly young. In a cold space of a second, she remembered what it was like to fail him, over and over. How it felt to want desperately to please him, to make him proud. To prove she deserved his love.

She remembered making love with him in sweet, mindless oblivion, only to wake and find herself disappointing him again. Overturning a raft, hanging from an evergreen, rolling down a mountainside . . .

Cora squeezed her eyes shut, but tears emerged beneath her lashes. *I can't go through this again*. Adrian kissed her forehead, then sighed heavily. Cora opened her eyes. His expression shifted from pure desire to a quiet assessment.

"Cora, before you can truly be my woman, there are some things about yourself you have to face."

"Oh, are there?" Cora's mood shifted, too. *The nerve*! "And what makes you think I want to be 'your woman'?"

Adrian smiled. He touched his lips to hers, allowing the pressure of his hips to increase against hers. Cora gulped a quick breath of air. Curse him! Her body responded with a hot rush of desire, of the promise of what might be between them.

Adrian's eyes glinted. "I think it's obvious, don't you?"

That patronizing tone. "Not at all." A weak and unlikely response.

"I've made you face your desire, and now I'll make you face yourself."

"What?" *The arrogance*! "My 'self' is none of your business!"

"It is. You are my woman. It is my duty to show you reality."

"I'm not your woman!" Cora squirmed violently to free herself. He held her still until she wearied of the effort. Cora puffed a furious breath and glared up into his face. "I suppose you—a man I haven't seen in nine years and dated only a very short while—know more about myself than I do?"

"Yes."

A low, sputtering growl was all she could muster.

Adrian propped himself up on his elbows, looking down into her face. He cleverly positioned his elbows on either side of her, preventing any escape.

Flight wasn't an option. Cora affected a disinterested and sarcastic expression, to be sure he knew his opinion wasn't important in any way. Unfortunately, she lay beneath him, so she couldn't cross her arms over her chest.

"First of all, you make your choices based on fear. Fear of what might happen, of what you can't do."

"That's not true!" It was true. Exactly true. She lived in terror of her failures, of all the things she couldn't do.

Her expression must have revealed her doubt. Adrian smiled. "You see yourself in the light of some crazy opinion you concocted years ago, probably when you were a child. You act on life as if that opinion were true. But it's only an opinion, Cora. And a warped one, at that."

Cora's mouth dropped. He aimed for her core, for those flaws in her character that cut most deeply. "How dare you! I know myself perfectly—"

"You don't know yourself at all. You think you're an artist, because that's what your parents expected of you."

Now he aimed for her vocation—the only thing that gave her life meaning. "This is vicious!" Cora tried to jam her knee into his groin, but he kept her legs flat beneath his.

"I'm not saying you're not good at what you do. You're smart, and you've learned how to paint, and how to sculpt. But you're not talented at those things because you don't have the innate desire driving you. I don't think you even like doing them. You're not acting on what's inside you, but on what's outside: other people's expectations, trying to disprove to yourself your doubts."

He went farther than even her worst fears, calling up faint premonitions she endured late at night—trying to sleep, wondering why her career never solidified. Adrian spoke of her failings calmly, and cut to the quick of her life.

Cora's eyes burned with tears. He'd never hurt her before. He admired her various concoctions, even if he didn't know what they were.

"I'm not trying to hurt you."

Her tears ran into her hair. "You are." Her throat tightened, as she fought against weeping. "You never said that in college."

"Cora, when you and I were together—" He drew an impatient breath, as if the situation should be obvious. "If you murdered my best friend, I'd have said you did it well. I adored you. I couldn't see you clearly then."

"Oh, thank you very much! Then maybe you'd just let me go, and leave me in peace?"

"You won't have peace this way, angel."

"Not with you—"

"Not with yourself. When we were together, I knew something was wrong. I thought if I tried harder, I could make you happy. I tried to protect you from reality, because I was young and didn't know any better. But I know now. You need to look into its eyes, and see what's true."

Cora rolled her eyes. "And I suppose your 'power' gives you insight?"

"It does." Adrian paused. "The insight was there all along. I was afraid of it. I'm not afraid anymore."

"You should be!"

He smiled. "I do it for you, Cora."

"I am not grateful!" She couldn't stop her tears. She felt alone and raw, staring her own failure in the eye.

Adrian placed his hands on either side of her face and wiped away her tears. "You don't know what you're good at because you've spent your life trying to please people, to prove you've got some kind of worth."

He kissed her forehead. "But you've had worth all along. And you've muddled along, and all the while you were trying to be something you're not, you've developed what you really are."

Cora sniffed miserably, her throat tight. "How would you know?"

"Jenny says you can pick a talented artist better than anyone. She says you know how to present their work, and that you've already launched several painters."

"Yes. And they're in big galleries now. Not mine."

"You care about people, because you have the sweetest empathy. You probably encouraged them to go where they'd get more money."

119

She sensed something not totally bad in this line of conversation. Something hopeful. "Well, yes. It was only fair."

Adrian kissed her cheek. "Because you are fair."

Cora peered up into his eyes. He didn't look angry or mean, despite his brutal words. "You said I should think positively, that I could do anything. Now, you say I should give up."

"Not give up. Find what you really want to do, and do it. If you spend your life making choices based on fear and warped opinions of yourself, you'll never be happy. You'll never get the life you want. If you find what you really want, you'll do it, and the fight will be much easier."

"What fight?"

"The fight to get there."

Cora's brow furrowed tight. No one ever told her she wasn't talented. Her mother said she should try harder, and paint more often. Her father said she should focus solely on sculpture. Her customers invariably asked what her creations signified. Cora hedged, they'd suggest, and she'd agree. Her only sales came from people who recognized her parents' renowned names and assumed hers was as prestigious.

She should be crushed. Heartbroken. Instead, she felt relieved. She felt as if a thick fog had cleared in front of her, leaving the bright, cold light of day. But when she looked into the day, she wasn't afraid anymore.

"I haven't painted in a long time." She spoke slowly, hesitant as the thoughts formed in her head. "I threw my last sculpture against the wall." Adrian watched her face, but he didn't speak. "I told myself it was because I was too busy with my gallery business, but the truth is, I liked that part better. Arranging showings, finding new artists. Having lunch."

Adrian chuckled, then sat up. He pulled her up, facing him. He looked casual.

She eyed him suspiciously. "What are you doing? I thought you were going to . . . ?" She stopped before reminding him of love-making, but he knew.

He eased her hair back over her shoulders. "You have work to do first."

Cora felt small and drained. "On my psyche?"

Adrian's brow furrowed. "On my hut. It needs personalizing. A woman's touch."

"Oh, does it?"

His dark eyes twinkled. "Make it a gallery, Cora."

The egg was cracking unpredictably. "I don't understand you."

Adrian glanced down at his crotch, then back to her. Cora glanced at his crotch, too. He was hard and well-formed, his erection distinct beneath his jeans. Cora bit her lip, remembering too much of their past. "Oh."

"You still ache. I still ache, too." Adrian ran his fingers in her hair, untangling it. "I want you to ache, Cora. I want you watching me, and imagining. I want you slippery and wet. . . . "

"Oh, help!" Cora struggled to her feet, eyes wide. "Must you be so blunt?"

He rose, too. "I don't want any misunderstandings between us. If I say what I'm thinking, and tell you what I'm doing to you, you won't be able to make up some bizarre explanation on your own."

"How very considerate of you!"

He nodded. "It should prevent any number of disasters." He moved closer to her. She had to look up to meet his gaze.

"I'm almost certain you've grown."

121

"I am not the man I was. I am a man of the past. You don't know what I'm capable of." Adrian's words stirred a tremor of apprehension, though Cora wasn't sure why.

"I don't think you know, either."

He hesitated. She was right. "I will do what I have to do, for my people. For you. That's all I need to know."

Adrian took her hand and kissed it. He turned and left the hut without another word. Cora stared after him. Her heart beat erratically, but she didn't feel sad. Her heart wasn't broken. She felt stronger, as if a great burden had lifted from her shoulders.

"My gallery was among the finest in New York." She spoke aloud, then looked around the little hut. "True, it was small, but visitors were always impressed, even when they didn't buy anything."

She waited a while in silence, contemplating her skills. She'd launched several promising artists. One had been homeless, and she'd found him drawing with a pencil. He was now living in a loft in SoHo.

She, of course, was still in the Bronx. Until now. So her life was more interesting, and she was with Adrian. Cora peered out the door. Adrian was walking through the campsite, looking pleased with himself. Despite his insight, she still saw the shadows of a cracking egg.

In contrast, Cora felt strong. An egg that considered itself hopelessly shattered, who looked in a mirror, and realized it was a nice, round, and fertile egg, after all. "I am a worthy egg." Cora clapped her hand to her forehead. "Oh, dear. I've even confused myself." Her hand slipped down. "But it's true."

She had good qualities. She was practical. Practicality was something Adrian obviously lacked. So he needed her, lest he go completely off the deep end with his new power.

Cora puttered around his hut. Maybe if she added a few of Laurencita's baskets. Another blanket. Some pottery. He held up a mirror to her, and she dared look in, albeit unwillingly. She saw what was truly there—herself. It wasn't what her parents wanted. It was just herself. But in that mirror, she saw all that she wanted to be. A woman free to choose her own path.

Chapter Five

Well done. Adrian walked through his father's campsite, proud. Cora would be puttering in his hut, arranging things. Her mind would wander. She'd think of what they'd almost done, and remember what they did so often nine years ago.

Her little body would respond. Adrian caught his foot on a horse tether and tripped. He caught himself and looked around. No one saw, other than the horse. He looked closer, and recognized the bay horse Tradman had ridden, the horse Cora de-bridled.

"My people take good advantage of situations." He patted the horse's neck. It already looked healthier, probably relieved to be free of Tradman's brutal treatment.

Adrian walked to the edge of the village. It was well-hidden and easily defended. Strange, how easily his mind turned to the needs of his father's time. He had power. He also had knowledge of the future, and a perspective denied those trapped in time. He could reason with his people's enemies. Maybe create a better life for them.

"What do you think of your land, my son?"

Adrian startled. He felt sure he'd never startled in his previous existence. Cora had started something. Tiotonawen eyed him doubtfully. *They both burst forth talking, out of the blue. . . .*

"Father." Adrian studied his father's face. It was like looking in a mirror. Tiotonawen was handsome, venerable. Adrian pictured himself at that age. Maybe less wrinkled. Of course, Tiotonawen didn't have the benefit of sunscreen. *I'm starting to think like Cora!* "My land?"

"We grew from this land, my son. Its bones are our bones. For now, and for always." He paused, as if hesitant to continue. "In the world to come, is it much lost?"

Adrian wondered what his father would consider "lost." "It is changed. People travel fast, and there are many more people then than now."

"White people?"

"Of many colors." He knew Tiotonawen held his breath. "Including red."

The old man's breath exhaled and he nodded. "There is a future."

"There is. But much has changed."

Tiotonawen's brow angled. "You don't need to tell me that, son. I've seen your woman."

Adrian repressed a smile. "Cora isn't typical of the future."

"Good. For all women to talk so much, it would be a hard world for a man."

"Cora has sweetness."

"You will not know boredom in her company. You will have much reason to laugh."

"And she's . . . " Adrian wasn't sure how to say "cute" in Apache. He hesitated.

His father nodded in understanding. "Pleasing to the eye." He sighed. "It is good fortune. Distract the ears with the eyes." Tiotonawen watched Adrian's face. "You fear losing her."

Adrian's heart took an erratic beat. "While I'm here, she is mine."

Tiotonawen smiled. "Keep her here."

Adrian's brow furrowed. "But if she wants to leave, how can I stop her? Should I even try?"

Tiotonawen set his hand on Adrian's shoulder, warm and strong. "What do you want, my son?"

Adrian stared across the campsite, through the rim of dark green junipers. "I want her here."

Tiotonawen patted him fondly. "Then she will be here."

Adrian's chin firmed, his lips curved in a smile. Tiotonawen nodded his approval. "The power is yours, son. Use it along your path, and the path clears. A woman doesn't know what's best for herself. The man knows. Make it so."

This wasn't right—some part of Adrian knew it. He wasn't a domineering person. When Cora left, he'd hoped to win her back, but he'd never thought of tracking her down. He respected her freedom.

That was then. Today felt different. Cora had no where to go. He had time. Yet if she truly wanted to return to her time, and leave him in his . . . "The whirlwind gives choice."

"Yes, but what a man keeps to himself is his choice. A man does not walk toward what he wants, and shoot his own foot in the doing."

Tiotonawen patted Adrian's shoulder again. "Make your days as you want them. Never walk from your forward path. Never let another pull you off. Pull her where you want to go. If you listen to that little one, you'll end up . . . " He paused as if struggling to find something truly awful. "You'll end up thinking like her."

Adrian shuddered. "What Cora doesn't know won't hurt her."

"That is true, and wise."

Tiotonawen's hand tightened on Adrian's shoulder. "You are my son." His voice cracked, and he paused. Adrian's heart throbbed with emotion. *My father.* "Your return brings hope to a people who stand on the edge of the forever gone." Tiotonawen sighed. "We fight for so long, and see no end. Your life shows there is victory, after all."

Adrian hesitated. "Our people are alive, but victory . . . Father, there is much grief to come."

Tiotonawen nodded. "Then I may yet fall in battle. It is an honorable death."

"You won't fall in battle!" Adrian contained his emotion. "Of all the things that separate our people from the white men, misunderstanding is the most dangerous. I have knowledge of the future, of their misconceptions now. I will use what I know to negotiate on your behalf. I will reason with them."

Tiotonawen didn't argue, but he looked doubtful. "What can you say that will make them leave us in peace?"

"They won't leave, Father. But maybe the blending of our races can be less tragic than it was. At least, for our people."

"Try your way, my son. If you fail, you walk in power. My heart tells me you will learn more of battle than of peace."

127

"No."

Tiotonawen fell silent, watching Adrian. "Your woman, will you win her by reason, or by power?"

Adrian started to answer "reason," then stopped. "Any way I have to."

"Yes." Tiotonawen smiled and nodded. "Yes." He turned away and returned to his hut, and Adrian stood alone.

A hawk lifted from the sparse trees and soared into the sky. He saw himself, Cora held beneath his own talons. Not an entirely peaceful image, but still powerful.

Power. It belonged to him as his birthright. He could use it to protect himself, and others. He could use it to convince others to his will. To find truth, to follow visions of the future. Not the future he knew, but the future he wanted.

He wanted Cora.

He suspected she wanted him, too. She'd stayed single. Better still, she'd stayed celibate. Not that making love with others necessarily dampened one's memory. He'd had many girlfriends, and he couldn't forget Cora. Sex wasn't the same as passion and love. It was physical release, but it wasn't bliss.

With Cora, it was bliss.

He'd almost taken her in his new hut, on the floor. But he'd looked into her eyes and saw her doubt. Doubt he couldn't change until she changed.

So he restrained himself. It wasn't easy. When Cora made love, she forgot her doubts. When she lay naked beneath him, or on top of him, or beside him, Adrian felt himself growing hard. He'd seen Cora without her fears, when all that mattered was what they could find together.

Adrian watched the hawk fly out of sight, then walked back to the village. He avoided the ground tethers this time. Cora wasn't in his hut. She was chatting with Haastin's wife, examining baskets with a bright, critical eye. Another woman emptied a basket on the ground beside Cora, and small carvings spread all over.

Cora clapped her hands and started selecting among them. Adrian wanted to oversee her actions, but she looked happy stuffing the carvings into a large basket. Haastin's wife seemed to be translating, and the women nodded in agreement. Adrian had no idea how they could understand Cora's thinking in any language, but they seemed to know exactly what she meant.

A group of young men sat in the shade, smoking. Adrian's eyes narrowed. He hadn't been in the village long, but he was accepted and admired already. His words had value. He strode toward them, but Tiotonawen emerged from his hut with a long pipe. He sat cross-legged among the boys, and lit his pipe.

Cora looked up from her business transaction, saw the same scene, then glanced at Adrian meaningfully. Adrian forced his attention back to the matter at hand. The young men were wreathed in smoke. His people's health could be much improved by early intervention.

Cora set aside her nearly full basket, and approached him. She almost swaggered.

"You're looking pleased with yourself, Cora."

Her lips curved, her brow arched. She nodded toward the smoking men, then shook her head. The effect was theatrical. "Awful shame, isn't it?"

"It will soon be corrected."

"I don't know. Laurencita tells me tobacco is sacred to your people. Your father traded many skins and a bunch of her baskets for just one pouch." She stopped and clicked her tongue several times.

"He doesn't understand."

"You'd better set him straight." She looked more smug than ever, as if she found humor in his situation. Adrian solidified his confident expression, then went to his father. Cora followed, looking pert.

"Father. . . . " Adrian eyed Cora, then reverted to the Apache tongue.

Tiotonawen held up his hand. "I have decided, my son, that we are to speak English more often. If it is spoken by my people in the future, we need it now, to be on level ground with our enemies."

Adrian hesitated. Cora beamed. "Sounds sensible."

"Ancient language has value, father. It is still spoken by many of our people."

"A man can have two languages. As many as he needs to stand on equal ground. I have overlooked its importance. Speak so these boys will learn."

Adrian sighed. "Very well." Tiotonawen blew a long series of smoke rings and looked pleased. Cora folded her arms over her chest.

"Impressive."

Adrian's temper cracked. "Deadly!"

The boys looked up and Tiotonawen set his pipe to the side.

"Son?"

Adrian regained control. "Smoking, father, is harmful to your health."

Cora nodded in support. "He's right, you know."

Tiotonawen didn't appear convinced or interested as he drew another long and thoughtful breath of smoke. "Tobacco is sacred, my son."

"I told you." Cora's voice took on a sing-song quality.

Adrian restrained his impatience. "I understand that you

consider this plant sacred. But it damages you inside. It causes cancer."

Cora nodded. "And it ages your skin."

"Right."

The young men continued to smoke, looking confused. Tiotonawen straightened his lame leg and tapped his pipe. "My son, has the future separated you so far from the sacred rituals? Have the white men deprived you of your right?"

He wasn't getting his message through. "White men smoke, too, and it's just as bad for them."

"Because it is not sacred to them, son." Tiotonawen's expression revealed sympathy. "It is sacred to you." He patted the rock beside him. "Sit, and learn the art."

Cora hummed. "I knew this would be interesting. Just glad I'm here to see it." She almost sang the words. Adrian stiffened.

"Father, you don't understand. You may think it's sacred . . . "

"It calms the soul." Tiotonawen took another puff, happy. "Cleanses the spirits which surround us."

"It's addictive!" He didn't mean to shout. But the old man wasn't listening to his advice. They all looked blank, except Cora, who looked smug. "That means once you start, your body becomes accustomed to the drug, and you can't stop."

"Because the body reaches a higher level of purity, son. Sit, and learn."

"Not a chance, man."

Cora cackled beside him and Adrian cringed. " 'Not a chance, *man*?' Well, that was inspiring!"

"Cora—"

"Go ahead. We're in the past, Adrian. Your world. I don't

think there's a surgeon general in these parts. And tobacco is—" She paused and smacked her lips. "Sacred."

Tiotonawen assembled a vile twist of tobacco for Adrian's benefit. "Talks Much is right. The white eyes has confused you, and led you astray. Here, you will return to the sacred ways."

No way.

Cora's face knit into a concerned expression. "What a dilemma! You, oh man of the past that you are, are in a serious pickle. On the one hand, you belong here, and that means 'ritual.' But on the other . . . " She paused and eyed his chest. "You've got those pretty, pink lungs to think about. Just think, all that fresh air you accumulated up in the Rocky Mountains. Do you remember making me breathe so I'd clear my lungs from any smog?"

He remembered. Adrian glared. "Health is important."

"Isn't it? In the future. Here, it's ritual that counts." Cora looked around and shook her head. "And you don't belong in the future, remember? You belong right here. Smoking."

She was trying to prove he didn't belong here. That no matter where he lived, he carried his life and his values and his knowledge with him.

Tiotonawen held up the tobacco. Adrian took it, but his lips curled in disgust. Cora held up her fingers and pretended to smoke. Her eyes glimmered devilishly as she blew a stream of air. She coughed, choked, then chuckled to herself.

He couldn't change what he knew. He handed the tobacco back to his father. "It harms the body. The body is sacred."

"Good comeback, Adrian!" Cora patted his shoulder. "That's one for the future."

He turned to her, but she just smiled and returned to the other women. The little demon was counting. It was like Cora to count. Weighing the evidence of where he belonged

132

most, in the past or the future. One thing she hadn't taken into consideration, and that was herself.

If they returned to the future, he would lose her. In the past, she belonged to him, and he would never lose her again.

Cora liked the past. She liked seeing Adrian de Vargas squirm. The smoking was just the beginning. "*Not a chance, man.*" Cora repeated the phrase aloud, pleased. "Kind of a cool Apache dude." She hummed to herself. "You can take the man out of the future, but you can't take the future out of the man."

Laurencita sat beside her, weaving another basket. "Your words are hard to understand, Cora. What is cool?"

Cora watched Laurencita's quick fingers weaving. She wanted to commit the art to memory, so as to give a good presentation at her exhibition. She wasn't sure what exhibition, or where it would be, just that she was determined to give one.

"Cool means a person isn't flustered by what happens to him. Everything he tries works. He's not floundering around, he's not scared of his own shadow."

"I see. You are cool."

Cora angled her brow, wondering how Laurencita could have misunderstood her description that much, but the woman turned back to her basket. Cora eyed Adrian. He was lecturing a group of boys. They looked tired, but respectful. "Maybe he'll influence a few."

Laurencita looked toward Adrian, too. "Or maybe they'll influence him."

"I don't know. Adrian has had it pretty easy in life, but what he values is very strong. There are certain things he'd never do. Smoking, for one. He doesn't drink. Now, I rather enjoy wine and sherry. An occasional cocktail. Adrian drinks sparkling water and thinks it's festive."

"That is well. Drink changes a man, both red and white men. I have seen that." Laurencita turned back to her basket.

"The soldiers who served under your stepfather?"

"Yes. He was at the fort in Tucson, but they have gone back to his home in California now. But many of his soldiers are at Fort McDowell near here. And we, the Tonto Apache, are their greatest enemies."

"Enemies? Really?"

"Often, our warriors ambush them as they pass by. And often, our warriors die. It is well your man is here. Leaders are few."

"Adrian wouldn't kill anyone! Anyone who thinks differently is in for a shock."

"A warrior kills, or is killed, Cora. That is the way of things. We must hold our freedom, or lose it."

Cora's light mood vanished. "Will they really expect him to fight?"

"Can't he?"

"Well, he has a bunch of stripes on his Black Belt." Cora paused. "But karate is for defense. He hates guns."

"Many warriors use bows."

"Archery. I see." Cora shook her head. "I don't think so. He didn't get far with the non-smoking issue. Killing . . . " Cora fell silent. Adrian had no clue what he'd gotten himself into. A chieftain's son with "power" was expected to lead. And leading meant fighting.

Not in a martial arts tournament, with respectful bowing. Not leading a group of fun-loving adventurers white-water rafting, or up a mountain, or down a mountain. But into battle. A battle where Native Americans more often used bows, and their white enemies came jaded and angry from the Civil War's bloody battlefields.

"Maybe he can convince his father that Native Americans don't win much by fighting. Passive resistance works better. Or perhaps reasoning with the enemy."

Laurencita didn't answer at once. She watched Cora's face, then sighed. "You don't understand a warrior, Cora. It is not the winning, but the honor of living as a man. At times, I think it might be easier to move out of the white man's reach."

"That won't happen, either."

Laurencita nodded. "Then there is no escape."

"There is peaceful coexistence, and respect between races." Cora's chin firmed. "Something tells me that's what Adrian will push for."

The morning passed quietly, but Cora's discontent grew. She watched the rhythmic procession of the people's day. Young men left to hunt, then returned with a dead deer. It was cleaned and skinned, which Cora avoided watching. Laurencita told her that a pregnant woman couldn't eat a deer's intestines. Cora hoped non-pregnant women didn't have to, either.

Adrian was with his father and a group of young men. They were dressed like warriors. Cora couldn't hear what they said, but she assumed they were briefing Adrian on their current situation. She noticed that he nodded a lot.

The women left their morning tasks, and turned to preparing a meal. An old woman spoke to Laurencita, but her gaze fixed on Cora. Laurencita looked uncomfortable, but she nodded.

"Toklanni says you must learn the ways of an Apache

135

wife." Laurencita sounded sheepish, and Cora guessed Toklanni was a formidable woman. Cora smiled at her. Toklanni's firm, wide chin elevated. Yes, formidable.

"I'd be happy to help. What do I do?"

"She says your instruction will begin with the gathering of plants. We need mescal."

"Okay." Cora paused. "What's that?"

"It comes from the century plant. We do much with it."

This clarified nothing to Cora, but she nodded. "If she'll tell me what they are, I'll pick them."

"She'll can't exactly tell you." Laurencita wouldn't meet her eyes. Cora's suspicions soared. "But you'll know."

"How? She doesn't speak English. How will she communicate?"

Laurencita winced, then shrugged. "She'll hit you."

Cora hopped back. "She'll *what?*"

"Not hard. Don't worry. A meal will be prepared for your man this night. You are expected to help."

"I don't mind helping. But being hit . . . "

"It's more of a tap. A firm tap."

"Adrian!"

Adrian turned immediately from his conversation. Toklanni seized Cora by the shoulder and led her from the village. Adrian looked a little nervous. Good!

He caught up with her before they reached a narrow, rocky path. "Where are you going?"

Cora tried to free herself from Toklanni's grasp, and failed. The old woman held on like a burr. "This woman is taking me to pick plants!"

"That doesn't sound so bad."

"If I pick the wrong ones, she'll hit me!"

Cora observed with irritation that Adrian fought a smile. "Pick the right ones."

136

"Oh, easy for you to say! What's mescal, and what's a century plant? Dear God! What's yucca?"

Adrian spoke in Apache to the old woman. The old woman nodded deferentially. Her harsh lips cracked toward a respectful smile. She said something to Adrian. Cora held her breath.

"It's all right, Cora. Toklanni understands."

Cora puffed a breath of relief. "Good. Then I don't have to go?"

"You have to go."

"But she won't hit me?"

Adrian hesitated. "Not hard."

"Oh, perfect! Just perfect!"

"Just a tap, to point you in the right direction."

Cora stiffened, her eyes narrowed to slits, so that only Adrian's dark face filled her vision. "I will remember this."

"She won't hurt you, Cora. You're my woman. You're expected to perform tasks befitting my wife."

"For the last time, I am not your woman! Especially now!"

"Calm down, angel. It will be interesting. Maybe you'll see a roadrunner."

Toklanni gazed admiringly at Adrian, then diverted her attention back to Cora. Her pleasant expression altered, her eyes glittered. She gave Cora a small shove. Laurencita passed her a basket. "You'll need this."

Cora took the basket, but Laurencita skittered away as if worse was yet to come. Her children hid when Toklanni walked by. Cora cast a final glance Adrian's way. He was grinning. She straightened her back and smiled formally. "This will only take a few minutes."

It took three hours. Cora checked her watch several times to be sure. She saw three roadrunners and a hare, but by the third hour, Cora wasn't impressed. They went only a short distance from the village, but the old woman was very picky about which plants were useful, and which weren't.

She spoke no English, so she pointed to various plants for Cora to pick. If Cora picked the wrong one, the old woman swatted her hand. It didn't hurt—much—but it grew annoying. Cora reached for what she guessed was a yucca plant. Toklanni reached down and smacked her wrist.

Cora felt tempted to smack her right back. Instead, she straightened and glared into Toklanni's dark eyes. "The basket is full." She indicated the basket. It wasn't completely full, but full enough.

Toklanni shook her head, then pointed up a small slope. Cora sighed, and walked on. Century plants were tall golden shoots with flowering buds, coming from a low bush with pointed leaves. Cora learned those soon enough, but yucca still confused her. Toklanni seemed to want her to take white flowers from some kind of cactus, then directed her to what looked like wild onions.

The old woman smoked tobacco rolled in an oak leaf while Cora labored over the plants.

"That's bad for you, you know."

The old woman didn't understand, and Cora sighed. She stuffed the various plants into her basket. The old woman didn't stop directing her activities until the basket overflowed.

Cora bent to pick up a fallen berry. Toklanni issued a brief grunt, then pointed toward the village. Cora's back ached. The basket was heavy. Toklanni didn't offer to help.

They walked back to the village in silence. Adrian waited for her, standing with a group of boys. This time, none of the boys was smoking. Apparently, he'd made some progress, after all.

He eyed her basket, smiling. "You did well, it seems."

"My back hurts. My feet hurt. And my fingers are sore from picking all these bizarre plants. I am not pleased."

"I'll take care of your back later. And any other part of your body that needs attention."

Curse him! His dark eyes twinkled, his sensual lips curved in a smile. Cora's heart fluttered, but she refused to acknowledge his appeal. He still wore his jeans and white shirt, but he had changed. His hair fell loose over his shoulders, bound with a twisted, red bandanna. He wasn't a cool, Southwestern yuppie anymore. He was a warrior.

"A new look?"

"Keeps the hair back."

Cora sighed. He looked so masculine that her knees felt weak. Her insides tingled. Power. Adrian didn't need more power. She was the one who could have used a boost, just to level them out. "It suits you."

Adrian touched her basket. "You seem to have returned unscathed."

Cora cast a dark glance Toklanni's way. The old woman looked subtly triumphant. "I prefer going to the grocery store. But thankfully, we are done."

Toklanni spoke to Adrian. He bit his lip. "Well . . . "

"What do you mean, 'well . . . ?' "

"About being done . . . "

They worked until nightfall. Toklanni supervised while Cora and Laurencita prepared the mescal. It was soaked in water, cut, roasted in a pit, and mixed with their other gatherings. While it soaked, Cora made some form of tea from yucca buds. It smelled appealing, but Toklanni wouldn't let her sample any.

Cora made a fist, which Laurencita grabbed. "It's for the men first. Then we eat."

"*What?*" Cora leapt to her feet. "That is unacceptable!"

Toklanni laid her large, firm hand on Cora's head and pressed her down. Laurencita struggled against laughter. "It is our way."

"Your way! Not mine."

Cora grumbled as the women made soup from bits of meat and roots. They made flour from grass and potatoes, and another group of women set about making bread. Cora sank to the ground and lay flat on her back.

Someone poked her with a stick. She didn't have to look. She knew who it was. "Toklanni. What now?"

Toklanni stood over her, holding a strange wad of herbs. It smelled like sage, and it was smoking. "What is it with you people?"

Cora peered at Laurencita, who looked very tense. "You're not going to like this."

"Probably not. What does she want?"

"The bread is ready. The meal is hot. We need one more thing."

Cora sat up. "What?"

"Honey."

"Oh. That sounds good. Where's the pot?"

Laurencita bit her lip. "It's empty."

"Oh, that's a shame. . . . " Suspicion formed. Horror dawned. "No!"

Toklanni grunted and spoke sternly. She held aloft the smoking plant. She dropped a sack onto Cora's lap. Laurencita's oldest son appeared with a small bow and quiver of arrows.

Laurencita helped Cora to her feet. "It's not that bad, really. My son will shoot the hive, and all you have to do is squeeze it until the bag fills with honey."

* * *

"I will never forgive you for this, Adrian de Vargas. Not as long as I live. Never, for the passage of all eternity, nor beyond. Do you understand? Never."

Adrian applied another wad of damp herbs to Cora's arm. Her wrist was swollen double its normal size. "I'm sorry. I didn't know."

Cora winced. "Careful!" She sat cross-legged while he knelt before her. She glared at his bowed head, willing him to meet her eyes. He concentrated on her bee stings instead. Probably afraid to face her. "And not knowing is no excuse. You brought me here, thanks to your boundless power. I shouldn't be surprised. Squeezing a hive!" Her voice rose as the memory assailed her. She closed her eyes to block the image of swarming, angry bees.

Low laughter rumbled deep in Adrian's throat. "I'm sorry."

"You're laughing?"

"No." He shook his head as emphasis. He was still smiling. "It's just the way you phrase things. Why didn't you tell me what they were up to?"

"Tell you? Tell *you*, the man who said that evil old crone wouldn't hit me *hard*?"

Laurencita delivered a fresh wad of herbs and passed it to Adrian. "She went in too soon, before Toklanni had smoked them all out. We tried to stop her, but she attacked the hive." Laurencita paused, looking thoughtful. "She was . . . cool."

Adrian looked up. Cora glared. "She means I panicked. Yes. Hard as it is to believe, I panicked."

Adrian's brow angled. "Usually, when a person panics, she runs away. From bees, from bears, from—oh, say—her lover in Kathmandu. What made you attack a hive of angry bees?"

Cora wasn't sure. "I lost my mind. It's been a long day."

Laurencita held up the bag of honey. Golden droplets oozed out the top. "She pulled the hive down and squeezed until the bag was full. Toklanni has added to her name."

"Does that mean I'm not Talks Much anymore?"

"You are Talks Much Who Fights Bees."

Cora considered this. "That's an improvement, I guess."

Adrian removed the herbal pack and studied her wounded arm. "How does it feel?"

"Extremely painful." Cora paused, struggling with conscience. "Better." A lot better, but she wasn't ready to tell Adrian that. She had attacked a beehive. She'd been stung, on her arms, while Toklanni waved her smudging herbs wildly to drive the bees away. All the while, Cora struggled with the hive, squeezing the honey forth. Her jaw still ached from gritting her teeth in determination.

Toklanni entered the hut carrying a sack. Cora hopped to her feet and squealed. "No!" She backed away, pointing at the sack. "What's that? Do I have to go fetch you a bear now?"

Adrian stood up, a grin fighting on his lips. Laurencita laughed. "She has a dress for you. What you wear now . . . " Laurencita hedged, gesturing at Cora's stained chinos. "For a leader's wife, it is not . . . "

Cora wanted to argue, but couldn't. Her pants were dirty, her T-shirt was twisted and had small cactus points sticking in uncomfortable places. She faced Toklanni and held out her hand, keeping a safe distance. "Thank you."

To Cora's surprise, Toklanni smiled like a friend. She said something in her language, which sounded almost warm. Cora looked to Adrian for explanation, but he didn't speak.

His expression revealed surprise and wonder, but he looked down as if . . . as if afraid to hope.

Laurencita took the sack and pulled out a large maroon-colored skirt and a full blouse of a lighter shade of maroon. "She says it was her dress when she first walked with her husband, the day he took her to wife. She says you have proven yourself strong enough to wear it."

Cora's eyes flooded with tears. She pressed her lips together to restrain an emotional outburst. One day among the Apaches had taught her they didn't favor outward displays of emotion. She bowed twice. "Thank her, please. I will wear it with honor!"

Adrian eyed the dress doubtfully. "Don't you have something in leather? Maybe a little shorter? Tighter?"

"Adrian!" Cora seized his arm. "Toklanni has *honored* me. Hush!"

"At least two of you could fit in that skirt, Cora."

"Nonsense. It's beautiful." Cora held the skirt and blouse up to her body. *Maybe three.* Adrian had a point. It wasn't exactly sexy, but maybe that was for the best. It would cover her swollen wrists, anyway.

Music came from the village center, soft drumming mingled with a flute. Adrian cast a final, somewhat self-pitying glance at Cora's new dress, then headed for the door. "I will join my father now. When you're ready, come to me."

"What? I actually get to eat with you?"

Laurencita looked at the ceiling, and Adrian at his feet. "Well. . . . "

"Don't tell me."

Laurencita patted Cora's back. "You serve your man, and wait while he eats. When he is finished, he gives his plate to you, and you eat what's left."

Adrian winced and darted from the hut as Cora gaped,

speechless. Laurencita closed her eyes and waited while Cora sputtered. "But what . . . what if he's very hungry?"

"We always find something. Now, you must put on your new dress."

Cora positioned a blanket over two upright sticks for privacy, and removed her dirty clothes. She pulled on the full skirt and adjusted the waist to fit herself. The hem was pleated and had a pink stripe for decoration. The blouse had loose sleeves, and ample space for large breasts. Unfortunately, Cora didn't have large breasts, so the blouse hung as if a five-year-old had crawled into her grandmother's nightgown.

"I need a belt of some sort."

She emerged from behind the blanket and Laurencita burst into laughter. Even Toklanni chuckled. Cora felt foolish and began to wonder if the old woman had set her up again. Toklanni seized a narrow, smooth rope and tied it around Cora's middle. She tugged at the blouse so that it flared admirably over Cora's hips.

Cora examined herself. "Sort of a Spanish look, really. Not bad." She imagined herself in a close-fitting, leather dress, her legs bare, emerging from the hut to meet Adrian. But this would have to do. She bowed to Toklanni, unsure if Apaches bowed or not. But Toklanni seemed to like the inherent respect. "Thank you for the dress."

Laurencita translated for Toklanni. Toklanni studied Cora's appearance thoughtfully, then spoke to Laurencita. "She says you need beads, a necklace. Of course, you can't wear bracelets just now, or I'd give you some of mine."

Cora reached beneath her blouse and drew out the bear fetish pendant Adrian had given her. Both Laurencita and Toklanni gasped in admiration, then fingered the pendant.

"It's beautiful, isn't it? Adrian always had such good taste. He gave it to me when we were dating, for my nineteenth birthday."

The two women looked at her in amazement. "He presented you with the symbol of bear." Laurencita spoke as if the pendant symbolized more than good taste. Cora wondered if Adrian knew.

"What does it mean?"

"Many things. The bear lives in the West on the Medicine Wheel. It is the place of what the future holds."

"Fitting."

"It also means looking within, to see from what the future comes."

"Also fitting."

"The bear is courage, to face fear, and to make your own future."

Cora's heart beat with sudden force. *He knew.* Because Adrian had power, even then. Cora looked out the door to the darkening campsite. She had been floundering through life, taking all the wrong paths. For a little while, here in the past, she imagined that he needed her. That somehow, she could be helpful to him. But Adrian de Vargas was now, and always had been, as far above her as the stars.

Cora wrapped her fingers tight around the little pendant and went out to serve his meal.

He'd only seen Cora Talmadge in a dress once, when he took her to an expensive restaurant for Valentine's Day. He'd spent the whole evening looking at her legs. Cora had beautiful legs, long and shapely, with delicate feet and ankles. Long enough to wrap around him as he made love to her.

145

Stop thinking about sex. Keep your mind clear. With Cora dressed in a garment that would be loose on a linebacker, it shouldn't be impossible. She emerged from his hut behind Laurencita and Toklanni. Her hair fell loose around her shoulders, soft and wavy, the amber highlights catching the fading, red sun.

Adrian swallowed hard. He couldn't see her legs or even her ankles because the skirt was wide and brushed the ground. The big shirt obscured her breasts, and the sleeves reached her fingers. She met his eyes and her lips quirked in a sideways smile, as if sharing a private joke: herself.

His heart pounded. A long spiral of soft golden hair fell forward over her left eye, and she pushed it back. His groin tightened. She walked to his side, and he saw the tips of her plaid sneakers beneath the dress. The image should have been funny, but instead, Adrian felt nervous. Because she was tall and slender, her ridiculous wardrobe didn't look ridiculous. And he realized something he'd never really known before—Cora was elegant.

She was elegant in plaid sneakers and chinos. She was elegant stuffed into a skydiving suit with goggles and a cap. She had been elegant in the wet suit she wore rafting—even when he pulled her from the white water, her eyes as round as saucers, her chin quivering. She had adjusted herself, folded her narrow, slender hands together and issued a silent prayer. Then she thanked him for saving her.

She had thanked him for a lovely evening when he took her powder skiing, even though she had ended up in a tree. She complimented him on his mountaineering skills while she sat in the emergency room waiting for her sprained ankle to be bound.

"No laughing, Adrian de Vargas. I know it's a bit large."

She seated herself beside him, her legs tucked under herself, to one side.

"I'm not laughing." Adrian looked into her soft gray eyes and he felt nineteen again. "You are beautiful."

Cora chuckled as if he was joking. "Well, thank you. So are you." Toklanni approached, and she groaned. "Uh-oh. I think I have duties. See you later."

Cora used his shoulder to prop herself up. Adrian looked up and she smiled. Her expression altered as if she didn't understand his mood. She touched his hair and his nerves tingled to his toes. "I'm supposed to get your meal. If I'm quick, I should be able to nab you some prime intestines."

I love you. "Wait in line, Cora. I'm not that hungry."

Her eyes twinkled. "Don't worry, Adrian. I have to eat your leftovers, remember. I won't pick anything too weird."

He watched her mingling with the other women. They instructed her with gestures, and Laurencita translated. Cora examined various offerings, selecting what he hoped looked appealing. She laughed and nodded, happy. Cora made a good Apache wife. *Wife.* Despite his words to her, he'd been living as if this time was temporary, but it didn't have to be. They could stay in the past for the rest of their lives, together.

He didn't have to convince her to marry him, to take his ring. She was already his woman. He wanted her to wear his ring, but first he had to prove to her that she wanted the same thing. He would make love to her, he'd take care of her. They would live a natural life, in contrast to what she had known in Manhattan. She'd be happy with him, and he'd casually give her the ring one day. When she had already accepted their marriage.

Tiotonawen seated himself beside Adrian, and Haastin sat beside Tiotonawen. Adrian tried to concentrate on their conversation, but his gaze kept wandering back to Cora. He noticed when she took a sly bite of bread, and another of what looked like stew.

"Talks Much adjusts well." Tiotonawen ignored the young woman who delivered his meal. Adrian smiled at her, to minimize his father's neglect. His people could use more balance between the sexes, but it would have to be done delicately. "She needs more fat on her bones."

Cora brought a large, wooden plate to Adrian and knelt beside him. "I don't know what most of this is." She leaned forward to examine his meal and pointed at a white root. "I think I picked that. No idea what it is."

The other men ate while the woman sat behind them, but Adrian felt awkward eating while Cora licked her lips hungrily. He slipped her a piece of bread. Somehow, that felt worse. Like slipping food to a pet at the dinner table. Cora made a small "woof" noise and Adrian cringed.

He ate sparingly, partly for Cora's sake, and partly because his nervousness took away hunger. He passed the plate to Cora, who devoured everything. "I don't know what this is," she said thickly, then swallowed, "but it's tasty, isn't it?"

Apparently, Cora wasn't nervous. No nervous person could eat that much. She sat with her back resting against his, intimate and sweet. He wondered if she felt his heart pounding. "It's a bit like camping." Cora took a sip of yucca blossom tea. "Did you try this, Adrian?" She passed him the cup. He drank, but his throat felt tight.

"Good."

"Isn't it?" Cora drank more. Evening fell over the ravine where the village lay hidden, and Adrian's nervousness grew. Cora peeked around his back to Tiotonawen. "So, sir." She spoke casually, at ease. "Adrian has been looking for his original family for years. We thought he was Navajo."

Tiotonawen braced indignantly. "My son is Apache. His blood reaches from this soil, and runs like pure water. Apache water."

"Why was he wrapped in a Navajo blanket, then?"

Tiotonawen's brow knitted into a tight frown. "It was his mother's weave."

"Why did she use a Navajo pattern, if she was Apache?"

Tiotonawen exhaled a strained, annoyed breath. "She was Apache because she was my wife, and I made her Apache."

"I see. What was she before?"

A long pause followed. "Navajo."

Cora chuckled, and Adrian restrained a smile. "I see. So in reality, Adrian is half Navajo. Anything else?"

"No. Navajo and Apache are alike. Red and strong."

"I always thought he had Spanish eyes." Cora studied Tiotonawen's face. "Like you."

Tiotonawen's jaw set hard. "A captive woman becomes of her husband's people."

Cora's eyes wandered to the side in confusion. "Meaning . . . " She paused. "Meaning someone back there captured a Spanish woman?"

"My father took many women. He had seven wives."

"And your mother was . . . " Cora sounded knowing.

"Mexican."

"I *see*." Cora considered his heritage while Tiotonawen fumed. "That means Adrian is, in actuality, one half Navajo, one quarter Spanish, and one quarter Apache. Well, well." She stopped and sighed. "It's certainly a beautiful combination."

Adrian felt shy. He hadn't felt shy since he asked Cora on their first date. He'd taken her to lunch in Boulder, then for a walk along the river. He'd held her hand, then kissed her cheek at her apartment door. Her roommate interrupted

149

them, and gave him a long list of rules, which basically meant he was a man, and men were evil, and he wasn't to set foot in their apartment after ten o'clock—despite the fact it was only five o'clock.

"Does he have any brothers or sisters?"

"I had a son who died from the poisoned food. I had another wife, and another son, later. They died, too."

"Oh. I'm sorry. What happened? Was he sick, too?"

Tiotonawen gazed across the campsite, toward the new stars. "He was not sick. He was Eschinaeintonyah. His mother died in childbirth, but he grew to manhood."

Haastin and the other men looked down, and Adrian guessed their grief was recent. "What happened to my brother?"

Tiotonawen met his eyes. "The white eyes named Tradman . . . "

Adrian's mind flashed to the scalp-hunter and his collection of black hair. "No."

Tiotonawen nodded slowly. "Eschinaeintonyah had a wife. She was seventeen years in age. Your brother was twenty-two. They had one daughter. Tradman hunts our people. Not for vengeance—for gold. He sells scalps to the Mexicans. He sold Eschinaeintonyah's wife and daughter's scalps, after he killed them."

Adrian closed his eyes. His heart filled with black rage, dark hatred. He heard Cora beside him, crying softly. He felt her hand on his shoulder. "My brother."

"Eschinaeintonyah went after Tradman alone. Tradman has no courage. He did not stand and fight. My son hunted him through the hills, to the white eyes Fort McDowell. Tradman hid inside the fort, knowing my son waited. My son waited, but Tradman did not come out. Eschinaeintonyah would not leave. He loved his wife and his daughter. Tradman would not come out, so he went in."

Cora caught her breath. "He went into a fort alone?"

"He walked in and they didn't stop him, because he carried a white cloth. He walked to the house where the white eyes drink. . . . " Tiotonawen paused searching for the word. "Bourbon. Tradman was there. My son took his knife, which was hidden in his boot." Tiotonawen sighed and shook his head. "Many soldiers there. Before he could take his vengeance, he was shot down. Tradman lives on, but he does not forget my son. The soldiers threw my son's body outside their fort, to lure us close, to kill us all. They know we would not go so close, where all would die. So they left him to the ravens and the coyotes."

Tiotonawen looked into Adrian's eyes. "Yes, you had a brother. You have a brother no more."

Tiotonawen's voice trailed. Adrian stared into the low campfire. His world, the reality he hadn't considered. Cora dried her eyes on her sleeve. "The men at the fort, why do they let Tradman in?"

"He is white."

"White murderers are as bad as any other color."

"Tradman says to them that my people kill the soldiers. We do, when they come to kill us."

"This is grim." Cora shook her head. "You've got a homicidal maniac on the loose. Someone should set those soldiers straight."

Adrian stood up and gazed down at his father. "Someone will. I go tonight."

Chapter Six

"You're not going anywhere!" Cora sprang to her feet, waving her arms violently. "The egg has shattered beyond recall, hasn't it, Adrian?"

"Cora, please. I must go."

"Are you crazy? He just told you those wackos killed your brother. What makes you think they'll listen to you?"

Adrian glanced at his father. "Did my brother speak English?"

"No English. He didn't go to fort to talk."

"Tradman is your enemy. He is their enemy, too. White soldiers were prejudiced, but they weren't all evil. They can be made to understand."

Cora issued a long, drawn out moan. "So you're just going to knock on the fort's front door and ask to speak to their leader? Dear God! They'll shoot you before you say two words! You're not going."

"Talks Much, a wife does not issue commands. She obeys commands."

"Ha!" She glared at Tiotonawen. "You can't let him do this. He's your son—the only one you've got left. Tell him he has to stay here and be safe!"

"My son does his duty. He is leader. His brother died without vengeance."

Cora shook her fist at the old man. "Some father! His first day with you, and you're getting him into trouble!"

Cora stepped toward Tiotonawen, her fist clenched to attack. Adrian thought of her battle with the beehive. He caught her and drew her back. Every muscle in her body was clenched tight in anger. "Cora." She couldn't understand, but Adrian knew. He had grown up in the future, and returned to the past. He had a purpose. He had his people's honor at stake, and he could help them to deal with men who would be forever after their neighbors. "I must go."

"What if they shoot you?" Tears glistened in her eyes. Her chin quivered.

Tiotonawen positioned himself at Adrian's other side, a safe distance from Cora. "My son has power."

"That didn't help your other son!"

"Eschinaeintonyah did not have power. He was young, he was brave, but he did not have power. Few men have the power. Who has it, walks safe and unseen."

"Oh, God! He can't make himself invisible, you idiot! That's nuts."

"He walks unseen."

Adrian stroked Cora's hair to calm her. "He means I have natural stealth."

"Oh, do you? Well, you'll need it. You're not going. Do you hear? No."

"Talks Much, bring my son's horse."

Cora leveled a dark look Tiotonawen's way. "I don't *think* so."

"It is the wife's duty to carry the saddle and bring the horse."

She sneered. Seeing her defiance, Tiotonawen nodded to the young woman who served his meal. She hurried away toward the tethered horses. Adrian slid his hand down her arm and took her hand. "Walk with me."

Her tears fell to her cheeks. "Where?"

"Anywhere."

She hesitated, then nodded. He led her from the fire to the edge of the village. They stood silently together, watching the stars. She sniffed several times. "I was just beginning to like it here."

"I have to go."

Cora turned to face him. "It was a sad story, I admit. That Tradman person is evil. But I don't think riding off into the night is a good idea."

"My people ride at night to avoid detection. I know my way to the fort—it's east of here, on the other side of the park." He paused. "What will be the park. I'll be fine."

"Oh, right! Maybe a nice park ranger will give you directions!" Cora contained herself, and her eyes narrowed as she watched him. A tremor of suspicion formed in Adrian's stomach. "You're going alone, I assume?"

"I won't risk any of my people. And one man alone will be less threatening to the soldiers." Adrian drew her hand to his lips and kissed her fingers. She looked up at him, her eyes shining with tears.

"I don't want you to go."

"I know."

"You're going anyway, aren't you?"

154

"Yes."

She bit her lip and drew a quivering breath. "Adrian, I believe you have power. But it's gone to your head. When I knew you before, you were perfect. You're perfect now, but you're in the wrong time. I don't care when you were born. You belong in the Nineties, you belong in the next century after. Not here."

"You're doing well enough here."

"I'm different. I never did fit in back there, but you did. Please, let's find a way back, and go home."

Home. Where she would fly back to Manhattan, and leave him in Phoenix. "That is impossible. More soldiers will come, Cora. My people may be destroyed completely. I can help them find some way to exist in the world to come."

"What if something happens to you?"

Adrian knew. His father would send her back to the future. "You'll be all right. I promise."

"You're here to look after your people. Who's going to look after you?"

"I have power." Adrian cupped her chin in his hand and tilted her face to his. "I hoped to use it to seduce you tonight, but that will have to wait."

She blushed, but she didn't look away. Her lips parted and he bent to kiss her. Her arms wrapped around his neck, and her kiss intensified. He felt the tip of her tongue against his lips, sliding between. Her fingers entwined in his hair as he answered her desperate passion.

He was a warrior, riding away to battle. She was his woman, waiting. Adrian kissed her face. "I'll come back, Cora. Don't worry."

She rested her forehead on his chest, then looked up at him. Her lips twisted to one side, and her eyes narrowed as if she were scheming. "I suppose you know what you're doing. I guess I can't stop you."

Her casual tone astonished him. She hadn't offered to go with him. He wouldn't allow it even if she did, but somehow, he expected her to offer. Maybe she viewed an armed fort like Mount Everest. Maybe she was right.

"If you're really going, you should start now."

Her sudden change seemed wrong, not quite real, but Adrian didn't have time to pursue the matter. A girl led his black-and-white horse to him. He took the reins. Cora stood back, still casual.

The men gathered around him. Haastin passed him a rifle, which he attached to his saddle. Laurencita gave him a pack. "Dried meat and water, for your ride."

Tiotonawen gave him a large, curved knife. "The White Eyes have scouts around the fort. They shoot before talk."

"I will be careful. I know these mountains."

He turned his gaze to Cora, then spoke in Apache to his father. "If I don't return, you will send her back where she belongs."

"I will."

Cora looked between them, almost as if she guessed what they said. She popped her lips, making a sound like a wine bottle being uncorked. Adrian knew that sound. It meant, solidly, that she was scheming. That her mind was working in cold, methodical action, to a rhythm so illogical that he couldn't begin to comprehend her plans.

He touched her face and she kissed his palm, then held his hand in hers. She didn't speak. She rose on tiptoes to kiss his cheek. He guessed she was overcome with emotion, and had no words. A first time for everything.

The others stood back for him to mount, but Cora clung

fiercely to his hand, her eyes closed as if in prayer. He kissed her forehead, then held her face between his hands, stroking her cheeks. "I love you, Cora." Her eyes popped open, glistening with tears. "I never stopped. I wanted you to know."

She drew a quick gulp of air, her chin quivered, her tears fell. "Adrian . . ." Her voice came as a whisper, but he laid his finger on her lips to quiet her.

"Don't say anything, angel. Just know. I'll come back, and maybe I can get back what I lost with you."

He didn't let her speak. He mounted quickly and turned his horse to the ravine path. He glanced back once. Cora stood in front of his people, her hands clasped in front of her body. He saw the toes of her plaid sneakers sticking out beneath her oversized skirt. The full moon glinted on her hair and her small, lovely face.

He knew, no matter what, he would come back.

Cora stood motionless as Adrian rode alone up the narrow path. His father stood behind her. She waited until the horse disappeared, then turned around. "Now, then, Whirlwind. You and I have a few things to get straight."

She took a deliberate and threatening step toward Tiotonawen. He backed up, an instinctive response to danger. Cora pointed her finger at him. "Stay put, you!"

To her amazement, he did. She realized that without Adrian beside her, his father feared her, as if he wasn't certain what she was capable of. So much the better.

"Adrian doesn't belong here. He belongs in the future, a lot more than I ever did. You're stealing from him a life everyone I know would envy. You're placing him in danger. Well, over my dead body!"

"My son belongs here." Good. He sounded nervous, too.

"We'll just see about that!"

"You fear for my son. As a wife should. Wait in patience, Talks Much. He will return."

"Oh, he'll return, all right. And he'll be perfectly safe. He'll be safe, because I'll be with him."

He looked thoroughly shocked. "Talks Much!"

Cora's eyes narrowed to slits. "I am Talks Much Who Fights Bees. And if I say I'm going, I'm going."

Cora stormed past Tiotonawen and aimed for the horses. Several warriors hurried after her, but she ignored them. She spotted Tradman's bay horse. *Fate.* "So, we meet again." The horse eyed her steadily, as if he recognized her from their earlier meeting. "One good turn deserves another, sir. I helped you get rid of Tradman. Now I need you to help me."

The horse touched his muzzle to Cora's shoulder and pushed gently. Cora scratched beneath his ears. "I shall call you Spot, for the star on your forehead." She paused. "Come, Spot." She led him to the collection of old saddles, and slapped the smallest on his back. She bridled him quickly and mounted, but the warriors blocked her way.

She affected a confident leer. "I'll be going now, and you won't be stopping me." She whipped her bear pendant from her shirt and held it up. The men looked confused. "He gave me this. He put part of his power in this necklace, and I have it. It means he needs me. So you will let me go, or else."

It worked. The men stood back. Tiotonawen looked like he wanted to argue, but didn't dare. Laurencita stood beside Toklanni, smiling. Toklanni looked proud.

"I will also need a pack." She paused. "And a nice blanket for sleeping."

Laurencita hurried off to fetch a blanket. Toklanni filled a bag with food. Cora hoped it didn't contained dried intestines or anything vile. She turned her attention back to

Tiotonawen. "Adrian is riding into a fort of white men. I am white, in case you hadn't noticed. Mostly. I have a distant ancestor who was Micmac. Anyway, if I'm with him, they'll be less likely to shoot first, ask questions later. I'll assure them he's perfectly trustworthy, and we'll set things straight about that Tradman fellow."

Tiotonawen clearly wanted to object, but couldn't think of anything convincing. Instead, he shrugged. "The soldiers are from the big war. They do not shoot white women."

Laurencita passed Cora a rolled blanket and Toklanni gave her the bag of food. Cora attached it to the saddle. "Oh, hell." She hopped off the horse, gave the reins to Laurencita, and darted into Adrian's hut. She fumbled in her chino's pocket and withdrew her tube of sunscreen. She returned to Spot and eyed Tiotonawen's hat. "I could use that."

His brow arched in disbelief as she gestured to his hat. "You want?"

"Your hat. You don't need it just now. It will keep the sun from my eyes tomorrow."

He removed his hat slowly, as if he didn't believe he was complying with her request. Cora took the hat from his hand and placed it on her head. It had a rounded top and a fairly wide brim, with a red band for decoration. Cora would have liked a feather, and decided to pick one up along the way.

"Thank you." She adjusted the hat, positioned her long skirt over her knees, and set off after Adrian.

Adrian rode until the first light of dawn. He stopped at a narrow stream to water his horse. He felt sure he heard another horse whinny in the distance, but when he stopped to listen, he heard nothing more. If something was following him, it wasn't in a hurry for confrontation. He doubted an enemy soldier would take that long to attack.

159

He hid his horse in a thicket of bushes where it grazed quietly. He set his camp beyond a rim of cholla cactus, remembering that the Apache used the bristling plant as a weapon long ago. He laid out his blanket a distance away, hidden beneath a Palo Verde bush and some junipers.

He was exhausted, but sleep didn't come easily. He ran over his upcoming introduction to the fort, to soldiers who viewed his people as animals. He would correct that impression by his education and calm reason.

His thoughts turned to Cora. He'd told her he loved her. She'd cried, but it had felt good to say the words. When he returned to the village, he would win her love. He wasn't sure if he'd lost it, or frightened it away, but she still cared. She certainly still desired him. He'd gone a long while without sex—he could wait a few more days. It hadn't bothered him much until he saw Cora again. Now, sex consumed his thoughts.

Even at nineteen, she had been so eager to learn, to please him. She liked everything he did. They had been desperate to blend, to become one thing. It hadn't been easy to get time in private. Luck wasn't with them, even then. They had seized their chance when her cantankerous roommate went to a movie, and they sat necking on her couch. He remembered vividly touching Cora's small, round breast and thinking he would explode from desire.

The Amazon roommate returned unexpectedly, and in disgust because the movie glorified romance and made men seem heroic. She yelled at Cora for defying the "rules." Cora apologized profusely. Not to be defeated, Adrian took her to his own apartment, because his roommate was out, too. They made it to his bed. She touched his arousal through his jeans. He unbuttoned her shirt. His roommate came back with a half-drunken girlfriend, and they proceeded into the other bedroom. The groans and banging bed ruined the atmosphere.

Determined and painfully aroused, he had taken her to a hotel. Their room was small, but it had a king-sized bed. Unfortunately, a high school football team had the rooms on either side of theirs, and across the hall. They seemed to be holding a practice in the hall. Cora had made that popping noise he remembered so well. She took his hand and brought him into the bathroom, where she suggested they make use of the shower.

He remembered that his hands shook too much to take off his shirt, so she unbuttoned it for him. It seemed they had persevered, until she turned on the shower. It burst forth in hot, then icy cold spurts.

They gave up. He took her back to her apartment, and they sat miserably on the steps together because her roommate wouldn't let him in. He had contemplated making love to her in his Jeep, but Cora deserved better. He kissed her, then went home to gather camping gear.

The next day, he took her up into the Boulder foothills. He sent up a tent, put her in a sleeping bag, and made love to her all night long. The memory still had fuel, though it had gone through his mind a thousand times.

Perseverance over circumstances defined his people. It defined his own power. He would handle matters with the soldiers, then return to Cora. He would hold her, and kiss her, and find what he'd longed for since he lost her.

Satisfied with that image, he closed his eyes and went to sleep.

"Hands up, pardner! This is a stick-up!"

Adrian bolted upright, fumbled for his rifle, then froze at the sound of a woman's laughter. He drew a breath and looked around. Cora sat on horseback, silhouetted against the high morning sun. She braced one arm on her leg, slumped like a cowboy. Laughing.

Adrian just stared. She still wore the over-sized shirt and full skirt. She had added his father's hat with a black feather sticking upright from the band. He blinked twice, but nothing changed.

"Waking you is such a trial, Adrian de Vargas. I rode around you twice, and you didn't notice." She hopped off Tradman's bay horse, removed the saddle, and tied the horse beside his.

"Cora. You're here."

"You noticed." She sat down beside him and rested her arms casually on her knees. "Hi."

"You followed me."

Cora shrugged. "It wasn't hard. I just stopped when you stopped. My horse followed yours."

"Well, you can just turn around and ride right back."

She gazed into his eyes. "Where you go, I go also."

"Sweet, but no way." For some reason, he felt nervous. She looked so pretty. Her hair fell in a long, loose braid over one shoulder, her face looked a little pink from the sun. "Did you forget your sunscreen?"

She whipped the little tube from her sock and held it up. "Of course not."

He eyed her hat. "You look cute."

She touched the hat. "What do you think of my feather?"

"Impressive."

She beamed. "I thought so."

"If you've followed me all night, you must be tired." His nervousness didn't abate. They were alone. Camping, more or less. A perfect opportunity presented itself. He hadn't

162

been shy in his hut. He'd been strong and powerful, able to arouse her, then restrain himself.

Cora watched his face as if she knew what he was thinking. "I'm not so very tired."

"Aren't you?" His voice was high. She angled her brow knowingly, then moved a little closer to him. He swallowed, looked at his hands, at a nearby prickly pear, then at her hat.

"You look cute."

"You said that."

I am not a nervous man. She touched his arm and he startled.

"Adrian."

"Yes?" He didn't dare look at her. He took a quick glance and saw that her gray eyes looked dark, her eyelids seemed low. Sensual. *Bedroom.*

"Lie down."

He seized a desperate breath, then lay flat on his back. She pulled off her hat and set it beside his cast-off boots. A slow, painfully sexy smile curved her lips. She cast a contemplative glance along the length of his body, lingered over his crotch, which he knew bulged from nervous desire, then returned her knowing gaze to his face. He'd admitted he still loved her.

She took a small pack from her saddle and pulled out a blanket. She laid it beside his, then positioned herself beside him. She propped herself up on one elbow, then touched his hair, casually. His heart throbbed as if she'd reached into his jeans. She ran her finger from his hair to his ear, then along his jaw. Her finger stopped at his lips.

Her hair fell over one shoulder, and curled in loose spirals over his forehead. "Cora, you're so beautiful."

She looked a little surprised, as if she didn't quite believe him. He touched her hair, then released her braid. Her long hair spread around her shoulders in rippling, desert-gold waves, soft and sensual. She leaned close to him, so that her face was just above his.

"Adrian, so are you." Her lips touched his, and her hand cupped his face as she parted her lips to taste him. His body went rigid. He wanted to grab her and take over, but she moved over him, so that she lay half across his chest.

She peered down into his eyes. "I've missed you."

"I've missed you, too."

She kissed his chin, then his neck. Her quick fingers unbuttoned his shirt, and her hand slid over his chest. She slithered down and pressed soft kisses across his skin, then rested her cheek over his heart. Her fingers crept to his waistband. The button popped loose, and he heard a quick "zip" as she opened his jeans.

Her deft little fingers slid purposefully over his underwear and found the solid evidence of how well she'd done so far. She kissed his chest again as she cupped his erection, then tasted his flesh with a low growl.

"You're not trying to delay me, are you?" His voice came hoarse and ragged. Cora ran her tongue over his nipple, then squeezed his concealed length.

"You supposed to sleep all day, and ride at night, remember? We won't be delayed."

Realization formed hazily, blurred beneath currents of desire. "We?"

She peered at him through half-opened eyes. "I am going with you."

"No, you're not!"

Her hand wormed its way to his bare skin, then clasped around his shaft. She massaged him casually, as if they'd spent every day of the past nine years this way. "I am."

His hips moved in irresistible response, but he fought for control. "Cora Talmadge, this tactic—" Her fingers tightened, and he groaned. "Is manipulative, and—" Her hand moved a little faster. Her palm grazed his sensitive, hot flesh purposefully. "So good."

He would let her persuade him into rapturous oblivion, then send her back to the village. Later. Adrian surrendered to her teasing fingers. Her mouth pressed against his. He felt her sweet, rapid breaths as she kissed him. Vigor. She kissed as if she loved his taste, his feel, everything. *Him.*

"Adrian." She gasped for air, then kissed him again. "I think of you so much. When I see a romantic movie, when I hear love songs. I think of you when I see hiking boots, or those beer commercials where everyone is athletic and outdoorsy and having fun."

He laughed, and she kissed his neck. "Thank you. I think."

She pushed his jeans down, and he elevated his hips to assist. "I think of you when I walk past a karate studio, when I see a river, when it snows. I read romance novels about Native Americans because they remind me of you. And I would pretend to be a beautiful girl who could do anything, and dream you loved me still."

Adrian reached up and touched her face. "Cora, you are, and I do."

She stared down into his eyes. "I don't care what I am anymore. I want you so."

Adrian caught her shoulders and rolled her over onto his blanket. He sat up and took off his shirt. He pulled his jeans the rest of the way off, and tossed them aside. She caught her breath as her vision fixed on his erection. She dampened her lips. She looked hungry. She reached for him, and he bent to kiss her.

165

He untied the rope belt around her waist, and the big, maroon shirt draped in folds around her middle. He slid his hand under the shirt, deliberately slow. "You know, there's something sexy about this outfit, after all. I think it's you."

He slipped the big shirt up, and realized she wore no bra. He considered Cora fairly conservative, with a tendency to wear white, cotton underwear, but instead, nothing. She bit her lip. "It's hot, so I thought I didn't need anything underneath."

"Good."

She sat up and he pulled the shirt over her head. He caught her bare shoulders in his hands and kissed her. Her skin felt soft beneath his touch. He pulled her closer, and felt the tips of her breasts against his chest. "Cora."

"Yes?" Good, her voice was high, too.

"Lie down."

She lay back. Adrian untied her skirt and edged it down over her hips. He pulled off her panties, which were white cotton, and drew them over her long legs. Her legs were soft and perfect. He took off her plaid sneakers and placed them beside his boots.

He looked into her eyes and smiled. "Do you want me?"

She gasped, then nodded vigorously. "How much, angel? Enough to let me do this?" He gently spread her thighs and knelt between her legs.

"Enough to let you do anything." Her voice came gravelly. Sexy. He didn't remember Cora sounding that way, but little shocks darted through his body at the sound.

Her chest rose and fell with quick, raspy breaths. Her stomach clenched as she waited. He touched her cheek, and ran his finger slowly down her neck, feeling her racing pulse. He ran his finger along the right of her collarbone, then the left.

He trailed a sensual line to the swell of her breasts, then circled the small peak. His heart drove pulses to his groin, fueling an already blazing fire. He brushed his palm over one pert nipple, then the other. Her eyes closed, her head tipped back. Her white teeth sank into her lower lip as he bent to taste her.

The little bud hardened still more against his mouth. He touched his tongue to the tip, and she shuddered. He laved it gently, then teased her until her breath came as fierce gasps. He moved his attention lower, pressing kisses against her stomach. He paused to admire the soft triangle of dark blond curls, then dipped his finger between her thighs.

She was damp and warm, ready for him. He found the tiny, concealed peak and grazed it with a light touch. Cora's eyes opened wide, glittering with passion. Her lips parted to allow for her breaths. She reached to him, seized his erection, and urged him closer.

Her legs wrapped around his waist. Her little toes curled as she squirmed close to him. She positioned his length against her moistened opening, then circled her hips to please herself. Adrian stared down at her, astonished. At nineteen, she had responded with vigor, but she never took control. He had treated her like a fragile doll, gently and carefully. Over and over, but never out of control.

His control weakened. She moaned and arched beneath him. She murmured soft demands as her fingers gripped and insisted. She met his eyes and she smiled. A knowing smile. A smile he'd never seen before. She knew what she did to him—how he hovered on the edge of abandon. Her lips curled still more, then parted. She dampened her lips purposefully, and her silver eyes burned. "Take me."

Mine. He thrust into her until she had all of him. She closed tight around him, welcoming him inside her. He was now where he'd always belonged, past or future. Home. He ached, and she ached, too. She wrapped around him like a blanket, and he withdrew to thrust again. "Cora." Her hips met his, and undulated in sweet rhythm. Desire fused, and flared beyond control.

He moved faster and deeper, rocking against her, feeling her soft inner flesh squeezing around his swollen length. He felt her pulse, her desire. "Cora, it's been so long."

She nodded feverishly. "Long."

"You feel so good."

"I do." She looked up at him, shocked. "I do now."

He moved slower, methodically, watching her face. He braced his arms straight on either side of her head. She gripped his forearms and balanced herself as she met his thrusts. As he watched her beneath him, he realized with a fiery shock that she wasn't his young lover anymore. She was a woman he'd known for two days. A woman who fought bees.

His desire flamed. She was a beautiful, elusive stranger. A stranger who teased him with erotic kisses, and urged him to make love to her. Her hair spread out around her head, around her shoulders, over the red and black blanket. Her teeth clenched as her pleasure soared. Her round breasts bounced with the power of his thrusts.

His power had brought him more than he bargained for. Her inner depths spasmed, her legs clenched. He watched her as ecstasy rippled through her. He heard his name on her breath. "Adrian, I love you."

Her words sank into his soul. His body quivered and his release came with a force he'd never imagined. Waves and waves of pleasure spilled through him, deep inside her. All the while, he watched her face in ecstasy. Their motion stilled. Her eyes drifted shut. A small, satisfied smile curved her lips.

Adrian sank down into her arms and she held him close, softening his hair. "I will protect you, Adrian." She spoke as if to a child, then kissed his forehead. It wasn't what he expected to hear.

They were together again. He was inside her. He wanted to stay. Her legs remained around his, her arms went around his shoulders. She nuzzled his neck and sighed.

Modern sensibilities made their way back into his thoughts. "I didn't use a condom."

She didn't seem bothered by his lack of restraint. Probably because she'd so thoroughly abandoned her own. "We didn't have a drugstore handy. And I owe you sons."

The morning light spread through the hills, peaceful. "Are you sure?"

Cora ran her hand over his shoulder, down his arm. "Isn't that what you told me? I'm your captive, aren't I?"

"I didn't exactly expect you to accept that."

"I didn't have much choice."

Adrian didn't respond. If Cora accepted being his woman in the past, would it carry to the future, too? Their sexual bond had always been strong. He had made love to her the night she left him in India. Twice. Each time, she'd murmured his name and said she loved him.

And she still left. Unexpectedly.

He looked into her peaceful face and saw two women. One was young and insecure—the Cora he knew nine years ago. One was a stranger. Until he knew this stranger better, he couldn't be sure she was truly his. Whoever she was, she was incredibly erotic. He felt himself growing hard again inside her.

She felt it, too. She moved slightly, circling him. They had to discuss her presence here, and why she couldn't continue on to the fort with him. Her inner walls clenched around him purposefully. He decided the matter would be resolved later.

"I am, of course, going with you."

She was already on her horse. *Tradman's horse*. Adrian considered pulling her off and leaving her tied. They made love, they fell asleep in each other's arms, and woke at sunset. They'd argued while the stars burst one by one into the night sky. "You're not going anywhere." He shook his head. "I mean, you're going back to my father's village."

"I'm going with you. You need me."

"I do not."

She looked hurt, and he wished he'd kept his mouth shut.

"Cora, we can't be sure what will happen at that fort."

"Why is it all right for you to risk life and limb, and not me?"

He scratched his forehead. He hated it when Cora used logic. "I would feel better knowing you're safe."

"Oh, would you? Well, I'd feel better if you walked around in a nice, soft bubble suit and a bullet-proof vest!" She lifted her chin, and he suspected his battle was lost. "I am going with you. I am a white, more or less Anglo-Saxon female. That term, incidentally, isn't terribly accurate. My heritage is mostly Scottish. The Scots were Celts, not Angles or Saxons. I think they really mean 'Germanic' when they call someone Anglo-Saxon. Anyway, I am going with you."

"You're white. So what?"

"Your father says the soldiers won't shoot a white woman.

170

They're Civil War types, you know. High on chivalry. I figure they won't shoot while we're together, which will give you time to talk to them."

"It could work."

"That's what your dad said."

"I don't like it."

"You're a very good lover. I thought I remembered what it was like to be with you, but not fully. You are wonderful."

He grinned. He couldn't help it. "What does that have to do with anything?"

"Not much. I just thought you needed reminding."

"You're trying to distract me."

"Maybe they'll give us a room at the fort, with our own bed."

"I don't think we can expect a bed and breakfast there, Cora."

"No. I suppose not."

Adrian relented. They belonged together, anywhere. "I can't force you to stay behind, but please, stay out of trouble."

"Of course."

He untied his horse and mounted. "I don't remember you being the adventurous type."

Her brow angled doubtfully as they set off. "I'm not. What gave you that idea? I simply think I can be helpful. I can't stand staying behind and wondering if you're all right. Also, you're a reasonable man. Something tells me the people of this time period aren't quite so sane. I, on the other hand, will have no trouble at all."

Cora eased her horse forward and took the lead. Adrian followed. He felt sure of his abilities, but Cora's words left a vague disquiet in his heart. The anger he felt when he heard of his brother's death had submerged, but it wasn't gone. He went to deal with men who thought nothing of a Native American man's death.

Adrian cleared his doubt away. They didn't understand his people, because no one had presented their case with sensitivity, understanding both sides. He had the lessons of history on his side. He knew how past conflicts were best resolved.

He had power. He watched Cora riding ahead of him, her long hair swaying with the horse's long stride. They were lovers again. Because he willed her back into his life. Because he used his power to regain her desire. Yes. He wanted her with him, so she followed him—against orders. He blinded her with desire, so she seduced him.

This seemed somehow askew, but Adrian couldn't find a more rational explanation. His father's hat perched on Cora's head. She wore the loose blouse and full skirt bunched up over her knees. She applied sunscreen sparingly to her exposed skin as she rode along. Yet even with the black feather sticking up from her hat, Cora didn't look askew.

Adrian's shirt felt awkward. He looked down and realized he'd buttoned it out of sync. This seemed more meaningful than it should. He adjusted the buttons in the proper order before Cora noticed, but his sense of awkwardness didn't abate. Cora's stolen horse walked faster than his paint, which jigged to catch up.

"If I'd known you could ride, I would have taken you on trail rides."

Cora glanced back over her shoulder. "I didn't want to brag."

"Why not? I can ride."

Her brow tilted slightly. "I see that. But you are an amateur, Adrian. Not to be insulting, but it's true. You don't even dismount properly. I, on the other hand, won several medals because of my jumping skills. I didn't want to embarrass you."

Their whole relationship was askew. He didn't know this woman. *Didn't want to embarrass him, indeed*! His attention wandered to her bare legs. She kicked her feet out of the stirrups and dangled her legs as if she knew what the sight did to him. She looked relaxed and happy. Hours of love-making did that to a person.

"When do we start using this stealth power of yours?" She burst into a torrent of giggles. Adrian had no idea why.

"What is the matter with you, woman?"

"I don't know." She collected herself. "I was just thinking: Stealth Bomber. Stealth Apache. Kind of an early rendition."

He'd forgotten the need for stealth. He didn't want Cora to know that, though. "When we get closer to the fort."

"What about the scouts?"

Good question. "I think I'm supposed to sense their presence."

Cora jerked Spot to an abrupt halt. "*Sense* their presence? How?"

Adrian rode up beside her and stopped, too. Their horses touched noses, then aimed simultaneously for leafy branches. "I'm not sure. Geronimo had the power, and no bullet could kill him. Probably because he could sense where his enemies were."

"Close your eyes and tell me what you sense."

Adrian closed his eyes. "I sense you've been celibate for too long, and we've got a lot of catching up to do." He peeked at her through one eye. She wasn't blushing as he expected. She smiled, a twinkle of seduction in her bright eyes.

"We do. What else?"

Adrian let his mind go blank and travel beyond his immediate desires. He went beyond himself. He found Arizona, its bones and its dry earth and rugged, mystical landscape. It was part of him. No matter where he went in the world, he carried Arizona with him. All he learned, all he found, he brought with him back to its soil.

"I see my land."

"Really? What's in it?"

His mind relaxed, and his soul took over. He felt the creatures that lived alongside his people. He felt the primal balance of life. He felt another presence, strong and demanding. A cataclysmic force, loud and discordant. It came like a tidal wave or an earthquake, and his whole body tensed. His father's enemies. White men.

He attained calm again, and his mind wandered farther. He saw himself surfing. "Um . . . I don't think this is working."

"Why not?"

"I just saw myself hanging ten on a surfboard."

Cora clapped her hand to her forehead. "You were surfing?"

He nodded. "I've tried it a few times, in the Gulf, and in LA."

"I suppose you were good at it."

"It's like skiing."

"Uh-huh." Cora rolled her eyes and slumped in her saddle. "You're supposed to be psychically searching out enemies, Adrian. Not riding the waves in Malibu."

"Right." He closed his eyes again.

"I wonder what surfing signifies?"

"I'm trying to concentrate."

"Sorry." A brief silence followed. "Riding the waves. Of humanity?"

Adrian opened his eyes. "I was thinking of the forces of nature, and how even the white men were part of it."

"Thank you for including my race in the balance of nature. So, you're surfing these forces. Very interesting."

"My mind wandered."

"Try again."

He sought out his place, and narrowed his range of perspective. He centered on the hills, and felt the presence of animals. He felt prey seeking food, watchful and nervous. He felt predators, intent and hungry. He felt two men, thirsty and bored. Men who were vastly separated from their own homeland soil.

His eyes opened. His mouth dropped. "I sensed two men, not far from here. They're not paying much attention. We should be able to pass by without being seen."

Cora looked a little scared. Not of the scouts, but of him. Adrian's heart beat swiftly, in excitement. A smile spread across his face. "It really works, Cora. I have power."

"Don't talk so loud. How do we get around them?"

Adrian pointed up the hill to their right. "We can go up farther and around. They're up here in the hills, figuring they'll see anyone who's out in the desert. As I remember, it's a narrow passage, but we can do it even in the dark."

Cora shrugged and held her horse back so Adrian could lead. "After you."

Adrian stopped his horse often to "sense" the presence of his enemies. He announced that one man was sleeping. Adrian chuckled to himself as if his hapless enemy amused him. Cora felt sure Adrian was slipping farther from sanity with every mile they progressed.

He was the best lover in the world. Her body still tingled. She couldn't wait to stop, to make love to him again. She had to be quiet, so he could concentrate, so she spent the ride imagining different ways of seducing him. Her morning at-

175

tempt had been successful beyond her wildest dreams. She'd found him sleeping, looking innocent and sweet and vulnerable. It was his vulnerability that sent her over the edge.

"I love you, Cora. I never stopped. I wanted you to know." Those words rang in her ears, with their haunting sweetness, the inner longing. She would do anything for him. She would die for him. She would give him sons and daughters and whatever he wanted.

So when she saw him lying alone, knowing he was in love and still afraid, Cora found another kind of power. A woman's power. The desire to please him filled her mind and her heart. Even the memory of his erection in her hand made her fingers tingle with wanting. It had pulsed with life, with courage and beauty.

She had lost her mind, just as when she attacked the beehive. She approached love-making with the same insane glee. But nothing ever felt better. Even her toes felt satisfied.

Still, more inspired her than lust. She had to keep an eye on Adrian. He went from confident assessment of unseen enemies to a nostalgic recollection of surfboards. Maybe all people had two sides. She felt certain she did. Her sides were coming together and congealing into a stronger being. Adrian's were pulling apart, shattering. Leaving him vulnerable and confused.

She feared for him. She wasn't sure what she feared, but as Adrian sensed his environment, she sensed a growing danger to him. Maybe the men at the fort would listen. If they could see beyond his long, black hair and the color of his skin. Which from what she'd seen so far, didn't seem entirely likely.

If things didn't go the way he expected, if the dark forces that destroyed his brother's family proved still powerful, then Adrian might end up at their mercy, too. He had something his brother didn't. He had Cora. She didn't have power. She wasn't strong or athletic or terribly brave. But she loved him with all her heart. And if he needed her, she would be there.

Adrian sensed five more scouting parties before they neared the fort. Cora initially doubted his judgment, but when he pointed out three men wearing blue uniforms in a low ravine, she was forced to concede his skill. When the fort was in sight, they stopped to make final plans.

"So, we're here. Now what?"

Adrian shaded his eyes against the morning sun. "If we sneak in from here, it will look suspicious. They might shoot before thinking. If we ride in on the main drag, it will appear that we've been let through their pickets, and we should gain entrance."

"Have you been here before?"

He hesitated. "Well, yes. A few years ago."

"That's good. What do you remember about it?"

"Not much." He looked a little sheepish. "I was here on a school field trip. In fifth grade."

"Fifth grade?" Adrian nodded, but Cora's heart warmed with affection. "I suppose you were racing around, pestering little girls and playing Indian."

"Actually, I was playing Star-Fighter."

For a reason she didn't understand, Cora's eyes filled with tears. "Didn't you ever play Indian? I even played Indian. Never cowboy, mind you. Just Indian."

Adrian shook his head. "I was more into science fiction and sports, I'm afraid."

"Adrian, you don't belong here."

His expression hardened. "I am a man of the past, Cora. This is my world. You are my woman. I brought you here, as my father brought my mother from the Navajo. As my

177

grandfather brought my grandmother from Mexico. This is my world."

"You seem a bit defensive." *A lot defensive.* "I'm afraid you're going to get into trouble here."

He looked smug. Odd. She'd never seen him look smug before. Self-assured, yes. But never smug. Smug implied just a little over the edge, just a thread from sanity. A cracking egg. She had often felt smug herself, so she knew. And it always, without fail, led to disaster.

"I will not 'get into trouble' here. I know exactly what I'm doing. I am guided by power, and a Higher Wisdom."

Adrian edged his horse forward. Cora gazed heavenward, "Uh-oh." She sighed heavily, then followed.

They rode down from the hills and onto a dirt road which bore signs of carts and horses. It looked well-used, the closest thing to a road Cora had seen since hurtling back in time. "Well, this looks promising."

"Stop right there!"

Cora nodded. She should have expected as much. A thin soldier wearing a blue uniform emerged from the bushes, aiming a rifle that resembled Mr. Cramer's. Perhaps more polished. "Good morning, sir." She couldn't detect his rank because his sleeve was crimped from aiming the rifle. She cast a sidelong glance at Adrian. "Why didn't you 'sense' him?"

"I did."

Cora mustered a formal smile. "We're here to visit your fort. I am Miss Cora Talmadge. This is Mr. Adrian de Vargas."

The soldier's eyes darted back and forth. "What'd'ya want?"

Adrian dismounted, properly, and tossed his rifle aside. "I speak for the Tonto Apache, who live on this land. I seek peace and understanding with you, and your leaders."

The soldier's suspicion was palpable. Cora cleared her throat. "Isn't that nice? I know you've had some trouble, but I'm sure we can clear everything up."

The soldier fixed his gaze on Cora. "Where'd you get her?"

"She is my woman."

The soldier called to someone in the bushes. A bearded man emerged, wearing a uniform with three stripes. He eyed Adrian, then nodded. "Keep him here, Wetherspoon. I'll tell the captain what we've got."

The bearded man darted away, and the fort's tall gate opened enough to let him in, then closed. Cora swung herself from the saddle, and positioned herself beside Adrian. If anyone shot at him, they'd have to go through her first. Adrian edged her aside, apparently with the reverse intention.

The gate opened again, and a man rode out. He was much cleaner than the first soldiers. He almost looked neat. His blond hair was trimmed to his neck, although it hung a little long over his eyebrows. He wore a mustache, as if trying to look older than his years. He looked both innocent and weary, as if despite his youth, he'd already seen too much.

Cora liked him at once. He was cute and boyish, and vulnerable. A potent combination. She relaxed, feeling more comfortable. Beside her, Adrian looked both put out and unfriendly. Cora had no idea why. The young man seemed much easier to deal with what she'd feared.

He sat very straight on his horse. He stopped when he saw Adrian, but he didn't seem afraid, just curious.

"Sergeant, did you capture this man?"

"No, sir, Captain. He rode on in with this here girl. Figured you wouldn't want him through the gates."

The captain folded his hands at the pommel of his saddle

and studied Adrian. His bright gaze moved to Cora and his expression changed. She saw both pity and wonder. His jaw firmed as if he'd been insulted.

"Good morning, sir. As your soldier may have mentioned, I am Cora Talmadge."

The young man dismounted and gave the thin soldier his reins. "Miss Talmadge, allow me to introduce myself. I am Captain Darian Woodward of the Eighty-Third Regiment."

Cora beamed. He was the first person to address her as if she could speak for herself. Tiotonawen's interrogation didn't count.

Cora stepped forward and held out her hand. He took it, but rather than shaking it as she expected, he bent and kissed the backs of her fingers. Cora eyed him doubtfully, then smiled. "How nice."

He met her eyes. He looked earnest and emotional. "Miss Talmadge, I give you my word as a gentleman that your dark times have passed. You are safe."

Cora hesitated. "That's very comforting."

The captain cast a quick, pained glance Adrian's way. "Take him."

The two soldiers moved in, rifles aimed at Adrian's head. Cora blanched with fear. "Wait!"

Captain Woodward took her arm and gently eased her from Adrian. Her heart raced in terror, her mind went blank. It couldn't go blank. Adrian needed her. "You can't shoot him! It will be . . . bad. Thousands of Indians will attack if you do."

The captain hesitated. "Thousands?"

Cora nodded vigorously. "This is Adrian de Vargas. If you'll listen, he can explain why he's here, and maybe settle a few matters. Peacefully. You'd like that, I'm sure."

"Peace? What peace can there be with a people who consider us invaders? A people with no God, to whom killing is like breathing?"

180

"Okay, it may take a while for you to see eye to eye. But *a*, you are invaders, and *b*, it's just this kind of prejudice and misconception that leads to trouble. Please. He isn't armed. He came here alone, except for me, and it's only polite to hear what he has to say."

For some reason, the word "polite" got through to the captain. "The last Indian we allowed to walk free into our fort attempted to kill a ranger, in cold blood."

"Yes, and if that ranger was Mr. Tradman, he had killed the Indian's wife and daughter."

A muscle in Captain Woodward's lean jaw twitched. He looked between Adrian and Cora. "He will be escorted inside, and I will announce him to General Davis. If he has something to say, we will hear it."

Cora puffed a breath of relief, then turned proudly to Adrian. "There! What did I tell you?"

Adrian's expression remained dark and unyielding. Cora moved closer to him, speaking under her breath. "You're perpetuating the stereotype here, Adrian. Dark and inscrutable. Say something."

"The man who killed my brother will answer for his deed, and the vengeance he sought will be won at last."

"Not that!" Cora groaned and shoved him behind her. "He doesn't mean that quite the way it sounds."

Darian Woodward's brow elevated, making him look even more aristocratic and Anglo-Saxon than before. "Doesn't he? I thought his meaning quite clear. But as for searching out the man who shot your brother," he paused, blue eyes glittering, "you have found him."

Chapter Seven

Vengeance involved blood. Also, a great deal of screaming and pain. Adrian walked behind Darian Woodward, contemplating a fitting end. He disliked the young man on sight. He sensed an enemy—a man who walked blind into his land, and took what Adrian valued most.

Woodward took Cora's arm protectively and she walked beside him, glancing back to be sure Adrian was safe. He was safe, but he wasn't happy. His hands were bound behind his back. Two grisly soldiers walked on either side of him, clutching their worn muskets as if they'd blow him away for sneezing.

His nose tingled at the thought. He would not sneeze. His eyes watered. Sneezing would ruin the moment. He tensed his lips and flared his nostrils to prevent . . . He sneezed. Twice.

Cora looked back, a smile playing on her lips. "Are you all right?"

Adrian kept his head held high. "Dusty." He glared at Woodward, who seemed to kick up an inordinate amount of dirt from the toes of his overly polished black riding boots.

Darian Woodward walked straight, his shoulders square. Adrian slumped a little more and ambled in contrast. The fort was filled with soldiers. Apparently, they were settled in enough to have their wives with them. He saw several women of various ages. An elderly woman spotted him, gasped, and darted into a small, wooden building. A red-haired soldier seized the opportunity to guard a pretty girl in a floral dress, as if Adrian posed some unimaginable threat.

Cora chatted amiably with Woodward, asking him about the fort and how the people lived. *As if he's a tour guide.* Cora clearly hadn't accepted the full reality of their situation. They were in an enemy camp, among men without scruples. No matter how well they dressed, or how innocent they looked with their big, blue eyes and golden hair, or how tenderly they kissed a woman's hand.

"How long have you been in Arizona, Captain Woodward?"

"I was sent West nearly three years ago, after the war ended, Miss Talmadge."

"The war? Do you mean the Civil War?"

Woodward glanced at her doubtfully. Adrian saw both wonder and tenderness in the young man's face. Protectiveness. Darian Woodward wanted to protect Cora—as most men would—but from *him*. "I served in the Civil War, yes, Miss Talmadge." He paused, as if hesitant to bring up a delicate subject. "Have you also been long away from your home?"

183

The idiot obviously believed Adrian had captured Cora and stolen her from her homeland. True, he had, but . . . the nerve!

Cora didn't seem sure how to answer. "Well, I was born in Halifax, but I live in Manhattan."

Woodward brightened. "Manhattan!" "My home is in western New York."

Adrian eyed the captain with disgust. "Practically neighbors." They ignored him as Darian Woodward studied Cora's face. Adrian felt sure he didn't see the dirt or the peculiar hat. He saw her pert nose and silver eyes, her soft, tempting lips. Lips probably still pink from Adrian's own kissing.

"How did you come to this place, Miss Talmadge?"

Cora glanced at Adrian. She'd learned not to say "I flew out," anyway. "Well, I was . . . Um . . . "

Woodward placed his hand over hers. "Please forgive me. How you came out is of no importance. You are safe now, among your own people. The rest is past."

Future. Adrian repressed a growl of irritation. Cora, however, didn't seem annoyed in any way. She looked up at Darian Woodward with interest, and perhaps admiration. "You fought in the Civil War."

She was trying to change the subject. Darian Woodward looked at his feet as they walked—a theatrical ploy meant to enlist sympathy. Cora leaned a little closer, concerned. "I did. I joined the Union Army when I was seventeen."

Not unusual for the times.

"Seventeen! You were just a boy!"

Adrian rolled his eyes as Darian Woodward smiled, wistfully. "My boyhood ended at Bull Run."

Adrian fought a groan, but Cora patted Woodward's arm. "I am sorry. It was a horrible war, I know."

"Then you do know something of the events back in America?"

"Oh, here and there. What I can remember from books and movies." Cora coughed. "From newspapers."

"You are an educated young lady, that is obvious." Woodward cast a disparaging, pained look Adrian's way, then turned his attention back to Cora. "No doubt your courage has seen you through this difficult time."

She didn't seem to know what to say. Instead, she diverted the conversation back to the heroic captain. "The war is over now, isn't it? Why didn't you go back to New York?"

Again, Woodward looked down—burdened by tragedy, no doubt. "War changes a man, Miss Talmadge. I returned home, thinking to forget. To regain the life I had known. I sat in parlors, listening to my mother and sisters playing the piano, singing. They wanted to forget the war, naturally. I tried. But I found I could not. It haunted my dreams and memory. I saw my friends . . . " He stopped, containing emotion. "I re-enlisted and came West hoping to build a new life, a new future. To escape the past."

Cora was thoroughly won over. Adrian wondered if the young fool considered Apache lives as he grieved for his "friends."

Cora placed both hands on Woodward's arm. Adrian's stomach tightened in fury. "I am so sorry. It's called Post-Trauma Stress. It affects people who've fought in wars, and who've been in disasters. It's not your fault."

Adrian couldn't stand it anymore. He quickened his pace, despite the rope tied to his hands. "Perhaps that explains why he murdered my brother."

Woodward cast a cold glance his way. "I 'murdered' your brother because he held a knife to a man's throat. I gave him fair warning, and a chance to surrender."

Cora's brow furrowed tight. "Adrian, I know you're upset because you never got a chance to know your brother, but it's not really Captain Woodward's fault. Your brother could have handled the situation better. If he'd explained about Mr. Tradman, maybe . . . "

Adrian's mouth dropped. His blood ran cold at her betrayal. "What, Cora? Do you think they'd listen when a red man spoke against a white? Will they listen now?"

Darian Woodward led them to a large, two-story building in the center of the fort and stopped by the door. "We will listen to what you have to say. But many times, we have listened to your people, only to be betrayed."

"Ha!" Adrian sneered. "There's a twisted version, if ever I heard one."

Cora winced. "Adrian! You won't get far with this attitude."

Adrian's fist clenched and unclenched. He didn't come here to attack. He came to reason with his enemy. To make a better life for his people. Anger could only damage his purpose. As the captain opened the door, Adrian realized he'd never really known anger before. He'd never been faced with a true enemy, nor pure injustice. Now that he looked it in its pale, blue eyes, he had no idea how far he would go against it.

A guard held open the door, but Woodward turned to Adrian. "You are invited in this room by my honor. But I warn you, we will not tolerate treachery, and we are well-armed. I can see that you have grievances. I am sorry for your brother's loss, because despite our differences, I assume family bonds have meaning to your people. Please understand also that General Davis lost one of his finest officers and the officer's wife to an Apache raid. Their deaths were grim. But speak wisely, and we may yet find a road to peace."

Cora clasped her hands over her heart. Her silver eyes misted with tears. Adrian's jaw set hard. Darian Woodward spoke with the flair of an orator. He met Adrian's gaze evenly, as if he meant every word. A true Anglo-Saxon prince. Adrian's dislike surged.

Woodward still held Cora's arm. Adrian saw them together, as a couple. Darian Woodward was taller than Cora, slender and delicate, as she was. They looked similar. Some women might find the young man attractive. Cora clearly wasn't repelled.

Adrian's pulse moved slow. He had her. She was his, here in the past. It never occurred to him that his claim could be threatened by another man. "Release my woman, or die."

Cora buried her face in her hands and shook her head slowly back and forth. Darian Woodward's cold blue eyes burned with challenge. "You are in no position to give orders."

Cora uncovered her face and drew a long, calming breath. "He's just being polite. These people are Victorians. Behave!"

Adrian's gaze shifted to Cora, then back to Woodward. "She is mine."

"Adrian! I am not a possession!"

Perfect! He'd offended her feminist sensibilities. Darian Woodward misconstrued her response and moved closer to her side. "The general awaits you."

Adrian walked past Woodward, pausing to administer a dark, threatening glance. He entered the front hall as Woodward scurried to cut him off. "There is propriety. Wait here!"

The two soldiers and the guard surrounded Adrian as

Woodward entered another room. Adrian heard low, formal voices, but he couldn't make out their words. Cora seized his arm and pinched hard.

"What on earth do you think you're doing?" She didn't let him answer. "You came here to make peace, remember? Not annihilate Western culture!"

"I will not allow my people to be abused."

"Use your head! Remember who you really are."

"I am Apache, the son of a war chief."

"No! In the first place, you're only a quarter Apache, and a little bit Spanish, and half Navajo. In the second place, you're none of that stuff. You're an Arizona businessman who grew up middle-class and beloved. You're *not* a warrior. Your brother was, because that's how he was raised. But you . . . you're more of a . . . a cool Apache surfer dude!"

Adrian's eyes narrowed to slits until all he saw was Cora's small, pert face. "I am a warrior and I speak for my people."

"You're going to speak your way to a hanging if you're not careful! Captain Woodward explained how your brother died. Now you explain to them about Tradman, and we'll iron things out. The captain seems reasonable."

"Oh, does he? You're seeing those stupid blue eyes and blond hair, Cora. You're looking at his overly pretty face, and not . . . "

Cora smiled so widely and so brightly that he lost his train of thought. "You're jealous!"

"I am not."

"You are. I never thought I'd see the day. Jealous. Well, well."

Captain Woodward emerged from the office looking formal. He motioned to Adrian and stood back. Adrian walked in, and Cora followed. A tall man stood behind a polished, mahogany desk. Adrian found himself wondering how it was transported from the East.

The general wore a lavish handlebar mustache and goatee, well-trimmed. Adrian had grown a goatee once, and had looked so masculine that women touched him in the supermarket. But on this polished Victorian gentleman, it looked . . . prim. The general looked him up and down, his lips curled in a sneer.

Woodward stood before the desk and turned to face Adrian. "General Davis, this is the man who we found at our gate. It isn't known how he passed the guards without being seen, but his final approach was straightforward. He claims to speak for the Tonto Apache."

"Tiotonawen." The general spoke his father's name with pure hatred. "Your father?"

Adrian nodded. "I am Tiyann—"

Cora hopped forward. "That's his Native name. He's really Adrian de Vargas. He lives in Phoenix. Um . . . around here, but as you can see, he went to college."

The general glanced at Cora, then back at Adrian. "You had schooling with white men, did you?"

Adrian hesitated. "Yes."

"So you can speak English. With a forked tongue?"

Adrian resisted the impulse to gag and cough at the clichéd and irritating phrase. "Let's drop the hokey analogies, shall we?"

Cora pressed her lips together to keep from laughing. "What he means is, he'll tell you the truth if you'll listen."

"The truth? About what would this man speak? And why should I listen?"

"We know about your officer and his wife, and we're very sorry."

Stobie Piel

The general's eyes darkened. "Then give me one good reason why I shouldn't string this red devil from his feet and split him limb from limb?"

"Oh, gross!" Cora turned in a complete circle, her wide skirt billowing with her speed. "Would you just calm down?"

Adrian seized her arm and pulled her back. "Cora, I will handle this." He couldn't react with emotion. He had to remain calm. "My father assures me that his warriors did not do this deed of which you speak. On the contrary, it was a man called Tradman who committed the murders."

The general burst into harsh laughter. "Tradman? The ranger? And pray tell, boy, why would Bill Tradman murder an army officer?"

The back door of the office opened, and Tradman emerged.

"Oh, crap." Cora lowered her head and sighed. "Wouldn't you just know?"

"We meet again, red man. But in such an . . . inhospitable place."

Adrian ignored the ranger's baiting tone, and faced the general. "I don't know why he wished your officer dead, or why he chose to blame my people. I do know he murdered my brother's wife and daughter. For this reason, my brother hunted him here—"

"And tried to cut my throat. Thanks to the good captain here, he failed. Just as you'll do, boy. What kind of fool walks into an armed camp trying to pull the same trick twice?"

The general smiled, cold and unfriendly. He nodded to his soldiers. "Take him outside the fence and shoot him."

A piercing scream shocked the men into silence. Cora

190

hopped from one foot to the other as if trying to jog her brain into quick action. "That's not a good idea! Do you people have a clue how many Apache warriors are looking down on you, *right now*? Yes! Thousands! Unless you want to be holed up here forever, I'd think twice about killing Whirlwind's last son!"

Darian Woodward came unexpectedly to Adrian's other side. "Miss Talmadge is right, General Davis. A rash act could worsen our relations with the Tonto Apache beyond our present ability to contain." He paused and glanced at Cora. "There is also the matter of Miss Talmadge herself." He didn't elaborate, but the general seemed to understand. Tradman frowned, but here, the weight of judgment belonged to the army.

"You're right, Captain. Thank you for reminding me of proper procedure. The commanders in Tucson don't like us to get . . . ahead of ourselves."

Adrian was educated. Intelligent. He could use those qualities to get past the general's obvious prejudice. "I grieve for your officer, General Davis. Even as I grieve for a brother I never knew. Both our races know pain and loss. The white man has come West. He will never leave. My people do not accept this, but it is true. The red man is born of this soil, and we will fight and kill to remain. The white man does not understand. Yet there is balance to be found, and kinship in humanity."

Cora sighed and Darian Woodward nodded his youthful approval. The general looked skeptical, as if he'd heard too many words, and believed nothing. "I can't punish you for another's act. For now, you may walk freely in Fort McDowell, and I will listen to your father's terms. For now."

Woodward moved to stand beside Cora. "What of Miss

Talmadge, General? Surely we can offer her assistance?" Adrian didn't like the way Woodward said "assistance," but he didn't argue.

The general eyed Cora's Apache dress in disgust. "Escort Miss Talmadge to the Ladies' Guild and locate a suitable gown in their wardrobe storage." He dipped a pen in ink and wrote a note, which he gave to Cora. "This will tender you your choice of dress, Miss Talmadge. We have a small collection from ladies who are no longer with us."

Cora fidgeted, obviously tempted by the suggestion, yet not willing to leave. "What about Adrian?"

General Davis glanced at Adrian, then offered Cora a patronizing smile. "He will be treated as a spokesman for his people. You may have noticed when you entered the fort that many of our best scouts are Indian, from many tribes. They are among our most trusted allies."

Adrian huffed and muttered under his breath. "Outcasts."

Cora shot him a warning glance, but the general ignored his quiet remark. "We want friendship, not war, Miss Talmadge. This man"—the general waved his hand in Adrian's direction—"is hot-headed, but if he can restrain his father's warriors, it is in our best interest."

The general adjusted a blotter on his desk, aligning it with an ink pot. His attention to detail was obviously extreme. "Captain Woodward will see to your needs, Miss Talmadge. It may surprise you to learn that despite this vast wilderness of rock and sand, the ladies of Fort McDowell live in civilized grace. Perhaps the finer accouterments are more precious here, where so much is hostile and unwelcoming."

Adrian frowned, but Cora brightened at the general's description. "Is there a place where I can take a bath and wash up?"

Woodward smiled and held out his arm. "I will be pleased to arrange such facilities for your use, Miss Talmadge."

Adrian didn't like the idea of Woodward "escorting" her anywhere. "She stays with me."

The general's expression revealed disdain. "You needn't fear for your skin, boy. You're safe without the woman. It is my duty to secure peace with the Apache. If you can assist that end, I will support you."

Adrian's teeth ground together. The pretentious fool believed he wanted Cora with him to ensure his safety. They probably thought he brought her along for that purpose, using her as a shield.

Tradman twitched with aggression. "You can't be serious about letting this red snake stay in the fort, Clem. Sure, he talks pretty. Had that fool Cramer believing him. But you're a hell of a lot smarter than Cramer."

"Cramer has had dealings with the tribe, and he's maintained civil relations. It may be he has developed a method of reasoning with them, Bill."

Tradman's lips curled in mimicry of a snarl. "Cramer don't know nothing about no Indians. He'll likely be stuck at night by these savage devils for his peace-keeping."

Adrian kept his attention on the general. "As long as Mr. Cramer refrains from violence, my people will leave him in peace."

General Davis nodded, but Tradman refused to relent. Adrian fought impatience. "This discussion would progress more smoothly with fewer people in the room."

Tradman fingered his holster. "You'd like that, wouldn't you, boy? Give you a chance to slit a White Father's throat maybe eat Brave Soldier's heart."

Adrian's patience shattered. "Chill out, man!"

"That's enough, Bill."

"Excuse me!" Cora tapped Adrian's shoulder, eyes glittering with amusement.

Adrian kept his gaze on the general. He had to gather his power, and use it. "What is it, Cora?"

"You just told this desperado person to 'chill.' "

Adrian frowned and glanced at her. She looked pert. "So?" He kept his voice low. Admirably restrained.

"Just felt I had to point it out. One more for the future, Man of the Past."

She knew how to get to him. And she was still counting. "Perhaps it would be better if you waited outside, after all."

She furrowed her brow seriously and nodded. "You're doing so well on your own."

"Cora." His voice lowered into a distinct warning.

"Gotcha."

The general looked confused, as men always did around Cora Talmadge. "Captain Woodward, if you would escort Miss Talmadge to the Guild."

Woodward held out his arm, beaming. "It would be my honor."

"I'll bet." Adrian hadn't meant to speak aloud. Cora shook her head and mouthed the word "jealous." Adrian twitched.

She placed her hand on Darian Woodward's arm and he guided her toward the door. She stopped and looked back over her shoulder. She winked, gave him the "thumbs up" sign, and clicked her tongue. "Later, dude."

"I can understand that you don't want to talk about it. What you've been through is enough to destroy a lesser woman."

Cora examined a blue dress and decided it was all wrong for her coloring. Darian Woodward sat on a stool as she rummaged through Victorian dresses. He had to sign a form for her to borrow a dress. The fort was run like a strict library.

Cora picked through a collection of underpinnings. Apparently, hoop skirts were no longer in fashion, and had been replaced by a slight bustle. She held up a chemise made of soft cotton, but Captain Woodward blushed furiously, so she set it hurriedly aside.

"It's not that I don't want to talk about it." Telling this kind young man the truth would be satisfying, but it probably wouldn't help. "It might be hard to explain, though."

He nodded, sympathy riddling his innocent face. "I understand completely. But tell me, what of your family? Where are they?"

"Oh, well they're back East." Cora hesitated. For the first time since she'd landed in the past, she wondered how the people in her future would take her disappearance. Her parents wouldn't find out for a while because they were both vacationing on opposite sides of the world. Her landlady wouldn't notice until her rent was late.

"I'm a little worried about my friend, Jenny. She was there when we . . ." She stopped herself, but Darian nodded.

"When this dark fate befell you. Somehow, your friend escaped."

"Well . . ." Cora's face puckered at the deception. She wished she could explain, but honest explanations were likely to brand her a madwoman. She needed the soldiers' trust if she was to help Adrian. After his bizarre performance with the general, she felt sure he needed her more than ever. "My friend was kind of . . . ahead, when—"

"I understand." Darian sighed. "The red men attack without warning. Without mercy. Even in war, there was gallantry. Rebel soldiers would wait for a fair prisoner exchange before again taking up arms against us. Pickets exchanged coffee. But this place. There is no honor to be had. To think, a lady as sweet as yourself should be forced to endure . . . " He caught himself and swallowed hard.

Cora's eyes wandered to the side. Yes, he'd thoroughly misconstrued her situation. He probably thought Adrian nabbed her from a wagon train, then had his way with her. Repeatedly. "It's not so bad."

He looked up at her, eyes filled with emotion. A suspiciously familiar emotion. A wave of intense guilt washed through Cora. "You are the bravest woman I have ever met." Cora eyed him doubtfully. Soon, he'd be calling her "cool." Somehow, the past had altered the outward perception of her character. Darian gazed at her with intense admiration. "My dear Miss Talmadge, allow me to contact your family. I will take you back to their care."

"Um . . . I can't really go back."

Darian rose suddenly to his feet and seized Cora's hands. He closed his eyes tight, then looked at her. Cora saw his young heart in his eyes. He looked so sweet, so hopeful. So enthusiastic.

"Maybe you're right. Maybe neither one of us can go back. You may think me young, Miss Talmadge, but I have seen so much. Too much. If you can't go back, then let us go forward, together. To California, perhaps. Leave this place, and that . . . that black-eyed devil who robbed you of your life."

"An interesting proposal."

Both Cora and Darian jumped at Adrian's low, overly controlled voice. Darian placed himself in front of Cora. Cora's heart expanded with pity, but she couldn't restrain a smile. She tapped Darian's shoulder. "Please, Captain. I'm perfectly fine. Don't worry about me."

He hadn't been worrying, exactly. She felt fairly certain he was propositioning her, but she hoped to spare them both embarrassment by deliberately misunderstanding. From Adrian's dark glower, she guessed he wasn't fooled by her reaction.

Cora puffed a casual, quick breath. "So. How did it go? Did you straighten things out with General Davis?"

"He's a stuffed shirt with an attitude. I didn't get far." Adrian eased himself between Darian and Cora. "We're staying overnight. He and I will talk again in the morning. On the bright side, that bastard Tradman has left for Tucson."

Darian blanched. "Sir! You do not utter such words before a lady!"

Adrian rolled his eyes. The wrong response. He wasn't doing much to placate the enemy. "Lighten up, will you?"

Cora coughed to suppress laughter. "So Mr. Tradman is gone. Well, that's a relief, anyway. A night in the fort will be nice. Captain Woodward says they have real beds here." Cora stopped short at the flash of anger in Adrian's eyes. He turned slowly toward Darian, who faced him with a challenging expression.

"Oh, did he?"

Darian's well-formed chin elevated. He wasn't as powerfully built as Adrian, but he was a little taller. They made interesting—and picturesque—adversaries. "Miss Talmadge will be given a room in the ladies' quarters, where she will be comfortable and well-tended and *safe*."

" 'Miss Talmadge' will stay with me, where she belongs."

"I won't allow it. Not here, and not while I'm alive."

Adrian's eyes formed narrow, black slits. "A minor hurdle."

"Adrian!" Cora hopped between them. "You and I make them uncomfortable."

"Isn't that a shame? Interracial couples make a lot of people 'uncomfortable,' Cora. But I never thought you were one."

He turned and left the wardrobe storage, banging the door as he passed. He called over his shoulder as he stormed down the hall. "She stays with me."

Darian touched her shoulder. "Please forgive me. I never intended for you to bear the brunt of his wrath."

"He's cracking like an egg." Cora sighed and her heart filled with love. She gazed dreamily at Darian and sighed again. "You mentioned something about a bath?"

He had never been so angry in his life. Adrian sat on the edge of a narrow cot in a "guest room" and glared out the window. It looked more like a prison cell. The mattress was no more than an inch thick. No pillows. One ragged blanket of cheap wool. There was a pitcher of brown water on a rustic table and a metal cup. An old oil lamp hung on the wall, stained with dirty fingerprints.

Adrian tried to clear his mind, but all he saw was Cora at Darian Woodward's side. *Come with me to California.* And why didn't Cora set the miserable, baby-faced boy straight?

Adrian rose from the cot and paced from one blank wall to the other. Another man wanted his woman. A man with a boyish smile and just a hint of sorrow in the most infuriatingly blue eyes he'd ever seen. Women fell for that kind of whiner daily.

Not that Darian actually whined. He was far too subtle for that. He hinted at a dark, tragic past. The Civil War had been grim, sure. But that didn't mean Capt. Darian Woodward was free to make off with Adrian's girlfriend. Now, or ever.

If he hadn't made that clear in the "Ladies' Guild," he would do so now.

Adrian aimed for the door and yanked it open. The final rays of golden sunset glinted across the newly constructed fort, then disappeared in the hills behind.

Music that sounded like an Irish fiddle came from the center court. It didn't have the mystical, ancient beauty of the native flutes and drums, but it moved with a pulse. It throbbed with an erotic pulse which started low and uneven, then built with gradual intensity. Someone joined in with drums. Adrian heard laughter, and a soldier danced around the square with an older woman.

Adrian stood motionless, watching. People danced to the music of what was presumably their ancestors. Women tended a large pot of stew, and men cleaned their muskets, laughing and talking.

He came from the future to see the past first-hand. He stood in its midst, but he wasn't a part of it, no matter where he was born. Two cultures clashed, and he couldn't stop them, or alter the outcome. They clashed because one was bigger and stronger, and still growing. Because one was bound to its sacred soil, and the other restless, had journeyed afar.

Like the sea rolling over the shore.

He didn't know where he belonged. The music grew, and it moved his heart despite his disgust at the invading culture. Another couple joined the dance. The woman held her hand palm-outward, and the man circled her, then placed his palm against hers. They circled around in time to the music, smiling. They danced without native passion, without the power of warrior and god. Yet they seemed unstoppable, driven.

The Europeans were just another tribe, after all. A tribe of conquerors, dancing to their own rhythm. And that rhythm was just as old and just as deeply ingrained as the blood of his own people.

Darian Woodward emerged from a building across the square. Adrian noticed that the windows of that building had white lace curtains. Soft lamplight glowed from inside. Even flower pots decorated the windowsills. Darian held open the door, and Cora appeared. The music slowed as the fiddlers turned to watch her. The drummer lost his timing as he gaped.

Adrian's arms hung limp at his side. His mouth opened, and stayed open. She wore a gown of dark red trimmed with black velvet ribbons. Her neckline was low and scooped, showing the soft, warm skin above her breasts. Something unseen had squeezed up her small breasts, making them round and tempting and full.

Adrian swallowed hard. The bodice of her dress fit snugly to her waist, then flared in soft pleats, gathered at the side where she held it in her small, gloved hand. She looked around, her head high. She was looking for him. The bulk of her hair had been pinned behind her head, and fell in waving ringlets down her neck, leaving loose tendrils to frame her face.

She seemed natural, at home. Captain Woodward held out his arm and she took it easily, as if born to the graciousness of the Victorian age. She spotted Adrian across the square and waved happily, having no idea what she had done to him.

Captain Woodward appeared less enthusiastic, but he led her around the cooks, then through the fiddlers as they resumed their lively music. Cora released Darian's arm and spun around, flaring her dress as she twirled. A portion of her long hair came loose and curled down her cheek. She blew it away and it fell back exactly as it had been.

Adrian stared. His mouth was still open, but he couldn't close it. She twirled to his side in time with the music. "What do you think? Isn't it pretty? I thought the green floral dress was more my style, but Captain Woodward suggested this one."

Adrian's lips twitched into a frown, which he felt sure the captain noticed and appreciated. "The neckline is a little low, isn't it?"

Her face fell, and Adrian cursed himself inwardly. He wanted to apologize. To tell her she was more beautiful than a queen, more tempting than Delilah. She was drifting away from him even as the erotic stranger he'd found in his arms grew stronger. Her beauty and grace shone until he hurt inside.

"Weren't you the one who wanted me in something short and leather?"

"Yes, but we were alone then." His throat felt tight. His heart moved in erratic pulses.

"We were in the middle of your father's village." Cora's head tilted to one side. She looked so disappointed. She felt pretty, and he'd criticized her. Because he was jealous that another man had picked her dress. Because she stole his breath and he couldn't tell her so. Because she looked like she belonged here, and he was an alien.

Darian seized the opportunity to look good in contrast to Adrian's floundering. "General Davis's predecessor, General Peterson, ordered this dress made for his wife in San Francisco. Unfortunately, he vastly underestimated his bride's appetite, and she soon grew out of it. But it suits you perfectly."

Darian's blue eyes twinkled mischievously. His full lips curved in a teasing smile. The man had elevated boyish charm to an art form. Cora's sad expression altered in response. "I'm so glad you let me borrow it."

"It is yours, Miss Talmadge. When General Peterson transferred to his new post in Tucson, his wife insisted this dress remain behind." Darian lowered his voice conspiratorially. "I suspect the sight of it reminded her husband to keep her from her favorite porridge."

Cora giggled, then turned her attention to the dancers. "That looks fun."

Darian positioned himself closer beside Cora. Casually. "Do you dance, Miss Talmadge?"

Cora sighed. "I was never a very good dancer, I'm afraid."

Adrian looked between them as if watching a movie. He knew what would happen, but he stood spellbound in horror as it unfolded before his eyes. He wanted to intervene, but Darian Woodward was too quick. "The steps are simple. Allow me to show you?"

Adrian's fingers clenched as if squeezing the captain's neck through his high, starched collar. Cora glanced at Adrian uncertainly. All his objections flooded to the surface at once, but Darian was ready for that, too.

"Unless you forbid a simple dance?" He sounded guileless. He effectively placed Adrian in the position of jealous boyfriend. Forbidding Cora would drive her away, and the baby-faced captain knew it.

"No."

Both Darian and Cora hesitated. Cora chewed her lip. " 'No,' meaning you won't forbid me, or 'no,' meaning I can't dance?"

"Of course, you can dance, Cora. If that is what you wish."

The music picked up tempo as if controlled psychically by Darian's conniving brain. He bowed, and Cora placed her hand on his arm. Adrian watched in sick fury as the blond demon led her toward the fiddlers, as they mingled with the other dancers.

Rolling Irish music took control of the dancers, and of Cora. She learned the steps as if she'd done them all her life. She held her palm outward, and Darian placed his hand against hers. They circled each other and twirled, then reversed. Cora was laughing. Darian was laughing, too.

Adrian endured an image of them together—Darian leading Cora to a room decorated with curtains and crystal lamps, peeling away her red dress, her head tipped back as the fiendish boy made love to her.

Apache fire burned in his veins. All his life in the future was forgotten. He had this moment, and no other. No man touched his woman. Adrian stormed across the square, seized Cora's waist in both hands and lifted her off her feet. A woman screamed. Captain Woodward cursed and drew a saber.

Adrian's eyes never left Cora's small, shocked face. The fiddlers didn't notice his interruption. They played on, oblivious to everything but their Irish strains. The drumbeats intensified, but maybe that was his own heart pounding.

He lowered Cora to her toes, then guided her with the music. It mirrored his own passion, a primal fury and a primal lust. She stared up at him in pure, feminine wonder. She knew he had claimed her, and she didn't resist.

"You are mine, Cora Talmadge. I will never let you go."

She placed her hands on his arms, and he gripped her waist, moving her sensually, closer and closer. Victorians didn't dance this way, but Adrian didn't care. He moved her hips in a sexual rhythm, barely touching, but leaving no doubt as to what he intended.

The fiddlers must have understood. They played with gusto, as if the passion of an Apache chief's son equaled

203

more closely their own violent ancestors than the prim Victorians surrounding them. Adrian felt passionately male this night, more aware of his masculinity than he'd ever been in his life.

Cora was female, sweet and yielding and ripe with need. He would drive the blond captain's gentle touch from her memory, fill her with only himself, until she saw her life through a passionate haze.

Adrian stopped dancing and released her. He stood back, his gaze still locked with hers. He smiled slightly and held out his hand. No one would doubt her acquiescence this night. Cora raised her arm slowly and placed her hand in his.

"That's enough of that!" Captain Woodward's voice came like a high chirp, but Adrian held Cora's stunned, sensual gaze. Woodward seized Cora's arm and drew her away. Her lips remained parted, her cheeks flushed with desire. "Miss Woodward, allow me to escort you to our guest facilities."

Her eyes widened. Adrian smiled at her immediately obvious sexual frustration. "The night is young yet." He spoke in a low voice, for Cora's ears only. "While you lie asleep in your 'guest' bed, know that I will think of you. I will dream that you come to me. . . . "

Woodward's face flushed hot and pink with both anger and embarrassment, but Cora caught her soft lower lip between her teeth, then breathed a quavering, womanly breath. Pure desire. Her desire was mirrored in his own pulse, in the passion of his soul. *I will have you tonight.*

As if guessing Adrian's intention, Woodward edged Cora farther away. "*You* will be given quarters beyond the barracks." Darian glared, as if thinking that short distance not nearly far enough. "You will not be placed under guard, but should you attempt any"—he glanced at Cora—"wrongdoing, know that I and my men shall not hesitate to do our duty."

Adrian eyed Darian with growing dislike. "By shooting me? That seems to be your M.O."

Darian appeared confused. Adrian didn't explain.

Cora looked between them. Her gaze lingered on Adrian. "I will go to my room now. And I am sure I will fall asleep immediately because I am so tired."

Adrian fought a smile. Only a fool would doubt her intentions this night. "I find that I am also . . . exhausted. In fact, exhaustion burns within me, pounding, out of control like fire . . . " He lowered his voice and she caught her breath. Darian glared suspiciously, then took Cora's hand and placed it on his arm.

"You will be summoned before the general early tomorrow morning."

"Early?" Adrian repressed a groan. "Not too early, Woodward."

Cora smiled, then allowed Darian to lead her away. Adrian watched her go. She glanced back over her shoulder several times, and even as she passed through the door to the guest quarters, he saw the desire in her eyes.

Drums and fiddles throbbed in Cora's head as she crept across the courtyard. No one noticed her as she eased behind the general's quarters, then aimed for the barracks. Her heart pounded. She had learned stealth here in the past—she felt like an Indian maiden, strong and swift and sure of her destination.

She imagined her lover's arms around her, the burning need flashing in his beautiful eyes. She hadn't been able to wait a half hour before coming to him. Desire turned liquid inside her, a fiery reaction to his power. To him.

She made her way to a small log building behind the barracks, checked for onlookers, saw no one, then touched the door handle. It opened before she turned it. Adrian stood before her, silent. Her knees felt weak.

He closed the behind them, and lowered the bar to lock it securely while Cora stood trembling. Adrian turned in the darkening room and smiled. She knew he didn't mean to reassure her with gentleness, but to promise her the rapture of passion. His passion. A passion she shared, because he was part of her. Because when he walked across that square, all her soul rose to greet him.

He ran his hand along the line of her neckline and his smile widened. "Beautiful woman."

Cora glanced at her bodice. "Not too low?"

"Not too low."

She seized a quick breath. "What are . . . ? I'm not sure—"

"Be sure, Cora. I'm going to give you everything you ever wanted. Tonight."

Those brown eyes burned darker and he caught her waist in his hands. He bent to her and kissed her, tasting her lips and the inner cavern of her mouth. Cora leaned against him. His dark hair fell forward and touched her face. His sexual energy burned with a power she'd never imagined, and it set fire to her own.

He kissed her face and her neck. He bent her back and kissed the bare flesh between her neck and her shoulder. He found the tiny buttons at the back of her bodice and unfastened them one by one. He lowered the bodice, exposing the borrowed corset and her high breasts.

He placed his hands on her shoulders and caressed her arms. "Cora, you steal my breath."

She reached to touch his face. "As you steal mine."

He caught her hand and drew her palm to his lips. His kiss

sent wild shivers up her arm and through her body. He kissed her wrist and she felt the tip of his tongue teasing her flesh. Her nerves tightened in wanton anticipation.

He removed her heavy skirt and it slid to the floor. Somehow, he guessed the workings of her bustle and petticoats, and they came off, too. She stood wearing her stockings and snug corset over a gauze-light chemise, with soft leather slippers on her feet.

"What happened to your sneakers?"

Cora smiled. "They're resting."

"You are a temptation, Cora Talmadge. Do you know how you fill my dreams? Do you know how I've missed you?"

Cora felt powerful. As powerful as he was. "Show me."

Adrian caught her bear pendant in his hand and lifted it from her breast. "Always, I am with you. No matter how far you go from me, no matter where you are. I am with you."

She nodded, and her eyes filled with tears. "Adrian, I love you so."

He lowered the necklace to her breast, and his knuckles grazed her flesh. He trailed his finger down her new cleavage and bent to press his mouth against her bare skin. Cora tipped her head back, delirious with pleasure.

He moved behind her and slid her hair over her shoulder, then kissed the back of her neck. He reached around and cupped her taut breasts in his hand. She felt his thumbs through the fabric of the corset, teasing and firm. "Do you see how you want me, Cora?"

His voice came low and mesmerizing. Cora's heart beat so fast that she felt weak. She tried to nod, but he kissed her neck, and her strength failed.

He circled her concealed nipples simultaneously until

207

they formed hard peaks beneath the corset. "Do you see how your body strains toward mine?"

"Oh." Her voice came as a small squeak, and he chuckled. She leaned back against him as he unhooked the corset and lowered it to her feet. Her stockings crumpled, leaving her hobbled. Her heart banged beneath her breast as he brushed his lips along her neck. She felt his breath, swift and strong as he again cupped her breasts in his beautiful hands. Only the thin, white chemise covered her skin, but he didn't tear it away. He circled her breast with his palm, using the soft fabric to tease her sensitized flesh.

"How much can you take before you have to have me inside you, angel?" As he spoke, he caught her nipples between his fingers, massaging the tips until she rose up on her toes. Molten fire coiled inside her, directed by his touch. The fever soared between them, he nipped at her ear and she turned her face to his. He tasted the corner of her lips and she twisted in his arms to kiss him. He pulled off the light chemise and tossed it aside.

Cora tugged open his shirt and kissed his chest. "Adrian, you do such things to me. Such perfect things." She pushed his shirt off his broad shoulders, and flung it aside. She stood back, her breath coming in short gasps.

"Do you want to look at me, angel? Have you thought of me in the night, and wished you'd spent more time this way?"

"How did you know?"

He smiled. "Look at me now."

Adrian wasn't shy, and he wasn't modest. He had a beautiful, strong body, and he knew it. He stood back, smiling. "Take your time, Cora."

She had seen him before, and admired him. Now, she

scrutinized his body boldly, without shyness. She devoured every muscle, every inch of his smooth, dark skin, knowing they would make love, that every portion of his body would please her.

She wet her lips, imagining his taste. She studied the defined, strong muscle of his shoulder and his arms. Her gaze moved purposefully over the wide expanse of his chest. His black hair hung against his skin, a raw, masculine image. His jeans had faded and loosened with wear. She caught him by the waistband and pulled him closer.

"These hinder my viewing."

He looked surprised at her boldness, but he unfastened the snap. His hands shook. Cora watched in pure amazement. His strong, lean hands really shook. Despite his supreme self-confidence and his perfect body, he trembled.

Cora looked into his warm, brown eyes, and her heart filled with overpowering love. The power of the man brought her to her knees, but his vulnerability claimed her soul. She placed her hands gently over his. "Let me."

Her hands weren't shaking. Her fingers tingled, but they were sure as she fiddled with his zipper. He kicked off his hiking boots, pulled off his pants and underwear in one swoop, and stood naked before her.

"This," Cora paused to catch her breath, "is better."

His erection stood poised from his body, full and dark with desire. Cora reached for him eagerly, but he caught her hand and kissed her fingers. "You've driven me as far as I can go, woman. Now it's your turn."

She had no idea what he meant, but he didn't give her time to wonder. He picked her up and set her to a bare table, positioning her close to the edge. He shoved aside a metal cup and it clattered to the floor. He knelt in front of her and

209

ran his hands up and down her bare legs. Cora gripped the table to steady herself.

"Do you know how sweet you are, Cora? How often I dream of you, of driving you crazy this way?"

Cora chomped her lip. He wanted her crazy? If she'd only known nine years ago!

He kissed the insides of her knees. "You are so delicate, and so soft."

"Thank you." She didn't feel delicate, but if Adrian thought so, and it affected him this way, so much the better.

He trailed the tips of his fingers up along her inner thighs, just grazing her feminine curls. Her flesh tingled, her muscles tensed. He took her legs and placed them over his shoulders, and Cora was lost. She quivered in anticipation, biting her lip to silence herself as his kiss moved inward, closer to her woman's core.

"You're elegant, even here."

Am I? She felt his deliberate breath, his slow teasing, and her questions fled. She closed her eyes when he parted her soft folds and whispered her name. Her toes curled tight when he found the small bud at the very heart of her desire. He tasted her and teased her, and made small circles with the tip of his tongue.

He tormented her gently, then with increasing demand until her legs wrapped tight around his shoulders. He slowed to almost stopping, holding her on the brink of sweet release. He began again and teased her until she writhed, oblivious to everything but him.

Her body quivered uncontrollably as pleasure spiraled tighter and tighter. Just as she hovered close to the edge of control, he drew away and stood up. He looked like a god, young and strong and potent beyond any time. His eyes glowed like fire. He pulled a thin mattress off the narrow bed and tossed it to the floor.

He lifted her against him, then lowered her to the mattress. "No other man, Cora. No other time. You are mine."

He sounded like a warrior. Cora lay on her back watching him, enchanted as he positioned his thick staff against her. He looked like a warrior, too. His black hair fell long and loose over his dark skin, every muscle in his body drew as tight as a bow.

She thought she wanted a gentle, tender lover, but when he knelt between her legs, she knew she wanted the warrior. Adrian had never worn more than the guise of civilization and a modern demeanor. She had been wrong about him. He was a man of the past, just as he claimed. He was powerful and overwhelming. A warrior.

His dark gaze met hers in both challenge and welcome. *Deny me. Resist me, but the battle is lost. You are mine.* He held her gaze as he entered her. She saw the harsh stab of pleasure written on his face as she closed snug around him. He moved to her pleasure, taking all he wanted, giving all he had. He cupped her bottom in his hands and directed her motion, deepening his thrust with every entrance, until her every breath was a moan, every moan a plea for satisfaction.

"You are mine, Cora Talmadge. Whatever I want, you will do. Whatever you need, I will give." Even his accent shifted, his tone grew lower, more resonant and deep. He spoke with the motion of his body inside hers. Cora twisted around him, close to her pinnacle, ready.

He stopped and withdrew, and she stifled a scream. He laughed, then turned her onto her stomach. He spread her thighs and entered her again, deeper this time, touching her womb with powerful thrusts. Cora gripped the mattress and

211

arched beneath him. Her head tipped back, and he bent forward to kiss her shoulder. She felt his teeth as he grazed her skin, she felt his lips as he kissed her neck.

He moved faster and deeper, groaning as his own control wavered. He touched her deeper than anything had ever touched her. He brought them to a primitive level shared by lovers from the dawn of humanity. He took her from behind, because it was the most primal position, and brought them both to elemental passion.

She was his, filled with him. She felt him, hard and engorged inside her, driving her through shuddering spasms of rapture. The tension inside her coiled to impossible tightness, then burst in a shattering cataclysm of energy. She sobbed his name, wracked with waves of pleasure. Deep inside her, his own release came. She felt every convulsion, every sweet shudder that rippled through him.

He stilled, then withdrew from her body. Cora lay flat on her stomach, stunned beyond motion or words. Adrian rolled her over, and wrapped a blanket around them. He held her against him, close. His chest heaved with short, uneven breaths. Cora looked up into his eyes and saw tears.

"You're crying." Cora touched his face, amazed. "Why?"

He kissed her forehead. "Because you're truly mine."

Chapter Eight

"Break it down! Now!"

Something splintered and crashed. Adrian opened one eye and looked up. Ten soldiers, at least, charged into his room and pointed out-moded muskets at his head. Adrian closed his eye and groaned. "I hate mornings. Is this a Monday, by chance?"

Cora lay tucked in beside him, in his favorite "spoons" position. His arm was draped over her waist, and his knee over her thigh. She took one look at the soldiers and disappeared beneath the blanket. "Oh, God! We're going to die!"

Adrian smacked his lips, rolled his eyes, and sat up. He counted five soldiers on one side, six on the other. Two were kneeling for better aim.

Darian Woodward stood in the doorway aiming a shiny revolver in one hand, a polished saber in the other. Adrian's lip curled in a morning snarl. "Of course. The heroic captain. Get a grip!"

A muffled laugh came from beneath the blanket. "*Get a grip.*" He felt sure she had added, "Man of the Past," and possibly, "there's another one."

Darian Woodward's bright gaze moved across the room as if he witnessed a bloody crime scene. He saw Adrian's discarded clothing tangled with Cora's red dress. *Good.* Maybe he'd get past his boyish infatuation and face facts. Cora belonged to Adrian, body and soul.

"What . . . what have you done to this poor girl?"

The soldiers looked askance at the captain's innocence. One man covered his mouth to repress laughter. Darian looked so indignant and so confused that even Adrian smiled. "Look, the bed was too small, so we're on the floor. What's the deal? And if you're so consumed with worry, why'd you wait all night before bursting in here like blood-crazed gangbusters?"

"The morning, sir, is half past. When I discovered that Miss Talmadge was missing from her room, I feared that much ill could have befallen the lady. Which, clearly, is the case."

Cora drew a pained breath and groaned beneath the cover. Very slowly, she peeked out. "I'm fine, thank you."

Several soldiers laughed. Adrian restrained himself, but his eyes watered with amusement. "If you'd get lost for a while, we'll dress and be out in a minute."

Something about his phrasing seemed to confuse the Victorian captain, but the soldiers lowered their weapons and retreated. Darian hesitated by the door, watching Cora's concealed body doubtfully. "If any harm has befallen her, you will pay with your life. Should I see one bruise on her dear face . . . "

214

Anger coiled in Adrian's stomach. "Get out."

Darian cast a final glare from his cold blue eyes, then followed his soldiers. "General Davis is waiting for you."

Cora waited until the door closed, then emerged from beneath the blanket. Her cheeks burned pink. "This is the most embarrassing moment of my life. More embarrassing then ending up in a tree, or in a river, or anything. It had to happen with you."

"He's such a geek."

"He's cute. Just innocent." Cora winced and chewed her lip in agitation. "I wasn't very considerate of his feelings. Of course, you had to turn into Seduction Man and distract me."

"He put a move on my woman. I saw no alternative."

Cora sat up beside him, then kissed his cheek. "You have become such a contrast, Adrian de Vargas. 'Put a move on,' is so . . . twentieth century. Yet you turn around and act like a marauding hun. I wonder which is the real you?" She kissed his cheek again and smoothed his hair. "Maybe both."

Adrian seized her red dress and pulled the chemise over her head. Cora eyed the corset, then set it carefully on the bare bed. "I don't like that much."

"If women of this time period would exercise, they wouldn't need these contraptions."

Cora's eyes wandered guiltily at his mention of exercise. "Well . . . I'm not exactly hard-bodied."

"What are you talking about? You're fit."

"I don't exercise, Adrian."

"You look good. I think you're stronger than you were in college."

Cora looked down at herself. "Am I? It must be all the walking. You walk a lot in New York, you know."

Cora assembled the red dress and Adrian helped her with the buttons. "Who did this the first time?"

215

She peered over her shoulder. "Well, Captain Woodward helped with my corset and stockings, but an officer's wife helped with the dress. Darian was too exhausted from sex to do that part."

Adrian's face heated in both embarrassment and from the visual image she presented. "Stay away from him."

Cora turned around and tapped his chest. "You are getting so bossy."

"Only about certain things."

Cora watched as Adrian dressed. "I hope I didn't hurt his feelings."

Adrian sat on a stool and laced his hiking boots. He needed a new pair. These were worn. He finished the tie, then realized this brand of hiking boots wouldn't be invented for over a hundred years. *If we stay here in the past, we won't live to see the Nineties. We may see World War II. Perfect. Just perfect.*

"What's the matter? You look worried."

"No. . . . just thinking. Since you're mine again . . . "

Someone knocked. Adrian didn't have to ask who. "We're coming, Captain."

The door opened, and Darian poked his head in the door. Seeing them dressed, he entered, uninvited. He looked shy and a little confused as he quickly assessed Cora's well-being. She seemed uncomfortable, but she smiled sweetly. Too sweetly. The captain's face softened into a wistful expression of love. *Infatuation.* Nothing more.

Adrian glared. "No bruises."

"It was very kind of you to be so . . . concerned for my welfare."

Adrian interrupted with a huff, but she shot him a warning glance, then turned her attention back to Darian.

"Your welfare, Miss Talmadge, is my only concern."

"Thank you."

Darian's soft expression turned hard as Adrian carefully wrapped his red bandanna around his head. "The general is expecting you."

"Good. It better not take too long. I've had about as much of this place as I can take."

"I'm sure you have. Miss Talmadge, however, may be more accustomed to genteel living than you can imagine."

"Miss Talmadge is coming with me."

Darian stood back as Adrian led Cora through the door. Those cold blue eyes narrowed in a surprisingly powerful challenge. "That remains to be seen."

"Tell your father we will leave his village unaccosted, as long as he sees fit to leave our coaches and riders unhindered in passing."

General Davis sat at his desk, going over papers Adrian felt sure meant nothing. "My father's village remains unaccosted, because none of you know where it is. My people move their site regularly, and thus, face little danger from your invasion."

The general's gaze whisked to Adrian, then back to his papers. "I sense you require more in the way of reassurance."

"Many of our hunters have been slain for no purpose. They hunt deer and elk, yet are shot down by your men. We are not targets. We are men."

A faint sneer gave away the general's true feelings on the matter. "As long as they avoid our property, and aren't involved in a war party, your 'hunters' may continue their vocation."

"Then it seems we have a truce. I warn you, it is temporary. Too often, the white man offers his hand in peace, then betrays his own word. That is the lesson of history, and why I will not trust you now. Actions speak loudest. It is your actions I will watch."

"You're an arrogant son of—"

Captain Woodward gasped and gestured at Cora, his face pale at the impending vulgarity. General Davis's lips curled beneath his lavish whiskers, but he controlled his outburst. "Tell your father we'll be watching him, too. You people are spread out all over this place, but threaten us, and we'll hunt you down, one by one. Where the white man settles, he stays. We are strong people."

Adrian nodded. "The red man is the same." He aimed for the door, fury in his gait. "Didn't you know?"

Adrian took Cora's arm. He couldn't wait to leave, to return to the sanity of his father's village.

"Not so fast, boy."

He turned slowly. The general rose from his chair and came around the desk. "The woman stays with us."

Adrian started to laugh, then realized the man was serious. "Cora is mine."

Darian positioned himself beside Cora. "Miss Talmadge belongs with her own people, where she will be treated with the honor and dignity she deserves."

They were serious. He wouldn't get Cora out of the fort with this blue-eyed monster guarding her. They believed Apaches were savages, that family meant nothing. That wives were to be used and discarded. He could play on their assumptions, and use his power to win.

Adrian shrugged. "Bring me two extra horses, and I'll leave her. That's a fair trade."

"*What?*" Cora's mouth dropped so wide that he saw all

her white teeth. "You're *leaving* me? Here?" Her eyes narrowed in suspicion. "Is this some kind of revenge for Kathmandu, Adrian?"

"I don't think the good captain has any intention of letting you go, Cora. Why risk my neck fighting the inevitable?"

"You are cracking in a very bizarre direction."

Darian laid his hand gently on Cora's shoulder. "You'll be safe with us, Miss Talmadge."

You'd like to think so. Adrian took her other arm. "If you gentlemen will excuse us, I'd like to say a final farewell to my woman."

Darian fingered his revolver. "Don't take her from this room."

Adrian edged Cora aside, turned his back to the men, and bent to whisper in her ear. She appeared highly suspicious, but not quite ready to believe he would abandon her. "They won't let us out of here together. I'll leave, hide the horses, and come back for you tonight. Be near the main gate at midnight."

"How will you get in? What if they shoot?" Her whispered response held a tremor of fear, but she controlled herself admirably.

Adrian looked into her wide, lovely eyes. "They can't shoot what they can't see."

Cora bowed her head miserably. "Just when I think you can't get any crazier."

Adrian stood back, slapped her shoulder in a friendly fashion, and winked. "See ya, babe. It's been real."

"The Apache version of English is hard to understand." Darian sat beside Cora as the sun set again over the fort. Adrian had ridden out with two extra horses, which Cora felt sure was stealing since he didn't really mean to trade her. It occurred to her that when Mr. Cramer offered to trade a horse and an extra chicken for her, Adrian had been appalled. It didn't take him long to stoop just as low. The man had changed.

"Adrian's version of Apache is probably pretty weird, too."

Darian looked confused. "He has altered your speaking as well."

"He's altered a lot more than that." Seeing Darian's shock, Cora cringed. "I mean, he's gotten me into all sorts of trouble." This sounded even worse, but she couldn't think of a way to correct it.

"I have seen red men before, of course. I served in the Nineteenth New York as a lieutenant. My division had two Onondaga brothers, Joseph and David Pratt. They were farmers, and well-respected. The Twentieth had a black soldier who won great honor. Even here, we have Apache and Navajo scouts. I have considered them inscrutable, but none has seemed so dangerous as that man who captured you."

Cora noticed that Darian never said Adrian's name. He always called him "that man," with an undertone of intense distaste. It didn't make sense, because Adrian was cleaner and more educated than anyone Darian could have encountered.

Maybe Darian was reacting on another level to Adrian, a man totally at ease in his body, with his sexuality, and with women—while Darian adhered strictly to Victorian sensibilities. Cora wondered what he would be like unleashed. What kind of woman would release the warrior in Darian Woodward?

Not herself. She and Darian were too much alike—sensitive, and a little bewildered by the world around them. "If I'd had a brother, I think he would have been like you."

Darian smiled. "As it happens, you remind me of my younger sister."

"Where is she now?"

"She died in childbirth while I was at war."

"I'm sorry." Cora studied his youthful face. His innate sorrow intensified. "Why haven't you married?"

Darian looked at his clasped hands. "I had a sweetheart in Le Roy."

Only Darian Woodward could use the word "sweetheart," and not seem foolish. Cora smiled fondly. "What happened?"

"I returned from war thinking to propose marriage. But when I saw her, she hadn't changed. I had changed. She wanted to dance and to take her place in society. I tried, Miss Talmadge, but it was like a waking dream. I tried until every day was an effort. I was restless. The slow leisure of my days gave me time to remember. A regiment was formed to go West. I joined, and asked her to accompany me. She refused."

"How mean!"

Darian shook his head. "In truth, I was relieved. I felt nothing for her but a memory of my boyhood. She had seen nothing of the war but fairy tale versions written in *Harper's Weekly*. She considered me heroic. But a hero is a man who has nothing left to lose, who has seen so much death that his own means nothing."

Cora clasped his hand tight. "Your life has value, Captain. You'll find someone, I know."

Darian placed his hand over hers. "I already have."

He meant her. Cora cringed. "I'm not sure I'm exactly right for you."

"Miss Talmadge, whatever he did to you is past. You are safe now."

* * *

Cora left Darian after supper and went to her new bedroom. It was decorated thoughtfully, with lace and some kind of desert flowers. She took off her borrowed gown and dressed in Toklanni's old clothes. After the snug bodice and cumbersome skirt, the Apache clothing seemed very comfortable. She replaced her satin slippers with her plaid sneakers, and stared at the Grandfather clock until midnight.

The fiddlers played again, and from her window, she saw Darian waiting. Her heart twinged with guilt knowing he hoped she would come down. She knew he believed he'd found a kindred spirit in her, a woman who had seen tragedy and hardship, yet wasn't shattered. But Darian had known real pain. She had known love.

He bowed his head, then left the courtyard, returning to the officer's quarters. Cora issued a silent prayer that he find a woman worthy of his gentle heart.

At eleven forty-five, she crept from her room and slipped out the door into the square. The fiddlers were gone and the fires burned low. She tiptoed along the buildings near the gate and waited.

Guards took position in tower posts, and kept keen vision on the landscape. Cora's heart beat in erratic pulses. If they saw Adrian creeping around, they wouldn't hesitate. They'd shoot. She fought panic. He had power. He wouldn't be caught.

"Please, please be safe."

"Did you ever doubt?"

Cora opened her mouth to scream, but he clamped his hand over her mouth. "Quiet!" She leaned back against him, too weak to stand. "Sssh."

She nodded, and he released her. She turned around and

he pulled her between two buildings. His face looked darker than usual. "What happened to your white shirt?"

"This is it."

"It looks black."

"I soaked it in mud. Walking unseen takes a little fore-thought, woman. Now be quiet, and follow me."

"Are you sure we can get out of here unseen?"

"No." He caught himself. "Yes. Come on."

Adrian took her hand and led her behind the building.

"Adrian, you have power to 'walk unseen?' What about me?"

He hesitated and a small scream threatened in her throat. "Do what I do, and you'll be all right."

He started off, but she waited a moment. Power. Cora took her necklace from beneath her blouse and fingered the bear fetish. *Where you go, I go also.*

She took a deep breath, then followed.

"What did you need with four horses?" Cora examined the product of Adrian's ingenuity. A big-boned, healthy gray and a smaller chestnut stood munching on shrubs while Adrian untied his black-and-white paint. With little effort, he'd stolen Spot, too.

"My people will make good use of extra horses."

"You're stealing."

Adrian grinned. "It was a fair trade. If I'd been in the mood, I could have haggled up to at least six horses, and a few chickens, too. Our noble captain would have sold his mother to free you from my dark embrace."

Cora frowned reproachfully, then tightened the girth of Tradman's bay and patted his neck. "I'm glad Mr. Tradman didn't see my horse."

"His horse. I'm not the only one willing to take advantage of the moment."

They mounted at the same time. Adrian reached to take her hand, and kissed her fingers. "Together again."

"I feel a little bad about leaving Captain Woodward that way. Maybe I should have explained."

Adrian released her hand and groaned. "I don't think he wanted to hear that you'd rather be at my side than in his protective custody."

"No, probably not. He didn't like you much."

"The feeling was mutual."

"If you gave each other half a chance, you could be friends. That's probably true for your clashing cultures, too. But for some reason, this seems more personal."

"No kidding. He's after my girlfriend. Why wouldn't I love the guy?"

"He's not really 'after me,' Adrian. He just thinks we have something in common."

"Ha! Like what?"

"Well, he's been through a lot, and he thinks I have, too."

"Right. Me."

Cora met Adrian's annoyed gaze. "He thinks you've taken advantage of me, and made love to me until I can barely walk, leaving me gasping and weak, craving base pleasures while you force me to do unspeakable things to your body."

"Quiet, woman. You're getting me hard."

Cora urged Spot forward, leading the chestnut behind her. "Come along, Adrian. We have a long ride before we can . . . relax."

Adrian's perception held true as they made their way from the fort, but he stopped as if listening when they reached the eastern foothills of McDowell Mountains. "We're being followed."

Cora cranked her head around, expecting a blue-clad cavalry to appear in the hills above them. "What do we do?"

"It's just one." Adrian looked more annoyed than concerned. "Ride on, and we'll start up into the hills."

"But won't whoever's following us know where we're headed?"

"He might."

His expression triggered a torrent of suspicion. "You're scheming. I thought keeping your father's village secret was really important."

"Just ride, Cora."

They entered the McDowell Mountains and made their way through the giant boulders before the first light of dawn. "Isn't this where we stopped when you showed me where Phoenix was?"

"More or less. Farther east."

"Have we lost the man who was following us?"

Adrian shrugged noncommittally. "Don't worry about him. We need to make camp."

"I think we could go a little farther. I'm not tired, and it's not light yet."

"We're stopping." Adrian dismounted and tied the horses. Cora sighed, and tied hers beside his.

"Bossy."

"I know what I'm doing, woman." He arranged a blanket for a bed, but he didn't seem as attentive as Cora expected or hoped. "I'm going to have a look around. Maybe shoot a hare for dinner."

"I thought you opposed hunting for sport!"

"Not sport. Dinner."

"I guess that makes sense. Wait a minute! The soldiers took your rifle!" Cora watched doubtfully as Adrian brandished his father's jagged knife. "You're going to *stab* it?"

He looked impatient. "Native Americans know hunting, Cora. You just relax here, alone." He paused and waved his arm in her general direction. "When I get back, I'll . . . have my way with you, then we'll eat."

"Have your way with me?"

Adrian gazed thoughtfully at the morning star. "I think I'll try something different this time. Something only Apache do to their women."

Cora's face twisted to one side. "Nothing weird?"

He glanced toward the bushes and a faint smile played on his lips. Yes, he looked devious. "Nothing weird." He paused. "Have you ever been hung by your feet, naked?"

Adrian left her standing speechless and climbed over the fallen boulders. She watched him as he disappeared in the darkness, then seated herself on a rock. "By my feet?"

"By my soul, Miss Talmadge, it will not happen!"

"Oh, no!"

Darian Woodward scrambled out of the bushes, his blue eyes glowing with courage and total indignation. "Come, quickly. I'll get you out of here."

"Captain!"

Adrian appeared out of the bushes, caught Darian by the neck in what closely resembled a martial arts move, and pinned him back. "You're a persistent little fellow, aren't you?"

Cora waited to see if Darian had any karate training. Apparently not, because Adrian held him fast. "You sneaky red devil!"

"I need a rope, Cora."

"Why?"

"To bind his hands."

"Adrian—"

He spied her belt and nodded. "That will do."

"I don't think—"

"Now!"

Cora pulled off her belt and passed it to him. "There's no need to be mean."

Darian didn't seem afraid, nor willing to ease his situation by pleading. "His kind knows nothing else."

Adrian tied Darian's hands, found the captain's revolver and tossed it away. He looked around, then pulled off his red bandanna.

"What on earth are you doing?"

Adrian stuffed the bandanna in Darian's mouth and tied it tight around his head. He stood back, pleased with himself while Cora looked on in horror. "Shall we go?"

"You're leaving him here?"

"Of course not. The crazy bastard would just follow us. He's coming along."

Darian's eyes widened, but his expression turned resigned. He looked like a man facing death, and accepting it.

Adrian saddled his horse and Cora's, and rolled up his blanket. "What are you doing? I thought we were stopping."

"A ruse, Cora. Which worked predictably well. Now we return with a prisoner. Good luck, isn't it?"

"You have lost your mind. I know I've said that before, but this is definitely it! You've gone so far over the edge—"

"Cora." Adrian looked sane. Sensible. He wasn't, but he still managed to pull off the illusion. "Do you think he'll stop and turn back because he's not welcome in my village? Hmm? Do you think if he finds our village, he won't give its locations to his oh-so-egalitarian commander?"

Cora hesitated. "I see no reason to gag him."

"I don't want to hear his whining."

Darian braced and Cora puffed a furious breath. "It might drown out your various complaints!"

"He's a danger to us. He'll squawk and bring down his whole damned army."

"You said only one man followed us. Who's he going to call out to? Anyway, I have a suspicion no one knows where he went."

"What makes you think that?"

"General Davis wouldn't send him out alone. He'd send out some soldiers, not Captain Woodward."

Adrian offered no immediate argument, but he didn't move to take off Darian's gag, either.

"You're just being stubborn. You're asserting dominance in some wacko primitive way because you're pretty much gone on this power thing."

"I am not."

"Prove it. Take off his gag."

Adrian yanked the gag off Darian, cranking the young man's neck in the process. Darian shook his head and glared. Cora tapped her foot vengefully. "There's no need to be deliberately rough."

Darian met Adrian's eyes steadily. "Thank you." He spoke with condescension and slight mockery.

Adrian looked around, his expression determined and extremely devious. "Have you seen an anthill around, Cora? I've got an idea what we can do with our good captain. All we need is some honey—you're good at fetching that—and a few stakes."

Cora sank to a rock and bowed her head. "Trapped with you two. What an evil fate!"

Darian wasn't moved by Adrian's threat. "You've taken

an officer of the United States Cavalry hostage. Do you know the penalty for this kind of act?"

Adrian sat beside Cora and cocked his head to one side. "What? Electrocution?"

Darian hesitated. "No. Hanging."

Adrian huffed. "Big deal."

Cora whimpered and clasped her hands to her forehead. "Death is death, Adrian."

"Release this lady, and I will spare your sentence."

"Oh, get real! Cora is my woman. My girlfriend. My—" Adrian glanced at Cora and angled his brow in a teasing expression. "main squeeze."

Darian looked appalled. He maneuvered himself to another rock and sat facing them. "You have taken a young lady in unholy union, beyond the sanctity of marriage, which to your kind is a brief and incidental affair, I know."

"Well, she dumped me before I could pop the question."

Adrian had lapsed into uncontrollable anachronisms. Darian seemed unnerved by the language. Cora cleared her throat and tried to smile. "He means he was going to propose marriage, but I . . . well, I left him before he got the chance."

"Left him?"

"It's a long story. You see, Captain, I'm afraid I haven't been fair or clear to you. Not quite sure how to handle the situation. Adrian and I are from the future. We met at college, and we dated. Meaning, we fell in love and went places together. But he could do everything, and he was so perfect. I wasn't, and the harder I tried, the more I failed. I couldn't face letting him down again, so I left. My friend, Jenny—I wish you could meet her—set me up skydiving because she'd met Adrian. . . . "

Cora turned to Adrian. "I haven't asked you about that. How did she know about us?"

"We went out for drinks after her first dive, and she mentioned you."

"Drinks? I thought you wouldn't touch alcohol."

"Soda water."

Cora nodded. "Go on."

"She mentioned your name and said you were coming out to Phoenix. I spit sparkling water all over the bar, by the way."

"Disgusting." Cora beamed. "I take it that perked her interest."

"It did. She knew you had a man in your past, and guessed it was me."

"So she set us up."

"I set us up. She helped."

Darian cleared his throat, a polite gesture. "The future?"

Cora tore her gaze from Adrian's smiling face. "You probably find that hard to believe. It's a Native American thing, I guess, special to Adrian's people."

Darian fixed an accusatory glare on Adrian. "What have you done to her? I have heard that your kind imbibes poisoned plants, which alter their minds—"

"Back off—I don't do drugs." Adrian turned to Cora. "You didn't expect him to believe you?"

Cora shrugged. "Not really."

"What you've done to this sweet girl is foul beyond telling."

"What I've done?" Adrian eyed Darian with palpable irritation. "I've made love to a woman I adore. What's wrong with that?"

Darian issued a derisive snort. "To make love is to issue gentle words of wooing and praise, expressing the fullness of your heart, making promises of an eternity together. Not . . . a bestial embrace."

Adrian laughed, but Cora sighed with feminine apprecia-
tion. "I think the term 'make love' meant something different to the Victorians, Adrian. It's sweet, isn't it?"

Darian nodded. "It is the honorable display of romantic
affection."

"Give it a rest, man. Your time period is known for
hypocrisy. There were more hookers during the Victorian
age than ever before." Adrian huffed. " 'Honorable display
of affection!' Right! He speaks sweet nothings to a 'lady,'
and gets laid by a whore."

"Adrian!" Cora swatted his arm, but Darian braced into
gentlemanly indignation.

"Your judgment is profoundly inaccurate. Yes, some men
stray from the ideals of fidelity. Many men lower themselves
by seeking out, perhaps, a lady of the night. But they do not
attain the level of true love that honorable chastity eventually delivers."

Cora's brow furrowed as she tried to decipher his meaning. She glanced at Adrian, who stared at Darian in amazement. "I think he means he's a virgin."

The fading moonlight illuminated Darian's coloring
cheeks. Cora's heart wrung with tenderness. "Captain
Woodward, one day you will make a lucky woman very,
very happy."

Adrian's brow angled. "How? He won't have a clue what
to do with her."

Cora elbowed him in the ribs, hard. "Didn't you have a
first time?"

"Sure. With you."

Her mouth opened, she exhaled in sweet wonder. "With
me?"

"Yes. With you."

"You were a virgin?"

231

Adrian fidgeted. "I was."

Pure bliss filled her soul. "Why didn't you tell me?"

He fiddled with his knife, then drummed his fingers on the blade. "I wanted you to think I was . . . you know, cool."

Cora's body went tight with emotion. She flung her arms around his neck and kissed his face. She kissed his high, smooth cheekbone, his temple, his nose, and the corner of his mouth. "Adrian de Vargas, I love you so."

"I don't know what you're getting so excited about."

She settled back beside him and rested her head on his shoulder. "I was the first."

Adrian kissed the top of her head. "And the last."

"You have delivered your brother's murderer to my hands. You have done well."

Tiotonawen sat cross-legged at the back of his hut, smoking. Adrian suddenly wished he'd kept Darian's involvement in his brother's death to himself. "There were extenuating circumstances to be considered, father. The captain did his duty. I wouldn't call it murder."

Tiotonawen angled his dark brow and eyed Darian. "Did you shoot my son?"

"I did."

Tiotonawen studied the young man's face for a long moment, then nodded. "He is brave to speak no lie."

Adrian relaxed. "As I said. Tradman is our real enemy."

"Tradman will be thrown to the ravens, and his soul will claw its way through the mire of doom. This man will die in honor."

Darian seemed to expect no more, but Adrian's blood ran cold. "But you just said . . . You can't kill him!"

Darian glanced at him from the corner of his eye. "What

did you expect? A lecture such as a school headmaster would deliver?"

Adrian shifted his weight. "Look, we're not killing you. So knock off the sarcasm."

"He will be bound to a stake and given to the women. They will, with axes and knives and burning sticks, extract vengeance for Eschinaeintonyah's death. When he is dead, you, my son, will have the honor of eating his heart."

A short laugh escaped Adrian's lips before he knew what he was doing. "I don't think so."

"You take into yourself his bravery. Assuming he dies without shrieks."

Darian straightened, proud. "I will die with honor."

"No, you won't !"

"I will."

Adrian raked his fingers through his hair, fighting for control. "I mean, you won't die 'with honor,' because you're not dying at all. We're not staking you out—"

"You threatened to do just that when you captured me."

"It was a joke!" Adrian seized a desperate breath. "No one is hacking you, there'll be no shrieking, and God! I'm not eating any part of you!"

Adrian spun in a full circle. *Cora.* How would he explain to Cora that her boyish friend was about to be tortured to death, then devoured? "Apaches aren't cannibals. It's not a Plains kind of thing."

Tiotonawen grimaced. "Not cannibals. The eating of the heart is ceremonial, an act of ritual. Not a meal."

"Whew!" Adrian caught himself. "Okay, so the revenge can be ritual, too."

"It is ritual. With each cut into his flesh, the blood of anger is released."

"That's not what I meant." Adrian swallowed hard. He didn't like Darian Woodward, mainly because he was jealous. But killing? Never. "Look, he's my prisoner, right? Don't I get some say in the matter?"

"You choose the time of his death."

"Good. I can work with that."

Darian frowned. "You would force me to linger, hoping I will crack and shed tears at my death. I will not."

"You really get off on misunderstanding everything I say, don't you?"

"I understand you, far more than you understand me. You see, I had a brother once, too."

Darian's tone sent cold dread down Adrian's spine. He didn't want to know what motivated this innocent, blue-eyed soldier. He realized he'd been in the past, without really feeling it. It had been a convenience, because he had Cora where she couldn't get away. But it was real. These men, Apache and white, were real. And their pain was real, too.

"What happened to your brother?"

"We enlisted together, and we fought side by side from Bull Run to Gettysburg. At Gettysburg, his leg was shattered by a cannon blast. His leg turned gangrenous, and the surgeons said it had gone too far. They couldn't waste time on a hopeless cause. So I took the saw and removed his leg myself."

Adrian shook his head slowly. "No. . . . "

Darian's eyes glowed, but no tears emerged. Suddenly, Adrian knew the young man couldn't cry. "He thanked me for my attempt, and then he died. No, you can't hurt me, and no, I will not scream."

Adrian met Darian's cold gaze and held it. "Captain, you will not die."

234

* * *

"You can't keep him here!" Cora stood with one hand on her hip, the other holding a bag filled with honey. Adrian checked her arms, but saw no evidence of bee stings.

"I take it you had better luck this time."

Cora eyed the bag of honey. "It's no big deal, really. You just have to smoke them out. . . . Don't try changing the subject, Adrian. What about Captain Woodward?"

He hadn't told her the full details, because he hadn't thought of way to avoid Darian's eventual death. He wouldn't let it happen, but he wasn't sure how to send the captain back, either.

"It's a little tricky, Cora. He knows the location of this village."

"So, move the village after he's gone."

"It's not that easy. Also," Adrian paused and looked casually around. "There's the matter of my brother's death. My father still considers the captain responsible."

"I have noticed that neither you nor Captain Woodward use each other's first names. Why is that?"

"I don't know. He's a pain. But nothing's going to happen to him."

"He's tied to a stake all day, walked like a dog on a leash, and confined at night. I'd say something has already 'happened' to him."

"He shouldn't have tagged along after you, then, should he?"

"That's not fair!"

"I'll do what I can. But this is a different world, Cora. They don't do things the way we do."

"It's a different time, but the same world. People are still people. Life still matters."

Stobie Piel

Adrian couldn't argue, but his father reacted to his objections about killing much as he had about smoking. The white man had deprived him of "his right," and with time, he would return to the Apache way.

Darian Woodward seemed to consider his captivity some kind of spiritual test of courage. He never complained, though he issued annoying and sarcastic comments on occasion. Despite his boyish manner, Adrian noticed Darian had a well-developed sarcasm, which—in someone else—might have been amusing.

Darian's predicament certainly solidified Cora's devotion. She brought him food and tea, she brought him a basin of water so he could shave. She even gave Darian her first sample of Cora-made bread, complete with honey. The man might die young, but he would be well-tended until the end.

Adrian eyed Darian, seeing in his resigned face the potential for a major falling out with Cora. He was tied to a crossed stake at the center of the village, watching women prepare the day's meal. He seemed curious, and was always polite when spoken to, except to Adrian. If a woman walked by, he smiled and nodded. Adrian felt sure if he had a cap, it would be doffed at every passer-by.

Cora smiled knowingly. "You like him."

Adrian's lips curved downwards. "I don't."

"I think you do. Your names even sound alike. *'Darian.' 'Adrian.'* You could be brothers. What you have is sibling rivalry!" The sing-song quality of her voice grated. "He's so cute. You'd have to like him. I know I do."

"That is obvious."

"You're still jealous. How flattering!"

Adrian drew a calming breath. "I am not jealous in any way. He's a . . . child."

"He's twenty-five."

"He seems younger."

"I don't know. . . . True, he's innocent, but in some ways, he seems so much older. I suppose because of the war."

Cora spotted Toklanni across the village and sighed. "I've got to go. Chores. Laurencita says there's a big party this afternoon. She was kind of vague about the occasion, though."

Adrian hesitated, trying to muster a casual response. He'd told Laurencita to keep the celebration of Darian's capture and ritual killing from Cora. "Just ceremony. I left for the fort before they could celebrate my return."

"Oh, good! Everyone's dressing up. I met the shaman—he's neat. And Haastin's brother is practicing his flute, there are drums all over the place. Should be fun."

Cora headed off, leaving Adrian standing by himself in the center of the village. He had solidified his position as leader by capturing his brother's killer. The villagers respected his time of choosing for Darian's death, but they were getting impatient. The Apache worked to a subtle rhythm, finding harmony and balance in ways Adrian couldn't bring himself to understand.

I'm in a bind. No question. He glanced toward Darian, and saw that the captain had overheard his conversation. Darian knew that his time was short, and that Adrian was busy deceiving Cora on the subject of his death. Darian's lip quirked at one side to indicate nothing had escaped him, and perhaps because he knew Cora would never forgive Adrian for what was to come.

Adrian glared. *You won't die.*

Darian glared back, smirking slightly. *I will.*

Adrian turned away. When he spoke those words in his father's hut, he had been sure he could back them up. But the Apache way seemed to roll toward him, and over him like an ancient tide. They truly believed they respected the white

237

soldier by offering him a brutal death which he could endure, thus proving his ultimate courage. Worse still, Darian seemed to expect it, even welcome it.

Twenty-five years old, and he'd lived through the bloodiest war in American history. He'd come out of it with his Victorian sensibilities intact, yet carrying a world of sorrow in his eyes. Yet still fully capable of stirring a woman's heart to pity, and perhaps more.

It wasn't Adrian's heritage that offended Darian Woodward—it was Adrian himself. Maybe because Adrian represented the cost of adhering to his social dictates. Because Adrian could lie with Cora and revel in sexuality, while Darian never sampled a woman's delights lest he somehow dishonor himself. *Pathetic.*

Adrian turned his gaze back to Cora. She stood with a group of young women, who chattered and laughed, getting ready for his celebration. He loved sex. He felt strong, and perfectly confident when making love. Sex with Cora had always been good. Even the first time—lying on top of her, looking down into her shining, trusting eyes. Bringing all his fantasies to reality as he edged slowly into her, holding himself in painful restraint lest he damage her.

He didn't damage her, and she loved every second, every thrust, every touch. It had been even better than he imagined, because his heart had filled with such overpowering love during that first time that no other lover would ever come close to Cora Talmadge.

And it was even better now, because he was aware of his masculine power, and Cora had learned to take charge when the mood suited her. But the passion between them had always been strong.

Even so, he'd lost her. That was what bothered him. He wasn't sure that it couldn't happen again. In the past, it had been her doubts that drove them apart. Today, it might be the result of two conflicting cultures. Darian might accept the reason for his death, but Cora never would.

Victorian gowns were pretty and supremely feminine, but nothing matched the sensual allure of the Apache's soft leather dress. Cora examined her outfit with glee. It was a soft camel color, with ceremonial paintings in blue and red of eagles and symbols which she guessed meant fertility and long life.

It had a fringe over her arms and at the hem, and a useful slit up her thigh. Adrian would like it. No question. Cora abandoned her plaid sneakers and selected soft beaded moccasins from Toklanni's collection.

Laurencita wore a long skirt decorated with beads, and wore many strands of coral and turquoise around her neck. "Are you sure you don't want some of these, Cora?"

Cora fingered her fetish bear pendant. "This is enough."

Laurencita pulled off several bracelets. "Take these."

Cora decided bangles would be good, so she hung them artfully over her wrists, then held out her arms to admire the effect. "Very good." She fingered her hair. The women washed in wooden basins, and her hair was now squeaky clean, but it required adornment. She added a narrow braid on both sides, stuck beads on the ends, then looked around for her feather.

She'd forgotten on purpose to return Tiotonawen's hat, but she'd lost the raven feather. It wouldn't do, anyway. "Where can I find a good feather or two?"

Laurencita's eyes lit, and she left the hut. Cora followed. Laurencita seized a hen, yanked out a tail feather and held it up victoriously. She presented it to Cora with pride. It was pretty, with brown and white stripes. Still, a chicken . . . "We'll say it fell off an eagle."

Laurencita smiled. "I always do."

Cora looked around for Adrian, excited about her new appearance. She smiled at Darian. He took one look at her bare legs, went pale, and closed his eyes tight. Laurencita eyed him doubtfully. "White men are so odd."

"I'm afraid he's a little odder than most."

"His face is appealing, though. I am sorry. . . . " She caught herself and looked uncomfortable, inciting Cora's suspicions.

"Why?"

Laurencita hedged as Cora's eyes grew narrow. "I am sorry he killed Eschinaeintonyah."

Cora sighed. "I think he is, too."

Chapter Nine

Apache women were treated as equal to their men in three ways: Drinking, gambling, and dancing. Cora faced off with Haastin as they tossed dice in the sand. A seven tumbled upright and Cora squealed. "I win again!" She seized a collection of red beads and stuffed them in her already-full bag, then offered the "thumbs-up" sign to Laurencita.

Haastin sat back and issued a torrent of Apache curses. Cora beamed and jingled the purse. "I'm going to put these in my basket, and bury them for the future. Thank you!"

He glared, but didn't speak. Laurencita tapped his shoulder and spoke in Apache. He huffed, then headed off to his hut. "Where's he going?"

"The dancers are making themselves ready. You kept him overlong at the game. He does not like to lose."

"Me, neither." Cora sighed happily. "Where's Adrian? I want him to see my new dress."

241

"He will come soon."

Cora stood up and stretched. A gasp of embarrassment reminded her of Darian's presence nearby. Apparently, she'd revealed too much of her legs again. "He's so stuffy." She thought of Jenny lecturing a Young Republican spokesman on the virtues of communal living, and wished Jenny and Darian could meet. "Curse the difficulties of time travel! So many good couples, never to be!"

Cora made her way to Darian's staked position. "There's supposed to be music and dancing soon, Captain. Maybe they'll let you dance, if you're interested."

"Certainly not! Miss Talmadge, I admire your ability to integrate with these persons, but I'm not entirely sure it's in your eventual best interest."

"You seemed to like dancing at the fort."

"I am an expert at the Virginia Reel. This is different. They're not . . . clothed."

"You know what's interesting? In the future, Native Americans dress quite conservatively. They're very restrained. But I'm afraid your descendants are the opposite. You should see what people wear to the beach!"

Darian looked like he didn't want to know, so Cora spared him a description of bikinis and topless beaches. She gazed around the village, and realized she felt at peace. Adrian would be with her soon, they'd watch the dancers like tourists. Maybe they'd even join in and learn the steps.

A group of men appeared, fully costumed, and Cora's excitement peaked. "Oh, look! How neat! I must get a costume to put in my basket. Think of the price I could fetch for it! Or maybe I'll just keep it on display. . . . "

Music started, and the dancers took position. Cora looked around for Adrian, but he wasn't there. "Drat! He should see this. I don't know how often they put on these events, and we could be gone. Oh, hell!"

Each warrior was costumed differently, with intricate masks, dyed feathers, and body paint. They wore cloth tied around their hips, covering very little, Cora noticed. She guessed the costumes represented gods, and wished she knew more about Native American legend.

A low fire burned in the village center, despite the heat of the Arizona sun. The pungent aroma of burning herbs filled the air, a heady and somehow erotic fragrance. Darian's eyes widened as if he watched a Satanic ritual, but Cora knew now what it meant to feel God. In the bones of the earth, in the souls of humankind, in the wind and the fire. Everywhere. She swayed to the drumbeat, moving her arms in peaceful timing.

"Isn't it beautiful?" She waved to Laurencita, who carried her baby son around the dancers and took position beside Cora and Darian. "What do the costumes represent?"

"Many legends. There is the Coyote, the Trickster. . . . " Laurencita indicated a dancer wearing a mask with a long nose. "The shaman"—she indicated an old man drumming ferociously—"he begins the music, and he will sing. Then comes the social dancing, when we all circle the fire. That is my favorite time."

"What are the steps?"

"The dancers know the music, and the gods speak to them inside their heads. For us, we dance as we feel."

Cora clasped her hands eagerly. "Wonderful!"

One dancer wore what looked like a loin cloth with turquoise and red patterns, and a red belt around his lean waist. He wore a red and white mask, and a long train of feathers and white fur. A red and black circle had been painted on his wide chest, with the same pattern covering his muscular forearms. He wore white fur around his ankles, but his feet were bare. "Nice legs."

Laurencita nodded her approval. "That one is—" She lowered her voice and looked around. "What do you call a man who is built strong, which makes a woman think of lying with him?"

"Sexy." Cora's voice assumed a low growl. She remembered Captain Woodward's indignant presence, and quickly cleared her throat, then effected an innocent expression which she didn't warrant. "I like what he does with his hips."

Laurencita issued a murmur of agreement. "He mimics what a man does between a woman's legs, just before—"

"Dear God!" Darian Woodward struggled at his stake, the first resistance Cora had seen.

"It's just a dance, Captain."

"This is obscene."

"Isn't it?" Again, Cora growled. Laurencita chuckled.

The sexy dancer picked up a painted red and black shield, then took a spear which was covered in red cloth. He moved with the other dancers around the firelight, possessed by the intensifying drumbeat.

"Damn! Where is Adrian? I want him to learn that."

Laurencita eyed her doubtfully. "Your man has power. He does not have to learn. He will know."

"Really?" Cora clapped her hands. "Great!"

The drumbeat shifted, and the dancers turned outward. The villagers entered the circle, moving in individual patterns. Cora looked desperately around, but Adrian didn't appear. "Oh, hell! He's probably gone off hunting rabbits again—with a spoon."

The dancers involved the watchers, drawing them into the passionate rhythm while Cora watched enviously. She spotted the sexy warrior and her cheeks warmed. She pretended to look around for Adrian, but she felt the dancer's approach.

He didn't speak, which made the encounter all the more embarrassing. He just moved closer and closer, beading in on her like a target. His motion became decidedly sexual.

Darian snorted in disgust. "These people are heathens to the core."

"Aren't they?" Her voice came as a muttered, stuttering squeak. Up close, the man's legs were very, very good. His chest glistened with some kind of herbal oil, which added definition to his muscles. He circled Cora, his sultry attention fixed on her as he moved. She caught a shuddering breath of raw embarrassment, then stole a surreptitious glance at his back as he turned. The sort of back a woman might sink her teeth into. "Oh, help!"

He separated her from Darian's staked position, and eased her toward the dancers. She backed away from him, and found herself caught in the flow of the moment. Dancers faced the fire, then turned away, then turned back. The drumbeat filled her head and her soul. Curse Adrian de Vargas for missing it!

Cora made up her own steps. She bent left, then right, then forward. It was fun. She found herself circling her sexual opponent, peering coyly up at his masked face before she realized what she was doing. She couldn't see his face at all. Somehow it made their encounter all the more erotic. She bit her lip hard, then whirled toward the fire. She heard him chuckle, and her blood burned in embarrassment. Erotic man.

Seduction Man.

Cora stopped, faced him, took a long look at his chest and legs, then burst forth in a wide smile. "Adrian!"

He moved closer. "Tiyannandiwahdi."

"Tee." She leaned toward him, her eyelids low. "You are so sexy." She didn't let him respond. She resumed her dance, feeling the wild power that drew them closer. She felt primitively female, aware of her power to arouse and to nurture. She felt . . . fertile. The spark that was *Cora* commanded every portion of her body, then reached out to draw him in.

Adrian was clearly male. His spark filled him with potent strength, and fueled every cell in his glorious body. Cora felt sure her spark centered itself in her womb, then ignited the power of sexuality. She had a fair idea where Adrian's spark settled, and the thought filled her with intense desire. *Lust.*

Her knees went weak at the full realization of how much she wanted him. She stumbled, then leaned back against his chest. "Oh, my goodness!" She swung her head dramatically around and looked into his mask. "Got any plans for tonight, sweetheart?"

"Whatever you desire."

Cora felt drunk. "I desire you"—she lowered her voice to a deep, gravelly tone, then winked at him—"baby."

He lost his rhythm, too. "*Baby?*"

She seized his spear and shield and set them aside, then resumed her sensual dance. She slid her hands up his arms, from his hands to his strong, painted forearms. They danced and played, and people sang. Adrian sang, too, and Cora hummed.

The sun blazed, then lowered, and the dancing continued. Cora wasn't tired. Sexual tension propelled her through the best afternoon of her life. Adrian removed his mask, and she reeled with giddy pleasure to see his face painted with red and white stripes. "Make-up becomes you, Tee."

She spotted a feather in his long hair, wound in a narrow braid like her own. "Chicken?"

His brow furrowed. "Eagle."

"Mine, too."

He caught her small braid and smiled. "Beautiful."

Cora grasped his biceps and peered up at him, her soul on fire. "I can almost feel you inside me. If we don't go somewhere alone soon, I may get, um, carried away right here, if you follow me."

He swallowed hard and exhaled a taunt breath. "Yes."

Cora looked around. "It's not dark enough yet. And if we go in your hut, we'll have to be quiet, and I don't want to be quiet."

"Okay."

"I'd like to hear you scream, too."

A tiny whimper came from somewhere in Adrian's throat. Cora studied the landscape. "How much can we do standing up?

He didn't answer. He grabbed her arm and pulled her from the dancers. He led her from the village, then into the cluster of boulders and juniper bushes where Toklanni had forced her to pick yucca. He pressed her back against a boulder, freed his erection from his painted loincloth, pushed up her leather skirt, and drove himself deep inside her.

Cora's primal groan became a low scream of delirious joy, and Adrian thrust again. She wrapped one leg around his, clutching his shoulders as he feverishly kissed her neck. Her orgasm came without warning, so intense that her toes seemed to lift from the earth. The drumbeat echoed from the village, throbbing in time with her rapture.

He lowered her to her feet, then rested his forehead against hers. Their breath came in short, shuddering gasps. Cora peered up at him. "You, too?"

He nodded. "Me, too."

Cora adjusted her skirt. Adrian centered his ravaged loincloth. They looked up at the same time and stared at each other. They smiled. Cora puffed a quick breath. Adrian did, too. He held out his hand and she took it, and they walked casually back to the village.

They returned to the village as night fell over the ravine. Toklanni was sharpening what looked like an axe. Another woman held a glowing spear point in the fire. Adrian went rigid beside Cora, grabbed her hand, and hauled her toward their hut. Cora tugged free. "What is the matter with you? The party's not over!"

"I think it is."

"Look. They're getting ready to cook something"—Adrian's groan cut her off—"and they're moving Captain Woodward closer. How nice! I wonder if they'll relax and let him take part in the ceremony?"

"God! Cora . . . " Adrian looked desperate. He seized her shoulders and held her firmly in place. "Stay here."

"Where are you going?" Adrian didn't answer as he ran toward the fire. Cora stood alone, watching. Darian looked toward heaven and his mouth moved as if he spoke. Adrian positioned himself in front of Darian and argued dramatically with Tiotonawen. Tiotonawen laid his hand on Adrian's shoulder and shook his head as if instructing a child.

In one sick flash, Cora knew. They meant to kill Darian Woodward, and Adrian had known all along. He didn't approve—no man could change that much, but he hadn't stopped it, either. Maybe he couldn't. He could, however, have set Darian free. If Cora had known, that's what she would have done.

She walked slowly because her legs felt stiff and heavy. Her heart beat in slow, even thumps, as if walking into a dream. She came up behind Adrian and saw that he was trembling.

"No. Not yet. It is my choice, and I'm not ready. I want him . . . I want him to suffer more!"

Tiotonawen bowed his head. "He has suffered enough. The time has come."

Adrian stepped back from his father. "I will not let you kill this man."

"This man killed your brother."

"I know. But he did it in defense of another, because he had no choice."

"These words you speak are white men's laws. You do not know your own people. Your head is too strong, and stands in your way." Tiotonawen gestured at Darian. "This man is not afraid. He does not cry out. He dies in honor."

Adrian stared at his feet while Cora held her breath. He looked up and held his father's gaze. "Father, if he dies, you must kill me, too."

Cora's eyes filled with tears. He meant it. But what if Tiotonawen accepted? "No—"

"Talks Much Who Fights Bees, be silent. This choice is my son's, not yours. If he says he will die with this man, he speaks true."

"You can't be serious!" Cora hopped in front of Adrian and shoved Tiotonawen in the chest. "You've hauled him back into the past, and now you're going to kill him because he's not willing to abandon everything he believes?"

"I will not kill my son. I will have him bound until the ritual is over. The choice is not his, and his belief is not dishonored."

"It's not the belief in life that matters, you idiot! It's life itself!"

Adrian touched Cora's shoulder. He was the strongest

man she'd ever known. He had power. While he lived, nothing terrible would happen. Despite her fear, Cora relaxed.

"The captain is prepared to die, Cora. There's nothing we can do for him now."

She started to nod, then realized what he'd said. "*What?*"

"We must respect—"

"Oh, no we mustn't!" Cora felt the blood drain from her face until she went dizzy from shock. She stared up into Adrian's warm, brown eyes, and she couldn't see *him*. She saw a tall, dark man wearing war paint, inscrutable and distant. She shook her head, then reached to touch him, to bring him to his senses. "You can't let him die. Adrian!"

Adrian turned away from her before she'd finished her sentence. He seemed relaxed, casual. "Father, this deed is done in blackness. Wait until the moon has disappeared beyond the hills, and I will not stand in your way."

Tiotonawen puffed with pride. "My son is wise, and has returned to his people. It shall be done as you say."

Darian Woodward bowed his head in prayer, but he didn't object. Cora looked from Adrian to the young soldier, and her heart quailed. Darian was afraid. He wouldn't show fear, but she knew he wondered inside if he could truly die with honor. He'd seen death, yes, but never endured his own. Cora went to him, stumbling as she walked, too shocked for tears.

She stood before him, looking up into his face. He looked down at her, and he tried to smile, but his expression seemed frozen. "Don't fear, Miss Talmadge. I am ready to die."

Her tears came in a hot rush. "No, you're not. You can't be. You're so young."

"My brother was nineteen when he died at Gettysburg. Twenty-five, that's not so young."

Cora looked back at Adrian. He stood casually with his

father and the other men. The warriors were smoking. She half expected him to join in, but when Tiotonawen offered his pipe, Adrian shook his head. He still protected his own body, yet would allow a noble young man to suffer a gruesome death. It didn't make sense. Could she have been so blind? Could he be so supremely selfish and unaffected?

"No. He promised."

Darian sighed. "I do believe he tried. But what is my life to that man? Nothing. He wears only the cloak of a civilized being, Miss Talmadge. Beneath that guise, he is as brutal and unrestrained as those you see around you. Perhaps more so, because as he disrespects our customs, neither does he follow theirs. I have noticed that during my stay in his village."

Darian spoke casually, as if still pondering Adrian's behavior despite his own certain death. Cora felt something she'd never felt before. *I'm the only sane one here.* Her chin firmed and her heart beat with growing confidence. *I'm the only one who makes any sense whatsoever. Therefore, it's up to me to end this madness. And somehow, I will.*

Darkness. If they performed this deed in darkness, so much the better. The moon was still high and full, shedding a light like the sun into the ravine. It would take awhile to disappear. She had time. Time for what, she wasn't sure, but time.

She touched Darian's shoulder. "I will come back."

"Please, Miss Talmadge, do not. Let us say farewell now. Promise me you will not be here when . . . " He swallowed to control himself, and a hot wave of nausea churned in Cora's stomach. "I don't want you to see me that way."

She tried to nod, but her head barely moved. "You won't die. I promise." She started away, aiming for Adrian's hut where she would plan his escape.

"Miss Talmadge, I love you."

251

She nearly buckled beneath the weight of guilt. She knew she had to look him in the eye and see all his young soul looking back at her. Cora forced herself to turn, she forced herself to smile. "You are a dear man, Captain. I am not worth your affection."

"Please, don't reject it." He looked so sincere, so pure. She couldn't bring herself to turn him away. "I can offer you nothing but a brave death in your honor. I know that man has affected your senses, and that you care for him. I ask only that you remember me, and know I have lost my heart to you."

Cora clamped her arms around her waist, in agony. "Oh, God, why?"

He smiled, sweet and young. "Because you are so brave. Because nothing that has happened to you, however foul and degrading, has changed what you are. I look at your sweet face, and I see a powerful woman, a woman who can do anything. I admire you, my dear Miss Talmadge, for your bravery as much as for your beauty."

"I'm not brave! I'm much too weird to be beautiful. What are you seeing when you look at me?"

"I'm looking at you, and I see what you are." He paused. "Maybe you don't see? Then if nothing else, I have done some good by telling you. You are the bravest woman who ever lived. And I love you with all my heart." He paused, weighing the situation. "You haven't turned me aside, so I will take that to mean some part of my vow has touched you. No matter what they do to me, I will die a contented man."

He didn't really love her. He was infatuated. Maybe subconsciously he saw himself in her, and what he could be. But he needed to know he wasn't alone. Cora went to him and placed both her hands on his chest. She stood on tiptoes and kissed his cheek. "You have given me such a precious gift. I will treasure it always."

She moved back, tears flowing over her cheeks. He smiled and nodded, and she turned away. Adrian stood behind her, a dark, glowering presence. She felt his fury, but it didn't affect her. She tried to brush past him, but he caught her arm and pulled her back. "A tender scene. You are easily moved by pity."

Cora yanked away from him. "Which separates us even more than we were! Leave me alone, Adrian. Or maybe I really should call you Tiyannandiwahdi. That's who you are now, isn't it? Whatever you were is gone. Yes, you are a wonderful lover. You touch something in me that is so primal that I feel the very beginnings of mankind when I'm with you. I assume that comes from your 'power.' But if your power isn't enough to save a good man, then what is it worth? Nothing!"

"Cora." He reached for her, but she smacked his arm away. "I don't want to talk to you. I can't." She leaned toward him, fire burning inside her. "I love you. I always have, and I always will. But it's not enough. Captain Woodward loves me. Love isn't fair. If it was, I would feel for him what I feel for you. . . . "

Her voice cracked and she ran to his hut, sobs racking her chest, tearing at her throat. She flung herself to the floor mat and cried. Something more powerful than grief, more powerful than heartache, rose inside her. She had to be strong for a few hours more. The captain depended on her, whether he knew it or not. Cora wiped her tears away and she sat up. She found her modern-day clothes, and changed from her leather dress back into chinos.

She located a small, but sharp knife. She tucked it in her waistband and slipped from the hut unseen.

Adrian walked around the village three times. Each circle reduced his hurt and fury, and restored his rational mind. He sat cross-legged in front of the fire, staring into the dark orange depths. He waited until no one was looking, then tossed a handful of sand onto the embers, lessening the glow. Haastin passed by, and Adrian fiddled with a stick. He waited until the warrior passed by, then doused another corner of the fire.

The moon lowered slowly. He watched as it moved from boulder to boulder, until it left the juniper bushes as dark shadows in the night. The moonlight shone briefly on his own hut, and he closed his eyes. He felt Cora's shock, her outrage. As much as it wounded him, it served his purposes, and convinced his father that he was a man transformed.

The moon faded to a thin line of white, and Adrian stood up. He made another circle around the village, then slipped behind a boulder. He waited until Darian Woodward's staked position was clear of villagers, then crept up behind him.

"Don't say a word. Just listen."

"You can't leave me in peace, can you?" That sarcasm, that annoying, disgusted tone.

Adrian ground his teeth together. He briefly imagined leaving the captain right where he was, and cheering with the crowd as he was hacked to bits. "I am here, you sniveling weasel, to rescue you." Adrian took his rabbit-hunting knife from his boot and cut Darian's ties. Darian made no move to escape, though he rubbed his wrists as if they were numb.

"Is this some despicable method of freeing me, perhaps so I'll be shot escaping in dishonor, thus to die in ignominy?"

Adrian twitched. "There's no dishonor in living, dude." He looked around reflexively, then issued silent thanks that Cora hadn't heard his latest slip. "I don't like you. I think you're a geek, and you're annoying, and you're after my girlfriend. But I promised you I wouldn't let you die. And I won't."

"You think I will linger less true in her heart if I flee?"

Adrian rolled his eyes. "I think I'll 'linger less true in her heart' if you don't." He paused to gather his wits. It wasn't easy to speak quietly when he wanted to shout. "Look, do you really want to die?"

"No. But there are worse things than death. Living in discord with one's higher principles, living in dishonor."

"Then do it for Cora. I don't think she can take seeing you die. She cares about you. Whether you believe it or not, I love her. I don't know what your death will do to her."

Darian studied Adrian's face calmly, in no hurry to leave. "Say my name."

"What?" Adrian's fists clenched. If he punched hard enough . . .

"Say my name, and make your request. Politely. That means using the word 'please,' in case you didn't know."

"You little—"

"I am two inches, at least, taller than yourself. Go ahead. I'm waiting."

At most, an inch. "Why? What the hell do you care what I call you?"

"You'll hate calling me anything but 'dude' and 'geek.' If you give up something, I'd be more inclined to give up something, too."

"What are you giving up? I'm saving you!"

"Keep your voice down. In case I decide to accept your

offer." Darian looked around, spotted the village shaman walking past the fire, and leaned back against the stake, casually. Adrian hid in the dark until the shaman went into his hut.

"He's gone. I've left a gray horse—"

"The one you stole from us?"

"Yes, that one. He's tied about two hundred feet up the path, behind a boulder."

"You haven't submitted to my request." Adrian growled. Darian smiled. "As I was saying, I am giving up the opportunity to die a heroic death, render myself immortal in Miss Talmadge's eyes, and know with certainty that you'll never share her bed, or whatever you might use, again."

"I could kill you now, myself. *Bare-handed.*"

"Yes, but you won't. Say it."

It took all his power and all his restraint. He imagined Cora's face, encouraging him to do the right thing. "Okay, fine. It would give me great pleasure if you would . . . please . . . let me save your miserable hide . . . save you . . . " His throat didn't want to comply. His tongue twisted to one side. "*Darian.*"

"Captain Woodward."

He felt like a human volcano on the verge of a horrendous eruption. His voice shook. "*Anthill.*"

"I accept."

The shaman threw a log on the low fire just as Cora approached Darian. She stopped and held her breath, but the glow hadn't reached the stake. She had seconds. Her hands shook so much that she could barely grip her knife. Another log was tossed on the fire.

She crept to the stake, drew a breath, then fumbled around for his ties. They were loose. So loose he could have escaped on his own. Two more logs crackled and burned, illuminating the square. Cora pulled off the ties. Darian gasped in surprise.

"Quick, run!" She reached to push Darian from the stake. Adrian de Vargas turned around and smiled.

"Adrian! What are you doing on Darian's stake?"

Every person in the village turned at once. The shaman issued a torrent of strange words. Toklanni dropped her axe and sighed. Laurencita laughed. Tiotonawen emerged from his hut, walked across the square and stopped beside the fire, shaking his head and muttering words that Cora felt sure disparaged the influence of white men.

Cora gaped at Adrian. He wore Darian's blue uniform. His hair was tied back in a ponytail and he wore the captain's wide-brimmed hat. "Does this mean the captain is now wearing your 'come-get-me' white shirt and jeans?"

"I can't believe I gave him my jeans. The shirt was torn."

"What about your hiking boots?"

Adrian held up one foot, hiking boots intact. "He kept his riding boots. Said they'd gotten him through one war, and they'd get him back to the fort."

"You let him go." Cora brushed away tears. "Adrian, I'm so sorry to be so wrong."

"I'm sorry I couldn't tell you."

"This is pathetic." Tiotonawen stood glaring between Adrian and Cora. "My son has the soft hand of a woman. You have disgraced me, shamed me. . . . "

"I did what I thought was right." Adrian sounded hurt, but sure of himself. Cora reached for his hand and squeezed it.

"*What you thought was right.* What of your brother's 'right?' Now, his soul flies above you unavenged, tied to the mortal world because of your weakness."

"Then maybe you sent the wrong man forward in time."

Tiotonawen's jaw set hard. "Maybe I did."

He turned away and walked to his hut. Adrian stepped forward to follow him, then stopped. Tiotonawen didn't look back. Cora touched his shoulder. "You did the right thing, Adrian."

"Did I?"

"Of course, you did! And your father will understand once he has time to think. He didn't send anyone after the captain. That must mean he accepted what you did."

"He sent no one because it would dishonor me further, thus dishonoring himself." Adrian sighed. "Nothing I do works."

Cora seized his arm. "Because you don't belong here, Adrian. You belong in the future, where you really can make a difference."

He gazed down at her. His expression chilled her blood. "Can I? I wonder. I have failed my father, my people. My brother. What next, Cora? You?"

"You have never failed me, Adrian de Vargas."

"Haven't I? I stood on a mountain alone, because I couldn't convince you how much you mattered to me. For all the passion we shared, for all the love I felt, I lost you. If we weren't here, you'd be back in Manhattan."

He didn't wait for her response. Cora didn't have one, anyway. She'd never seen him doubting anything. He'd always been so sure. Adrian cracked, until he finally became . . . her. He left her standing by herself, and headed off alone. Cora started to follow, then stopped. He needed to think, he needed privacy to come to terms with what he was, and what he wanted to be.

The villagers separated, some returning to their huts, some around the fire. No one seemed to resent her interference. Toklanni silently offered her a bowl of soup, and Cora sat down to eat. Darian Woodward was safe, on his way back to the fort. But Adrian had reached a point of no return.

He didn't make love to her when they returned to his hut. Cora tried not to be disappointed. Maybe he was sated from their quick passion at the boulder. She had been sated, for awhile, but she kept imagining him in his costume, with his primal warrior appeal, and she began to feel restless inside. But Adrian just lay on his back, staring at the thatched ceiling.

"You were very heroic, Adrian. You've always been heroic, but this was really special. You saved a man you don't even like. Of course, I think you like him underneath, but still . . . "

He didn't respond. He sighed, but he said nothing. Cora waited awhile, then moved closer beside him. She rested her cheek on his arm. "You didn't have a choice. You can't change what you value. It's just part of you."

Nothing. Cora began to feel impatient. If he could get past his depression, he might turn to brighter thoughts, and that might involve sex. She kissed his arm. "Are you angry with me?"

"No."

She waited for something more effusive, but he lapsed back into silence. "I can't stand it!" She jerked upright, waved her fists and growled. "Say something! I know your father hurt your feelings, but talk, would you? Talk!"

His eyes shifted to her, and his brow furrowed in confusion. "Are you all right, Cora?"

"No, I'm not all right. You're not saying anything. I don't know what you're thinking."

He held out his arms. "Come here."

She flopped down against him and he held her against his

259

chest. He kissed the top of her head. "I'm sorry, angel. I've got some things on my mind."

"I don't suppose you want to share them?"

"Not tonight. Okay?"

She puffed a breath. "Okay." She rested her cheek against his smooth, strong chest. "Sometimes, you can be such a . . . man."

"Kind of born that way."

"I don't like this strong, silent stuff, Adrian."

"I'm sorry. I just need time to think."

Cora hesitated. "Yes, but the way you're thinking lately, you're apt to come up with something really weird. The next thing I know, you'll be engaged in some bizarre Native American custom like roasting in a sweat lodge, or leading a war party, or . . . "

Adrian went very stiff as if her words triggered a thought. "Oh, no!" she said.

"A war party. . . . "

Cora sat up again. "Don't you dare!"

His eyes were narrow. Scheming. "A war party is a show of power. Not necessarily violent."

"Adrian, *war* isn't a nonviolent concept."

"Our hunters have been ambushed several times. My father seldom rides with them, so they are left with lesser warriors like Haastin to guard them. They need a leader."

Cora clamped her hand over her forehead and groaned. "Not you. No, no, no."

"I have the power."

"You have a screw loose!"

He smiled. He looked smug. Disaster approached, and Cora couldn't see a way to stop it. "You're trying to regain your dad's favor. I understand. I've tried for years to win my parents' approval, but—"

"I must prove my honor to my father."

"Your honor isn't in question."

"You do not understand the Apache way, Cora."

"Neither do you!"

He wasn't listening. Cora recognized defeat—at least, for tonight. There had to be another way of protecting him from himself and his peculiar ideas of Apache honor. Cora felt strong. A woman capable of determining her own destiny, and protecting the man she loved.

As she drifted toward sleep, she realized she truly was a woman of the past. She snuggled closer to Adrian. The man of the future would return to where he belonged, and she would be the one to bring him home.

"Women do not ride in war parties."

It was too much. Cora—the same woman who refused to swim in water over her neck, who fled Kathmandu rather than climb a mountain, who likened downhill skiing to a blood sport—was now seated astride the horse she'd stolen from a desperado, and she was holding a gun.

She offered a pert, happy smile. "I don't know how to use this, exactly. But just holding it makes me seem dangerous."

"You can say that again!" Adrian made his way through the mounted warriors and held out his hand, then pointed at the ground. "Off."

She wore her chinos and plaid sneakers, with a beaded leather vest over her white T-shirt. She wore his father's hat, with two brown-and-white feathers sticking straight up from the band. She fingered the gun, a small, rakish smile curving her lips. One brow angled. She spun the gun around her finger, then stuffed it in her waistband.

"I'll be riding in your war party, Adrian. So mount up, and let's get started."

Adrian bowed his head, fighting for patience. "Women do not ride in war parties."

"On the contrary, they do. It's not the norm, true, but Laurencita tells me that there's a well-renowned Apache woman named Lozen who rides with Geronimo. Incidentally, she's known to have power, too. You should meet her."

He looked her straight in the eye. He firmed his jaw, he flowed with confidence. "I forbid it."

She laughed. "Get real, Adrian. Like I have to obey!"

"I could pull you off this horse, this *stolen* horse, I could tie you up, gag you—"

"Kinky, but you're not getting around me by promising me a fun night."

"I love you."

She smiled, her expression soft. "I love you, too. That's why I'm going along. You said this would be a nice, non-violent war party. So what's the big deal?"

Adrian hesitated. "It is my intention to be peaceful in the protection of my people. The whole thing is for show. Power in numbers." He paused again. "I guess you can come along. But stay out of trouble."

"Thank you for your permission for what I was going to do anyway." Cora turned her attention to Haastin and studied the streaks on his face. "I'd like some of that."

"You are not wearing war paint. No."

Cora nodded to Toklanni, who held up two small saucers of red and black chalk. "I need yellow instead of red." Laurencita translated for Toklanni, who produced a pot of yellow dye for Cora's use. Cora dipped one finger in the black saucer, and another in the yellow pot. She applied the paint over her nose and along her cheekbone, then dabbed a spot of mixed yellow and black to her forehead.

Adrian watched, shaking his head. "What is that supposed to signify?"

She straightened in her saddle, looking proud. "The Bee. I am the Conqueror of the Bee, Adrian. This is my symbol."

"It looks like mud."

"As leader, you could use some decoration, too."

He eyed the pots, put white on one finger, and black on the other, then applied them to his forehead. Cora watched with misgivings. "A yin-yang? Oh, that's *so* Native American!"

He frowned as he retrieved his horse. "It's the only thing I could think of."

"Lucky you didn't think of a surfboard again."

Adrian mounted and rode to the front of his group. Cora stayed behind him, looking casual. He turned in his saddle to address his men. "We'll ride out ahead of the hunters, then take position in the hills as cover. Haastin says a herd has been spotted not far from Cramer's ranch."

Cora turned in her saddle, too. "And no stealing Mr. Cramer's chickens!"

"Right."

They rode off single file, and scaled the ravine cliff. Cora leaned forward as Spot surged up the final, steep level. "I'm used to English saddles, of course. But this is fun."

Adrian eyed her bottom. "I like your position."

She settled back down as the reached the plateau. "It's the correct position for going up steep hills. It puts your weight over the horse's shoulders and helps him balance."

"Nice bottom."

She winked. "Yours, too."

Riding with Cora was fun. Adrian wished he'd learned of her ability with horses during their first romance. It might have solved a lot of problems. They reached the desert flatland, and broke into a gallop. Cora's horse was fastest, but she kept it reined in alongside his. Her loose braid flew behind her head, and she was smiling.

"I hope I don't lose my feathers!"

Cramer's farm was positioned near what would one day be the Pinnacle Peak road. Adrian saw it as a small speck in the distance. Something felt wrong. He sensed . . . something gone. He held up his hand, and his men brought their horses to a sudden stop. Cora rode on, oblivious to his command, noticed he wasn't there, then stopped, too.

"What's the matter? Isn't the herd up past Mr. Cramer's farm?"

Adrian felt nauseous. It wasn't the riding. He felt hot and cold at once. "Something's wrong."

Cora rode back to him and studied his expression. "What's the matter? Were we going too fast?"

Adrian's gaze fixed on Cramer's distant farm. "We need to pay Cramer a visit. Now."

Haastin eyed him doubtfully. "He does not so much welcome us. And he has not many chickens left."

Cora frowned reproachfully. "Adrian, you didn't come here to steal. You don't need any chickens." She paused, then touched her feathers. "I wonder if he has any with interestingly colored feathers?"

Time flew short. Adrian urged his horse into a sudden gallop, catching the others off-guard. The desert flew by beneath the horse's stride, yet he urged it faster still. Desperation drove him, as if he knew it was already too late. The whole world was shaking as if about to open wide. And his people would be caught in the middle.

Cora's long-legged bay caught up with him. "What's going on?" She held the brim of her hat as the wind rushed in her face.

He couldn't answer. His heart beat sick and uneven, and his blood flowed like ice. Cramer's decrepit ranch grew larger as they approached. A black cloud of smoke hovered in the air nearby, then moved slowly eastward with the high clouds.

It filled Adrian's vision like a grim specter. They reached the broken fence, and Adrian slowed his horse to a walk. Cramer's barn had burned to the ground, and the fire smoldered low. Haastin and the warriors rode in around him, silent.

Cramer's livestock pens were empty. A bramble rolled by in a dry, hot wind. One chicken raced around the corner of the burning barn, clucking wildly. Cora shaded her eyes against the sun. "What happened?" Her voice shook, her face went white. "Mr. Cramer!"

The dead air grabbed Cora's words, and they fell into silence. Adrian dismounted. "Stay here." He looked up at her. "I mean it." Adrian nodded to Haastin, who leapt from his horse carrying a rifle.

Together, they walked toward the farm. The silence was overwhelming, eerie. *There has been a fire. Mr. Cramer must have taken his son and fled, probably to the fort. Fires happen all the time.* They walked around the corner of Cramer's house, and the truth became brutally real.

Cramer's body lay in a distorted heap, his head face-down on the dry ground. At least twenty arrows pierced his back. Adrian took another step forward, and his stomach heaved without warning. The man had been scalped. Adrian sank to his knees and threw up.

Haastin stood silent beside him, then laid his hand on Adrian's shoulder. "It is not done by the Apache, or by any other tribe." He strode forward and examined the body calmly while Adrian's thoughts whirled in a horror of revulsion and shock. He forced himself to stand and to join Haastin.

"What do you mean? How can you tell? These look like Apache arrows to me."

Haastin pointed at two arrows. "These are Apache, but not Tonto. They are Chiricahua. These"—he gestured at several more—"these, we made. Those with blue paint, those are Papago, and the shorter ones are Mescalero Apache."

Adrian couldn't think, his limbs felt heavy and cold despite the blazing heat. "So?"

"These arrows, all of them, they are stolen. They are used to make this death as if done by our hand."

Adrian's muscles tightened with such rage that he stood unable to move or to speak. He pulsed with fury. "Tradman."

Haastin nodded. "It is his way."

"But so many." He pointed at the tracks of horses. "There was more than one man here."

"Tradman, he kills alone, or with one Mexican man. His Mexican man died to our arrow, so Tradman kills alone. He shoots straight with gun. Not with arrows."

The past came real and swallowed Adrian's life in its grim reality. He had no point of reference. Nothing he had known in the future prepared him for this. He had watched the TV news about gang violence, read the newspapers, and considered it a shame, the product of a vast civilization. It never touched him. He'd never seen a man die.

If it devastated him, what would it do to Cora? Adrian found a tattered saddle blanket hanging from a post and placed it over Cramer's body. Haastin scanned the area, but Adrian returned to Cora. From the moment she saw his face, she knew.

"Adrian?"

He placed his hand on her horse's shoulder and leaned

against it, his head down. He looked up at her. "Cramer is dead."

Her soft eyes filled with tears, but she didn't scream or panic. She touched his face, then closed her eyes. "I'm sorry." She swallowed hard, then looked around. "Archibald?"

Adrian's heart stopped, then bounded. "I don't know."

Cora hopped off the horse. "Where is he?"

"I don't know. I didn't see him."

"Archibald!" Cora dropped her horse's reins and raced around the farm calling the boy's name. She saw Cramer's covered body, but the sight didn't stop her. "Archibald! Where are you?"

She was crying, but she didn't surrender to panic. She stopped in the middle of the yard as if gathering her wits. "Would whoever did this take him?"

Adrian stood by her side, trying to think clearly when his senses were ravaged. "My people took children prisoner, and adopted them into their clans. But this wasn't done by warriors, Cora. I think Tradman is behind it." He paused, and misery soaked through his soul. "I don't believe Tradman would take the child. I think—"

"He would kill even a little boy."

"Yes."

Cora wiped away her tears. Her expression cleared as her determination formed. Adrian stared at her as if transcending all time and all tragedy. Her strength astounded him. She took his hand and squeezed it protectively, as if she knew what this day had done to his soul. "Tell Haastin to look in what's left of the barn. We'll look in the house."

Chapter Ten

Haastin picked through the smoldering rubble of Cramer's barn as Cora and Adrian entered the house. They went through every room of the house, but found nothing. A make-shift desk had been rummaged through, papers lay scattered around the floor.

Cora found a silver frame with a painting of a young woman. She picked it up and examined it closely. Her eyes filled with tears, and she passed the picture to Adrian. "This must be his wife."

Adrian looked at the portrait. The woman had a round face that looked made for laughter, yet was held in a solemn, dignified posture. She had red hair. Cora took the picture. "We must keep this for Archibald, in case we do find him."

She still hoped. Adrian had gone beyond hope, but Cora studied the cabin's main room carefully. "This frame looks valuable, but it wasn't stolen." She gestured at the papers strewn across the floor. "But it looks like someone went through his papers. I wonder why?"

"I don't know. But the boy isn't in here, Cora. We must go."

They went outside. Haastin met them and shook his head. Archibald wasn't in the house or the barn. He wasn't lying dead in the yard with his father. He might have been taken, but if Tradman was the murderer, that didn't seem likely, either.

Cora pointed to the empty pen. "Maybe he escaped on one of the horses."

"It's possible."

"Can you sense anything, Adrian?"

His power was gone. Maybe it had only been imagination, after all. "No."

She seemed to understand. She patted his shoulder gently. "It's not your fault."

Adrian's heart beat slow and cold. *What have I done*? "Isn't it?"

"Of course not!" Cora eyed the well near the smoldering barn. Her expression altered toward surprise. She walked toward it, and Adrian followed, confused.

"Cora?"

"The bucket, Adrian. It's down in the well."

"Is it?"

"Yes." Cora went to the well and leaned over the edge. "Archibald! It's all right. We're here to take care of you."

Adrian stared at her in astonishment. "Is he—"

Cora looked back at him and smiled. "He is." She pointed into the well, and Adrian looked in. Large, round eyes peered up at him, glowing with terror, but alive. Alive. Relief and joy rushed through Adrian.

269

"You're safe now, little fellow. You'll be all right—"

The little boy yanked up a gun, aimed at Adrian's head, and fired.

Fortunately, the kid wasn't a sharpshooter. Adrian glared at the well as the shot rang in the still air. Cora bit her lip. "He's terrified."

Adrian exhaled a long, strained breath. "Guns need to be abolished." He heard a click from below, followed by a muffled curse. The boy had fired his last shot.

Adrian looked back in the well. "Listen, kid. We're not going to hurt you. But whoever did this might be back. So you're coming with us."

Archibald was too scared to respond. Haastin looked in from the other side, and cranked the bucket up from the well. Archibald appeared, his red hair glittering in the sun. "I can fight!"

Cora held out her hand. "We know that. We're here to help you."

The little boy looked at Cora's hand, he looked at her face. She moved a little closer. He hesitated, then flung himself sobbing into her arms. She held him tight, and kissed his head. "It's all right now. We'll take care of you."

He looked into her face. "My pa's dead, ain't he?"

"Yes, Archie, he is. I'm sorry."

Adrian watched Cora with the child. She turned madness back toward gentle humanity. Life's cruelty, and its ugliness never had power to change Cora Talmadge.

Adrian seated himself on the edge of the well. "Archibald, do you know who did this?"

Archie eyed Adrian with utmost suspicion and cuddled closer in Cora's arms. Cora stroked his hair and leaned her cheek against his small head. "We saw your barn burning from a long way off. What happened?"

"Don't know."

This seemed unlikely. Adrian wanted to press the matter, but the child was probably still in shock.

Cora nodded thoughtfully. "You were very bright to hide yourself. Did your papa tell you to go in the well?"

"My pa told me to hide in the well if there was ever trouble."

"You were very good to do as he asked you. He would be proud. Did he tell you there was trouble?"

"I knowed."

Cora didn't press. She waited patiently. Archie seemed to relax, although he kept his gaze fixed on Adrian. "I knowed, because I heard folks coming in the door. You knocked when you was here. Those folks didn't knock. Pa weren't there to stop them. I climbed out my window and I called Pa. He didn't say nothing, and the barn was all afire. The horses were run off, so I figured either Pa took 'em, or the Indians got him already."

Adrian frowned at the assumption. "What makes you think Indians did this?"

"Indians does everything."

"Not this."

Cora adjusted the boy's brown shirt like a mother would have. "Did you see anyone?"

"It weren't even morning. I seen men." Archie paused. "There weren't no whoops. One man said, 'get the letters.' "

Cora looked at Adrian hopefully. "He said that? In English?"

Archie didn't seem to understand the significance. "I figured Indians, they'd be a whooping and screaming, but this time, they was quiet. They just whispered like, all hushed up."

Hoofbeats echoed in the dry air, the ground rumbled.

Adrian's warriors rode into the barnyard leading the others' horses. "Soldiers."

Cora went pale. "What do we do? They'll think we did this!"

Adrian leapt from the well. "Get out of here."

Archie held fast to Cora's skirt. "Don't leave me!"

Cora patted the boy's hand. "The soldiers will take care of you."

A dark fear grew in Adrian's heart. "Tradman is often at the fort. If he had something to do with this . . . We'll take the kid with us."

Cora swung herself onto her horse, and Adrian held out his arms for Archie. "I'll give you a lift."

Archie backed away. Across the desert, Adrian saw a cloud of dust as riders approached. It wasn't the full cavalry. No more than ten, a reconnaissance party perhaps, but they were coming fast. His people could hold their own.

Adrian relaxed his muscles, then jumped toward Archie, seized him in one quick motion, then plunked him behind Cora. "There. Did that hurt?"

The little boy glared. "Yep."

Defiant little . . . Adrian turned to his men. "If we run, we look guilty." He knew he was responding with twentieth century sensibilities, but it seemed the wisest course. "Cora, take the boy and ride back to the mountains. We'll catch up with you."

She turned the horse away, then looked back over her shoulder. "I don't want to leave you."

Stubborn woman. "The child needs you, Cora. I'll be all right. There aren't many soldiers, and—" Adrian eyed the galloping riders. The high sun glinted on over-long blond hair. "And our faithful Captain Woodward is leading them."

"Is he?" Cora sounded predictably cheered and relieved

by this revelation. "Well, then. You'll be fine. Archie and I will just ride on ahead, because I don't think the captain will want Archie with you. And he might not believe Mr. Tradman did this."

"Go!"

"Right." Cora urged her horse away from the others. Archie clung to her waist. "Ready?" She sounded cheerful, as if they were going on a child's expedition. The little boy cast a final glance at his father's ravaged farm.

She rode away, and Adrian mounted his horse. He positioned his men strategically around the farm. "We outnumber them, and they're likely to believe we've got more men hidden in the hills. The captain is a pain, but he's no fool. I don't want this to become a battle."

Haastin looked disappointed, but he nodded, then took cover around the corner of Cramer's house. Adrian waited until his men were concealed, then rode out to greet the soldiers.

Darian Woodward still rode the big gray horse Adrian had left for him. Despite his rank, he rode at the fore, fearless. Adrian endured an embarrassing wave of pleasure that Cora wasn't nearby to witness the captain's display of courage.

Darian spotted Adrian, and held up his hand to stop his men. He spoke to them, and they formed a circle. Darian rode on ahead. Adrian rode out, too, but his soul seemed to hover at a distance, like he was watching an old movie. A silly western, where he played the Indian complete with war-paint, and the blond heartthrob starred as the valiant hero. Two young leaders meeting in a vale of death.

Darian rode to within ten feet and stopped. "I should have known we'd meet again."

"It had to happen."

They nodded at the same time.

Darian eyed him more closely. "What's that on your forehead?"

Adrian felt a little foolish, but he kept his expression stoic. "A yin-yang. It's an Eastern symbol of balance."

Darian looked predictably confused, but apparently wasn't interested in pursuing Adrian's choice of decoration. He looked toward the burning barn. "I see you've managed to wreak havoc in a short time."

"You're not going to believe me, but my people had nothing to do with this. We're a hunting party."

"You're painted like warriors."

"We're an escort to the hunters. We've had trouble with our hunters being shot."

"Yes, I know. It is an issue to the commanders in Tucson, and General Davis has been asked to refrain from unwarranted attacks, for the purpose of peace-keeping."

"I bet he loved that."

"No."

"You are so literal."

Darian ignored Adrian's slight. "Cramer is dead, I assume?"

Curse him for guessing! Adrian had intended to reveal this himself, thus proving his own innocence. "He is. The method of his murder was designed to make my people look guilty. He was shot with arrows, then scalped."

Darian didn't look repulsed or horrified. He looked like a man who had seen so much death that nothing really frightened him anymore. "Cramer had a son. Dead, too?"

"He's with Cora."

Darian's eyes widened in true horror. "You forced Miss Talmadge to ride with you?"

Adrian slumped. "You don't know her, do you? I'm not sure I know her, either. There was a time she was scared to go swimming. She insisted, okay? I didn't have much choice. And I didn't think we'd see anything like this."

"You could have tied her up."

"Kinky, but I couldn't distract her with fun."

Darian didn't understand, but he looked suspicious. "Where is she now?"

"I sent her on ahead, in case your men started shooting."

"We are cavalry soldiers. We don't shoot without assessing our target."

"That's not what the history books say."

Darian studied Adrian's face. "I believe you are deranged. Be that as it may, it is useful that you speak a version of English. Walk with me around the farm. Show me what has happened, and explain to me why I should believe you innocent." Darian waved toward Cramer's house. "And call off your warriors to a safe distance, across from my men. Then you and I will walk together."

A heroic suggestion. Adrian tensed with dislike. "I was about to do just that."

Darian smirked, as if knowing the thought had never entered Adrian's mind. "Of course."

Adrian called in Apache to Haastin, who emerged with the others. They rode out from the farm, and formed a circle mirroring the soldiers. "We outnumber you, you know."

"Yes, but our weapons can fire three times before one arrow flies."

"This time period could benefit from serious gun control."

Darian started toward the farm, and Adrian followed. Darian looked thoughtful. "You know, I often thought during the war what it would mean to have no guns. If we had to charge each other with our bare hands, look each other straight in the eye before we tried to kill each other." Darian paused and sighed. "Ah, but humanity didn't become thus over one night, during one war. Our ancestors fought with sticks, then arrows. We are a race doomed to conflict."

They entered the farmyard and dismounted. Adrian gazed around and his heart labored beneath the truth of Darian's words. "Nothing is created without conflict, Captain. The Civil War created a greater country, like the Revolution before it. There's a dark side to everything. We can't get rid of it. Maybe we shouldn't try. What we need is a balance."

"Where is the body?"

Adrian hesitated, then led Darian behind the house to the burning barn. He pointed at Cramer's covered body, but Darian's attention wavered to the ground nearby. "What's that?"

Adrian saw what the captain was looking at and cringed. "I threw up."

He expected a well-aimed taunt at his expense, but a gentle smile grew on Darian's face. "You have never seen a man die before?"

"No."

"I did the same during my first battle." Adrian met Darian's even gaze, and saw understanding. Even sympathy. "We handled the sight better than some, you and I. The man beside me fainted."

Darian knelt beside Cramer's body and removed the cover. He examined the arrows, then the scalp wound. Adrian forced himself to maintain the same clinical expression, but it wasn't easy. "My warrior says these arrows were stolen. He says they come from several different tribes."

"I see that."

Darian Woodward was still annoying. "We checked the house, and nothing appears stolen—except by Cora."

Darian glanced over his shoulder. "Miss Talmadge stole something? I can't believe that."

"She took a picture of Cramer's wife for Archie."

"She is a dear woman, with a kind and sensitive heart."

"It looks like someone went through Cramer's papers, though."

Darian stood up and surveyed the destruction. "What could a man like Cramer have for papers? I am surprised he even wrote."

"I thought of that, too."

Darian gestured at the smoldering remains of the barn. "This was done for no purpose. To attract attention, perhaps. It was done before Cramer was killed. See, his face is charred as if he came too close to the fire in its first blaze. It was done before dawn, to draw him from the house, so that he was easily killed. He is wearing his nightshirt."

"Why would they want him outside?"

"If they'd broken in, he might have shot them. He has a rifle, see." Darian edged the body aside. Cramer's old rifle lay beneath.

"I see." Adrian paused, not liking Darian's superior analytical abilities. "So?"

"They didn't want to shoot him in his bed. They wanted this to look like an Indian massacre. Also, we found two loose horses grazing north of here. They weren't stolen. Your people never make such an oversight."

Adrian frowned. "My people make use of what circumstances they can find."

"That is called 'theft.' " Darian paused. "Did the boy see anything?"

"Just men."

"I didn't think this was done by a pack of wolves."

Adrian's fingers twitched. "The boy hid in the well, but they were apparently looking for him."

"Not thoroughly, or they would have found him. No, they wanted Cramer dead. But why?"

"Tradman had association with him, and they weren't friendly. Maybe Cramer knew something threatening."

"I don't admire the ranger, though he is often a guest at the fort. His reputation is shady, but I doubt he'd be threatened by anything Cramer could know. It's too easy for him to slip away, to evade capture or responsibility. He has nothing to lose."

"Could he have done it to protect someone else?"

Darian didn't answer at once, but his youthful face hardened. "Yes."

"Well? Who?"

Darian glanced back at his soldiers, then Adrian's men. "Go back to your village. Keep hidden. Whatever I suspect, it will do you no good. My men have seen what's happened here, and I can't keep it from being reported. You will be suspected. You didn't make a particularly good impression on General Davis."

"Oh, really? Well, he didn't make a great impression on me, either."

Darian sighed. "You are so arrogant. There's only one thing General Davis hates more than an Indian, and that's an educated Indian. He wants a full brigade at the fort—he's been pressing Tucson for months. He wants a battle."

Darian's voice trailed, his brow furrowed. "Some men, they like war. The general is one such. His glory was in war. But he fought in the West, in Kansas, where no leader restrained his men on either side. The tales I have heard are grim indeed. I believe he has become like a man who drinks liquor and can't stop."

"You mean he's addicted? To war?"

"Perhaps. We have disagreed on much since I arrived at my post. He was ready to demand forces to avenge my capture."

"I set you free!"

"As I told him. I sent a private message to Tucson, and the forces were denied." Darian looked back at Cramer's body and sighed. "For this, I do not know. Many people are moving west because of the gold and silver mines. They will need protection."

"Then my people need protection, also."

Darian held Adrian's gaze for a long while, then nodded. "Yes. I believe they do."

"I ain't playing with no girl." Archibald stood stubbornly in the center of the Apache village, glaring at Laurencita's daughter.

Since Adrian had brought the boy to the village, he had refused to play with the other children, though Cora noticed he had eaten a large, filling meal. Adrian's people accepted him at once, and Haastin appeared to have adopted him, but Archibald wasn't impressed. Cora suspected he would run away at the first opportunity.

The little girl made a face, picked up a handful of dirt, and flung it at Archie's head.

Cora winced as Archie's face flamed with red fury. "You're gonna die, little girl!" He hurled himself toward the girl and flipped her onto her back.

"Stop that! Archie!"

Laurencita placed her calm hand on Cora's shoulder. "Watch."

The little girl made a quick move with her legs, braced her feet on her attacker, and hurtled him backwards. Archie was stunned. He hesitated before going after her again. "Real girls don't fight."

The little girl made a fist, spoke something in Apache which sounded distinctly threatening, then took a menacing step toward the boy. Archie paled. "You ain't real!"

279

The children dashed off, Laurencita's daughter in determined pursuit. "Haozinne is strong and fast."

Cora sighed happily as the children raced behind the huts. "Isn't she? Oh, dear, I think she's caught him. . . . "

Wild screams indicated the truth of Cora's assessment. Adrian joined her. "What's going on? He isn't hurting that little girl, is he?"

Archie let out a blood-curdling yelp, then raced from behind the boulder. His shirt was torn, and his eyes were wide with terror. "Help! She's after me!"

Haozinne crept like a small panther from boulder to boulder, drawing ever closer. Archie stumbled toward Adrian and hid behind his legs. Adrian's brow elevated. "Whatever's after you must be really bad if you've come to me for help."

Archie nodded. "The worst."

The little girl slipped soundlessly up behind him, tapped his shoulder, and affected a dangerous leer. Archie screamed at the top of his lungs and tried to crawl up Adrian. Adrian laughed and picked him up. "You'd better get used to it, kid. Women are devils."

Cora kissed his shoulder. "And don't you forget it."

Laurencita spoke quietly to her daughter in Apache. The little girl's face furrowed, but she nodded, mumbled a few words, then backed away. "She says she won't chase you anymore today, Archibald. I have made you a bed in our hut, and Haozinne will show you where we get water—"

"Not for washing, ma'am?" Archie sounded horrified at the thought.

"No washing. Little boys don't need to wash."

Archie breathed a long sigh of relief, then slid from Adrian's arms. "Good! My pa had me washing two times a year!"

Laurencita's brow knit in sympathy. "That is too much here."

"Too much anywhere!" Archie eyed Haozinne suspiciously, but followed her to a small hut and they disappeared inside.

Cora observed Laurencita's mothering skills with approval. "Are you really only going to make him wash once a year?"

"Only once. But he will go splashing in the river with the other children. He will be cleaner than his worst fears."

Something crashed in the hut. Laurencita sighed, then went after the children. Cora stood with Adrian, feeling at home and at peace. "I want to be a mother."

He took her hand, but he said nothing. Cora studied his face. "You look worried. Didn't Captain Woodward believe you?"

"He did, but he doesn't have much authority at the fort. He implied that the general has built up a vendetta against me. The man's itching for battle."

"Why?"

"I don't know. The captain seems to feel the man is suffering pangs of loss for the Civil War, but I suspect there's more to it than that. He's got something to gain by driving my people off. He's the type who wants control. If someone comes along who can speak for the native people of this land, it's a threat to him."

"You."

"Me."

"That means he'll want to get rid of you."

"So he can annihilate my people without angering the commanders in Tucson, yes."

Cora chewed her lip. "I guess that means you have to stick around long enough to assure their safety. That's all right, Adrian. I'm in no hurry to get back."

His expression looked a little strange, almost guilty, but he didn't comment. Cora ran her hand along his arm. "Do you have any idea what to do?"

"No. I've sent Haastin with a group as scouts. I'm riding out with another this afternoon. My father is prepared to move the village at a moment's notice. We'll be all right, Cora. For now."

Adrian gazed down into her eyes. He looked sad and tired. Cora took his hand. "Maybe you should rest first."

"I can't." Adrian touched her cheek. "I'm sorry I got you into this, Cora. It was fun, but it was selfish. I don't want you in danger."

Haastin rode into the campsite, preventing Cora's response. He jumped off his horse and ran to Adrian. They spoke in Apache, but Cora knew from Adrian's expression that soldiers had been spotted nearby.

Adrian issued an order, and Haastin called for more warriors. The camp burst into purposeful action. Cora seized Adrian's arm. "What happened?"

"The whole damned cavalry is moving toward the desert. We're heading to higher ground up in Cave Creek, where we've got a better defense."

"Why? They don't know their way here."

"No, but the honorable Captain Woodward would feel bound to disclose this site."

Cora couldn't argue, but her heart labored in disappointment. "I'm sorry to leave. I was getting used to the place." She sighed. "Home."

The villagers tore down the grass huts with speed and precision. Cora helped, and even Archie carried a pack of dried food. He and Haozinne had made some kind of truce, and shared the burden of a large basket between them. Toklanni deposited two bags of honey into Cora's care, attached a strap to Cora's head which supported a canvas of firewood, and slapped her shoulder.

Cora didn't argue, but when Adrian walked by, she cast him her most forlorn glance. He wore a pack—his parachute pack. Hers dangled from his side. He hadn't given up the hope of returning, apparently. The sight settled Cora's jumbled nerves, and she resumed her duties.

Cora found her treasure basket, and debated whether to bury it here, or take it with her. Toklanni added more wood to her log carrier, and Cora relented. She looked around for a site that looked identifiable and permanent. She went to the bottom of the cliff, found a square-shaped boulder, and removed her firewood carrier.

She dug as fast as she could and both Archie and Haozinne joined a hand. "It looks deep enough, miss. What are you burying?"

Cora pointed at her basket. "These are things people here have given me. There's a few small baskets, some dolls, and the costume Adrian wore at a party. Also, some necklaces and bracelets that Toklanni gave me. And a really sexy . . . um, *pretty*, dress."

Cora lowered her basket into the ground and covered it with sand. "Very good!" She clapped her hands, then eyed the marking boulder. She found a small rock and began engraving her name for future reference.

Cora ran her finger over her name. "I wonder if I can get my name legally changed?" She shook her head, banishing the thought. "I guess not. It wouldn't work on checks."

The village moved at nightfall. The men rode, and the women walked, carrying what Cora felt sure were the heavier burdens. Adrian rode off with a group of scouts, so she couldn't enlist his aid in escaping her chores.

They walked silently north for hours, deep into the night. They walked up ravines, and around boulders, then down onto the flat desert. Cora nearly bumped into a giant saguaro before realizing the possible consequences. Just before dawn, they reached an area of massive rocks and boulders. Silhouetted against the clear night sky, they looked like a giant's playground.

They made their way up and through the rocks, still progressing north around what Adrian called Black Mountain. The trek became a hardship by dawn as they squeezed through narrow passages and crossed gorges by makeshift bridges.

Cora's firewood got stuck in a small passage. It took two warriors and Toklanni to wedge her through. She was too tired to care. She just hung there, suspended by firewood, waiting as they tugged and shoved to extract her. She came loose with a pop, and crumpled to her knees. The others walked on.

Cora sighed miserably, got up, and followed. When the sun rose, she found they were in a small clearing between massive boulders, high above the desert. She spotted the tall, golden century plants and spreading prickly pears, and felt curiously at home. "What a nice spot!"

She was the first person to speak above a whisper since they left. Laurencita eyed her doubtfully. "The walk was long, and far from the desert."

Cora looked around. Her face lit when she spotted a stream racing over a rock. "Look! A little waterfall!"

"Water is nearby, that is true. But there is much walking to gather food."

"Is there? A shame." Cora deflated somewhat, but the scenery still kept her interested as they began to assemble the grass huts and campsite. A hare hopped out into the midst of the villagers, panicked, and darted away. "There's another one! Aren't they cute? If I lived here, I'd make a nice desert garden so all these animals would come by. Look at those little fat birds!"

Adrian rode into the campsite, stopped his tired horse, and stared. Cora waved happily. "What do you think? Amazing, isn't it?"

"Cora, soldiers are hunting all over the desert. If they find this camp—"

"They won't find us here. Laurencita says your people have used this place for generations, and it's never been discovered. We're safe."

"For how long? General Davis is fixated on destroying my people. Apparently, Darian's word—"

"*Darian's word?* You're calling him 'Darian' now?"

Adrian's eyes formed dark slits. "What of it?"

"Oh, nothing. Go on."

"Davis wants us gone. I've placed you in danger, Cora."

"You've placed yourself in danger, true, but you did what you had to do. I'm proud of you, Adrian. I think your father is, too."

Adrian bowed his head. "Cora, we need to talk."

Something in his voice convinced her talking wasn't in her best interest. "Well, just now I'm supposed to be helping Toklanni make a meal. Something with mescal. And hare, I'm afraid. I couldn't stop them. But you know, they hunt hare with rifles, Adrian. I thought you should know, so you don't make a fool of yourself going after one with that knife."

"I guess our conversation can wait. I must return to the scouts. Since you're safe—"

"I'm fine. We're all fine. Even Archie and Haozinne are getting along." Cora paused. "All right, she tripped him once on purpose and he pulled her hair. But other than that, everyone's getting on fine. When are you going to sleep?"

"Later."

Haastin and several warriors rode into the clearing. They spoke to Adrian, and he relaxed. Cora tapped his knee. "What did they say?"

"The soldiers have withdrawn, for now. They found our old campsite, but apparently, they don't have a tracker capable of following us here. They've left a few scouts, but it's my guess they'll send for reinforcements before searching out these hills."

"You think they'll persist? Why?"

"I don't know. Just a feeling."

"Captain Woodward will reason with them, I'm sure."

"Oh, are you? You have a great deal of faith in him."

"Jealous."

Adrian started to object, then stopped. "Maybe I am, Cora. Maybe when I see you with him, I see you with the kind of man you need. The kind of man I can never be."

Adrian didn't wait for her response. He turned his horse and rode from the village, leaving her stunned by his words. She'd spent years thinking she wasn't right for him, that some other woman would make him a better wife. Now Adrian was doing the same thing. It didn't make sense. Or maybe she'd been so caught up in her own fears that she never noticed his.

Adrian returned to the new campsite at nightfall. His muscles ached, his head pounded. Not only from weariness, but from the full knowledge of what he had done. He'd brought the woman he loved into the past, and into disaster.

He stopped outside the camp and watched his people. Cora tossed a makeshift ball to Archie, then to Laurencita's daughter. The little girl pelted Archie with the ball, but he caught it and tossed it gently to Cora. Adrian's heart felt swollen with love. She adjusted to whatever circumstances she found herself in, and made the best of it.

I love you so.

Adrian dismounted and went to tether his black-and-white horse. Tiotonawen joined him, and stood silently, head bowed. *My father*. He hadn't expected the hurt he'd felt at Tiotonawen's rejection, but it lingered as a dull ache. He realized he'd never disappointed anyone before. Now he had alienated the father he barely knew. If Cora knew the truth, he'd lose her, too.

Adrian braced for criticism, but Tiotonawen didn't seem angry. "You have proven yourself leader today, my son. You have buried your failure with the white officer."

Adrian eyed him as if he were joking. "I've led us into disaster."

Tiotonawen lay his hand on Adrian's shoulder, a fatherly comfort. "You were right to set the boy officer free. Now, he is your friend. Now, he will speak for you."

"If they listen. He isn't in command, Father."

"Maybe he will be. Then the Tonto Apache will have a friend, too."

"Right now, we've got an enemy. Maybe more than one."

"This is why we hide. This is why our scouts watch the land."

Haastin rode into the clearing with several warriors. They led a man on a horse, with a sack over his head. Adrian eyed his father doubtfully. "We have a prisoner?"

287

"Not at all!" The man struggled beneath his mask, and Haastin reached to pull it off, revealing the youthful face of Darian Woodward.

Adrian groaned. "Just how many times will I have to save you?"

Darian swung his leg forward over the horse's neck and hopped down. "Incorrect dismount." Adrian checked to see if Cora noticed. She waved happily at the captain, and he doffed his cap.

Darian turned back-to, revealing bound hands. "Didn't have a choice."

"What in hell are you doing here?" Adrian asked, untying him.

"I surrendered myself to your men." Darian gestured at Haastin. "I recognized him from Cramer's farm. I assumed he wouldn't kill me because of our earlier meeting."

Darian looked around the campsite. "Well done! We'd be hard-pressed to get through here, in our current condition."

"Did you come to assess the enemy, or do you have something to say?"

"Both!" Darian looked cheerful. Adrian considered strangling him. "I also have something to give you." He removed a pack from his saddle and gave it to Adrian.

Adrian examined the contents. "My jeans! Great!"

"Their fit is too tight around the hips, even on myself, and I am thinner than you—although, of course, I am taller." Darian waited for Adrian to glare before continuing. "It is indecent for a male to wear such garments."

Adrian folded his jeans carefully. "I'm assuming you had a more pressing reason for angling your way up here."

"I don't like the way things are going at the fort. The general nearly demoted me for not instigating battle against you. I reported that my findings indicated a deliberate mur-

288

der, not an Indian massacre, but it affected his judgment very little."

"So now what?"

Darian met Adrian's gaze. "The general has ordered troops from Tucson. I believe this time he will get them. Even so, we might not penetrate this hold, but you would be effectively sieged. That would mean starvation and eventual death to your people."

"I know what it means."

"You are a stubborn man. Be that as it may, I am here to warn you."

"Why?"

"Because I am an honorable man. I do not believe you killed Cramer. I have reason to believe Cramer's death was linked to the death of our officer."

"The officer who was transferring here?"

"Yes. He stopped at Cramer's farm just before he was murdered. Tradman was there, also."

"I told you—Tradman is responsible."

"He may well be the killer, but he is not acting for himself. Until I learn more, your people are in grave danger."

Adrian looked the young officer in the eye. Beneath the layers of honor and dignity, he saw a crafty mind. "You suspect General Davis is behind this, don't you?"

Good. He'd finally one-upped the little fiend. Darian's mouth dropped in a satisfying display of shock. "The soldiers at the fort are loyal to me. They won't fight unless I give the order. But if General Davis brings in troops from Tucson, the matter will be out of my hands."

Adrian smiled and shook his head. "You don't look like a mutineer, Captain."

"Don't I?" Darian angled his brow. "How little you know me!"

Adrian grinned. "How little I want to!"

"I am likewise uninterested in your fate. The fate of your people, however, is important to me. There are families here. Women and children. Miss Talmadge."

"Cora will be safe. Even if you don't see her again, know she is safe."

"How?" Darian held up his hand, probably suspecting Adrian's answer would involve the future. "I don't want to know. I will trust you in this, so it's best I don't hear your implausible answer."

"Can't you warn the commanders in Tucson about your suspicions?"

"I can, but I have no proof. The commander fought along-side Davis early in the war. He won't find the general's betrayal easy to believe. General Davis has convinced them that you are a threat, that you are the new leader of the Tonto Apache, and that you came to our fort for the purpose of learning our positions and weaponry. Cramer's death will be used as evidence of your aggression and threat to the stability of this area."

"How long do we have?"

"It will take a while for the messengers to reach Tucson. Longer for them to assemble troops."

Adrian turned to his father. "We could move again."

"Where to, my son? Wherever we go, we will end up facing the same enemy."

Darian nodded. "He's right. You won't move unseen now. There are too many scouts."

"Then we stay." Adrian clenched his fist. "Trapped."

Tiotonawen picked up a stick and drew a shape in the dirt. A whirlwind. "You are not trapped. Not then, not now."

Adrian studied the shape and closed his eyes. He could escape. He could take Cora with him, and trust what they'd found together here in the past would last. He looked around at his people, even Darian. "I can't leave. I survived for a purpose, Father. That purpose has come."

Not the purpose he hoped, of winning Cora, of making her his. But of sacrifice, of defending his people against a new threat. He watched Cora as she lectured Laurencita's daughter for hitting Archie. Maybe her trip into the past had helped her, after all. She was stronger than she had been, her confidence had blossomed. She would find a life without him. But without her, there was no reason to endure.

Darian didn't question Tiotonawen's cryptic remarks. "A man does not run. But he is only trapped by what he holds in his mind. It may be that you and I won't meet again, but I wish you well . . . Adrian." Darian held out his hand.

Adrian looked from the officer's hand to his face, and saw a friend. He took his hand and shook it. "Good luck, Captain Woodward."

The two men faced each other silently. Then Darian mounted his gray horse, doffed his cap again to Cora and Toklanni and rode away alone.

Chapter Eleven

"Cora, we need to talk."

Cora opened her eyes and saw Adrian standing over her. It looked like morning, with a pale golden light inching its way into the clearing. She hadn't slept in a hut because she was waiting for him to return. He looked rested, but he hadn't slept with her. "Good morning, Adrian. Are you all right?"

"No. Yes. No. We need to talk."

She yawned and stretched, then got up. She was still wearing her chinos, but morning in the hills was surprisingly cool, so she added her new leather vest. "I'm ready. What do you want to talk about?"

He looked hesitant. "Not here."

Cora eyed the campsite, then spotted the little stream. "Maybe we can go for a walk along the river. You took me for a walk along a river on our first date, do you remember?"

He didn't meet her eyes. He seemed sad, as if facing something he didn't want to face. "I remember."

"You held my hand and I was afraid my palms were sweaty from nervousness."

A far-off smile crossed his face. "You were wearing gloves, angel. It was snowing."

"My hands were really nervous."

Adrian led her from the village. He watched his feet as he walked. His hair fell forward like a dark veil. The stream rushed past them, birds chirped, and a hare hopped into their path. Cora beamed and pointed, but Adrian didn't seem to notice.

Cora squeezed her fingers around his. "What's bothering you, Adrian?"

He stopped beneath a steep slope and leaned back against it, facing her. The expression in his dark eyes chilled her blood. "Do you know how much I've loved being with you again? When I'm with you, I'm seeing everything like it's the first time."

"You're in the past, Adrian. You *are* seeing everything for the first time. But I know what you mean. Every moment is special, every day has meaning."

"Because we're together?"

"Why else?"

"I'm not sure." He tilted his head back and drew a long breath. "Maybe I had no right. . . . I do love you, Cora. Never forget that."

Cora took his hand. "I won't have to forget. I'm here with you."

"What have I done to you?"

Cora started to answer, but he held up his hand to stop her. "We'll talk later. I need time to think. Go back to the village, Cora. I need time."

Cora watched as he turned from the path and climbed the slope. All those years of rock-climbing had paid off. He moved like a handsome, dark-haired and well-muscled spider. He scaled the first boulder, then ascended the next until he disappeared from her view.

The egg cracked, and left a vulnerable man, a man she loved. A man who could be hurt by the least likely person imaginable—herself. He was afraid. The way she so often had been herself. He asked her to talk, then took off without her. His actions seemed familiar. He was behaving like . . . her.

Cora eyed the path he'd taken. It looked sheer. Sheerer than anything she'd tried to climb before. The last time she tried something similar, she rolled to the bottom of a cliff and twisted her ankle. Cora patted the cliff wall, testing it. It wasn't totally sheer. There were little nooks and crannies where toes and fingers could hook. Assuming she didn't look down at any time—the mistake she made in her first attempt.

Adrian had gone up. She wanted to be with him. He was up on the top of the mountain, and there was only one way to reach him. Cora stuck her fingers in a cranny, hoisted herself up, and started to climb.

Climbing was harder than rafting. Cora felt sure of it. Her fingers dug into a narrow crevice and her knee ached from banging against the rock wall. *This is hell*.

She leaned her forehead against the rock, looked up to see the top about ten feet higher, then resumed her effort. She reached the top and discovered a flat plateau led to another collection of huge boulders. Adrian sat on the very top, looking out across the desert. The dry wind tousled his dark hair, a haunting and exquisite image.

Cora drew a long breath and proceeded across the plateau. She reached the fat rocks, picked her way through the first ones, then aimed to scale the last. Naturally, the rock Adrian chose for a seat was the sheerest. She made it half way up. She spotted another nook, aimed for it, and caught it. Just enough space for both hands to grip solidly.

Cora released her feet and swung over. Unfortunately, there was no foothold beneath her spot.

I could call him. He'd help me. Oh, hell! Cora's legs dangled while she fought surrender. She felt sure her arms were turning blue and stretching into long, thin lines. *That will be attractive. I'll reach the top and look like a chimp.*

Her arms weren't strong enough to hoist her body up, but her knees provided enough leverage so she could bring her right knee up to her hand position. With a grunt, Cora propelled herself up and over the top. She fell flat beside Adrian, gasping and uttering small moans.

He looked down. She looked up. She cleared her throat, smiled, and got up. His mouth was open, his brows were elevated in an expression of perpetual surprise. Cora dusted off her chinos, then sat down beside him. "Hi."

"How did you get here?"

"I flew up." She elbowed him gently. "What do you think? I rock-climbed. You taught me."

He gaped at her as if he'd never seen her before. "I'm sorry, angel."

"Why? I did pretty well. True, the last bit was hairy, but I'm here. Okay, so my arrival wasn't exactly spectacular——"

Adrian bowed his head and stared at his hands. "I'm sorry I brought you here, sorry about everything."

Her stomach tightened, her skin felt cold. "Why?" Maybe he didn't want her, after all. Maybe it had been the memory of an old romance he clung to. Maybe what he called love had been infatuation. All Cora's fears flooded to the surface. She went tense, blocking life, blocking hope.

She closed her eyes tight and knew she was trying to protect herself by blocking what she longed for. At nineteen, that fear had determined her fate. Not now. *I want you.* Cora opened her eyes and looked at him carefully.

"What are you afraid of?"

The dry wind ruffled his hair, the golden sun warmed his dark skin. He was beautiful, a sensual young warrior from a time apart. But for all the things that separated them, for all their differences, they were the same. "Adrian?"

He drew a long, weary breath. "It's all been a lie, Cora."

"What?"

"Everything. I brought you here with the intention of capturing you."

Cora's mouth slid slowly open. "You *meant* to skydive us into the past?"

"No. That part was an accident. But once I realized where we were, I decided you'd be mine whether you wanted to or not. Don't you understand, Cora? I knew from the moment we joined Haastin and his men that he wasn't taking us to Phoenix."

"Well, he couldn't could he? There is no Phoenix."

"No, but there will be."

"Adrian, you've had a rough time—"

"You can go back, Cora."

She hesitated. "Back where?"

"Home. To the future, to the world you knew. To Manhattan, if that's what you want. I told you that you couldn't go back. I lied. The whirlwind answers my father's command. It can answer mine, too. I could have sent you back at any time."

"I know that."

His eyes sparkled in surprise. "You knew?"

"It only makes sense, Adrian. If you can go back, you can go forward."

"You've known all along that I was lying?"

"I wouldn't call it lying, exactly. I assumed you'd tell me when you were ready."

Adrian's lips twitched into a frown. "I wasn't going to tell you at all."

"You just did."

"Semantics, Cora. I took you captive."

"Yes, and I was very flattered that you wanted to."

"I've gotten you in trouble, endangered your life, and—"

"You've vastly improved my sex life."

He blushed. Cora warmed with affection.

"This is serious, woman. We're about to be under attack by the cavalry."

"Exciting, isn't it? I don't think Captain Woodward will let them hurt us, though."

Adrian stared into her eyes, long and hard. Cora waited. "If you weren't mine already, would you want him?"

"Darian?"

"Yes, *Darian.*"

"Adrian! Of course not! True, he's cute, but he's not my type. I don't think I'm his, either. He'd be better with someone like Jenny."

"Jenny? The woman with the 'WARNING—I DON'T BRAKE FOR CONSERVATIVES' on her bumper?"

"Exactly. They'd be perfect together."

"I will never understand the way you think." He shook his head, then sighed. "You can go back, Cora. I've got your parachute."

"I'm not going back without you."

"You may have to, angel. If the soldiers decide to attack, it is my duty to defend my people."

"You don't have to do anything. You can come with me, and we'll go back to where we belong."

"I can't go back now. I can't leave my people this way."

"Then I'll stay with you."

Adrian fell silent as the dry wind echoed from the distant desert. Cora gazed across the plain and saw swirling sand. "Whirlwinds."

"They lie within the bowl of the Great Spirit, waiting to be summoned. My power comes from that wind."

"That's the part of sex I like best—when you're spinning inside, faster and faster. . . . " Cora stopped and cleared her throat. Adrian smiled.

"I brought you here to change what went wrong between us. But I can't. The sex is great—it was great then." He paused. "Maybe it's better now because you've turned into Temptress Woman, but we always had passion. Don't you see? Nothing has changed."

She didn't like his words, but she refused to panic. "Nothing has changed? *Nothing has changed*? Adrian, we're in the past. I never thought I'd see you again, and here we are, lovers. You've befriended a Civil War soldier who has a crush on me, I've seduced a masked dancer, you've infuriated the entire cavalry of the United States Armed Forces, and—" Cora's voice grew high and shrill, echoing from the mountaintop across the desert. "And I've just climbed a mountain that's as flat as glass! I'd say a few things have changed!"

Adrian smiled, but tears filled his beautiful eyes. The morning sun deepened gold and glistened on his dark skin. "I had no right to keep you this way. No right to force you. I

Free Falling

love you so much, Cora, but look what I've done to you. I've
hauled you back into the past, and now I have to leave you."

"What do you mean, leave me?"

He stood up and touched her face. "I don't have a choice,
Cora. These are my people. If I don't act, they'll die. You and
I, we were a sweet dream. You were the gift to my life. But
you don't belong to me. We don't even belong in the same
time. I was sent forward to evade death, so I could return and
save my people when the time came. You were caught in the
winds of something that was never meant to be."

Cora rose slowly to her feet. He caught her face in his
hands and pressed his lips against her forehead. She tilted
her face up, and he kissed her mouth. She tasted his tears
mingled with her own.

Adrian drew away from her. "I love you, Cora, but we
come from different worlds. We don't belong together. I
have to stay here and fight. You must go forward, and live."

She wanted to argue, to make him see reason, but with
each word, her spirit crumbled. He was really ending their
love affair, once and for all. Because they weren't "right" for
each other. Weren't those the same words she wrote to him
in Kathmandu?

"I'll get your chute ready, and learn from my father how
the transition is performed. It shouldn't take long. You'll be
gone before the cavalry attacks." Tears glistened on his high
cheekbones, but he didn't relent. "I'm sorry." He turned
away and climbed down the mountainside without her.

Cora stood alone, stunned beyond words, beyond tears.
Her heart beat in slow, even pulses, her breath came deep.
The dry wind filtered through her hair, lifting it and tossing
it behind her head as she stared out over the desert.

High above the hills, a hawk circled. A fat, brown rabbit

hopped innocently across the plateau beneath Cora's position, and the hawk circled closer. "No!" It was too late. The hawk dove and seized the rabbit in its talons, then lifted.

The rabbit twisted violently. Cora had thought rabbits always froze, but not this one. It pitched and fought for its life. Cora's eyes filled with tears. *Helpless, but still fighting, still wanting life.* The hawk's balance shifted as it struggled to keep its prey. The rabbit squirmed again, and the hawk dropped it. It circled vengefully, then flew away.

Cora watched the rabbit as it first scrunched itself, then looked around. It hopped with a limp, but it kept going.

Wild fury erupted from Cora, like fire from a deep well. It surged to the surface with such sudden, overpowering force that she shook all over. *How can you leave me? You know how much I love you! You said you loved me! How can you leave?*

Her hands trembled with anger. She seized her bear fetish pendant and ripped it from her neck. She held it up to the sun, drew her arm back, and prepared to fling it as far as it would go.

Just as he had done nine years before.

Adrian!

Her hand dropped to her side. Her fingers wrapped tightly around her pendant. Adrian had stood alone on a snowy, frozen mountain. She stood beneath the sun and tied the pendant back around her neck. "I will never, never ever let you go."

Cora sank back to the rock. The golden sun gleamed on the rocks and the sprawling prickly pears. Tall century plants swayed in the breeze. Cora tilted her face upward, then she remembered her lack of sunscreen. But for one moment, she couldn't hide her face. The sun warmed her soul, and she found herself looking into its core.

All my life, I have been afraid. Of what this world will do to me, of what I can't have. I've been afraid it will burn me and destroy me, so I've missed all the ways it nourishes what I am.

It seemed so simple. She stared directly into the sun, something she'd never done in her life. *"Stare at the sun, and you'll go blind, Cora." "If you stay out too long, you'll get wrinkles, get cancer, and die."*

She didn't go blind. Her skin didn't burn. She was lost in time amidst an Apache camp, surrounded by cavalry, and she wasn't afraid. Didn't even think of it.

"I've missed so much, all because I was afraid."

With a shocking certainty, Cora understood the true nature of power—the ability to gather what's inside you, and use it to create the life you want.

Adrian had power—he used it to connect himself to his world, and to share it with those around him. And suddenly Cora knew—her power had been there all along.

Cora rose up from the rock, and her blood flowed with power. *I've wanted Adrian de Vargas from the moment I first saw him. I thought I couldn't keep him because he was so much stronger than I am. But I was wrong.* Cora looked down from the mountaintop and saw the village below. *Maybe it's time I show him just how powerful I am.*

By the time Cora descended the mountain, Adrian had ridden out to join the scouts. The delay didn't bother her. She assisted Toklanni finding a new beehive to squeeze. She helped prepare the evening meal of mescal and roots. She sent Archie and Haozinne to collect berries, and helped Laurencita find bark strips for basket-making.

When the sun lowered beyond the highest rocks, she went for a walk alone. She followed the river toward its source, and found what she was looking for. A slender waterfall splashed into a round pool, then sped downhill. Satisfied, Cora turned around and went back to the village.

Adrian wasn't back yet, but the first scouts were returning for the night, while another group took their places. Cora positioned herself in the middle of the village. She motioned to Laurencita who came to stand beside her.

"I have an announcement to make. Since a lot of your people still don't have a firm command of English, I hoped you'd translate for me."

Laurencita nodded. "I will." She called to the villagers in Apache, and they gathered around.

Cora cleared her throat. "As you all may know, I am Adrian's woman." She paused and glanced at Laurencita. "Feel free to use his Apache name in translation."

Laurencita repeated her phrase in Apache, then waited for Cora to continue.

"When I first knew him, he was perfect. He's basically cracked like an egg since we came here, but if possible, I love him now even more than I did."

Laurencita hesitated. "I'm not certain how to translate the part about the egg."

"Paraphrase."

Laurencita issued a long, seemingly complicated explanation, then stopped. "Go on."

"Right. I'll be going for a walk along the river in a few minutes. When Adrian arrives, I'd appreciate it if you'd tell him where I've gone, and tell him I have an important message for him."

Cora waited while Laurencita translated. The men looked confused, but Toklanni's face lit in a broad smile of approval. *Women. The most logical beings in the world.*

302

"Now, I want to make it clear that absolutely no one besides Adrian is to follow. Is that understood?"

Laurencita chuckled, then repeated Cora's comments. "They understand."

"Good. I shall be on my way, then. Thank you all for your time. I appreciate your help in this delicate matter."

Laurencita said two brief words which Cora hoped meant "thank you." The Apache looked pleased, and even Tiotonawen nodded his approval. He approached her as she made her way from the campsite. "Talks Much Who Fights Bees, you have grown."

Cora smiled, confidence flowing in her veins. This time, she wasn't afraid of its force. "No, Whirlwind. I have not. I've just seen how big I really am."

Everyone but Cora seemed to be awaiting Adrian's return. He rode into the village and dismounted. A girl hurried to take his horse, and another ripped off his saddle. The women of the village watched him eagerly, as if expecting something. He wasn't in the mood for conversation tonight.

He looked around for Cora, but she wasn't there. Maybe she was angry or hurt. Probably both. Maybe she didn't want to see him again until it was time to leave. His heart fell and he walked through the village to his makeshift hut.

The villagers gathered around, and Laurencita called to him. A cold, sick fear flooded his senses. Cora wasn't there. If something had happened to her . . . "Cora. Where is she?"

Laurencita patted his arm in a motherly fashion. "Your wife has gone along the river. We think you should go after her."

Adrian relaxed, though the term "your wife" cut into him like a sharp knife. "The river?"

303

Tiotonawen shoved his way through the crowd and took position beside Laurencita. "My son is slow to act. When a coyote is slow to attack, another may steal his prey."

"What are you talking about?"

"Your woman has gone walking. You should follow."

Adrian hesitated. He wanted to talk to her, yet if she tried to change his mind, he might still waver and succumb. If she cried, if she begged, He wouldn't stand a chance. "She'll be all right. I'll see her later."

"She will be well." Tiotonawen nodded thoughtfully, though Laurencita appeared disappointed. "She will be well, because the pale-haired boy captain is with her."

"*What?*" Adrian spoke in unison with Laurencita, who coughed, then cleared her throat.

"Your father speaks true. Captain Woodward came back and took Cora for a walk."

Tiotonawen fingered his pipe. "He had offer to make. Alone."

"I think they went to the waterfall." The way Laurencita said "waterfall" incited Adrian's suspicions.

"What waterfall?"

Toklanni joined Tiotonawen and nodded. The waterfall is a place of mating where my husband first walked me when he meant to lay with me."

Laurencita tapped her lip. "Do you think Captain Woodward knows what happens when a man meets a woman beneath a waterfall?"

Sex. Mindless, passionate, ravaging sex. Adrian's thoughts formed a fiery blur. The little twerp might be a virgin, but he would learn fast. Cora was hurt. It was like the blond fiend to take advantage of her confusion. Sneaking back to the village . . . Darian Woodward knew exactly what he was doing.

Adrian seized a rifle from Haastin's hands, wondered briefly why the warrior was grinning, then took out his jagged knife in case he couldn't get a clear shot. He didn't wait. He ran along the river, leaping the boulders and rocks that hindered his way. His lungs burned with fire as he sped from the village.

Something reached his ears as he ran. Soft, muted laughter. It came from the village. Adrian didn't slow his pace. The little worm had been after Cora since he first laid eyes on her. Virgin! Hell! Probably a story he always used in seduction. He'd probably had more women than a sheik.

The river was long, with twists and unexpected turns. Of course, Darian would take her far from the village lest Adrian's people guess his intentions. If he was too late . . . No, Cora would cry first. Darian would comfort her, maybe cradle her head on his shoulder while she wept. He would stroke her soft, wavy hair. His hands would wander down her back.

If the rat was as experienced as Adrian imagined, he'd have her shirt off in seconds. He ran faster, his breath came harsh as he strained for more speed. The river disappeared beneath low pines and juniper. Adrian crashed through the bushes and emerged at the end of a small, crystalline pool.

"So good of you to come."

His mouth dropped, he braced his hands on his knees and gasped. From beneath the soft spray of the waterfall, Cora Talmadge emerged. Naked. Alone. And smiling like a goddess.

He hardened instantly. She waded through the water toward him, then stopped in the pool's center. Water dripped from her long hair, over her round, firm breasts, down her stomach, down her thighs. Adrian groaned. "Oh, my. . . . Cora."

Her sensual gaze moved from his face to his overly-tight jeans, then back again. "You're glad to see me."

He was too shocked to answer, too shocked to move. Cora didn't seem to require an answer. Her hand slid sensually down her side and she dampened her lips. Slowly. He caught a quick breath and held it.

"I take it you got my message."

He swallowed. "Message? About Captain Woodward?"

Cora's brow furrowed doubtfully. "Captain Woodward? No. Why would I give you a message about him? I asked Laurencita to tell you I had a message for you."

Adrian stared. They'd tricked him. His own father had tricked him. The laughter he'd heard was his people chortling over his gullibility and quick jealousy. "Nothing. I must have been confused."

"And not for the first time." She moved a little closer, revealing her shapely calves. She looked different. The way she stood had changed. Her shoulders were straight, back in a posture of pure confidence.

He'd never seen Cora look that way before. She used to stand with her shoulders clenched slightly forward, as if protecting herself, as if afraid to open lest she expose herself to some unimagined threat.

No longer. Her new posture had the effect of making her round breasts seem fuller, larger. More . . . in evidence. Her whole body seemed to radiate feminine allure. His gaze ran up and down her body, lingering on her firm, delectable bottom. She waited as he gawked, then came out of the water to stand before him. "Do you want to touch me?"

"God! Yes!" He caught his breath and tried to control himself, but she laughed, a soft, husky woman's laugh. She took his hand and placed it over her breast so that he felt her swift heartbeat beneath his palm. She moved his hand slowly over her soft flesh, over her rosebud nipple. She shuddered at his touch, as if she would please herself with his body despite him.

"Take off your boots."

He yanked off his hiking boots and flung them aside. Cora didn't wait for the rest of his clothes. She took his hand and led him along the edge of the pool to the waterfall. He was shaking. His body felt hot as if burning inside. Desire spun inside him—like a whirlwind.

She went beneath the waterfall still holding his hand. He hesitated, and she gave a sharp tug, pulling him under, too. He wanted to hold her, to run his hands along her damp, sweet body, then plunge his aching length inside her. But Cora just tilted her beautiful face to the water and let it spray over her. Her hair rippled down her back like a warm river.

She turned into his arms and fingered the buttons of his shirt. The shirt clung to his skin and she peeled it away. She dropped it to the sparkling rocks, then fingered his belt. That came off, too. Cora sank to her knees and drew the leather strap off, over his hips. He watched her, mesmerized as she tapped one leg, then the other. He stepped out of his jeans, and she tossed them away, too.

She knelt before him, looking up, her gray eyes shining with something he recognized, yet had never seen in its fullness before. Power. The water sprayed cool on his heated flesh—he thought it might sizzle from the heat of his body.

"You have a way, Adrian de Vargas, of getting me into so much trouble."

He didn't expect her to accuse him of anything. Not now. But Cora slid her hand up his thigh to his hip, and his arguments fled.

"You send me down rivers, down mountains, out of the sky. You've sent me through time, and to the edge of war."

Brutal, but true. He couldn't deny her accusations, but they still stung.

"Do you know what I've been thinking through all of that?"

His throat felt tight. "What?"

Her devious hand slid from his hip to the base of his erection. The cold water couldn't dampen its size, nor could her words. He wanted her no matter what. "I was thinking, 'How soon?' "

"How soon? How soon what?"

"How soon will we be alone?" Her fingers played lightly on his hard flesh, teasing. "How soon will we do this again?" She trailed her finger along the underside his shaft, then circled the rim. "How soon before I can take off your clothes and look at your body, and do everything that fills my mind day after day, hour after hour?" Her hand closed snug around his shaft. She pressed her soft mouth against his swollen tip and flicked her tongue to taste him.

His knees went weak. His legs quivered. His stomach was so tight he thought he couldn't breath. "How soon can I taste you, and hold you, and have you inside me where you belong?"

"Oh . . . my. . . . "

Her lips parted and she took his tip inside her warm, wet mouth. The waterfall roared around them, spraying fiery droplets over her face as she took him deeper. He felt her tongue teasing and swirling. And all the while, her beautiful eyes stayed focused on him, watching every reaction, sparkling with female delight when he moaned and clenched his teeth to prolong the pleasure.

She mimicked love-making fiercely, lost in the moment. Her hand gripped him tight and moved in accord with her mouth. He fought against surrender, but she drove him closer and closer to heaven. His body quivered, his breath came in harsh pants, then groans of pleasure. Every muscle drew tight.

Cora released him and slid from the waterfall edge into the pool. Adrian stood stunned, his erection glistening beneath the water's spray. She emerged half-way across the pool and motioned to him with her finger. He felt sure she winked.

He wanted her. She wanted him. Passion united them. And everything had changed. Adrian dove into the water, swam beneath the clear surface, caught her around her legs and lifted her.

She wrapped her arms around his neck and kissed him with wild, sweet passion. "Someday . . . " She kissed his jawline, then his cheek. "Someday you'll have to teach me that."

"Diving?"

She nodded, then kissed his shoulder, licking the droplets, then nipping.

"I thought . . . you were afraid to dive." His voice shook. She slid down along his body, reached between them, clasped his erection and massaged it firmly.

"Not anymore."

"Cora." She looked up at him, and he kissed her mouth. "I'll teach you anything you want to learn."

"Touch me." She placed her hands on his shoulders, closed her eyes, and tipped her head back. He didn't know where to start. At the top, and work down. He placed his hands on the top of her hand, and felt her wet hair against her head. His fingers grazed her cheeks, then her neck. He ran his palms over her shoulders, down her arms. Her skin seemed vibrant beneath his touch, warm over her swift pulse.

He felt her shoulder blades and her spine, down to the small of her back, to the flare of her perfect bottom. He traced its shape, then spread his palm over her stomach, feeling her skin quiver.

She was aroused, sure of her power to inflame him. She knew what she did to him. Her fingers gripped his shoulders firmly, supporting herself as he caressed her body. He directed his touch up her sides, over her ribcage to her breasts. His heart slammed in his chest with such power that he felt dizzy.

He cupped her breasts in his hand, then bent to taste the taut peaks. She moaned softly, her breath came even and swift. She tasted of clear water, damp and feminine. He suckled gently, and she gasped. "Adrian." She caught his face in her hands and bent to kiss his mouth.

She slipped her hands from his face to his arms and wrapped her fingers around his. She moved back, drawing him with her. "Where are you taking me, woman?"

Her eyes twinkled. "You'll see."

She turned and led him from the water. Adrian tripped over the bank because he was focusing on her legs and not where he was going. She chuckled, low and throaty, a vixen's laugh, then led him along the rock path past the waterfall. She bent to pass beneath a pine bough, and Adrian nearly crumbled at the sight of her well-positioned bottom.

She cast a seductress' glance over her shoulder, lowered her eyelids meaningfully, then passed beneath the bough. She waited as he followed, then pointed to a small tent. Four sticks had been propped up at angles, supporting soft leather sheets. "Who did this?"

"I did!" Cora indicated painted symbols. A yin-yang beside a bee. The bee had flared its wings and seemed to be inviting the yin-yang closer. "Actually, Laurencita and the other women helped me with the tent part and I painted the symbols. It's kind of like a tee pee." She paused, looking thoughtful. "Your people don't seem to know much about tee pees, but I wanted one, so they helped me."

She sounded so proud. *How can I leave you*? "It's beautiful. Amazing. Where's the bed?"

Cora held back a flap and gestured inside. "It's not exactly a down-filled sleeping bag, but it's the best I could do." Adrian looked in and saw a blanket over pine boughs. In the corner was a basket decorated with yucca flowers and juniper.

He looked into her shining eyes and saw all the life he wanted. Cora, his wife. A home built together, formed with a love that wouldn't die no matter what came between them. Adrian held out his hand and she took it. He eased her into his arms, picked her up, and carried her into the tent.

He placed her on the blanket and knelt beside her. Her damp hair spread out like a halo over the blanket, rippling like the desert sand. "I love you, Cora. No matter what happens, we are part of each other."

Cora propped herself up on her elbows. Adrian felt sure she assumed the posture for the effect of her jutting breasts. He dampened his lips, but she reached to touch his face. "You and I are going to make love." She glanced at his erection. "I know, because you are very hard, and I think you'd do anything to be with me."

A low, broken moan was all he could muster. Cora appeared satisfied by his response.

"I called you here to correct an impression you have." She adjusted her legs, bending them at the knees.

"Impression?" His voice sounded strange, small and weak. He'd never sounded that way before.

Cora nodded. "You think your father tossed you forward in time. But you're wrong."

Adrian hesitated. "He is my father."

"Yes, he is. But that's not what happened. You didn't come forward in time to save yourself. You came because I called you."

Adrian smiled. "A sweet thought, but . . . "

"But nothing." Cora sat up, facing him. "You were four months old when the whirlwind took you. Four months. Doesn't that ring any bells for you, Adrian?"

"Um . . . no."

Her head tilted to one side. "You are four months older than I am. You were sent forward on the day I was born."

"I don't know the day I was sent forward."

"I do. June twenty-seventh—the day you came forward, the day you went back, and the day I was born."

"I suppose it's possible."

"You were sent forward for me. There is no question. And I will prove it."

"How?"

She wriggled around and sat on her knees. She guided him to the blanket and pressed him down. She straddled his thighs, seized his erection, and positioned herself over it. She lowered until his staff rubbed against her damp curls, then stopped. "How does it feel? Good?"

"Good." He spoke in a shuddering moan, and she moved against him, slightly. His whole body drew taut in expectation, but she didn't satisfy his demanding ache.

"I ache inside, you know. I've been thinking about this all day, and most of last night, so the ache is very strong."

"Is it?" Now, a squeak. She chuckled, then maneuvered her hips back and forth. His staff met her small peak, and she growled with pleasure. Not a soft moan or a feminine breath—a growl.

"Stronger still." She moved again, deliberately teasing

herself. She caught her lower lip between her teeth as if prolonging her pleasure.

His pulse throbbed. He was swollen beyond endurance, every touch shot fire straight through him. She lowered herself enough to take his tip just inside her warm, silken folds. He arched upward, but she evaded his thrust.

"I will decide."

It became a battle. She braced her hands on his chest, her elbows locked straight. He thrust, and she teased. She took him deeper and he groaned with relief, but she pulled back. Adrian propped himself up, and she bent forward to kiss him. Their tongues met in a passionate dance. She teased him there, too. Her tongue flicked along his teeth, but when he answered, she withdrew and teased his lips. He tasted her mouth, and she suckled his tongue fiercely, then pulled away.

It was torture. "You're doing this on purpose, woman!"

"Yes."

"I can't take it."

"You can. You take things so well." She ran her hands boldly over his chest as if reveling in his strength. "You wanted me aroused—I am aroused. You wanted me looking at you, and thinking of you. I never stop." She kissed his mouth, then drew away before he could capture her thoroughly. "I want you hard, Adrian."

He squeaked, he groaned, and she laughed—a temptress' laugh. "I want you looking at me, and thinking of how good it will be."

Adrian groaned and flopped back on the blanket. "I never stop."

She leaned forward and kissed his jaw. "You never will."

She sat up, her shoulders square—confident and determined. She caressed his hard length until his whole body shook. Then she sank down above him, slowly, so that he felt every tiny motion inward, every portion of her damp flesh surrounding him. She took him into her very core, then stopped, holding him impaled inside her.

He was too aroused to move. She gripped his shoulders and moved for him. "It's too much. Cora, I can't wait."

She moved a little faster, then stopped, her breaths short, her eyes wild. "There's a whirlwind inside me, and it spins so fast. When it explodes, it will be like an earthquake."

"A volcano."

"To each his or her own disaster, Adrian." She bobbed up and down on him, pleasuring herself. Adrian thrust upward, and she responded with hoarse cries of delight. A blinding storm raged inside him, so far beyond his control that he couldn't begin to contain it. He looked up, and knew Cora rode the storm to her own pleasure. Maybe she called him through time, after all.

Her body glistened. Her hair bounced around her shoulders, over her breasts. She quivered inside, tightening around him, growing hotter and hotter as she approached her rapturous pinnacle. He fought his own release, waiting for her, striving against the need to spill himself inside her.

She was fighting, too. The battle continued. She met his gaze in a glittering challenge as she writhed above him. She dared him to defy her power, to delay himself from what he wanted so much. Her sensual lips curved in a vixen's smile, then parted to allow for erotic moans and sweet gasps.

He couldn't stand it. She was winning, and he couldn't help wanting to lose. Her motion ceased. She stopped without warning. "You are so strong." She puffed a quick breath. "I must find something you can't endure."

She moved again, but not up and down. She adopted a circular motion, around and around, circling just his tip, allowing no more inside her. When she sank over him again, his control shattered. His hips thrust upward as waves and waves of pleasure crashed through him, into her. Her breath came in triumphant gasps, knowing she had won.

His release triggered hers. Her body tensed around him, her hips rocked against his. Her inner walls squeezed tight, demanding his full release. She writhed above him, then collapsed against his chest gasping. Gasping and weak.

Cora slid from his body and tucked herself in at his side. "That was fun."

"Fun!" Adrian groaned from the depths of his soul. "You ravaged me, woman."

She peeked up at him. "Are you offended?"

"I will never be the same."

"No." She rested her cheek on his arm. "You will be much weaker from now on, because you'll know the things I will do to you. Your resistance will waver. Soon, I'll just have to touch you, or perhaps smile, and you'll be putty in my hands. Hard, well-formed putty. I'll do whatever I want with you."

"You're a monster."

She sighed happily and kissed his shoulder. "I am."

"That was the best thing that has ever happened to me. I felt it in my toes. In my hair. Everywhere."

"Me, too." Cora squirmed closer into his arms. Adrian ran his fingers through her hair, sifting it to fall over her shoulder. He felt her heartbeat racing its descent, her muscles relaxing, her breaths deepening. She placed her hand over his heart, at peace. "You responded to my message better than I expected." Cora yawned. "I was afraid you wouldn't come to me, and I'd have to fetch you. But there you were, crashing through the trees, breathless."

Adrian glanced at her small, restful face and decided to

keep the issue of Captain Woodward to himself. "When Seduction Woman calls, men answer."

Cora nodded, liking the title. "I am a woman of many names." She paused, her sleepy eyes only half open. "You know I'm not leaving you, don't you?"

"Cora, I won't have you starving or killed in war. You have to go back."

"Do you know what you're asking? You are the joy in my life, Adrian."

"I'm the reason you're staying. I could be the reason you die."

"Where you go, I go also. Give it up, dude. I'm not going anywhere." She yawned and her eyes closed.

Adrian lay watching her face as she drifted toward sleep, contented and happy. He studied every feature until his vision blurred, until the image of her this way ingrained in his mind.

Cora Talmadge had become everything he had seen in her eyes nine years before. Beneath the shyness and insecurity, there was a woman so strong and so beautiful as to defy his imaginings. He'd probed to find her, and found glimpses, but when he tried to make her his forever, she had fled.

They were together now. Maybe this moment was all they had, but he couldn't tell her that now. If he left, if she had nothing to cling to, she would go back where she belonged. Tiotonawen would see to that. There had to be another way—a way for them to stay together, to marry and raise children and *live*.

Tonight, his power wasn't enough to guarantee the future he wanted. As much as he loved her, he could lose her again. But tonight, she lay in his arms, sated and in love. The waterfall she chose for her sweet seduction echoed in endless rhythm, and Adrian surrendered to sleep.

* * *

"The pale-haired captain gave Haastin this note. He says it is for you."

Adrian stood shivering outside Cora's small tent, examining the letter Laurencita gave him. She'd woken him carefully, without disturbing Cora—something that was possible only because his sleep had been fitful and restless, anyway.

He read Darian's smooth, flowing script, and his heartbeat slowed with every word.

> *The general has received word from Tucson. You are to be taken alive and brought by coach to the headquarters in Tucson for the purpose of interrogation. The commanders believe you may benefit the cause not only of the Tonto Apache, but of the Chiricahua led by Geronimo as well.*
> *Darian Woodward, Captain, U.S. Cavalry.*

Adrian handed the note back to Laurencita, then looked around in the gray morning light for his hiking boots. He found them discarded by the pool, a visual reminder of his passionate encounter with Cora.

"You are leaving." Laurencita watched him tie his boots, her expression neither approving nor critical.

"I have to go. There's hope of a reconciliation, of progress toward peace."

Laurencita gestured toward the tent where Cora lay sleeping. "What do I tell her?"

"Wait until I've gone, until the scouts report my capture by Woodward's men. Then give her this letter." Adrian paused and gazed at the waterfall. "Tell her one night can count for a thousand."

Adrian glanced toward Cora's tent. The bee with its widespread wings, the yin-yang, struggling forever against itself—an interpretation he'd never considered before. But the bee, straightforward, purposeful—that was Cora.

He wanted to wake her, to say good-bye, to reassure her. He went to the tent and held open the flap. The faint morning light touched her sleeping face, and his heart twisted with love. Her hair fell over her face, but he saw that she smiled in her sleep. She looked peaceful. Happy. He wanted their farewell be the sweetness of the night, not the cold bitterness of the morning.

Adrian took a final lasting look at her as she lay sleeping, allowing her image to soak into his soul. *I love you, forever, through all time.* "Goodbye, my love."

He closed the flap quietly, and returned in silence to the campsite below.

Tiotonawen was waiting as if he expected Adrian's decision, and didn't like it. "My son does not walk bare-handed to the enemy."

"The captain thinks I might help ease tensions between our two races. Can I turn that chance aside?"

"The captain is a boy, with eyes the color of a fast stream, and hair like sand. His skin is smooth like a baby's. The general has dark eyes, dark without sun. His hair is the color of mud, and his skin is rough like bark."

Adrian's eyes wandered to the side as he tried to decipher his father's meaning. "And this means . . . ?"

"The general will crush the boy captain, and what the boy has started will go astray."

"They're sending me by coach to Tucson. Once I reach the commanders there, I'll have a chance to state our case and that of all Native American tribes—with the benefit of knowing history as it will happen. Father, it may be we can avoid much of the hardships and tragedies to befall us. I must try. The captain has given me a chance. I intend to take it."

Tiotonawen looked around as if searching out an ally. "What of Talks Much? Does she agree?"

Adrian smiled. "Since when does a warrior require his woman's approval?"

Tiotonawen's brow angled into a deep furrow. "Since the warrior took Talks Much Who Fights Bees for a wife."

"Cora is sleeping. She won't know where I've gone 'til it's done." Adrian hesitated, then placed his hand on his father's shoulder. "If I don't return, you'll send her back."

"She will refuse."

"Father, if I'm gone, there's no reason for her to stay."

"It will be done. If she fights, I will have the warriors tie her to a board. I will stand at a safe distance, and give orders."

Adrian repressed a grin at his father's fear of Cora. "That seems wise. I've told Haastin how to assemble the parachute. Just make sure that's attached to the board, too."

Tiotonawen looked long into Adrian's eyes. A cloud of tears surfaced in his dark eyes, but he didn't cry. "You are a great man, you are strong, and your life has force. But you are going where I cannot reach you. When you were a baby, your life was mine to protect. Now, you go beyond. Take care, my son."

Adrian kissed his father's forehead. "All my life, I've known where I was going. But I never knew where I came from. I am proud to come from you."

"Ride in peace, my son. Your woman will be safe."

A woman brought his horse, and Adrian mounted. "The captain will meet me in the desert. With luck, he'll send word to you of my progress, and when I return, the fate that might have been will be that much brighter."

Tiotonawen stood by the horse's shoulder and laid his hand on Adrian's knee. "You do not control the wind, my son. You ride its unseen waves. Don't fight its power, and

319

don't try to change it. You never will. Ride it as it moves, and you will survive."

Surfing. His father had described surfing. A bizarre farewell, if ever there was one. Adrian offered a weak smile, and rode off to meet his enemies.

Cora took one look at Darian's letter and her heart pounded furiously. Her hands shook so much that she could barely read his signature. She closed her eyes in prayer, then turned to Tiotonawen. "He's gone?"

"He rode out this morning."

She fought a wave of thick nausea. She stood up, still shaking, so weak she felt she might crumple. "How long ago?"

"An hour, no more."

"Then maybe there's still time." Cora looked around for Spot, struggling to maintain her senses when terror closed in all around. Tiotonawen took her arm.

"Talks Much, my son has chosen his path. The boy captain is his friend. He speaks for my son, and together, they may be heard."

Cora whirled, fighting tears. "Don't you understand? Captain Woodward didn't write that letter! It's a fake. Someone's setting Adrian up!"

Tiotonawen's face drained of blood. "That cannot be. You cannot know this."

"I know. I've seen the captain's handwriting when he signed a form about the dress I borrowed."

"If not his words, then whose?"

"I know that, too. General Davis wrote this note himself. I noticed his handwriting in his office. Dear God! He wants Adrian alone, but why?"

"The chief in Tucson wants my son, but not for his wisdom. For his death. It is a proud feather to this general to

320

capture my son. To hang my son, that is a victory to please even the white fathers in the East."

Cora placed her trembling hand on Tiotonawen's arm. "What do we do?"

"I will ride with my warriors, and we will fight."

"You'll fight and die, and everything Adrian came here for will be lost." Cora squeezed her eyes shut, trying to force her brain into logical thought. "You wouldn't reach him in time. The soldiers have better weapons, and there are more of them than you. Even if you fight, you can't help Adrian now."

She was afraid. More afraid than she'd ever been in her life. Adrian de Vargas shared his power, and led her to her own. Cora fingered her bear pendant, and her mind cleared. "No. Let them think you believe them, that they're winning. Where an army fails, a woman alone can succeed."

"No. No, no, no, no. No. I will not allow—"

"Fetch my horse! I'm off to save your son!"

He winced, reeled back, then limped off to find Tradman's long-legged bay. Cora worked with calm, supreme precision. She found her hat with its two chicken feathers, she put her leather vest over her T-shirt, then retied her plaid sneakers. She took a dark, Navajo blanket and draped it over her shoulders like a cape. She used the rope belt from Toklanni's over-sized blouse and fixed it around her waist.

She found a round stone that fit into her palm and stuffed it in her pocket. She found her small knife, and placed it carefully in her belt. Tiotonawen returned with Spot, then stood back while she mounted. She urged the horse forward, but Tiotonawen called to her.

"Talks Much Who Fights Bees, may you ride with the wind at your back."

Cora glanced back over her shoulder. "Whirlwind, I always do."

321

Chapter Twelve

An empty desert spread wide before Cora's desperate gaze.
No cavalry, no Indians. She'd ridden down from the hills expecting to be greeted by an army. Instead, nothing. She had
to find Adrian, but he was gone. Tucson was south. But the
letter was a lie. He could as easily have been taken to the
fort.

He could as easily have been shot on sight.

Cora closed her eyes. *No. You can't die.* One place her
eyes couldn't see, and that was on the far side of the hills.
She urged Spot forward, and circled around. She rounded a
bend and saw white tents set up across the desert. Soldiers
galloped to and fro, some stood on guard facing the hills
where the Apache hid in defense.

Cora hesitated. They probably wouldn't shoot a single
rider, but it would be safer if they knew she was a woman.

She unbound her braid and let it fall loose beneath her hat. Then she gathered her reins and galloped toward the campsite. A scout rode out to greet her, and she stopped.

He drew near, and she recognized Darian Woodward's bearded sergeant. Despite his burly appearance, he was a gentleman—with reverence for "ladies." She waited until he drew near, she tumbled deliberately from the saddle, weeping in what she hoped was Victorian style. "Help me! Oh, please!" The sergeant reacted with predictable concern. He took her arm and helped her to stand. "I have escaped the Apache . . . after . . . No . . . " She buried her face in her hands. The sergeant went white. "I can't say. Please, where is Captain Woodward? I must see him."

The sergeant hesitated, looking uncomfortable. "The captain, he's not free to take visitors, Miss. But I'll take you to General Davis."

Cora straightened. "I must see Captain Woodward."

The sergeant's jaw twisted to one side. "That's impossible, Miss."

Cora's breath held. "He's not . . . dead, is he?"

"Worse than that, ma'am. The captain's been imprisoned."

"*What*? What for?"

"For challenging Davis on the 'rules.' " The sergeant's tone revealed his true loyalty. Cora's mind worked methodically, dealing with the new circumstances.

"His imprisonment sounds dreadfully unfair. I fear General Davis has lost command of his senses."

"If he goes ahead and hangs the captain, he'll lose command of a lot more than that."

"If only the captain could be freed, somehow. . . . "

"Davis has a few loyal guards. They've got a watch on him. They don't let any of the captain's men near."

"Surely you outnumber them."

"For now. But there's troops coming up from Tucson. Freeing the captain would see all our necks wrung."

"Not if General Davis himself is imprisoned for, say, defying orders, instigating war with the Apache, and wrongly accusing a Civil War hero such as Captain Woodward."

"For a little thing who just busted free from them Indians, you've got a clear head."

Cora met his gaze steadily. "They took my husband. I want him back. Darian can help me."

The sergeant's mouth dropped, his eyes widened to round pools. Her hasty disclosure may have ruined everything. He laughed so loud that Cora jumped back. "Is that a fact? Well, little Miss, you're in a fine mess."

"Not for long. Get me to Captain Woodward, and I'll find a way to break him free. Then you and your men will take over the camp, imprison the general instead, and have matters well in hand by the time the troops arrive. How's that for a bargain?"

"Sounds good, if you can pull it off."

Cora huffed. "No problem."

She wasn't sure when she first became sneaky. Her deviousness just crept up on her, then took command. Cora shuffled toward the tent where Darian was held prisoner, spit once, then approached the armed guards. "Morning, sirs. Brung the poor fella some soup."

The guard examined the soup Cora carried, then glanced at her face. She kept her head down and puffed up her cheeks to resemble the fat servant she was impersonating. The woman had hair of a similar color, tied in a fat bun, which Cora emulated easily enough. She wore a loose, baggy dress, which Cora padded with pillows.

Apparently, her disguise was good enough. The guard stood back and let her in. Darian Woodward sat slumped in a corner, his hands and feet bound. He hadn't shaved in a few days. His growth of beard was surprisingly substantial, and he looked more masculine than she remembered. Not like a young war hero, but a . . . desperado.

He didn't look up when she entered. His brow furrowed as if in constant vengeance, and his lips curved in a deep frown. "I'm not hungry."

Cora knelt beside him. "Captain. It's me, Cora Talmadge. Sergeant MacLeod helped me sneak in to visit you."

He turned slowly. His eyes widened bit by bit as his mouth opened wide. "No . . . Miss Talmadge." His posture snapped to gentlemanly attention, he lifted his chin, but Cora smiled. She'd seen another side of Darian Woodward, and she wasn't likely to forget. *Desperado.*

"The general sent a message to Adrian, supposedly from you."

"I know." Darian's blue eyes hardened. "That is why I'm here."

"I figured you knew about it. The note said they were taking him to Tucson, but I guessed it was a lie."

"That part is true, Miss Talmadge. He is going by coach to our headquarters, but not for a meeting. They are taking him to his hanging."

Cora's blood ran cold, but she fought to keep her senses. "Why? Why go through such a procedure, if they want him dead?"

"They are using him as an example to all war chiefs. Davis was afraid I'd interfere, which I would, so he imprisoned me. He has threatened to hang me before I can bring the matter to trial."

"How long ago did the coach leave? Can I catch it?"

"You! No! Certainly not."

Cora sat back, watching Darian struggle against his ties in an attempt to stop her. "All right. Could a man riding catch it?"

Darian ceased struggling. "Riding fast, possibly. It's a two-horse coach, but it's not fast. But Miss Talmadge, catching the coach wouldn't avail you, or should I say, a 'man?' Adrian's guard is Bill Tradman."

"Oh, no!" Cora scrambled to her feet. "What if he kills Adrian before they reach Tucson?"

"He has orders to deliver the Indian. Should trouble arise, he will kill."

"We'll just see about that." Cora lifted her skirt, pulled out a Colt revolver and a knife, and cut Darian's ties. She placed the gun in his hand, then tore off her disguise. Darian went pale, but he didn't stop her.

"Captain Woodward, are you ready for a mutiny?"

"Miss Talmadge, I am more than ready."

The mutiny went well. Cora stood back and watched as Darian incapacitated his two guards, then mustered his men to arrest General Davis. The procedure took forty-five minutes.

Darian stood before the officer's tent, issuing a long list of grievances and broken regulations to the furious general.

"Woodward, you'll pay for this with your miserable hide! I'll have you strung up, gutted, and left for the crows!"

Cora grimaced, but Darian remained impassive. "Sergeant, a gag might be in order here."

The sergeant grinned and wrapped a dirty handkerchief in the general's mouth. "We've heard more than enough from you, boy."

The general's eyes blazed in fury, but Darian resumed his list of complaints. Cora watched him for a moment, as if from a great distance, as if glimpsing the true beauty of the past. "Captain, you are a brave and heroic man. I am proud to have known you."

She led her horse to his side, stood on tiptoes, and kissed his cheek while the general glared. "I'll be on my way now. I don't think you and I will meet again, but I will remember you."

Darian turned his back to the general. "I should go with you in your rescue attempt."

"If Tradman sees you or any of your soldiers, he'll kill Adrian."

"What if he sees you?"

"He won't. I ride unseen, and fast. I know what I'm doing."

"I hope so. Cora Talmadge, you are a woman of amazing virtues. The greatest of all is the power of your love." He paused, a small smile on his lips. "I hope *that man* knows how fortunate he is."

"I will tell him when I see him."

"I hope one day I find a love as pure. You and I are much alike. Together, we would have peace, but I see now that love is more than peace. When two well-matched persons marry, there is no chance to become something greater than you were. But when two souls come together from afar, there is no limit to what can be."

Cora clasped her hands over her heart. "You are so romantic." Her eyes misted with tears. "I hope you find it, too."

Darian took her hand and kissed it gently. "Don't worry about me. By the time the Tucson forces arrive, I will have the matter well in hand. When he placed me under arrest, General Davis issued several incriminating remarks, indicating his past association with Tradman. They've sold scalps to the Mexicans, instigated several bloody battles against the local tribes, and contrived to kill my predecessor. It seems the former captain was transferring for the purpose of investigating General Davis's association with Tradman, thanks to information gathered from the Apache."

"Well, that should fix him! Good!" Cora mounted her horse and swept Tiotonawen's hat from her head. She bowed dramatically and Darian smiled.

"Miss Talmadge, may you ride with the wind at your back."

"Captain Woodward, I always do."

"Boy, you're going to hang by the neck and twist in the wind. That's what you've got to look forward to in Tucson." Tradman settled himself back against the coach wall, smoking a foul cigar. Adrian studied the ranger dispassionately, as if researching a case study at college. The lines of his face were hard, and touched with no mercy. He had small hands. Curiously neat, the fingernails well-trimmed.

"You have just about the smallest hands I've ever seen on a man."

Tradman's dark eyes narrowed to slits. He flung his half-smoked cigar out the coach window and drew a knife. "If I'm in the mind to do it, boy, I could add a few choice touches to your worthless body before delivering you to Tucson." He aimed the knife at Adrian's crotch, twisting the blade to catch the fading sunlight.

The man lived to provoke fear. Adrian angled his brow doubtfully. "Since I am on my way to my hanging, how I am 'delivered' matters little. The men of my culture are disciplined to endure pain."

Tradman's lip curled into an expression of pure evil. "I've

seen 'em begging for mercy, screaming out—you ain't no different from the rest."

Adrian's stomach churned—not in fear for himself, but in anger for what his people had suffered. As he watched Tradman, he realized it wasn't just for his own people, but for any race victimized, for any living thing suffering for no cause of its own. Victorian sensibilities flowed strong in men like Darian Woodward—they were inescapable. But whatever his own age was termed carried its own values—just as deep, and just as inescapable.

I am not a defender of race. I am a defender of man.

"Tell me, what did my people do to anger you?"

Tradman snorted vengefully. "They live and breathe, boy. That's enough."

Adrian tried to stretch his bound legs to relieve the ache from confinement. His hands were bound behind his back—he had lost feeling in his fingers hours ago. "It may be enough, but in your case, there's more to your hatred. You have spent time with my people."

Tradman spat on the floor, then sucked his teeth in agitation. "How do you know that?"

"The good general has an Apache scout. When I was bound, you gave him orders—in his own language."

Tradman smirked. "Got to know their cursed tongue to tell 'em how they're going to die."

"And you learned it from a university study program? Perhaps an Apache dictionary?"

"I learned it from the heathens themselves, boy. Straight from their poisoned lips."

"I see. You have spent time among my people. As a guest?"

His words drove deep. Tradman's jaw tightened. A muscle in his cheek twitched. "Yeah, I've done my time. But your kind ain't people. They're animals. Guest!" Tradman spat again. "The Chiricahua took me prisoner—ripped six boys off a wagon train heading West."

Adrian's mood shifted, his heart quailed. "A massacre?"

"Massacre! You're a soft-hearted bastard, aren't you? Them Indians wanted us boys for working. They didn't have the stomach to stick around and fight."

"If you were brutalized, I am sorry."

Tradman's jaw set to one side, he glared out the window. "Damned ugly land, this Arizona territory."

"To each his own." Adrian paused. If Tradman had suffered trauma, perhaps his vengeance made sense. "It is better to face the cruelties inflicted on you as a child rather than to deny them and let them eat away at you."

"They weren't nothing but savages. Had us working like dogs, side by side with their own kind."

Adrian's compassion faded. "You did the same work as their children? What's wrong with that?"

Tradman sneered. "Had to eat with 'em, live alongside 'em. A few of the boys that got taken along with me, they didn't see no wrong in it. They started speaking the tongue, playing games with them red boys. One damned fool took up with a squaw girl—ain't no problem if a white man gets his relief from a squaw, but he put a ring on her finger and took the vows."

Adrian stared. He was too stunned to feel anger. He fingered the ring that hung around his neck. Cora's ring. The ring he'd never gotten a chance to give her. "And that's it? They didn't beat you, torture you? Just offered you an incredible opportunity to join their culture, learn how another race exists?" Adrian shook his head. "Well, man, you'll be

330

glad to know that within a hundred years, men and women from all races marry at will, legally."

"What're you talking about? Future!"

"Let's just say I'm psychic. A sage, if you will."

Tradman's face contorted in suspicion, as if he believed a native man capable of any number of dark arts. "You shut your mouth, boy. You don't know nothing about the future. In a hundred years, there ain't going to be no one in this land except white-skinned people."

Adrian smiled in deliberate provocation. "I'm sorry you won't be around to see it." He settled back in his seat. "So burdened by interracial contact, you made your way to freedom. Or did they kick you out for being a fool?"

Tradman's eyes lit with such evil that Adrian drew back. "I set up with some ranchers near Tucson—put 'em on the Indian campsite. They went through the village—cleaned it up real nice."

Loathing swarmed Adrian's senses, and his stomach churned in nausea. "Meaning, they slaughtered Native American women and children to give themselves a sense of power and security that all such pathetic fools lack."

The length of Adrian's sentence confused Tradman. He might be crafty, but he wasn't an intelligent man. As Adrian suspected, General Davis pulled the strings. "Who're you calling 'Native Americans,' boy?"

"The native people of this lands. Indians. Those people descended from ancient hunters who moved eastward across the Bering Strait, probably Asiatic in origin—"

"They ain't no Americans."

"On the contrary, my people are the original Americans. You are visitors at best—invaders at worst. We know this land. You would be wise to learn from what we know."

Adrian gazed out the window at the high, jagged rocks. His home. For all the places he had traveled, and all the wonders he had seen, nothing came close to Arizona.

He hadn't been raised in a Native tradition. He'd been raised by a loving couple who wanted children and couldn't have their own. They'd adopted nine children, babies to teenagers, and loved them all.

He didn't know his Apache brothers, but he knew his modern-day siblings. They came from all cultures; Vietnamese, Haitian, Hispanic, Cambodian. Adrian spoke French, Spanish, and could sing a Cambodian wedding song from his brother Nyuygen's wedding. When he was thirteen, the entire family traveled to Mexico City to meet his twin brothers' grandparents.

Adrian's eyes filled with tears. His family would never know what happened to him. He wouldn't see them again, or share holidays, or see his younger sisters or brothers graduate from school, marry. He wouldn't see his new nieces and nephews. But knowing them all, and sharing their lives, had given him something death couldn't take.

"Every culture has a gift, Tradman, to share with the whole of humanity. Every person has a gift, which he offers to the world around him." He studied the ranger with an analytical eye. "People such as yourself serve a purpose, perhaps, by presenting an obstacle. A contrast to what's right and what's good. I am sorry you never found your gift."

Tradman looked confused. Adrian had seen that expression before—on the faces of those listening to Cora Talmadge. He felt disoriented, but good. Maybe in such moments Cora felt that way, too.

He shouldn't have left her. He imagined her waking without him, learning where he'd gone. She would hope, because Darian's letter offered hope. It would be days, perhaps, before she learned the truth. By then, he would be dead.

Adrian closed his eyes and allowed himself to imagine the life he wanted. He wanted to bring Cora to his family, where she would be accepted and loved. She had envied his large family—he wanted to share it with her. She would learn Cambodian songs quickly, she would love Mexican dances. His family would love her.

He wanted to raise children of their own, giving them a life of magic and happiness Cora carried inside herself.

He opened his eyes, and the sun set over Arizona. There was no moon, but the coach pressed onward carrying him closer to death. He had no future, but he had the memory of Cora. Cora, wide-eyed and terrified about to jump from an airplane because she'd rather die than back down in front of him. Cora, tapping her foot in annoyance because Cramer didn't take care of his animals properly. Cora facing his father, and somehow seizing the advantage. Cora fighting bees, and winning.

The woman he loved, awaiting him in a sensual swirl of glistening water, because she loved him every bit as much as he loved her.

Adrian watched the last light ebb and turn to black. The value of a man's life wasn't determined by how it ended, but how fully it was experienced. For a little while, he'd shared her life and her heart. That was enough.

Darkness crept slowly across the desert, turning plants and rocks into shadows, obscuring the landscape's detail. Shadows enveloped the distant coach, and Cora urged Spot faster. She'd kept herself a mile behind to avoid detection, but the coach kept an even pace southward. It never stopped. If the coach moved on, Adrian was alive.

With the darkness came a moment Cora had never known before: Do or die. All her life, she'd avoided ultimate conflict, the point of no return. But something meant more to her than safety. Adrian. He needed her. Truly needed her. His life depended on her ability to think straight and fast, to act with perfect timing, not a moment too soon or too late.

Her confidence wavered. She wasn't a physically skilled woman. But she could ride. When she was a child, she had learned to ride because she loved horses—their warm muzzles, their friendly eyes. She hadn't realized she had skill until she won her first medal. Her skill came because she hadn't been worrying about her ineptness, but because she had been focused something she enjoyed, cared about.

Never in her life had she cared about anything the way she cared for Adrian de Vargas. Never had she enjoyed anything as she enjoyed being with him.

Cora's confidence returned. She would use her one skill from childhood and she would find a way to be with the man she loved again.

The sky still held grayness. *Too soon.* Cora decreased the distance between herself and the coach, so that she trailed it like a distant shadow. The moon would rise around midnight, giving her a limited chance to operate in the dark. Too soon, too late. She rode a fine line.

An hour passed as she edged ever closer. Adrenaline saved her from weariness—and a tireless horse who responded well to kind treatment. The coach stopped, and Cora's heart stopped, too. *They've seen me!*

She side-stepped the horse behind a bush and held him perfectly still. She heard nothing, no shots, no shouts. Cora peeked around the bush. Two men were standing outside the coach, facing away from her. Both assumed a peculiar posture, shoulders slumped, arms in front of their bodies. They both tugged at their pants, then returned to the coach.

"Oh, how foul! They're peeing!" Cora grimaced. She had made use of a good, private spot with useful leaves for cleanliness. "What about Adrian?"

Adrian came around the other side of the coach, and Cora relaxed. He'd taken his private moment where it belonged—in private.

This is probably more about this journey than I need to know.

The coach moved on, but Cora made a wide arc around their stopping point. The night deepened until she only saw a pin-point of light from the coachman's lantern, but she heard its wheels grinding over the silent desert. Her heart pounded in her chest. The moment drew near.

She urged the horse into a canter, then a gallop. The dry, night wind swept her face, her braid bounced rhythmically on her back. The coach appeared like a ghost, and she slowed to a smooth, steady canter. Despite the darkness, the coachman kept his team at a brisk trot. Cora slowed Spot, hesitating. She'd counted on the coach slowing to a walk in the darkness. Her plans faltered, her fear rose.

She stared hard at the coach, willing it to slow, but it moved on over the dry ground. *What if I fail?* Inside the coach, Adrian sat bound, tormented by a man willing to scalp people for a few pieces of gold.

Cora's fear hardened to determination. She urged Spot gently into a canter, and closed the distance to the coach. Up close, she could make out the coach's shape and features. There was no window in the back. Fortune turned her way, after all. There was a step for the coachman to load baggage onto the coach's roof.

335

The roof had a heavy trunk attached at the center, but otherwise, the space was clear. Cora inched closer, holding her breath lest her approach be noticed. If the coachman or Tradman spotted her, all was lost. If they shot her, there would be no one to save Adrian.

Then we'll meet in heaven, my love.

Heaven wasn't good enough. Cora wanted life—she wanted it with Adrian de Vargas, she wanted children, a home. Everything. Her will solidified, and she brought her horse's nose within reach of the coach. He seemed to understand. He neither slacked nor quickened his pace. He kept even time with the harness horses as Cora rose up in her stirrups.

The coachman sat to the left of his seat, so Cora edged to the right. She pushed her horse forward until his shoulder was parallel to the rear corner of the coach. *Not unlike parallel parking.* The coachman's lantern cast a light to both sides, but not behind. So far, she rode in darkness.

Cora guided Spot with one hand and assessed the coach for positioning. She saw a metal handle meant for climbing to the roof, for luggage purposes. *Perfect.* A small rim was enough for feet.

This is it.

Cora took a deep breath. She tied her reins in a knot, then patted Spot's neck. She closed her eyes and issued a silent prayer. *Please, let me do this. I know I've failed many times. Maybe I've disappointed you because I was so timid, but I can make up for that now. Please, let me save him. Please.*

Three "pleases" would have to do. God must know how much she loved Adrian. She believed that God honored people who used everything they had to create what they wanted. Adrian had done that all his life, but she had been afraid. She was afraid now, too, but Adrian's life meant more.

She gathered every speck of her strength, every speck of her courage, and swung her right leg forward over the horse's neck, balancing on her left stirrup. She released her reins to fall loose on his withers and focused on the metal handle. The coach bumped and jerked, but Cora kept time. It tilted toward her, and she swung forward.

She caught the handle just as Spot swerved away. From the corner of her eye, she saw him canter away, surprised at the sudden release. She hung with both hands to the handle, fumbling for her footing. Her toes met the rim, and she pressed her forehead against the coach, shocked at her success.

If I'd fallen, I would catch Spot, and try again. No problem. Now comes the hard part.

She'd climbed a mountain. She could climb a coach. Cora scrambled up the back and flung herself over the top. The coach creaked and swayed. "Whoa!"

Oh, no! The coachman pulled in his team, and stopped. Cora's heart slammed so loudly she felt sure its beat would be heard like drums across the desert. She perched on the roof like a flag. The coachman got up from his seat, and Tradman opened his door.

I'm done for now! Cora dropped behind the trunk and huddled into a bunch. She pulled her cape blanket over her body and closed her eyes tight.

"What the hell are we stopping for, Belmont?"

"Thought I heard something, sir."

Cora couldn't see, but she knew Tradman was looking around. She opened her eyes and saw the moving lantern as they checked out the area. It lifted, and she covered her face. She felt naked, as if the dark light of hell shone on her like a beacon. But the light moved on and the coachman circled the area.

"Don't see nothing, sir. Must have gone over a rock."

"Fool! Get moving!"

They got back into the coach and started off again, but Cora couldn't move. Her heart raced, her limbs felt numb. Lying pressed to the roof, she heard Tradman's muffled laughter. "Don't get your hopes up, boy. Your kind don't do no heroics. Your red hide ain't worth nothing, even to them."

Fury boiled in Cora's veins. The close call drifted from her memory as she gathered herself for the next attack.

She had to warn Adrian of her intentions so he didn't give anything away by surprise. Tradman had gotten out through the right door, which meant Adrian must be on the left. She maneuvered herself to the left, and looked around for a foothold. The trunk was bound to the roof by several thick ropes. *Perfect. Just the right distance.*

Cora stuck her feet under the ropes, and twisted around so that she lay face-down. She squirmed forward until she could see over the edge. The window was a little farther up. She adjusted her foothold and repositioned herself closer to the front. She wormed her way forward again, then a little more until she hung over the edge.

Curse the bumping! Her braid fell forward and hung down over her shoulder. Just a little lower. Cora stretched her legs straighter, and the ropes dug into her ankles. She took a breath, then peeked into the window.

Tradman snored. The man hadn't bathed in years, and now he snored like a train. Adrian sighed and closed his eyes. Not to sleep, but to hide his own mind. He wanted to remember the joys of his life. He wanted to remember Cora, and the last days at her side.

He'd never thought of dying, certainly not by violence or primitive execution. Now, he would die surrounded by people who hated his race, who feared him like an alien. He was afraid. He'd never been afraid before. Life had been so easy. His people struggled and fought to survive. He moved through life like a . . . surfer.

Adrian smiled despite his fear. *Cool Apache surfer dude.* No wonder Cora adjusted so well to the trials of the past. Her life in the future hadn't been easy. Her parents divorced, and both were involved in their art, selfish by necessity. Cora had no one to lean on—she'd spent her life trying to please, to fit in.

She never quite succeeded. Adrian's eyes filled with tears. *I love you so.* He wanted to give her a family. He wanted to hold her until she felt safe. He wanted to save her. . . .

Something tapped his window. Probably small rocks pitched up from the wheels. It tapped again, and Adrian opened his eyes. His gaze shifted to the window. To Cora Talmadge's pert face. *As she hung upside down from the roof of the coach.*

No! Adrian's mouth dropped open. He blinked. She smiled. She tried to nod, but seemed to find that difficult when hanging upside-down.

I am dreaming. No, I have lost my mind and I'm hallucinating.

Cora arched her eyebrows and pointed at something. Tradman. Adrian uttered a low whimper, then shook his head. *No! Get off the roof, you lunatic!*

She knew what he wanted. Her lip quirked to one side. She looked smug. *Oh, no!*

She mouthed words. *I'm saving you.*

Adrian shook his head, then lifted his bound wrists and motioned her away. In the gloom, he thought he saw her wink, and his blood moved like ice. *Cora, no!*

Fear swarmed through Adrian, leaving him numb and helpless. He couldn't stop her. Whatever the crazy woman intended, he couldn't stop her. If Tradman woke, if the coachman noticed her motion. Adrian closed his eyes and prayed.

The coach's balance altered slightly to the right, and his heart missed a beat. Tradman grumbled in his sleep, but he didn't wake. Adrian held himself motionless, staring at the right window. He saw the braid first. His breath came in short, stilted gasps. He fought to keep himself quiet.

He saw the top of her head, then her little face. He had no idea what she planned. She tapped the window, and Adrian shuddered. Tradman stirred, then jolted awake just as Cora disappeared from the window. "What was that?"

"Rocks. We're going through a rocky area. Haven't you noticed? It happens all the time." His voice rushed shrill. Tradman's eyes narrowed to slits and he drew a gun.

Adrian's blood drained from his head. Tradman looked furtively around, then opened the coach door a crack, then a little more. He looked out. A small hand came down, holding a big, round rock. It thumped on Tradman's head, and he jerked up his gun. Adrian fought against his binding, but he couldn't move.

The rock came down again, harder. Tradman reeled, and Cora whacked him again. He slumped, and she shoved him back into the coach, then disappeared again. Adrian waited, his heart pounding like war-drums. He heard her shuffling on the roof, but the coach moved on, oblivious.

He saw her feet—in plaid sneakers. Then her chinos pushed up over her calves as she swung down, and stuck her foot in the open door. She kicked it open, then lowered herself into the coach. She beamed with pride, still holding her rock. "Hi."

Adrian was shaking. His fingers were white from terror. "Cora—"

"Hush." She held her finger to her lips. "I'm saving you."

Tradman moved, and Adrian tried to move. "Get out of here!"

Cora eyed Tradman. He lifted his head. She frowned, held up her rock as if positioning a baseball, then gave him another solid thump. "I wonder how long something like this lasts?" She chuckled. "In the movies, when they're out, they're out, you know?"

"This isn't . . . the movies."

She cocked her eyebrow doubtfully. "I know that, Adrian. In the movies, you'd be saving me, and I'd be screaming helplessly at the top of my lungs."

She whipped out a small knife, clamored over Tradman's limp body, and cut Adrian's ties—first the ankles, then his wrists. She leaned forward and kissed him. "We'd better get out of here before the coachman notices anything fishy."

He felt too weak to move. Cora crawled back over Tradman. "I almost forgot!" She pulled a rope belt from her waist and tied Tradman's hands behind his back. She looked around, then fixed he bright gaze on Adrian's head. "I'm sorry you have to lose this." She snatched his red bandanna from his hair and stuffed it in Tradman's mouth. "There! That should hold him for awhile." She paused and glanced toward the front of the coach. "Maybe I should incapacitate the driver, too."

"No!" Her mad intentions stirred Adrian into action. "Let's get out of here while we can."

She nodded a little regretfully, then made her way to the door. She coach progressed at a crisp trot, and she hesitated. "Are you okay? Can you jump?"

He stared, beyond wonder. She wasn't afraid. She was

worried not about herself, but about him. He nodded, unable to speak. Cora smiled lovingly, then shoved open the door. She peeked toward the coachman, then motioned at Adrian. "All clear."

Adrian took Tradman's gun, then followed her onto the narrow ramp. The ground sped by in darkness. She took his hand and squeezed tight. "Jump!"

They jumped. They tumbled and rolled, then bumped to a stop side by side. Cora scrambled up to check him. She knelt above him just as the moon rose above the southern horizon. It glimmered behind her head like a halo. Her braid fell loose over her shoulder, her eyes sparkled with tears.

Adrian gazed up at her, amazed and in love. A slow smile grew on his lips and he reached to touch her soft cheek. "My hero."

"Now what?"

Cora gazed dreamily down at Adrian. *I am your hero—at last.* Her eyes misted with tears, mirrored in his. "I love you."

"I love you, too."

Cora pressed her mouth against his. He kissed her deeply and her heart felt swollen with love. She sniffed away tears, then rested her cheek against his. Adrian stroked her hair and hugged her.

"I don't think we're out of the woods yet, angel."

"Out of the desert, you mean." She sighed and sat up. "You're probably right. Tradman will wake and start thumping around until the coachman notices. He won't take losing his prisoner well."

"Especially if he knows you're the one who bested him— for me. The man doesn't favor interracial relationships."

Cora held out her hand and pulled Adrian to his feet. "It's none of his business." She looked around, left and right.

"Now, I left my horse around here somewhere. He should be just north."

She held up her arms, gauged the northern position, and marched off. Adrian caught up with her and touched her shoulder. He pointed right and smiled. "North, angel. That way."

Cora smacked her lips, then repositioned herself. "I may have to improve my sense of direction one of these days."

Adrian took her hand and kissed it. "Please, don't. I don't want to be intimidated by a woman who does everything right."

Cora considered this, then nodded. "Very well. Perfection can be off-putting, I suppose."

"You thought I was perfect, didn't you?"

"I did. But I was wrong. You use everything inside you, but you're not perfect. I have noticed that you can be stubborn, jealous, proud, um, let's see . . . vain, and occasionally, hot-headed."

"Oh, thank you very much!"

"You can also be shy and nervous, which I never noticed before. But I think you always were. I was just too fixated on my own fears to notice yours. I'm sorry, Adrian. I should have saved you long ago."

He smiled. "I never gave you the chance, angel. I was too stubborn and proud and nervous. . . . " He paused. "I'm not vain."

Cora rolled her eyes. "You're vain."

"I'm not."

"Since we've been here, you've cleaned your teeth every day, at least twice—you've probably even found a way to floss. You've managed to wash your hair and bathe—I notice it's combed out nicely even now. The red bandanna was decoration, Adrian. You're vain."

Cora's head felt bare. Her eyes widened, and her lips formed a fierce pout. "Oh, hell! I dropped my hat, and I didn't even notice where! Curses!"

Adrian's brow angled. "*I'm* vain?"

She grinned sheepishly. "We're *both* vain. Let's go find my horse."

They walked hand in hand across the desert, moving northeast toward the mountains. Cora whistled, but Spot didn't appear. "He's got to be around here somewhere. We need a horse! I couldn't think of a way to keep him near when I jumped onto the coach. Damn!"

"I can't believe you jumped onto a speeding coach."

"It wasn't speeding. Just a fast trot."

"Still. . . ."

She nodded. "It was impressive."

Adrian chuckled and squeezed her hand tight. "It was."

They walked on, and Cora's weariness caught up with her. She stumbled, and Adrian caught her arm. "Are you all right?"

"Just tired. I'm fine. We have to keep going."

A horse whinnied nearby, and Cora whistled. Spot came out of the darkness, his reins hanging to one side. Adrian caught him, and led him to Cora. "Up."

"Shouldn't you get on first?"

"You're saving me, woman. Not the other way around. Up."

Cora mounted, and Adrian got up behind her. He wrapped his arms around her and kissed her neck. Cora turned her face to his and he kissed her mouth. Spot stopped, waiting. "Do you know where we are, Adrian?"

"We're south of Mesa, along the Salt. I want to reach the hills, where we're out of sight, then we'll rest."

Cora yawned. "That sounds good." The reins slacked in

her hands. Adrian took them from her open fingers and guided the horse toward the mountains.

Cora snored. Adrian smiled and kissed her head as a small rumble came from her open mouth. She slept with her head against his chest, her hands folded on the pommel. They had reached the hills and the horse picked his way slowly through the boulders. He tripped often, but Adrian pressed onward until he felt sure they wouldn't be seen.

He stopped by a narrow stream and dismounted, carrying Cora with him. She didn't wake. She leaned her head against his shoulder, and resumed snoring. Adrian laid her carefully on a patch of sand and tucked her blanket around her limp body. He tied Spot near the stream so he could drink and eat the nearby shrubs.

Adrian returned to Cora. He lay down beside her, and tucked her close. She murmured his name softly in her sleep. He heard her words clearly: "Seduction Woman strikes again." She chuckled, then sank deeper into sleep, quieting. He smiled.

In the aftermath of heroism, Cora dreamt of making love. Adrian felt sure of it. She was weary to the bone, drained by his rescue. And she still dreamt about sex. Adrian felt himself tighten at the thought, but he resisted waking her. They had time.

He was exhausted, but he couldn't sleep. He'd faced the end of his life, and realized how much more he wanted. He had been helpless, his fate totally out of his hands. And the woman who loved him gave him back the chance to live. When he'd been most afraid, Cora had come to him. Adrian smiled. Sometimes, even the bravest man needs a hero.

The sound of hoofbeats and grinding wheels echoed across

the desert. Adrian rose silently and gazed down from the hill. Tradman's coach raced northward, and Adrian knew their trials weren't over yet. Tradman would return to Davis, and they would launch an assault against Tiotonawen's people.

It would take Tradman awhile to reach the camp. Longer still for Davis to muster his men. But Tiotonawen had to be warned. Adrian returned to Cora's side and reluctantly woke her. "I'm sorry, angel. We have to move on."

She opened her eyes and smiled as if she'd seen an angel. "Adrian? What's the matter?"

"I saw Tradman. He's headed to warn Davis of my escape. We've got to warn my father."

Cora chuckled—inappropriately to the situation at hand.

"Cora, we're likely to be cut off from my people if we don't move fast."

"I don't think you have to worry about General Davis."

"No?" Maybe she wasn't fully awake yet. "Why not?"

"He's got a lot on his hands right now."

"What?"

"A mutinous officer, and a bunch of angry soldiers."

"Mutinous?"

"I can't think of a better word to describe Captain Woodward. Except possibly 'desperado.' "

"Cora, you've been through a lot. . . . " Adrian huffed. "Desperado, indeed!"

"You obviously haven't seen him with a beard. Lie down, Adrian. Darian will take care of Tradman."

"I find that exceptionally hard to believe." Yes, he was still jealous.

"You'll see. Go to sleep." Cora held out her arms. Adrian hesitated, then lay back down beside her. She snuggled close, and he forgot his fear.

He felt her warm breath on his neck, and his pulse quickened. *Think about something else. She needs rest.* She nuzzled his skin between his neck and his shoulder, then pressed a leisurely kiss on his throat. Despite his best intentions, he hardened.

She murmured softly, something about feeling an "ache." Her leg wormed its way between his, and her tongue tasted his flesh. His skin heated but he restrained himself from rolling her on her back and satisfying his own ache. She was half asleep. She didn't know what she was doing.

She moved so that her breast touched his arm. Her nipple felt taut. He ground his teeth together to hold himself back. She puffed a soft, impatient breath, then bit his shoulder.

"All right!" Adrian seized a shuddering breath, pushed her onto her back and kissed her passionately. "Is this what you want?"

She opened her eyes and smiled. "There's a price for my rescue, my little save-ee. I want it paid in full. Tonight." Her hand wound its way between them and she grasped his arousal in firm, meaningful fingers.

They stripped away their clothing and lay naked together on her blanket, flesh against flesh. Cora's legs wrapped around Adrian's neck, and he held her bottom in his hands as he drove inside her.

"Woman, I've dreamt of this for years."

Her toes strained and curled, and she tipped her head back in delirious pleasure. "Me, too."

He touched her deepest core, and she accepted his. They met and joined, and fused. When he reached his release and felt hers around him, he knew nothing could take her away—not death, not a world, and not time.

The moon rose high at midnight, and cast its blue light across the ancient desert. Adrian withdrew from Cora's body and she fell asleep in his arms.

Chapter Thirteen

The army had moved, probably back to the fort. Adrian and Cora reached the foothills of Cave Creek, but the tents were gone. "Does this mean your people can return to their old village?"

"They can, but they probably won't. For now, they're safer in the high ground."

Cora shaded her eyes against the early morning sun. "I hope Captain Woodward is all right."

"You said he had things in hand. I wouldn't worry."

"I don't know. He had changed. I can't explain how exactly. You know how he was somewhat prim?"

"I'm glad you noticed. He's a Victorian yuppie to the core."

Cora's brow furrowed. "He *was*. But not anymore. He's almost . . . reckless."

"Ha! That man could never be reckless."

"He led a mutiny, Adrian. That sounds reckless to me."

Adrian couldn't argue, so he maintained an obstinate silence. Cora smiled and muttered the word, "jealous." "True, he's much sexier this way. . . . "

Adrian growled a warning and Cora chuckled. They rode higher into the hills, and made their way to the Apache camp. Tiotonawen sat in the center of the clearing, legs crossed, his eyes closed. Cora eyed him doubtfully. "Is he meditating?"

"He is conversing with the spirits. For us."

They rode into the village, and everyone circled around, silent and in awe. Not of Adrian, but of Cora. Toklanni met Cora's eyes and nodded. Laurencita beamed with approval. Haastin fingered his dice thoughtfully, as if forgiving her for his loss. Tiotonawen looked up, saw his son, and tears fell to his high, strong cheekbones.

He seized Toklanni's arm and shoved himself up. Adrian swung his leg back over the saddle and jumped down. Cora nodded her approval, then swung her own leg forward over the horse's neck. "I'm living dangerously."

Adrian shook his head, then faced his father. Cora half expected praise from the grumpy old man, but she wasn't surprised when his attention fixed on Adrian. "It is a wise man who takes for his woman such a force as this." He gestured at Cora, but he didn't look her way.

Adrian smiled. "I am a lucky man."

Tiotonawen turned slowly to Cora. He still looked a little wary. Cora found she liked the sensation of dangerousness. "Talks Much Who Fights Bees, you have earned your place among my people. From now forward, you are among the honored women, and will have much respect granted you."

Cora bowed. "Thank you." She paused. "Does this mean I get to boss other women as Toklanni does?"

Tiotonawen hesitated, as if reluctant to give her more authority and fearing what she'd do with it. Cora wasn't sure, either, but she liked the idea. "You would be a good Medicine Woman, with training. They boss."

Cora thought of her gallery—the one she had planned featuring Native art and historical exhibits. She sighed. "I will learn what I have to learn to be useful to you."

Adrian looked at her, his expression doubtful. "Do you want to stay, Cora? Here, in the past?"

She took his hand and kissed it. "Where you go, I go also. If this is what you want, I'll stay."

"What I want . . . " Adrian's gaze shifted to his feet. "I must serve my people."

Tiotonawen laid his hand on Adrian's shoulder, then touched his chin in a fatherly gesture. "My son, you already have."

Adrian shook his head. "I've done nothing but get you into trouble."

"Is that why you returned to us? To save us from what must be?"

Adrian met his father's gaze. "I could have made things better for you, if I'd kept my head, if I'd been able to reason with the general."

"How can you reason with a man who is driven by anger and greed?"

Cora nodded. "Good point, Whirlwind."

Adrian sighed. "I didn't do as much as I could."

Tiotonawen gripped Adrian's shoulder tightly. "My son, you have give me all I prayed for when I sent you through the whirlwind."

Adrian didn't appear convinced, but Cora's eyes filled with tears and she clasped her hands over her heart.

"How can you say that?" Adrian asked. "I have failed you."

Tiotonawen smiled. He looked wiser than Cora had noticed before. "Fail me? You have returned to me, so I know my son lives. Not only does he live, but he is strong and proud, undaunted by enemies. He talks to a pale-haired white boy like a brother—a brother he fights with too much, but a brother who answers his call."

"I wouldn't call Woodward a brother, exactly."

"My son is not beaten. I hear of his life in the tomorrow world, and it is good. He does what he wants. He flies in the sky, and takes white men with him."

Cora nodded again. "And women."

Tiotonawen ignored her. "This sacred land is strong in you." He paused. "You must learn to take tobacco into yourself, but there is time." He paused again, grinning. "*Man.*"

Cora chuckled, but Adrian shifted his weight from foot to foot. "I don't think—"

Tiotonawen held up his hand. "Don't deny me in this, my son. I will carry the hope you will find your way to the sacred plants."

"And I will carry the hope you'll quit and find a new habit that isn't a carcinogen."

Cora sniffed. "You are so right, Whirlwind. Adrian is very close to the earth. I know that's kind of New Age, but it's true. He shared it with everyone. He tried to share it with me, too, but I was so afraid of the earth. And it's not just the earth—it's the body and the mind and the spirit. I was afraid of those things, too. He tried to show me, but I couldn't see." Her tears resumed and dripped down her cheeks.

Tiotonawen nodded. "I know. Talks Much, you are the reason my son returned to this time."

351

Cora glanced at Adrian, who looked equally surprised. "I am?"

"You are." Tiotonawen looked at Adrian's face. "You did not come back to save your people, my son. You did not come back to tell me there is a future. I could have lived and died not knowing that truth. It eases my heart to know, but that is not the reason you returned."

"Cora is the reason?"

"If you had not returned, there would be no future."

Cora and Adrian looked at each other, confused, then back at Tiotonawen. "Why not?" They spoke at the same time.

"You were lost from each other, there in the future."

Cora hesitated, feeling the full purpose of her life rising. "We were."

"Without Talks Much, there would be no children for you."

Cora liked the idea, but it didn't seem plausible. "I think Adrian would have married eventually. Women go pretty much crazy for him, you know. And he had other girlfriends, so I'm sure—"

"I would never marry."

Adrian sounded so sure. Cora turned to face him. He looked at her, new wonder in his eyes. "Never, Cora. I knew that after I ended my last relationship. No woman could ever have what already belonged to you. I wanted to feel differently, but it was impossible."

Tiotonawen looked smug at his accuracy in prediction. "You, Talks Much, would have married. You would have association with a sad-faced and pale-haired boy much like the boy captain. You would pity him, and marry him because he loved you." Tiotonawen leaned toward Cora, eyes gleaming. "And your heart would die because you betrayed its truth."

"I knew it!" Adrian turned in a full circle, then seized her shoulders. "You are not going back to the future. You're staying right here, where there's no chance of you meeting some disgusting reincarnated version of Darian Woodward!"

Tiotonawen chuckled. "There is no longer reason to fear, my son. Talks Much has changed, and her destiny changes with her. No fate is carved in the earth's bones. All paths are possible, into darkness and into light. Each step we take changes its course."

Cora puffed a breath of relief. "Good."

"Now you are both strong enough to carve your own future. And together, you will grant my seed a future, too."

Cora glanced at him uncertainly. "Your seed?"

"He means our children, Cora."

"Oh!" Cora beamed. "We will have children. How many?"

"Talks Much, do you want nothing left unknown?"

"Yes. No."

"I will say no more." Tiotonawen backed away as if fearing Cora's reaction. She tilted her brow dangerously, and he stepped back again.

"Very well. We'll find that out on our own."

Tiotonawen stepped around Cora, then put both hands on Adrian's shoulder. "You give me joy, my son." He kissed Adrian's forehead, then pointed up the hill. "Together, we will walk to the highest rock. There, once again, I will see you to your future."

"You need me here, father."

"I need you there more. Go, and find life, find peace."

Adrian hesitated. "I can't leave you."

Tiotonawen sighed heavily. "If you stay, you will die."

Cora gasped and clutched Adrian's arm. "No! Do you see his future if he stays?"

353

"I see the future of a stubborn young warrior who frightens the white men with his knowledge. They fear us for what they don't understand. They would fear far more a man who understands their world, and can use it against them. Yes, he will die if he stays. The white general will not forget him."

"Cora says Darian Woodward arrested the general. We have nothing to fear from him."

A faraway gleam lit in Tiotonawen's eyes. "About the boy captain, I have nothing to say. He has much to change, like an onion."

Cora's brow angled. "An onion?"

Adrian nodded. "An appropriate analogy." Cora elbowed his ribs.

"An onion, Talks Much. You were an onion, too. Many layers hide the center. The outer layers have grown hard, formed tough to protect the inside." Tiotonawen paused. "You were maybe more like the nut."

Adrian chuckled. "You can say that again."

Cora elbowed him again. "Hush! What do you mean, 'nut'?"

"The outer shell was very thick, and grown to protect what was inside. Once removed, the real Talks Much came forward in one swoop. You became Talks Much Who Fights Bees. For the boy captain, the outer shell is not so hard, but it runs deeper, like the onion."

"Oh dear! I hope the captain will be all right."

Adrian snorted derisively. "You're already pitying him. I have to get you out of here." He paused. "What will happen to him?" He tried to ignore Cora's knowing glance.

"There are many paths before us all, my son. The captain's fate is already altered by his time with you and Talks Much. His journey toward the future alters, too, and I cannot see its ending."

Cora's lips twisted to one side as she pondered Darian's fate. "He'll be all right. I know it. You should have seen him lecturing the general. He was so strong. A little arrogant, maybe." Cora paused. "He seemed like a real pirate."

Adrian groaned. "This is nauseating. A pirate! He'll be back to his old stiff-backed Victorian yuppie self in no time. Trust me. Let's go."

Cora said good-bye to Toklanni and hugged Laurencita. "I wish I had something to pay you with for everything you've given me."

Laurencita kissed Cora's cheek. "You have given me hope for my children. I will give hope to them. That is better than gold."

Haastin stood beside Laurencita. Cora smiled at him, then gave him Spot's reins. "Please tell Haastin that I am surrendering my horse to him, because in a way, I'm chickening out of our future gambling matches."

Laurencita translated, and Haastin straightened, then took the reins as his due. Cora patted Spot's neck, then pressed her cheek against his soft muzzle. "You've gotten me through a lot, Spot. I wish I could take you with me, but these people know horses. You'll have a good life."

Archie ran by with a group of small boys. Haozinne followed close behind, ignored but determined to equal their efforts. Archie darted toward Cora and gave her a quick hug. "I've decided to stay on with the red folks." He cast a dark glance at Haozinne, who appeared to be stalking him. " 'Cept for her, it's real good to have folks to play with."

Laurencita touched his curly, red hair. "I will be as mother to him. Haastin will teach him the ways of our men. His life will be good."

Cora brushed away tears. "He is a lucky boy to have you

355

taking care of him. Adrian was adopted, too. He knew how much he was wanted and loved, and he always felt special. I used to envy him, but I think I understand my own parents now. They didn't plan for a child—I was born at an artist's colony. They didn't know what to do with me, but they got married and tried to be normal. They didn't know how, but they tried. When I get back, I will tell them both that I love them as they are."

"You are a brave woman, Cora. You are cool."

Cora started to shake her head, then remembered her heroism rescuing Adrian. "Yes. I am."

Adrian came to her carrying their parachute packs. "It's time, angel."

The villagers stood in the center of the clearing, silent as Tiotonawen led Adrian and Cora up the long path. Before they walked out of sight, Cora turned around and allowed the image to soak deep into her soul. She held up her hand in a still wave, and Laurencita waved back. Cora's throat tightened with emotion and she turned away.

Having proven herself by climbing onto the coach roof, Cora felt under no obligation to climb the rock unaided this time. Adrian helped her up and began assembling their parachutes. Tiotonawen stood silent and still gazing out across the desert. In the distance, small whirlwinds formed and began moving toward the hills.

Cora's heart pounded with excitement. They were going to jump into a whirlwind, and fly heaven knows where. They would fly together. She wasn't afraid.

Adrian seemed nervous. In his hurry, he tangled the parachute lines, swore, and knelt to fix the problem.

"What's the matter, Adrian? The whirlwinds are still forming."

He looked up at her, an emotion she didn't recognize in his dark eyes. He looked . . . young. Cora touched his hair, softening it from his forehead. "Adrian?"

He swallowed. Yes, he was definitely nervous. She had no idea why. "It's nothing, Cora." He stood up and gaze out across the desert. In his face, she saw an ageless man, the son of an ancient race, all power at his command. But beyond that strength, she saw his vulnerability. Because he was a man, because he wanted and cared and dreamed.

Tiotonawen looked between them, a smile on his face. "It is time, my son. Time for you to leave me, and to begin again. I believe now you can claim what is rightfully yours."

Adrian nodded but he still seemed tense. "It's time, Cora."

She eyed him quizzically. "I heard that." She hesitated, wondering if panic would surface, but it didn't. She fastened the parachute straps between her legs and put on her diving cap. Adrian popped the goggles over her head, leaving them loose around her neck. To her astonishment, his hands were shaking.

He adjusted his own parachute and positioned himself behind her. He bound them together so tight that she felt his every muscle. "I like this. I liked it the first time, too."

Adrian chuckled and shuffled her to the edge of the cliff.

Tiotonawen moved aside, then held up his hand in farewell. "Live well, my son. And you, talks Much Who Fights Bees, I don't have to tell you to take care of my son. I know that you will."

"I will."

Adrian looked once more to his father. "I love you."

Tiotonawen nodded, then turned to summon the whirlwind.

Cora watched it dance toward them and her heart beat with eternal wonder. "We're going home."

Adrian wrapped his arms around her and hugged her, then kissed her cheek. He drew a tight breath, then another. His smile seemed shy. "I have something for you."

Cora peered over her shoulder. "Now?" The wind swept faster, tossing his dark hair behind his head. Her insides tingled.

Adrian pulled the black cord from around his neck and took off the ring. When she looked into his beautiful eyes, she saw all the power of his heart shining there. "Cora Talmadge, will you marry me?"

Her vision blurred with tears. She pressed her lips together. "I will."

He smiled, but he was crying, too. He took her left hand and slipped the ring on her finger. It fit, because it had been made for her. Cora held his hand and kissed it. "I love you so. Whatever happens, I am yours forever."

Adrian pressed his cheek against her head. "Where you go, I go also." He lifted her goggles and put them over her eyes, then put on his own. "Are you ready, angel?"

Cora closed her eyes. "A leap of faith."

The whirlwind spun toward them, growing larger and darker as it approached. It lifted and danced, and the wind howled. Tiny rocks flew up and battered Cora's goggles like rain, but she kept her eyes open. The desert disappeared in a cloud of violent dust, and the whirlwind swept around them.

Her feet left the ground, then bumped back again. Adrian felt strong and solid behind her, but his heart slammed. The wind tugged at them. Cora resisted briefly, then gave herself over to its force. They lifted from the rock and spun. She couldn't tell where it carried them, but they seemed to go up rather than down.

Adrian released the parachute, but Cora couldn't tell if it

expanded above them. The whirlwind spun faster and faster, until Cora's thoughts blurred. Her vision took in only whirling dust, but she didn't close her eyes. The funnel pitched them up and out without warning.

"Flare!"

Cora pulled her straps in toward her chest and down. The parachute sank inward above them and they skidded toward the ground. "Hold on, angel. This is it."

Cora stuck her legs up, but too late. They landed on their feet, ran a few steps in unison, then stopped. They both looked down.

"Adrian . . . we're on pavement." Happiness flooded her soul. "We're home."

Adrian unhooked their straps, turned her in his arms, and kissed her. Cora wrapped her arms around his neck and kissed him back.

"What a landing! Wow! Nice going, Cora!" Jenny ran toward them dragging her parachute pack. Adrian and Cora gaped, speechless. They glanced at each other. Jenny's brow angled. "I see you've had time to get reacquainted."

Cora blushed. "Well, yes. We talked a bit." She hesitated and a foolish grin spread across her face. "We thought, since we've missed each other so much, that we'd get married."

Jenny's mouth dropped as Cora held up her hand to display her engagement ring. Jenny squealed in delight, flung herself at Cora, and hugged her wildly. "I knew it! The minute I saw those big, brown eyes, I knew you'd never go back to New York."

"Maybe for a visit. I have to sell my gallery and pack stuff." Cora peered at Adrian. "You'll come with me, won't you?"

"I will."

"Maybe the Demons will help us pack." Cora chewed her lip thoughtfully. "Then I have to purchase facilities for a gallery out here. I already have display items, of course."

Jenny's eyes wandered. "You do?"

"Yes. It's kind of a long story. We'll have dinner . . . ?" She paused. "Tomorrow night?"

Jenny nodded. She seemed shocked by Cora's apparently sudden transformation. "Good. We'll explain it all then. Just now, Adrian and I need to take a drive."

Adrian shrugged. "Where to, my angel?"

Cora rolled her eyes. "To the first village. You can find it, right?"

"I think so, but why . . . ?"

"You'll see when we get there." Cora turned back to Jenny and hugged her again. "I have my future to thank you for, Jenny. I have spent all my life afraid of not being good enough to get what I wanted. If you hadn't convinced me to get on that plane, I would have married a handsome blond man who was all wrong for me, and been miserable for the rest of my life."

Jenny stared, then shrugged. "Okay. . . . " Her attention shifted to the light-haired businessman. She winked at Cora, then headed off with her new friend.

Adrian took Cora's hand and kissed it. "How will you find your buried loot?"

"Not a problem! I buried it beneath a large rock, where I carved my name." She paused, triumphant. "Talks Much Who Fights Bees."

"You saved your dress." Adrian held up the tight leather skirt, admiring it.

Cora puttered around his house, opening cabinets, checking all the rooms. "You are so tasteful, Adrian. Look at all this stuff!"

She fingered a *kachina* doll, then stood back to view a painting of Canyon de Chelly at sunset.

"The skirt is just right," he said. "Perfect little slit up the side. . . . "

She went into the kitchen and examined the contents of his refrigerator. Adrian heard a small moan. "Look at all this health food. I hope there's a fast food restaurant nearby."

"How lucky this is a two-piece dress! I can slid my hands under . . . " Adrian sighed.

Cora emerged from his kitchen and flopped into a Southwestern-styled arm chair. "This is just the kind of house I pictured you in. Spanish architecture. I like the round windows and the painted adobe stuff. It's so . . . cool."

"And the leather is just thin enough to show your breasts."

Cora peered over at him. "Would you like me to put it on?"

Adrian nodded eagerly. "Would you?"

"Only if you put on your Erotic Warrior costume."

Adrian set her dress lovingly aside. "Maybe we should marry in these."

"If they're not worn out by then."

Adrian smiled. "It's only three weeks, Cora."

"Exactly."

Cora leaned back in his seat and gazed out his patio window at the flowering desert. A roadrunner pecked at seeds, and a cactus wren peeked out from Adrian's prized saguaro. A fat hare hopped by. Cora sprung up from her chair and raced outside.

"There's another one! Unbelievable!"

Adrian smiled to himself, then joined her on the patio. He slipped his arm around her waist and wondered if she'd ever tire of spotting fat rabbits. Cora studied the landscape as if expecting something amazing to emerge at any second. With her at his side, anything was possible.

A herd of javelinas made their way around his small pond. Adrian waited for Cora to notice. She watched the rabbit hop away and sighed in disappointment. "I feel certain I could tame one of those. . . . "

Adrian tapped her shoulder and pointed. She took one look at the little gray pigs and squealed. The javelinas stopped, looking concerned. Cora clamped her hand over her mouth, but she nearly hopped with excitement. Adrian watched her face as they drew closer, then positioned themselves lazily around his Palo Verde tree.

She turned to him, beaming. "This is so wonderful. I want to stay here forever."

Adrian drew her into his arms. "You will."

He led her from the patio, then out a side entrance to his pool. Cora's face lit as if she'd entered paradise. "A pool. . . . "

She cast a deliberate and thoughtful glance around his yard, studying the high adobe wall which separated him from his neighbors. She tapped her lip, then made the popping noise which portended . . . Desire flooded through his body, sudden and overwhelming.

"Adrian, I was thinking . . . "

He nodded eagerly. "Yes?"

"That wall is high. No one could see if you and I . . . " She eyed his diving board. "But I am a changed woman. I have to enter this pool in a manner which reflects my own particular idiom."

"Idiom?"

"Yes." She didn't wait to explain. She pulled off her

clothes and left them in a pile. Adrian stared as the warm sun reflected on her pale gold skin, highlighting every curve.

Cora marched to the diving board, positioned herself at the end, muttered instructions to herself as if recalling a swim class from her childhood, then poised her head between outstretched arms.

Cora, who refused to swim in water over her neck, was about to launch herself into the deep end of his pool. Adrian tore off his clothes and slid into the water just as she hurled herself out and down.

He swam to meet her, to save her. There was no need. Cora emerged in front of him, beaming. Love filled his heart, mingling with the desire he felt for her. Cora as a sweet-faced innocent girl had enchanted him. Cora as a woman would enthrall him forever.

Very gently, he reached to touch her cheek. "My hero."

Dane Calydon knows there is more to the mysterious Aiyana than meets the eye, but when he removes her protective wrappings, he is unprepared for what he uncovers: a woman beautiful beyond his wildest imaginings. Though she claimed to be an amphibious creature, he was seduced by her sweet voice, and now, with her standing before him, he is powerless to resist her perfect form. Yet he knows she is more than a mere enchantress, for he has glimpsed her healing, caring side. But as secrets from her past overshadow their happiness, Dane realizes he must lift the veil of darkness surrounding her before she can surrender both body and soul to his tender kisses.

___52268-3 $5.50 US/$6.50 CAN

Dorchester Publishing Co., Inc.
P.O. Box 6640
Wayne, PA 19087-8640

Please add $1.75 for shipping and handling for the first book and $.50 for each book thereafter. NY, NYC, and PA residents, please add appropriate sales tax. No cash, stamps, or C.O.D.s. All orders shipped within 6 weeks via postal service book rate. Canadian orders require $2.00 extra postage and must be paid in U.S. dollars through a U.S. banking facility.

Name_____
Address_____
City_____State_____Zip_____
I have enclosed $_____ in payment for the checked book(s).
Payment <u>must</u> accompany all orders. ☐ Please send a free catalog.
    CHECK OUT OUR WEBSITE! www.dorchesterpub.com

THE WHITE SUN

STOBIE PIEL

Sierra of Nirvahda has never known love. But with her long dark tresses and shining eyes she has inspired plenty of it, only to turn away with a tuneless heart. Yet when she finds herself hiding deep within a cavern on the red planet of Tseir, her heart begins to do strange things. For with her in the cave is Arnoth of Valenwood, the sound of his lyre reaching out to her through the dark and winding passageways. His song speaks to her of yearnings, an ache she will come to know when he holds her body close to his, with the rhythm of their hearts beating for the memory and melody of their souls.

___52292-6 $5.50 US/$6.50 CAN

Dorchester Publishing Co., Inc.
P.O. Box 6640
Wayne, PA 19087-8640

Please add $1.75 for shipping and handling for the first book and $.50 for each book thereafter. NY, NYC, and PA residents, please add appropriate sales tax. No cash, stamps, or C.O.D.s. All orders shipped within 6 weeks via postal service book rate. Canadian orders require $2.00 extra postage and must be paid in U.S. dollars through a U.S. banking facility.

Name_____
Address_____
City_____ State_____ Zip_____
I have enclosed $_____ in payment for the checked book(s).
Payment <u>must</u> accompany all orders. ❑ Please send a free catalog.
     CHECK OUT OUR WEBSITE! www.dorchesterpub.com

DESPERADO
SANDRA HILL

Major Helen Prescott has always played by the rules. That's why Rafe Santiago nicknamed her "Prissy" at the military academy years before. Rafe's teasing made her life miserable back then, and with his irresistible good looks, he is the man responsible for her one momentary lapse in self control. When a routine skydive goes awry, the two parachute straight into the 1850 California Gold Rush. Mistaken for a notorious bandit and his infamously sensuous mistress, they find themselves on the wrong side of the law. In a time and place where rules have no meaning, Helen finds Rafe's hard, bronzed body strangely comforting, and his piercing blue eyes leave her all too willing to share his bedroll. Suddenly, his teasing remarks make her feel all woman, and she is ready to throw caution to the wind if she can spend every night in the arms of her very own desperado.

___52182-2 $5.99 US/$6.99 CAN

BETRAYAL Evelyn Rogers

By the Bestselling Author of
The Forever Bride

If there is anything that gets Conn O'Brien's Irish up, it is a lady in trouble–especially one he has fallen in love with at first sight. So after the Texas horseman saves Crystal Braden from an overly amorous lout, he doesn't waste a second declaring his intentions to make an honest woman of her. But they have barely been declared man and wife before Conn learns that his new bride is hiding a devastating secret that can destroy him.

The plan is simple: To ensure the safety of her mother and young brother, Crystal agrees to play the damsel in distress. The innocent beauty has no idea how dangerously charming the virile stranger can be–nor how much she longs to surrender to the tender passion in his kiss. And when Conn discovers her ruse, she vows to blaze a trail of desire that will convince him that her deception has been an error of the heart and not a ruthless betrayal.

___4262-2 $5.99 US/$6.99 CAN